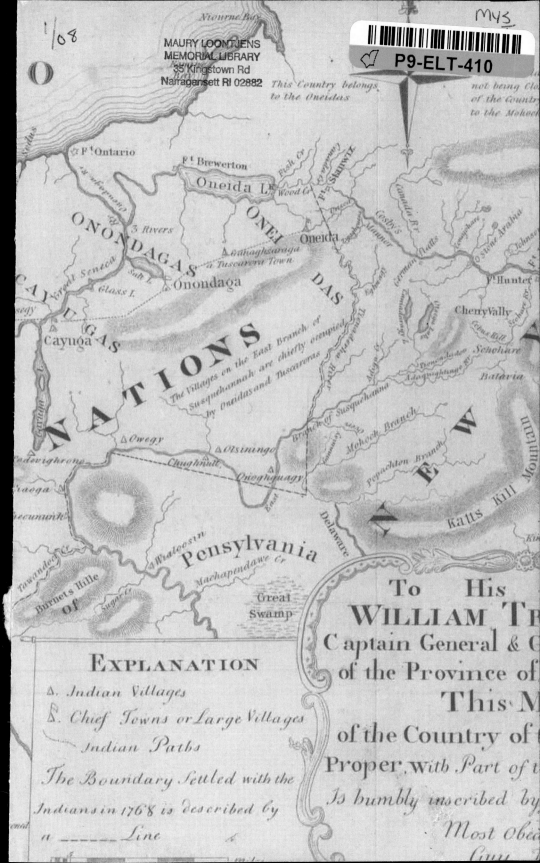

O

Niourne Bay

This Country belongs to the Oneidas

not being Clo of the Country to the Mohoc

F^t Ontario

F^t Brewerton

Oneida L^e

Wood C^r

Fish C^r

ONEI

SHAWIL

Oneida

ONONDAGAS

3 Rivers

Great Seneca

Glass I.

Salt L.

Achnughsawaga
a Tuscarora Town.

Onondaga

DAS

Costby's

Manner

Canada R^r

Germans Flatts

O Stone Arabia

Johnso

F^t Hunter

CAYUGAS

CherryVally

Cayuga

N A T I O N S

The Villages on the East Branch of Susquehannah are chiefly occupied by Oneidas and Tuscaroras

Schoharie

Batavia

Owegy

Otsiningo

Onoghquagy

Mohock Branch

N

Pepachton Branch

E

W

Katts Kill Mountain

Tadevighrono

Claghnut

East Branch

Susquehanna

Chaoga

Tawandee

Pensylvania

Wialoosin

Machapundawee Cr

Delaware

Great Swamp

Burnets Hille

Of

Sugar a

EXPLANATION

Δ. *Indian Villages*

Ͽ. *Chief Towns or Large Villages*

— *Indian Paths*

The Boundary Settled with the

Indians in 1768 is described by

a _____ Line

To His

WILLIAM Tr

Captain General & G

of the Province of

This M

of the Country of t

Proper, with Part of t

Is humbly inscribed by

Most Obe

Bone Rattler

Bone Rattler

Eliot Pattison

Counterpoint

Berkeley

With gratitude, and apologies, to
James Fenimore Cooper and Thomas Macaulay

This is a work of fiction. Names, characters, places, and incidents are the product of the
author's imagination or are used fictitiously. Any resemblance to actual persons, living or
dead, is entirely coincidental.

Author's Note and Time Line are available at the end of the book.

Library of Congress Cataloging-in-Publication Data

Pattison, Eliot.
  Bone rattler : a mystery of colonial America / Eliot Pattison.
    p.cm.
  ISBN-13: 978-1-59376-185-1
  ISBN-10: 1-59376-185-6

  PS3566.A82497B665 2008
  813'.54—dc22

Interior design by Maria Fernandez
Printed in the United States of America

COUNTERPOINT
2117 Fourth Street
Suite D
Berkeley, CA 94710
www.counterpointpress.com

Distributed by Publishers Group West

9 8 7 6 5 4 3 2 1

Chapter One

September 1759
The North Atlantic

HOPE, DUNCAN MCCALLUM HAD DISCOVERED after two months on an English convict ship, was the deadliest thing in the world. It wasn't scurvy that was killing his companions, nor any of the other shipborne diseases his medical training warned him to watch for. Hope was their poison, for hope was the seed of despair, and on the dark, dank prisoner deck those who had embarked with the greatest hopes were now dying of despair.

Had he time, and paper and ink, Duncan could have penned a treatise on the fatal contagion of despair, recounting how it consumed each prisoner differently, the final chapter being a description of himself. For Duncan, with strange detachment, had not missed his own symptoms. He had seen the sunken eyes looking back at him from his reflection in the water butt, observed the trembling hands, the absence of appetite, his abrupt obsession with memories of his Scottish boyhood, the only contented time of his twenty-four years. He had embarked for the New World clinging to vague ambitions about a fresh beginning, but the realities of the convict's fate had overtaken him, and now the dim spark of his life was fueled only by his compulsion to decipher the ghastly death of his friend Adam Monroe.

"Give way!" Duncan heard a man near the bow shout, followed by the sound of feet running toward him. Springing up from his hiding place between two barrels, he launched himself onto the shroud lines. He had prayed to evade attention this time, had even convinced himself he could return unseen in the mist to the prisoners' hold, but if they were going to beat him again, by God he would first make them work, wear his keepers down so he would have time to solve the anguished riddle that had caused him to steal away from the morning slops line. If his own despair had an antidote, Duncan knew where to find it.

As he climbed, the faces of the dead once again flashed before his mind's eye. Ian, the handsome young printer, arrested hours before his wedding, who had started the voyage singing about love. On his last day, a fleet westbound packet had overtaken their ship, pausing to deliver mail that included a letter from his fiancée breaking their betrothal, saying her parents forbade union with a criminal. He had stared at the letter for hours, then that night had crept away to the head, lain down, and filled his throat from the bucket of sand kept there. And Stewart Ross, the stone mason and engineer who, after receiving news that his only son and heir had died in the war with France, had chewed open a vein in the middle of the night. But it was Adam, Duncan's one true friend among the prisoners, whose face always lingered. Adam had been laughing one day, betting with wooden buttons as he urged on his entry in a weevil race, then had grown abruptly morose the next, transformed by something or someone unseen by Duncan. He had watched helplessly over the next twenty-four hours as Adam's face had seemed to rot away, the life fading from his eyes as steadily as if it had been his blood, not his spirit, that had been trickling out of him.

Duncan climbed without looking down, instinctively pushing and pulling on the lines with hand and foot as he had so often in the Hebrides boats of his youth, swinging from one spar to the next, the spray of the wind-whipped waves soaking his threadbare shirt, stinging the open welts left from the last time the keepers had bound him to the mast and whipped him. He was taking the same route, spar for spar, as Adam had taken two days earlier while Duncan, pinned in the grip of the keepers, had helplessly watched. Adam had lingered in the maintop platform, scratching something into the wood of the mast, then lifted his hand in mock salute to the officers and others gathered near the bow.

As Duncan hurried upward, he heard the helmsman cry out in a fearful tone, doubtless concerned that one of his pursuers would fall as the great square-rigged vessel, eight weeks out of Glasgow, pitched forward into the heavy sea. Fog swirled around the masts as he frantically climbed, knowing they would never stop their vengeful race. Breaching the rules of confinement was no different from spitting on the king, the captain had declared, and had offered half a crown to the man who brought Duncan to him if he went missing again. Duncan had escaped three times already, the last time tasting the freedom of wind and sea for half an hour before they found him clinging to the bowsprit. He had become something of a reviled mongrel at the whipping post, the favorite of every bully among the sailors. The captain had vowed that next time Duncan would receive forty lashes and be tied to a mast all night to let the salt spray work on his raw flesh.

He climbed with grim determination, swinging from the foremast, finally reaching the maintop, the platform high above the deck where Adam had lingered, working on the wood. His heart leapt as he saw the lines scratched with a nail, then sank just as quickly. There were no words of wisdom, no explanation of what had so abruptly destroyed Adam, no secret instructions to explain the cryptic legacy he had left for Duncan. His friend had left no words at all, only two crude drawings—one a plump creature with a round tail and outstretched wings, the other two parallel, curving lines joined at the top and bottom, like a hollow letter *S*. The last meaningless gesture of another life wrung dry by the king.

Adam had no sooner finished scratching on the mast than he had slipped down a line onto the port rail, running along its flat top, sprinting as the keepers closed in. Duncan had broken free as he saw the empty grin on his friend's face, and had been racing toward him as Adam scooped a set of chains off the shoulder of a keeper, draping it around his neck, then sped toward the stern. He had kept running when he reached the end of the rail, hugging the chain to him. Duncan reached the stern an instant later, in time to see that his friend made no effort to surface, had just spread his arms and dove deeper, his last mortal sign the bottom of one pale, naked foot kicking toward the depths.

Duncan extracted a small, dark object from his pocket, a four-inch piece of carved black stone. That terrible morning when they had climbed onto the deck for their breakfast slops, Adam had clamped a hand around Duncan's shoulder, spoken into his ear, then leapt into the rigging so quickly Duncan had not at first realized he had thrust the stone into Duncan's palm, bending his fingers over it as though to conceal it. Only several agonizing minutes later, after Adam was gone, had he become fully aware of the object, and of the exact words Adam had spoken.

"I am sorry," his friend had whispered to him. "She is done with me," he said, as if the stone were alive. "I failed her. 'Tis you she needs now." In his few moments of privacy since, Duncan had studied the disturbing black thing, expecting it to yield some explanation. But it was nothing more than a stone shaped into a lumpy, ugly creature with fat haunches and a broad head lowered between two thick front legs, as if it were bowing. In a hole in its bottom, a small note had been wedged. *I despaired because only a ghostwalker can understand what must be done,* it said. *But now I see you become one. Let the old one take you where she needs to go.* On the back, more lines had been added in a hasty scrawl. *Duncan, I vowed not to befriend you, but I never thought to find us so alike. I do not expect your forgiveness for what I have done to you and your clan, but I do pray that one day you will at least understand. What they say they want the Company for, they mean the opposite. They mean to use you, then they must kill you. They know who you are.*

Something as black and cold as the stone settled into his gut as he stared at the crude etchings in the wood. Duncan had been so certain he would find an answer to assuage his hopelessness, a meaning to Adam's strange words, some thin thread that might keep him connected to the world. But he had escaped for nothing, and would now have the skin flayed from his back for naught but scratchings left by a man gone mad.

They know who you are. Why would Adam have included such words in his riddle? Of course they knew who Duncan was, just another broken Highlander, adrift, with no prospect of ever finding an anchor again.

The marks on the wood were a nonsensical epitaph, not just for Adam, but for Stewart and Ian as well. It was no coincidence that three of the best-educated men of the Company, its natural leaders, had now died, for they had seen the biggest world, had nurtured the biggest dreams; they had been wise enough to see that, having been wronged by English judges, all doors had now been slammed shut, that if they lived, for as long as they lived, all their dreams would be nightmares.

He stared at the drawings until a wisp of fog swept in front of them, then he looked up. The ship had entered a low fog bank, its thick white cloud blanketing the world under the maintop. No sound came from below except a few shouts, not of anger now but of fear, and a strange mournful wailing. Duncan was alone, washed in the sunlight that pierced a gap in the gathering clouds. He heard only the groan of canvas and creak of rigging. Suspended above the dense, churning whiteness, Duncan had a sense of floating between worlds, and a sudden, desperate longing to be with Adam.

The wind began to push the fog, and the sea became visible a cable's length away, with the ship below still covered in the edge of the low, dense bank. Huge swells swept toward the horizon, which was lined with clouds as black as ink. Duncan felt strangely thin, impossibly light. He would float away into the storm if he just let go.

A stark and terrible beauty had overtaken him, seemed to be

seeking him, calling him from the world. *Rejoice in this moment,* something inside said, *this is freedom, or the closest to it you will ever find again.* But his heart was gone, replaced by the chill, empty thing that was spreading through his body. Adam's pained, confused words and his insane scratching had simply been his final gift to Duncan, leaching away the last drop of Duncan's hope. With an odd sense of relief, he felt the rot inside finally break through to the surface.

He did not know how long he gazed out into the storm, into the nothingness of wind, water, and swirling cloud, but gradually he became aware of someone speaking from a vast distance.

Stare into the raging sea and ye'll meet the eye of y'er god.

It was the voice of his grandfather, released from a chamber in his mind he had kept closed for years. When, as a boy standing on a sea cliff in a rising storm, Duncan had first heard the words, he had taken them as a somber warning. But now, as the old man's raw, dry voice echoed across the span of nearly two decades to reach him, a melancholy grin split Duncan's face. The words had been not a warning but a taunt. Duncan somehow knew now that when a British corvette had blasted the sloop his grandfather used to smuggle rebels, the old clan chief had glared into the dark waves and shouted a Gaelic curse at his god while the violent, frigid waters of the Hebrides crashed over him.

Duncan found himself fingering the runelike shapes on the mast. He had misunderstood. He did not need resolution, he needed release. Adam had shown him, his grandfather was showing him again. There were fates worse than death, and a way for a dying clan to triumph over those who imposed servitude. Duncan was ready to stare down his god.

The ship pitched forward into a trough of the angry sea and was suddenly clear of the fog. Duncan clutched the mast and dared a glance over the edge of the maintop platform, wary of being spotted again. Any moment they would be upon him, this time with clubs and chains, this time planning to strip his back raw.

"Lift up thy hands!"

The sudden command from below stabbed like a blade. Duncan thrust himself back against the mast, the welts on his back afire again, then slowly straightened his tall, thin frame, studying the treacherous rigging above. He would climb higher, to the tip of the tall mainmast. Then it would just be a matter of waiting for the right wave, when the ship would heel over and put him above the raging water. He would not go down to the deck, not ever again.

"Rise up to meet the lamb!"

Duncan froze as he reached for the ropes, then peered back over the edge at a group of men huddled near the bow, where a bearded sailor waved a black book. The calls had not been for him, but for the other sailors gathered around the man, listening to what? A service for the dead? But there was no shrouded body, no solemn officer in formal dress to recite the words prescribed for burial at sea. In fact there were no officers on deck at all, he saw as salt spray slapped his cheek, though the deck and masts should be crawling with sailors to reef sails and ready the ship for heavy weather. He realized the ship had been deathly still since the other prisoners had been taken to the hold an hour before. Even the helmsman seemed about to abandon his duties, for he stood beside the wheel, one hand on a spoke as he stared uneasily at the waters behind the stern. No one had been pursuing Duncan after all. The alarms had been raised for another reason.

From the group at the bow came the uneven chorus of a prayer, the sound growing more distant as Duncan turned his gaze toward the churning waters ahead. The deck seemed to be receding, drifting out of his consciousness. There was no need to climb farther.

They had reached the edge of the storm. He released one hand, letting the wind swing his body away from the mast, yielding at last to the emptiness that was swelling within. He selected a massive black wave in the distance and gazed into it as it approached, letting his hand slip around the curvature of the mast, defying his god to meet his gaze and hear Duncan's own venomous taunt.

Suddenly strong fingers clamped around his arm, pulling him back.

"'Tis a terrible final thing, lad."

Without looking, Duncan recognized the gravelly voice of the eldest of the keepers. "Just an autumn gale, Mr. Lister."

"Do not trifle with me, McCallum," the older man said. "Have I not seen such a look too many times this voyage? I ken what's in y'er eye even if ye do not."

Duncan glanced back at Lister and paused, confused at the pain on the man's scarred, weather-beaten countenance. Lister was a prisoner himself, as were all the keepers assigned to watch the others, a trusty not confined to cells or locked holds. He had served at sea most of his life, had been in the navy, then second mate on another of the merchant ships that plied the Atlantic, until he was condemned for some unspoken crime. Lister had been the only keeper to show him any kindness, had often spoken with Duncan about the sea, had only the night before pushed the lantern closer to the barred door of the prisoner hold to give Duncan more light as he sat writing at the threshold. The black wave reached and passed the ship, and the two men fixed each other with inquiring gazes as they gripped the rigging and rode the heave of the mast.

When he finally replied, Duncan's throat seemed dry and scratched. "Adam," he said, with a gesture toward the crude drawings.

"A cruel, rotten thing," Lister muttered, venom in his voice, then saw the question in Duncan's eyes. "Me mind has no reason to ken it, but in me heart I know what we saw plain before us was a murder, as sure as if we watched a blade planted in Munroe's back. His dying was different from the others. Adam didn't want to die. He had to die."

Something unexpected stirred within Duncan. The old sailor had found the words that had been struggling to rise from Duncan's own heart.

"'Twas that bastard redback," Lister added. "Our bluestocking prig."

The emptiness ebbed for a moment. Had Duncan misunderstood something about Adam's death? "Lieutenant Woolford?" he asked. There was only one member of the king's army on board.

"Ye were there. Ye heard Woolford report our destination had

changed, that we be bound for Edentown, in the New York colony."
Lister fixed Duncan with a grim stare. Prior to Woolford's declaration, the Company leaders had let the men assume they were sailing
to Virginia or Georgia, whose tobacco and cotton plantations
employed legions of transported criminals. "Adam had been in the
militia," he added soberly, as if it explained much. "New York be
where the war lies. In the wild lands."

He searched Lister's face, remembering once more Adam's last
words. *They mean to use you, then they must kill you.* He had known
Adam had spent years in the Pennsylvania colony, but Adam had
always evaded Duncan's questions about his former life in the New
World, diverting him with tales of colonial towns and taverns,
promising him that one day he would show Duncan mountains and
lakes that rivaled those of Scotland. "Are you saying Adam died
because of something that happened in America?"

"I saw his face go white as snow when Woolford spoke those
words. That night he asked for a writing lead and a scrap of paper.
Next day he was dead."

"After he declared our new destination," Duncan recalled,
"Woolford tried to see him. Adam had me tell Woolford he was ill,
that he would have to return the next day." But there had been no
next day for Adam. Duncan was silent a moment, considering
Lister's words. "Adam would not fear the French."

"Did I speak of the French? There's fates in those wilds God
never meant for man." Lister clenched his jaw and gazed toward
another huge wave, as if he, too, had begun to see some message in
the rapidly building storm.

After a moment, Duncan gestured again to the strange animal
shape scratched on the mast. "Do you know it?"

"A beaver, I'd wager."

Duncan touched the lines with his fingertips. "I have never
glimpsed a beaver." He knew of the lush beaver hats that were the
rage of fashion on high streets across England, but had no certain
notion of the animal's shape.

"A great round rat with a tail like a skillet. Except," Lister added in a confused tone, "this one's got wings." More frightened cries rose from the deck, followed by the angry shouts of officers.

Duncan's fingers went to the cold black stone in his pocket, and he began to withdraw it to show to Lister. "What does it mean, Mr. Lister?"

But the old mate was gazing in the direction of the chaos on deck and misunderstood. For the first time, Duncan saw the darkness along the right side of his face, the greyness around his eye. Someone had hit Lister, hard. "The captain sends for ye," the keeper said without looking up.

"To lift more skin from my back." Duncan glanced toward the rigging above. Even if Adam was right and the Company leaders needed him for some secret purpose, they apparently did not mind if he were scarred and broken.

"Not today. 'Tis terrible trouble. Nigh all the hands refuse to work. There be a medical question. They'll n'er take the captain's word on it. We searched for Professor Evering," he said, meaning the scholar who took passage with the company of convicts, "but he's nowhere to be seen. No doubt hiding from the storm in the holds. The cook might do, but every time a storm rises, the lubber drains half a jug of rum."

Duncan eased the stone back into his pocket. "I'm no doctor."

"The men say ye studied anatomy and such. Ye be the closest thing we have. Whether ye choose to toss y'er life away is between ye and y'er god. But there be a hundred other souls on board who don't wish to die this day. The devil hisself's at work in—" The words choked in his throat as the old sailor glanced over Duncan's shoulder, cursed, and threw an arm around Duncan's waist, seizing the mast with his other arm.

The second huge wave broke over the bow of the ship, submerging it, roiling toward the stern as men below cried out and lunged for the nearest rail or line. For a long, terrible moment, the entire main deck disappeared in swirling foam, and Lister and

Duncan were alone, with the three great masts like trees sprouted from the sea, and the wind gusting through their square limbs, ripping apart the topgallant sail above them.

A moment later the ship lurched clear, the deck draining of water, and the sea grew flatter. The damaged sail tore free of its stays, the wet canvas fluttering toward the deck. Two sailors ran to it as it lodged on the port rail against the shroud lines. The canvas slipped toward the sea as they reached it, and one man stretched over the side to capture the sail. But the sailor reeled back without the canvas, jerking his companion away, terror on his face as he fled toward the praying men at the bow. "It's too late!" he moaned. "They've come for us!"

Lister eased his arm from Duncan and pushed him down, to sit on the platform. Glancing at the panicked crew below, the keeper shook his head grimly. "Mostly Cornish men and West Indians. Each fool more superstitious than the one before. If the captain does not restore order soon, the ship is lost. I prefer to live, lad," he added, his tone hollow with desperation. When Duncan offered no reply, he searched Duncan's face and sighed. "'Twere McCallums on the west Highlands coast nigh Lochlash, lairds over the small islands. They be y'er people?"

Duncan stared uncertainly at the keeper, then slowly nodded as he studied the terrified men below. There was no still no sign of the other keepers who liked to make sport of escapees. Surely, as an old ship's mate, Lister would be hounding the crew if he believed the ship were in peril. But then Duncan remembered Lister himself was a prisoner. "A proud, stubborn lot," Lister continued, "as brave as any in Prince Charlie's army. Fought aside me own clan at Culloden, they did," the keeper confided, referring to the last desperate battle of the Jacobite Scot rebels against the English army, in 1746.

Duncan looked up, astonishment on his face.

Lister glanced about and lowered his voice, as if the mast had ears. "I always sign me ships' books as Lister. They think me of English blood, raised in Glasgow. Few ken me true name be McAllister."

The old mate fixed Duncan with a level, knowing stare. Hidden Highland roots were a dangerous thing to reveal, a secret that could cost Lister his status as keeper, and much more. The day before they had sailed, the Company, nearly all of whom were Highland Scots, had been assembled to witness the hanging of a shepherd for keeping an illegal cache of swords and plaids.

After a moment the keeper glanced down at the quarterdeck, where the sailing master had appeared, blasting the helmsman, shouting for men to reef the foresail. When no one responded, Lister spat a curse and looked back with worry in his usually steady eyes. "They were hard years, lad. And ye have the look of one who's crawled from the battlefield. But ye would have been a wee bairn then, in y'er mother's aprons."

"I was in school in Flanders. And by then my mother had ripped all her aprons into bandages," Duncan replied in a taut voice. "Someone brought me a newspaper with the story of the battle," he added, fighting a sudden flood of emotion. "It told how scores were hanged afterwards as traitors to the English king, with orders for no one to cut down the bodies. It listed the names. My father, and all his brothers, left to rot on the king's scaffolds. A few weeks later when they got around to seizing our house and lands, my mother stabbed an English officer in the arm. She and my sisters never made it out alive. Nor my six-year-old brother. Only the two of us away at school survived." The painful words rushed out, surprising Duncan. He had not spoken of those dark days for years.

More fearful shouts rose from the deck. Men were pointing past the stern.

"'And the sea shall give up its dead,'" a hopeless voice declared.

Duncan looked down as he recognized the words. A sailor was reciting from the Book of Revelations when he should be protecting the ship from the gale. A chill crept down Duncan's spine. It was true. Although the wind had ebbed for the moment, the full fury of the storm lay close ahead, and the ship's crew was seized by an inexplicable, paralyzing fear.

"We're bound for the New World, lad," Lister said. "New lives can be made."

"I had a new life," Duncan said despondently, his eyes back on the clouds. "Cousins in Yorkshire raised me. They never let me speak our true tongue out loud, never let me speak of my dead parents. A proper Englishman they made me. The best schools in Holland and England. I had completed three years of medical lectures, was set to join the chambers of a doctor in Northumbria. Then six months ago the last of my great-uncles appeared at my door, asking me to hide him in my rooms. Over eighty years old. I had thought him in the far northern isles, hiding all these years. Our last clan chief."

"I'm asking y'er help now, as he did," Lister said, urgency now in his voice.

"Three weeks later they came for him, claiming he was a reiver," Duncan continued, referring to the highwaymen of the Scottish borderlands. "I was arrested for aiding him, sentenced in the name of the king to seven years' imprisonment. After four months they dragged me out of that moldy hole, more dead than alive. Threw me before a judge who said the king had decided to be merciful, that I would instead do seven year's hard labor in the colonies. Transportation, the judge called it," he added bitterly. "A pilgrimage, in order to reflect on my sins." He looked back into the keeper's weathered face. "I had a new life, and now I have none." Duncan knew he would never be a doctor now, never fulfill his secret dream of becoming wealthy enough to buy back his family's Highland lands. Adam had seen something in Duncan's path that Duncan was blind to. There would be no freedom after seven years' labor. They were going to use him, then kill him. Adam, too, had somehow been used and killed. Despair seized Duncan again, a cold vise on his heart. "There is a letter in my hammock, Mr. Lister. Perhaps you could get it to my brother in New York." Duncan had spent much of the night before in writing the letter as the other prisoners slept, to his brother who had likewise been forced to leave the ways of the clans behind. *The English king,* he had written at the closing, *has wreaked its final vengeance on our family.*

"God knows I'm sorry, lad. But there be many good men on this ship who once wore the thistle," Lister declared, invoking the ancient symbol of Scotland. "They, too, will die without your help. And the ones in the ratholes," he said. Duncan cringed at the mention of the locked cells in the rear hold of the prison deck, reserved for the most violent of the transported prisoners, murderers all, separately bound under the king's warrant for the deadly sugar plantations of the West Indies. "Every last one taken from the courts in Glasgow, condemned by English judges," Lister continued. "I know this ship. The foretopmast is weakened, and she'll snap like a twig when the gale blows. 'Tis likely she'll stove in a hold cover when she falls, and the hull will slowly fill. Those in the cells will die first, drowned in their locked boxes. *Redeat,*" he uttered after a moment. It had started long ago as a Jacobite oath, *May He Return,* for the return of the Scottish Stewart prince. But it had become something of a prayer for all Highlanders, an invocation, as it were, of the Scottish gods. "The Ramsey Company will die without a chance to prove itself," he added, referring to the great lord named Ramsey, to whom all the prisoners outside the cells were bound. A community of troubled souls—as Reverend Arnold, the Anglican pastor who escorted them, called the Company—on its way to redeem itself in a New World paradise.

A furious voice thundered from below. An officer was chasing two sailors as they ran with an elegant chair out of the cabins. "What possesses them?" Duncan asked as the sailors dumped the chair over the rail and another man appeared, throwing bottles of brandy over the side, uttering a fearful prayer with each toss. They were making offerings to the sea.

"The devil awoke this morn. Ye must put an end to it."

Duncan swallowed the question that leapt to his tongue. How could he possibly stop the madness below? "Whatever inside me had been capable of helping other souls," he answered in a bitter voice, "drained out onto my prison floor." He could see lightning now, long, jagged bolts rending the horizon. Adam's face still lingered at the edge of his consciousness, as if calling Duncan to join him.

"Why today, lad?"

"We're due in port soon. I'll be given no chance to break free again. A member of the Company has but one way to express his freedom. My clan will not end in slavery."

"'Tis but seven years, McCallum. Don't be so prideful. Y'er still young."

Duncan's gaze drifted back toward the wind-whipped waves. "Are you suggesting, Mr. Lister, that for people like you and me long lives are worth the living?"

It was Lister's turn to grow silent and turn his gaze toward the sea. "Y'er great-uncle?" he asked after a long moment.

"They dragged me from my prison to make certain I was a witness. From the gallows they pronounced him an unrepentant traitor. He danced a jig, then spat as the hangman lowered the noose."

"Y'er brother. Older?"

"A year younger."

The announcement seemed to stir something in Lister. His eyes grew wide with a sudden, intense curiosity. He studied Duncan as if for the first time, a strange fire kindling in his eyes, then grimaced as though unhappy with what he saw. "Look at ye then," he growled, "is this how ye treat all those who go before?"

It was impossible, but the chastising voice Duncan heard was that of his grandfather, as was the disapproving cast in the old sailor's eyes. Duncan sensed something twitching inside him, and he grew very still, no longer aware of the storm. Lister had opened another long-barred chamber in Duncan's mind, a chamber of nightmares in which the rotting corpse of his father pointed at him from the gibbet, accusing him of forsaking the clan to become an Englishman.

"Have ye forgotten what it means to be the eldest?"

"I didn't . . . I couldn't . . . ," Duncan muttered after a moment, in a voice cracking with a new emotion. There was another chamber, often visited by Duncan, that held memories of long days spent with his grandfather, watching with awe as the fiery old Scot performed the duties of clan elder, protecting the innocent, filling the larders of the impoverished, dispensing rough justice among the tenants of the far-flung islands traditionally bound to their clan, even saving the drowning, for his grandfather had been the best swimmer in the isles. "My clan is extinguished."

"As long as ye and y'er brother breathe, there be a clan."

He gazed at Lister in wonder. During all the days of his torment since his arrest, the thought had never occurred to him. His uncle's executioners had made Duncan clan chieftain.

"God's eyes, McCallum!" Lister spat. "Ye must forget y'er own misery! Ye are blood-bound to y'er clan, living and dead, to all them who wear the thistle. Death stalks this ship, and if any survive, 'tis Scots who will be blamed. What will a clan chief do about it?"

Duncan looked from Lister to the gale, now nearly upon them. He could find no reply.

"What if it be true," Lister pressed, "what Reverend Arnold said not a quarter hour ago, that ye may be the one who could save the ship?"

"Arnold?" Arnold was the one who had snatched him from court, who had committed him to the prison ship. "I owe him nothing."

"Then what if it be true, that the professor needs y'er help?"

Duncan twisted his head toward the old sailor. "Evering?"

"That last night as he sat by the hatch, Adam told me to say to you that Evering found the key to save us all but knows not how to use it. He said to help McCallum protect the professor."

Duncan looked back at the waves, not wanting to betray his surprise, to acknowledge the sudden ripple of hope in his sea of despair.

"He said to heed how Evering explains his comet," Lister added in a perplexed tone. "Save us all," he repeated. "As if we all be going to die elsewise."

Duncan gripped a rope and leaned out, as if the wind might clear his mind. The storm still called him, but in a corner of his brain something was recounting ways he might reach Evering hiding in the holds below. No, it was impossible to descend without being snatched by the other keepers.

"My grandmother was a McCallum, came from y'er islands,"

Lister ventured when Duncan did not reply. "My own clan is shattered, lad, ashes lost to the winds. Long ago we came from those same islands." The old mate's voice cracked as he spoke.

"What are you saying?"

With a strange contemplation in his eyes, Lister ran his fingertips over Adam's scratchings on the wood, then fixed Duncan with a solemn gaze. "I petition for protection, Clan McCallum," he said in a slow, deliberate voice, using one of the old ways of addressing a clan chief. "I swear me blood to ye."

Duncan felt a bitter grin tug at his mouth. "You pledge yourself to a condemned convict? This is playacting, Mr. Lister. I am nobody. Less than nobody." Duncan was but a thin shadow of his grandfather. But his grin froze as he saw the earnest, hurt expression on Lister's countenance. It was an ancient tradition, that Highlanders who shared blood ties with a clan could offer their loyalty in exchange for its protection.

"I swear it to the laird of the McCallum clan."

Duncan stared numbly as Lister spat into his hand and extended it toward him.

"As God is my vow," the old sailor solemnly declared.

"People want me dead," Duncan said. "And I don't even know why."

"In the place of our birth, lad, that be a badge of honor. 'Tis my experience that the best of the clan chiefs be tougher than a shaggy ox to put down, and when they finally die, they do so on their own terms. It's easy for a king's convict to die. But a clan chief is duty-bound to stay alive, just to spite him."

At home there had always been a grand ceremony when a chief was installed, with pipes and sword dancing and, in the tradition of his own clan, the beating of the earth beside the new chieftain with knotted ropes to drive out the demons, then the presentation of a bundle of dried thistles. But in a world where pipes and tartans were outlawed, traditions were thin.

Duncan let Lister's callused hand close around his own, then returned the grip uncertainly as the sailor squeezed. As he did so the wind rose again, shifting, pushing the ship about so that for a moment it rode before a steep, following sea.

"Jesus, Mary, and Joseph!" the old mate moaned, and grabbed the mast as tightly as a landsman.

As Duncan followed Lister's gaze, something frigid clutched his spine. A man was suspended in the wall of water behind the vessel, his pale face fixed on the ship, his arm gesturing as if beckoning the crew to join him. It was what had terrified the two sailors who had followed the lost sail. *It's too late,* one had cried, *they've come for us.*

"The dead shall rise up," Lister said in a haunted tone. For the first time real fear entered the keeper's voice.

Duncan did not will himself to move, only seemed to watch as his body leapt to the side of the platform, grabbed a line, and quickly climbed down.

"Prisoner!" a keeper shouted as he bounded toward Duncan. An arm hooked around his neck. Another man slammed an elbow into Duncan's side, trying to knock him down. Duncan twisted free, running for the port rail.

"'Tis McCallum! Leave him!" Lister called out behind him as a young sailor leapt onto Duncan and began wrestling him to the deck.

"He isn't following!" Duncan shouted, pointing to the rail. "He's being dragged!" The sailor released him with an uncertain look, then helped Duncan untie the tangle of knots lashing a barrel to the rail. Duncan pointed to a rope tied at the base of the rail behind the barrel, chafing the wood where it hung over the side.

"A lifeline!" the sailor gasped as they pushed the barrel aside, and began hauling the rope with Duncan.

Lister appeared at his side and joined in the task. "What good's a lifeline," the keeper muttered, "if no one be there to see ye tumble o'er the rail? 'Tis an accident, nothing more," he added as if to assure the gathering men. But when they heaved the grisly thing onto the deck, even Lister shuddered and stepped back with a moan. The rope was not fastened around the man's waist. It was tied around his neck.

"Professor Evering!" the young sailor gasped, clutching his belly as he retched over the rail.

Duncan's heart lurched. He forced himself to look at the bloodless face, its empty brown eyes gazing up in surprise. It was indeed the kindly middle-aged professor who traveled with them to join the Ramsey family as private tutor; it was Evering, who had found the key that might save Duncan from those who would kill him.

"The rope," Duncan observed in a hoarse whisper. "His arm was tangled in the rope. It's why he appeared to be waving for us."

"It be the work of man, not demons," Lister declared to the terrified sailors, who gave no sign of hearing. He grimaced, then pulled Duncan away toward the hatch in front of the helm. "The captain," he said with foreboding.

A moment later they were in the chamber that the sailors called the compass room, where, amid crates painted with the name of the Ramsey Company, the ship's carpenter had raised a stanchion for the elegant compass that Lord Ramsey had ordered from a London craftsman, set out for final calibration during the voyage. Lister pushed Duncan toward a circle of grim men that included the bearded captain with his first mate; Reverend Arnold, the stern Anglican who regularly prayed over the Ramsey Company; and Lieutenant Woolford, the army officer taking passage to New York with them. Behind, in the shadows, several sailors lurked, some watching the captain and his companions with wild eyes, one kneeling, frantically praying as tears flooded his cheeks.

Lister leaned into the captain's ear for a moment.

"Your damned fool scholar!" the captain snapped to Arnold, then spun about to face Duncan. "Was Evering's chest split open?"

Duncan stared at him in mute confusion.

"Is it so difficult to tell if a man's lost his heart?" the captain demanded. "Speak up, damned your eyes!"

"His body appeared intact," Duncan stammered, scanning the faces of the others in vain for some explanation.

The captain spat a curse, dispatched his mate to the deck, then abruptly grabbed Duncan's shirt and pulled him into the circle. "There! Tell me, you wretch! Is it a man's?" The captain's voice was full of anger, but the fear in his eyes was unmistakable as he pointed toward the compass.

"I don't understand what—" The words choked in Duncan's mouth as he saw the instrument. It was covered in blood. On the floor below, arranged in a small circle, were the feather of a large bird, two stacks of small bones, a huge black claw, a metal buckle, a two-inch-wide yellow eye, and, resting on a pile of salt, a large, bloody heart. At the edge of the circle, opposite the stanchion, was a small brazier, the kind the cook sometimes used, which held the smoldering remains of a twist of tobacco. Above the gruesome circle, hanging on one of the brass swivel pins, was a colorful medallion on a leather strap, a medallion Duncan had often seen hanging inside Adam Munroe's shirt.

His eyes fixed not on the circle but on the medallion. It was as if Adam had returned, to remind Duncan of his duty. He found himself stepping backward, until the captain seized his collar and shoved him toward the stanchion, where he fell to the deck. "Not a man jack will climb the masts!" he bellowed. "They listen to the old fools who say we are bewitched, who say one of their own had his heart ripped out, that those who died this voyage have returned with this storm to claim us." The captain clenched his jaw, seeming to make an effort to calm himself. "Half the crew hide below, so we cannot even get a count to know if one is missing. Ye may be an insolent scofflaw, a damnable thief who steals from honest passengers, but now—"

"I never stole—" Duncan's protest ended in a gasp as the captain kicked him in the belly.

"—but your good reverend tells us you are an anatomist, that you love God and serve the Company, that the men will listen to you. Surely the eye be from a great fish. But the heart . . . . Tell my crew they have nothing to fear. Tell them no man was killed. The cook lies passed out in his hammock. The damned rogue has animals, to provide fresh meat for the galley. He could tell us if it is from one of his livestock. But we cannot wait. Break their damned enchantment! Tell them now, McCallum!"

But Duncan did not look at the bloody heart. His gaze went from the medallion to the Anglican priest, the lantern-faced man in black. Duncan had barely exchanged a word with him since boarding the ship. During most of the voyage the Reverend, like Lieutenant Woolford and Professor Evering, had stayed in the spacious forward cabins, where, it was rumored, another passenger, too ill to walk, stayed confined to bed.

"Reverend Arnold would have you tell us so," the captain added in a taut voice, as Arnold offered a stiff nod of encouragement. The words had the sound of a threat.

As Duncan looked up he saw that the officer's hand rested on the butt of a large pistol in his belt. "Do you understand, sir!" he roared. "My crew has been reduced to puss-gutted fools! Without them, this ship is lost!" he pulled the pistol from his belt and aimed it at Duncan's head. "Be it man or be it beast?"

Duncan's hand went not to the heart but to the long mottled feather, rolling its shaft to see it better. It was not from a seabird, but from a hawk, a land bird of prey. It had been weeks since they had been near the home of such a bird. Near its top the feather was painted with two diagonal vermilion stripes. He used the shaft of the feather to roll over the heart. A round silver object was jammed into one of the arteries. He touched the claw, thinking of using it to dig out the object. It was as large as his index finger, its point as sharp as a razor. It was of no creature he had ever seen.

"'Tis how the demons dug out the heart!" someone in the shadows moaned.

"Black arts of the Highlands!" another crowed. "Toss over the damned clansmen!"

Duncan glanced up, feeling Lister's stare. Scots would be blamed, the keeper had warned, and a clan chief had a duty to protect them.

"Who is given access to this chamber?" Duncan asked, raising his head toward the captain. With his gaze on the pistol in the man's right hand, he did not see the left fist that slammed into the side of his head.

The captain cocked the weapon. "You damned Highland filth! I won't abide an escaped convict putting my vessel at risk," hissed the officer. "There is but one way for you to be alive sixty seconds from now!"

"Dearest father," a sober voice interjected, "guide this wretched soul in the hour of our greatest need."

As Duncan glanced up, wondering to which of the wretched souls present Arnold referred, a new sound rose from above, a thin wailing that was not the wind, followed by more frightened shouts.

One of the men in the shadows darted out of the room, then another. "A sea witch!" a fearful voice cried out from the deck. As the captain turned, Duncan sprang away, grabbing Adam's medallion, leaping past Arnold and through the open hatch, Lister at his heels, the captain's curse close behind.

A dozen men were on the main deck when Duncan reached it, the medallion stuffed into his pocket. Three were sitting against a crate lashed to the deck, their arms thrown over their eyes, one holding an ax between his feet as if for protection. Two more struggled with a long rope stretched from high on the foretopmast, fastening it to a heavy rail stanchion, a foul-weather backstay meant to strengthen the mast, which Lister had proclaimed weakened. All the others were staring in abject terror at a pale apparition on the lower arm of the foremast, the bare cross-spar high above the deck. It was a young woman in a white dress, her long, dark hair swirling about her head, her feet bare.

It was impossible. There were no women on board, except the captain's stout wife and some murderers kept permanently locked in the cells far below. He glanced at the keeper. Lister was looking not at the woman but at Duncan, with the same disapproval he had shown earlier, as if Duncan were to blame for her escaping and choosing suicide. Lister had reminded him that all those in the cells were Scottish. As they locked eyes Lister uttered a single fierce word, barely audible over the rising wind. "*Redeat.*" His prayer for all Scots.

The woman seemed to float along the spar, oblivious to the wet, treacherous footing, moving toward its end—one hand on the slender diagonal stay that connected the tip of the spar to the mast, her face forward, toward the blackening horizon, the other hand extended, fingers uplifted toward the sky.

"Banshee!" the sailor nearest Duncan cried. "She summons the storm!" One of the sailors securing the brace rope dropped the loose end, pulled two wooden belaying spikes from the nearest pinrail, and hurled them toward the woman. She gave the projectiles no notice as they flew past her head.

"Banshee!" another man echoed as the captain appeared on deck. The officer's curse died in a strangled groan as he saw the woman.

Lightning lit the horizon. The deep snarl of thunder seemed to be coming from the sea, not the sky.

"Dearest Lord, I beseech thee!" a frantic voice gasped. Reverend Arnold was at the captain's side now. "Woolford!" the clergyman cried, turning back toward the compass room.

The woman halted a moment. She turned slowly to gaze toward Duncan and the men behind him, revealing a graceful face, hollow with melancholy. Then she faced the sea and stepped over the end of the stay line.

The cries ceased. Even Arnold stopped his frantic praying. All eyes were on the woman as she released her grip on the line, both hands free and uplifted to the sky, one bare foot balancing on the swaying spar, the other braced against the base of the line. It seemed she would surely tumble to the deck as the ship rolled back, sending the tip of the spar high over the deck, but by some magic she held her balance. As the ship righted itself, Duncan saw Lister leap onto the foremast shrouds, desperately climbing toward the woman, followed a moment later by Lieutenant Woolford. But as the ship completed its roll, dipping the end of the spar toward the sea, the pale figure raised her hands higher toward the heavens and lifted her foot from the line that anchored her.

She seemed to hang in the air as she left the spar, tumbling slowly downward, her white dress billowing against the black sky and blacker water, her pale arms ever upward.

No one spoke. No one moved but Duncan. For suddenly, without thinking, he had grabbed the ax, cut the backstay loose with one violent swing of the blade, and was tying the line to his waist. In the corner of his eye, Duncan saw the pistol raised toward him. "Seize him!" the captain bellowed, and flame belched from the gun barrel. Duncan's ribs exploded in pain, then he was on the rail and over the side, diving into the swirling blackness below.

Chapter Two

UNCAN'S HELL WAS A COLD black place at the bottom of the sea. In his youth he had endured more than a few sermons describing other torments the unrepentant might expect, and when he awoke in the darkness, frigid, wet, and shivering, he spent several terrible moments wondering which particular hell his lost spirit had found.

Suddenly the floor under him began to roll, and the wrenching pain in his ribs told him he had not died. He fell against a wall of heavy planks, then a violent pitch of the floor propelled him against another wall a few feet away. He threw his arms out and stood, desperately trying to understand what part of the ship he was in. It was a small chamber, barely seven feet long and even less wide, not quite high enough for him to fully straighten his six-foot frame. The floor was covered with moldy, rotting straw. One wall was canted inward at the base, and he sensed motion in it, or beyond it. A creature on the other side was groaning, pushing the wall with a furious power, as though trying to force its way through. No, he realized with a stab of fear, he was below the water line, and the thing clawing at the planks was the ravenous sea. Desperately he explored with his fingers, finding a long swatch of sailcloth hanging on a peg in one corner, and a heavy door in the wall opposite the hull. But the narrow door had no latch, no means of opening.

A gasp of despair escaped his lips, his chest tightened. He was in one of the cells where the murderers were confined. Lister had declared that the ship was going to sink, and he was locked in a box, where he would drown like all the other rats. He paced back and forth, his heart racing, touching the moist, matted skin on his side where the captain's bullet had grazed him, futilely trying to recall what had happened after the black water had closed about him. What had he done to be sealed into this oversized coffin? He had wanted so desperately to die, then after speaking with Lister and seeing Adam's medallion, he had wanted so abruptly to live.

Frightened shouts rose from the decks above. Someone called for pumps to be manned, someone else for a Bible. He heard the sound of water running past the door and with a wrench of his heart felt a puddle forming at his feet. He pounded on the door until his fists throbbed; then the ship lurched, his head slammed into a wall, and he sank into unconsciousness again.

"Black snake wind, black snake wind, make yourself known."

The thin eerie chant echoed in Duncan's nightmare as he struggled back to awareness, the meaningless, haunting words repeating themselves endlessly, from nowhere and everywhere. He pinched himself in his dream and pushed at his eyes, trying to make certain they were open, then pressed the wound in his side. The flash of pain jerked him upright.

"Black snake wind, black snake wind, make yourself known."

He was awake but the nightmare would not fade.

The storm, however, seemed to have passed. The sea no longer fought with the hull, the water had drained from his cell. He stripped off his wet clothes, wrapping the sailcloth around him, then sat in the black emptiness, listening to the chilling, melancholy chant a few minutes, realizing it was not a trick of his mind, but the utterances of a forlorn woman. He stood, trying to understand how he could hear her voice so clearly. Searching the locked door with his fingertips, he discovered a six-inch-square hatch halfway up the door, hanging open on a leather hinge. His hands shaking, he put his mouth to the hatch and shouted.

"It was a pig's heart!" As the terrible reality of where he was sank in, he repeated the words in a hoarse, desperate voice. "Not a man's! No man was killed!" There was no response, no movement in the darkness. He was on the prison deck, abandoned, alone.

Not entirely alone.

"Black snake wind, black snake wind, make yourself known!" The sad voice seemed more urgent now, almost frantic, and its source became clear. The woman was in the cell next to his. Duncan tightened the scrap of cloth around his waist.

"Who are you?" he asked, futilely pressing his eye to the hole, seeing nothing but a dim line of light at the bottom of a door several feet in front of him. "Are you ill?"

"Take the skin you are," the woman replied in a thin, plaintive tone. "You will see this is the real earth circling about."

He had found a new level of hell after all. He was wounded, trembling from the cold and damp, imprisoned in the dark without explanation, and his sole companion was not only a murderer, but a lunatic murderer.

"It was a pig's heart!" Duncan cried again, shouting the words, continuing despite the low curses they now drew from cells farther away, stopping only when he realized they were coming out in long sobs.

"Fresh meat!" cooed a coarse voice from the darkness. "The storm washed up fresh meat for our pets!"

He dropped to his knees as he realized the prisoner down the passage was speaking of him, then sank backward against a corner, listening to the murmur of the sea until finally, gratefully, he found slumber.

When he awoke, Adam Munroe was with him, squatting in the opposite corner, urging his weevil forward, tossing from hand to hand the wooden buttons he was using for betting. This was the grinning, roguish Adam whom Duncan had come to know, the one who softly sang Highland ballads in the middle of the night and cracked jokes when Company spirits sagged. Except this Adam had seaweed in his hair. Duncan, trembling, spoke his friend's name. Adam looked up, cocked his head, and, his grin fading, extended his open palm with his betting pieces toward Duncan as the tail of an eel began squirming out of his ear. Duncan recoiled in terror, pressing against the wall, his heart thundering, as Adam slowly faded into the blackness.

When he stirred again—was it hours, or only minutes that had passed?—there was a new sound, someone whispering low, rhythmic words that had the semblance of prayers. Their meaning seemed to linger at the edge of his consciousness, as if he should recognize them, but the words were not in English, nor in Gaelic, nor in any other language of Europe.

"Haudenosaunee! Haudenosaunee! Ohkwari! Ohkwari!"

Through the darkness he could not discover the source, only knew that the longer the whispers were spoken, the more they made his skin crawl. They could have been from the murderer next door or from another down the corridor, or even from someone roaming the aisle itself. Or something clinging to the hull outside. The dead were trying to take over the ship, the sailors had insisted. Or perhaps they were just trying to share their secrets.

He began shivering, though his wound burned like a hot poker. In the fever that took hold, questions and faces swirled in his mind. Lister. Evering. The ghostly woman who had drowned. Adam Munroe, again and again Adam, whom Duncan would dishonor because he was incapable of grasping his friend's dying bequest. Nothing of that terrible day made sense, but he knew better than to think everything unconnected. Someone had performed the work of the devil in the compass room, leaving Adam's strange medallion, then the melancholy angel had materialized on the mast and chosen to die by leaping into the raging water. The captain and Arnold had wanted him to prove no one had died. But instead he had shown them that Evering had died, and not, Duncan knew, in the way it appeared to the crew. Evering, who held the key, had died before Duncan could learn how to save himself.

Redeat, he kept hearing Lister say, over and over, and he kept seeing the chastising way the old Scot had looked at him. Surely it was just a bad joke, that anyone, even a dried-up old sailor, would consider Duncan a clan chief.

He slumped against a corner of the cell, the visions strangely congealing like the blood on his ribs. Adam and Evering, supporting the porcelain white angel between them, ran on the surface of the ocean, pursuing the ship, shouting something to Duncan that he could never quite discern. The captain poked a crimson-hot iron into his ribs. His father whipped him with thistles.

When he awoke again, much later, his mind was clear of the fog brought by the fever. A dim light shone down the corridor of cells, from a lantern hung on a beam. A crock of water had been left inside his door, and he gulped it down before noticing that his wound had been bound with a strip of cloth tied around his ribs. By the door lay another piece of cloth, an extra bandage. Not a bandage as such, his fingers told him, but a linen handkerchief, something from the traveling kit of a gentleman. Inside its careful folds was a small metallic object. He held it up to the meager light seeping through the hatch, touched it to his tongue. It was a button, a silver button with flecks of dried blood.

For the first time in a week he felt hunger, a ravenous, piercing hunger. As he lifted his britches from the peg, ready to pull them on, he explored the pockets, hoping to find something, a scrap of leather, even a chip of wood to chew. But then his fingers touched the hard, cold stone Adam had given him, and his appetite vanished. Beneath the stone was the medallion, which he examined for the first time, his fingers running over it in the dark. The storm was gone, the real world had returned, and he could no longer rely on demons or ghosts for explanations.

He had never known Adam to take the medallion from his neck, but someone had taken it, only to leave it on the bloody compass two days after Adam's death. He had sometimes glimpsed the colorful pattern on the leather circle inside Adam's shirt, the shape of a black bird like a crow surrounded by red and yellow concentric rings, but he had always assumed the pattern was made of beads.

Now he found they were not beads, but rows of flat strands—not glass, not reed, waxy-hard yet flexible. It was not of the Old World. He explored the bulge at the back with his fingers, surprised to discover that something small was sewn inside the soft leather. Without knowing why, he draped the amulet around his own neck and covered it with his shirt, then pulled on his britches. He sat, clutching the carved stone, squeezing it until his fingers hurt, hating it, irrationally blaming it for Adam's death, then, as his senses surrendered to despair again, slowly pounding his fist against it. Finally, his strength and emotion spent, he leaned against the hull, listening in the dark to the rush of the water, sensing changes in its rhythms, wondering if somewhere in the sounds were the last words of Adam, spoken as he swam downward, leaving his unfinished earthly business in Duncan's unready hands.

He fell into a languid trance, the carved stone clutched to his chest, his ear to the wood, his thoughts tangled with images of Adam and Evering and the disturbing, unintelligible whispers he had heard, until suddenly he bolted upright, wide awake. "The buttons!" he cried, understanding the first meager piece of the puzzle.

Voices rose in the distance. Kneeling at the hatch, he saw for the first time past the door, into an antechamber with a heavy table and a steep ladder stair that led to the upper decks. A shadow moved along the cells, pausing at each one, then dropping a small, hard crust of bread and a rotting apple into his own cell before disappearing, closing the outer door with the loud snap of a bolt. The voices, he realized as he ate, were those of inmates down the corridor, speaking to one another through their door holes, the meal having resurrected them. Duncan could not make out distinct words, only the hopeless tones in which they were spoken.

"Are you there?" he whispered through his own tiny hatch after he had gulped down the food, suddenly yearning for any human company, even that of the madwoman. "What did you mean about the black wind?" What was her crime, he wondered, what awful thing had she done to deserve condemnation to the deadly tropical plantations? He had once heard of a woman sent away for killing her infant. "I was frightened of the storm, too," he offered, his voice weakening, shamed at his desperation for a single word of acknowledgment. "Did you hear those words earlier? Like some dreadful spirit speaking through the hull. Have you heard it before?"

But no reply came. Had he indeed imagined the words? Was he losing his mind?

In the hours to come, he learned how the prisoners distinguished between night and day. Night was when the rats came.

He woke to the rattle of iron. A figure stepped into his cell, pulling the door behind him, squatting with a dim, hooded candle lantern.

"Brought ye a blanket," the man whispered, handing Duncan a tattered wool sheet and another crock of water. "How be the ribs?"

"Better, thanks to you, Mr. Lister," Duncan said after he nearly drained the crock. "The ship?"

"Captain wanted to make for Halifax for repairs. Reverend Arnold would have none of it. Foretopmast is gone. Prisoners on the pumps these past thirty hours. They had me clean the compass room."

"It's where you found that button? The thing jammed in the heart?"

"Aye. A cold, angry deed. A map was engraved on it, finely worked. A lord's jewelry. Whoever stole it likely realized he best not be found with such a thing on this boat." He extracted a piece of salt pork from his pocket and extended it toward Duncan. "Christ on the cross!" he exclaimed. "Y'er hands!"

Duncan held his fingers in front of the dim light. Blood oozed from a dozen small, swollen bites. "The wound on my side was still bleeding. The rats wanted to feed." He pointed to two dead rodents, lying where he had slammed them against the wall.

The keeper uttered a low groan. "Close the hatch after meals are delivered," Lister instructed as he bent and tossed the dead things into the passage. "At night, block the bottom of the door." He glanced nervously back toward the door. Lister was not, Duncan recalled, one of the keepers authorized to be on the cell deck.

"Surely I need not bear another night of this," Duncan protested. "Let them confine me to the prison hold. I did nothing to—"

The old mate leaned forward, his raised hand cutting Duncan off. "The captain was like a madman. Kicked away the one trying to revive ye after they hauled ye up, tried to heave ye back over the rail. Reverend Arnold took him aside. Ye would have thought ye were a Ramsey firstborn the way he carried on, not a Ramsey slave. When they finished speaking, two sailors carried ye down here, the captain shouting that he would haul ye by the heels for sharkbait. He's brought charges against ye. Two counts of escape on the day of the storm. Deliberate sabotage of the ship. He says fer that one he has the right to try ye and hang ye from a yardarm. Arnold had ye put in here as much to save ye as to punish ye, lad. Show y'erself to the captain and he's liable to drive a spike through y'er neck. There's bartering goin' on as we speak."

"Bartering?"

"The captain drew up a bill of damages alongside his charges. He demands payment from the Ramsey Company. The Reverend counters, claims it was the negligence of the ship's crew that nigh caused us to be lost, that with the crew at their stations Professor Evering would n'er been lost, that the captain owes him for loss of the Company tutor."

Duncan twisted his hands together, staring at the filthy straw at his feet. "Who decides the outcome?"

"All I know is that ye be the prize. The mate says if the captain wins, he's goin' to tie ye into a shroud with ballast rocks and drop ye over the stern."

For a long moment there was no sound but the murmuring of the sea. "Was there a proper funeral for her at least?" Duncan asked in a hollow tone.

Surprise creased Lister's brow. "Ye don't remember? Ye brought her up, lad!" the old keeper declared, wonder in his voice. "We thought ye were gone for certain, what with a half second to tie that knot and the captain's bullet in ye. A chance in a thousand. She was mostly drowned. When they carried you away, I saw Reverend Arnold working on her, pushing her belly, but then I was needed aloft and saw no more."

Duncan's head shot up. "She lives?"

"There's been no burial."

The news brought an unexpected rush of emotion. The angel had fallen and he had plucked her from the sea.

"But who . . . ?"

"The invalid from the front cabins." Lister leaned close to Duncan, whispering now. "I've seen her before, I'd swear it. Last autumn. I was on an eastbound merchantman, full of timber for Liverpool. She was a passenger. I'd not forget that face, so young and graceful yet so old. Like all the beauty had been burnt out of her. Stayed in her cabin nigh all the time. Traveled with a Greek gentleman."

"Greek?"

"Put me in mind of the sponge divers I'd seen in the Aegean. Dark, silent. Learned. Genteel enough. Walked the deck all hours of the night. Drew diagrams of constellations, pictures of the great fishes. Had me teach him sailors' knots. Carved me a little wolf, 'cause I'd said I had a dog like one as a boy. Socrates Moon, he was named."

"Who was she?"

"A princess, he said. A princess in exile, in danger somehow, so her name could not be spoken."

"You make it sound a fairy tale."

"Not my words, but his."

Duncan rose and put his hand on Lister's shoulder as the old mate turned to leave. "The day before Adam died," he said. "Someone's chest was broken into. The captain accused me of theft."

"Ye ship with dogs, everyone gets fleas," Lister declared with a sigh. The Ramsey Company included several slipfasts and pock-etmen in its ranks. Possessions of the sailors, even officers, had sometimes appeared on the prison deck, always prompting a flurry of barter and, sometimes, betting.

"But a new horde of trinkets appeared that day," Duncan explained. "Sewing needles. A flint striker. A horn drinking cup. Musket flints. Wooden buttons." Adam had never had wooden buttons until the day before he died.

"His honor the lobsterback."

"Lieutenant Woolford?"

Lister leaned closer, as if unwilling for even a rat to hear. "After we recovered from the storm, he turned out every man in the Company, with the captain's best bullies at his side, searched the prisoners, then searched every hammock. He cursed the lot of them, demanded the return of his property. He had a club in his hand and fire in his eyes. Even Cameron was scared," he added, referring to the short-tempered, barrel-chested man who led the keepers. "He said Woolford knows the ways of the heathens, who can inflict pain we have never dreamt of. He struck those who resisted, clipped young Frasier just for asking questions. A trunk in his cabin was broken into."

"What did he recover?"

"A bullet mold. A steel ax head. The horn cup. Things for America. He went through Adam's kit, twice. Seemed fair kicked about when he finished."

"You mean he did not find what he sought?"

"Most of his property he recovered, 'cause he said none be punished if they surrendered it then and there. But I'd say what he wanted most of all he didn't find. I'd say he was confirming to himself that Munroe took it with him."

"Took with him?"

"We all saw it. All of us near the bow that day. Woolford. Arnold. Cameron. When Adam was on the maintop after scratching those marks, he raised his hand. Something small was in it, something black. Put me in mind of a lump of coal. But t'ain't a piece of coal that worries our soldier," Lister said and reached for the door. "A black bag of jewels perhaps. The instant Woolford saw Adam swing off the mainmast, he began running to reach him."

It was true, Duncan recalled. Woolford had arrived at his shoulder, gasping, as Adam had disappeared into the water. When Duncan turned, the lieutenant had looked like he had been kicked by a bull. He fought the temptation to touch the black stone in his pocket.

"What questions?" Duncan asked. "What was Frasier seeking?" The young Scot, barely out of his teens, was from a remote Highland family, raised by a maiden aunt after his parents had been taken. One of the Company's many poorly kept secrets was the fact that his aunt had paid for him to be made a trusty keeper.

"About the Company recruitment. Why was Woolford at every court session? Saying that if the Company was just a scheme for pressing men into the army, he'd as soon stayed in jail. Quick as you can say Jack Pudding, the bastard was on the boy, throttling him. Took three of us to pull him away. Woolford was drunk. Sober as churches all voyage, and now he carries a flask."

"Is it so, what Frasier said?"

"Near as we can tell. I spoke with the boy. He says he canvassed every man, and every one recalls Woolford in his courtroom, though most thought nothing of it, since the army sometimes recruits from the courts itself. Says that to the army, men like us be like lambs kept for mutton. He says," Lister added hesitantly, "that English terriers are rightly sent to the kennels of the murderers."

Duncan chilled as he heard the words. "There is only one of the Company sent to the cells," he whispered. Adam had kept Duncan connected to the men of the Company, more than a few of whom spoke resentfully of Duncan's English upbringing. "I had nothing to do with what happened."

"He says favors ain't granted for free."

"Favors? Imprisonment in this rathole?"

"Frasier's half sick with hate and fear. He's been tossing salt in dark corners, speaking old words, words I ain't heard since I was a wee bairn. Reverend Arnold is assembling the Company twice a day for readings of the Bible. He says the only thing they need fear when men take their own lives is too great a distance from God.

"That's what they would have us think," Lister continued after glancing out the door again. "A herd of weaklings already being culled out by the wilderness, that's what Cameron says." Lister looked up into Duncan's eyes. "But ye and I know 'tweren't weakness that killed Adam Munroe. That last night when he sat by the door, I fetched him a cup of tea. He looked so low, I thought he were building a fever. He stared into the steaming mug, not speaking for a long time, then suddenly he looks up and starts firing questions, waiting for nary an answer. Asked me if I had ever thought about what God looked like. Asked if I'd ever been married. Asked if the navy were as heartless as the army. Said he had done terrible wrongs to people without knowing it. I asked if he had gotten into some rum.

"He said the Company would be used to set the price for changing the world. A tear rolled down his cheek, and he said his friend Duncan was about to fall into a black pit. He said the army was going to chew you up and spit out your bones."

Duncan drew in a shuddering breath. "I've nothing to do with the army."

"Perhaps," Lister suggested, "if we were to believe young Frasier, we all have something to do with it."

Duncan drank from the crock again. "It's because of what Adam said that you came up the mast for me."

"Cameron always gives me the late watch, in the small hours. Mostly I sit at the hatch, thinking about those inside, listening to their songs and the things they cry out in their sleep. All I knew was that I'm weary of seeing what happens to the fresh blood of the clans."

"The bruise on your face, Mr. Lister, how did you come by it?"

"It be nothing, an accident."

"No. Someone hit you."

The old sailor went silent for a long moment. "The day after Adam died, I asked about him, asked Cameron. He struck me with nary a word. Then told me to keep me nose pointed straight ahead."

"What exactly did you ask about Adam?"

"Who brought him on board. Did Adam come with Evering."

"But Adam was just another prisoner."

Lister pulled a piece of paper from his pocket, a remnant from a news journal, folded very small, compressed as if it had been flattened by an iron. "This was in Evering's cabin, pushed into a crack in a beam. It's from a paper in Argyll, where Adam came from. And ye remember how Adam carried things, paper things, small things?"

"In his shoe," Duncan recalled as he accepted the paper. "Folded into his shoe." Duncan had once thought Adam kept papers there for warmth, like some of the other men. But then Duncan had seen him reading them, when Adam thought himself alone. Duncan bent to the light and instantly his breath caught. It was an account of the trial of Duncan and his uncle. "Why would Adam have . . . ?" he muttered when he could speak again. "Why give it to Evering?" But he knew neither he nor Lister had answers, only more questions.

Lister pulled another slip of paper from inside his shirt. "And there was this, inside Evering's waistcoat when I was helping clean the body."

Duncan took the slip as Lister pushed the lantern closer. *McCallum*, it said, *6 bells first watch.* He looked up at Lister. "He wanted to meet me before dawn. It must have been for the next day, a message to give me at the morning slops." But Lister's pointed gaze meant the keeper understood the conclusion everyone else would reach, that Evering had met Duncan the day he died, at the likely hour he had died.

Lister pulled the slip away from Duncan. "Can't have this on y'er person, lad," he warned. As he turned to leave, Duncan touched his shoulder.

"What you said on the mast, about the McCallum clan chief."

"About ye, lad."

"No. That's what I mean. I know you meant well. But I was wrong to pretend about such a solemn thing. I am no clan chief. I can never be. You spoke of all those who came before. I can do them no honor."

"What would be wrong, lad, would be to pretend their world still exists. There be the rub of it."

"The rub?"

"Ye'll never have their world. But ye'll always have their name."

The words hung in the air a long time.

"Sometimes, at the edge of sleep," the old mate said as he turned to the door, "I hear pipes and smell the heather. I used to help me father bring the long-haired cattle from the hills." Lister's voice suddenly grew hoarse. "He would raise me onto the back of a shaggy cow and walk beside me singing."

For a moment Duncan's heart rose so far up in his throat he could not speak. "In prison," he said at last, "they left me in a solitary stone cell without light, for nearly two months. I thought I would lose my mind. I survived by picking a day of my youth and reconstructing what I might have done, for every hour of it, from the moment my mother roused me from the blankets. Festival days. Days with my grandfather. Sometimes it's summer, with a blue sky and a fair wind, and I am sailing, with seals all around." He put his hand on Lister's arm.

Lister stayed, and they sat on the cell floor, the lantern between them like some dim Highland campfire, as they spoke of the life each had known. Duncan told stories he had not put into words for years, and Lister's grizzled face broke into a grin as he spoke of long-dead aunts who danced with him as a boy, of drinking *athole brose,* the Highland drink of whiskey mixed with honey, oatmeal, and cream, on festival days. Duncan's own stories leapt off his tongue without forethought—of bonfires on St. John's Eve kept lit all night to ensure fertile crops, of helping his grandfather sprinkle whiskey over fishing boats before they first embarked in the spring, of tying juniper sprigs to the cattle tails, of the island women lined up around lengths of tweed, singing their waulking songs as they pounded and stretched the cloth, and of two score other memories of the lost Highland ways. An hour passed, and though Duncan could not name why, he felt more at peace than he had since his arrest months earlier. Lister felt it, too, Duncan knew, for the old keeper's voice grew lighter, even gleeful, until sitting in the shadow,

Duncan was hearing the boy who had romped in the heathered hills half a century earlier.

"*Tapahd leat*," the keeper whispered when he finally rose. Thank you.

As Lister pushed the door shut, Duncan leaned into the little open hatch. "You did not name him," he said to the retreating figure. "The one who revived me when I was hauled on deck."

"The devil hisself," Lister replied. "Redshanks. But for him and Arnold, the captain would have put a knife in y'er gills and tossed ye back to the sea."

Duncan watched through the hatch as Lister closed the outer door. *She lived.* The mysterious woman in the white gown was safe, he told himself with an unexpected exhilaration. Not for an instant had he considered that he might have been successful. He had saved her, and she was no prisoner but the sick, secret passenger—the banshee, the princess, the angel—who had stayed in the forward cabins with Arnold and Woolford. And Evering.

He pulled the black stone carving from his pocket. Adam had wanted the others, especially Woolford, to believe the stone had gone into the sea with him. Duncan turned it over and over in his fingers, trying to understand why it could be so important. With an abrupt, uninvited realization, he knew the shape was of a bear, a fat, fecund bear. A she-bear. *She is done with me,* Adam had said. *'Tis you she needs now.* Surely it was not possible that Adam had died for the bear, just to mislead Woolford and Arnold into thinking it destroyed. He unfolded the linen bandage and lay the stone on it, beside the silver button, staring at them in the dim light. Old World and New. Flotsam of the deadly tide surging through the Company.

Hours later, after more fitful sleep, the haunting words came again, in the strange singsong tongue that had made his flesh crawl, the soft liquid cadences filled with *S*'s and *Q*'s. Without conscious thought, he raised the stone to his ear to see if it was the bear speaking, then, shamed, shoved it back into his pocket.

"Be still, you witch!" came a shout from the end of the corridor.

Duncan bent to the hatch door, strangely relieved. Someone else heard the voice.

As if in defiance, the words grew louder, the syllables more distinct, though still unintelligible. *"Haudenosaunee! Haudenosaunee!"* At last, as the volume rose above a whisper, he realized they were coming from the madwoman in the next cell. More curses rose from the end of the corridor. She was frightening her fellow murderers.

He listened at the small square hatch a long time, until the voice descended to a whisper and fell away.

"Do you know where you are bound?" he asked the woman abruptly, feeling a sudden urge to distract her, to comfort her. "Jamaica? The ship stops in New York first. Surely they will let you out on deck there, to breathe fresh air." He alternately placed his mouth, then his eye to the small hole. "The Ramsey Company disembarks in New York. But the captain needs to deliver you healthy. He will let you exercise when we . . . ." His voice drifted off as he realized that for all he knew he, too, could be bound for the deadly tropical plantations or, even more likely, might never leave the ship except over the rail with a rock at his feet. His life was in the hands of Reverend Arnold, a man he despised, a man who had shown only contempt toward Duncan.

"I have a brother in the New York colony," he said after a long silence. "I have read in the journals about the beautiful mountains and lakes there, with wild beasts unknown back home. I had a plan once, I wrote him about it last year," Duncan continued, louder now. "I said when he leaves the army we could build a farm together, on a hill by a lake. We'll have cows and sheep. My mother always loved the sheep. When I was a boy she would keep the orphaned lambs in the house." Duncan realized he was speaking in a tight, boyish voice. It felt somehow as if he were asking for forgiveness, not knowing why he spoke the lie, why he pretended to her that he would be free to find his brother. "My brother's in the war . . . ." A slender arm, naked and pale, appeared from the next cell, slowly moving up and down as if it were exploring the shadows. His brother Jamie had been raised as an Englishman in the lowlands, and before he had come of age, the second cousins who had raised him, lying about his birth date, had rid themselves of him by purchasing a commission in the king's army, which assured he would never go back to his Highland ways. Now Duncan's plan about a farm had become one more forlorn dream, and his brother's army, Adam had vowed, was going to destroy Duncan. The army that, Frasier insisted, had some secret connection to the Company. Adam's note had said that whatever the Company declared it was going to do in the New World, it intended the opposite. Duncan had often heard Arnold state the purpose of the Company. To spread goodness and virtue, to make the new land like a peaceful, orderly England.

Suddenly, without thinking, Duncan extended his own arm through the small hatch, reaching toward the next cell, his arm filling the opening so that he was unable to see where the woman's arm was. He brushed her hand, then stretched out his fingers. Her hand found his and they touched, their fingertips overlapping. There was too much distance between them to grip each other's palm, but they entwined the ends of their fingers.

"My name is Duncan," he offered. Her fingers were soft, not those of a woman accustomed to labor. Women of wealth, he reminded himself, could also kill their children. Indeed, without wealth such a woman would likely have been hanged in her own town square.

She spoke a few words in her strange language, then squeezed his fingers and fell silent. Asian. He had never heard the Oriental tongues, but knew they were quick and filled with singsong rhythms. She must have been raised in one of the Asian colonies and was relapsing to another, happier time of her life. It was, he well knew, one of the ways despair played with the human spirit.

"How may I call you?" he asked. The woman's only reply was the sound of a choked laugh. "You are Flora, then," he declared.

She did not reply, but did not pull away.

"She would sing to them, Flora," he whispered, an unexpected aching in his heart. "My mother. She would hold the orphaned lambs and sing to them in the middle of the night, when she thought everyone asleep. I would stay awake and steal to the kitchen door just to listen. She never knew I was there. I think the songs had as much to do with those babies staying alive as the milk she fed them."

The woman squeezed tightly, and he kept speaking, forgetting for a moment the doom that was closing around him, telling of the ancient stone house they had lived in, of sailing with his grandfather, even how once his grandfather had stripped naked and leapt on the back of a passing fin whale, leaving Duncan alone in the open skiff as the old man roared with laughter and sang a Gaelic traveling ballad to the great leviathan, which had stayed on the surface, an odd contentment in its huge black eye. Eventually, realizing he had not confided so much to a woman in years, Duncan quieted, their grip continuing in the silent dark. Her fingers were the only warm thing he had felt for days.

Suddenly there was a creak of wood and Flora snatched her hand away. Someone was approaching through the outer door, carrying a lantern. Duncan retreated, crouching in the corner of his cell. A moment later a key turned in the lock of his door; the entrance flew open and two men appeared, their faces obscured in shadow.

"The captain's compliments," one announced with a guffaw.

As the man leaned into the cell, Duncan recoiled in terror. The captain had struck his bargain, and had sent for his prize. He twisted and rolled, evading the man's reach for a moment before the man landed a kick in his belly that left Duncan doubled up on the floor. Short, vicious blows reached Duncan, kicks to his legs and back, and the sailor laughed as Duncan kept up his vain, frantic resistance, trying to avoid his boot. They were going to render him unconscious, and he would not revive until he hit the water tied inside a shroud.

Suddenly the man was pulled away by his companion, who carried a length of heavy, knotted rope with which he began beating Duncan. But after the first blow Duncan felt nothing, only heard the sound of the strikes. He thought he had gone numb, then realized the man was striking the walls and floor on either side of

Duncan, while loudly cursing him. After a minute the man stopped, dropped something near Duncan's head, muttered quick words, then stepped away. The first man reappeared with a bucket and emptied its frigid seawater onto Duncan, then with a cruel laugh slammed the door shut, snapping its heavy lock closed. Duncan stood, shaking off the water, forgetting his pain as he crawled to the hatch to look after them. Had the captain lost his negotiation?

He held up the object left by the second man. It was a dried, pressed flower. A thistle. Suddenly the rushed, whispered words echoed clearly in his mind. *Redeat, Clan McCallum.* Lister, he slowly realized, had used the visit of the captain's bully as a cover. The stubborn old Scot was not going to let Duncan turn his back on his past. Lister had beaten the planks for demons and presented the traditional token. Despite the blood dripping from his reopened wound, a bitter grin tugged at Duncan's mouth. The ceremony for installation of the last McCallum clan chief had just been completed.

Two piles of tiny bones, a buckle, an eye, a claw, a feather, a heart on salt. At first the objects from the compass room drifted in and out of Duncan's consciousness, then he focused on them, until in his mind's eye he had their placement by the compass fixed. Next, like the orderly bits of facts from his medical lectures, he assembled in his mind all he knew about Evering's last few days. Adam must have confided in Evering, must have entrusted the professor with the strange amulet he wore around his neck. But why had he saved the stone for Duncan, why had he chosen Duncan for his legacy and not Evering? Why, he kept asking himself, would Adam say, *They know who you are,* as if there were something the leaders of the Company knew about him that Duncan himself was blind to? Why had Evering died so soon after Adam, and why so soon after that had the angel on the spar sought her own death? He lifted the stone bear for the hundredth time and pressed it to his forehead in frustration.

He slept, plagued by a recurring dream of a beautiful woman

suspended in the water beside him, her fingers ending in long black claws, pointing at him the way his father did from the gibbet of his nightmares. When he awoke, two large sea biscuits had appeared on his cell floor, apparently dropped through the hatch. For several minutes he tried to extract the worms from them in the dark, then gave up and ate them intact, as many of the sailors preferred. He spoke through the hatch again, calling to the madwoman, extending his arm to blindly search for her fingers in the shadows. Flora was there, for he heard her cry out several times, as though from nightmares, but she no longer sang her songs, no longer offered her soft, desperate touch.

Sleeping again, he was awakened by the sound of his door shutting, and by dim light once more reflecting through the little hatch. A stack of folded clothes had been left inside his cell door. In the corridor, the door to the outside was open, and Duncan could see that the table held a paper and two large candle lanterns.

He dressed slowly, watching the empty table. The clothes were plain and sturdy, though not cheaply made—the austere dress of a servant to a great house. As Duncan slid on the buckled shoes, his door groaned open, and he looked out to see Lieutenant Woolford retreating toward the table, where he took a seat as Reverend Arnold stepped from the shadows, closed the door to the cell corridor behind Duncan, and settled beside the officer. A stool across from the two men awaited Duncan.

"It was not a human heart," Duncan ventured as he lowered himself onto the stool.

Woolford frowned. "The cook eventually revived and explained that it was from a pig he had butchered the night before," the officer confirmed in a brittle tone, stroking his square jaw as he studied Duncan. The scarlet uniform coat the officer usually wore was oddly lacking in brocade or any other adornment of rank. Never had Duncan seen Woolford wear over his chest the small brass gorget that was so treasured by other army officers. Indeed, despite the aristocratic bearing that betrayed Woolford's origins, there was a restless, feral quality about him that Duncan had never before seen in a man in uniform.

"The ship weathered the storm," Duncan offered.

"That particular storm, McCallum," Woolford snapped, "is one *you* still have to weather. Evering died, precious time was lost fighting the weather because you failed to assure the crew with the truth, then you cut the brace for the mast just as it was needed. Most of us thought ourselves dead."

"Half the furnishings in the captain's cabin," a more patient voice observed, "were heaved overboard by those trying to placate the sea demons. We have obligated the Ramsey Company to bear the expense of replacement and the repairs," Arnold explained with a sigh. "We have given our covenant you will cause no more harm."

"I am as powerless in the prisoner hold as I am in here," Duncan offered in a low tone, with a troubled glance toward the corridor of mildewed cells.

"You have proven otherwise," Woolford shot back. "If you saw the fire in the captain's eye when your name is mentioned, you would be grateful to be locked down here." The officer coolly studied Duncan. "He has reminded us that under our own rules you are owed forty lashes for escaping."

The complaint that leapt to Duncan's lips died with the officer's last words. The still-healing flesh of his back crawled at the mention of the whip.

"The captain considers you our most dangerous criminal," Arnold interjected in a chastising voice. "But," he added in a softer tone, "we remain aware that while you perhaps endangered every soul on board you undoubtedly saved one life."

Duncan's gaze drifted to the papers in front of Arnold. The clergyman's elbow rested on the corner of the paper, a wide parchment curved at the ends. Beside it were quills, a pewter pot of ink, and a black lump of cloth.

Arnold leaned backward, letting the silence take hold as he might from the pulpit before making a profound point. "The Company has suffered a terrible blow," he declared. The Reverend, Duncan realized, was not wearing his stiff black waistcoat, but a stylish brown frockcoat and shirt with lace cuffs—the attire of a successful merchant. "Our Aristotle has been called to a higher temple."

"Professor Evering will be missed," Duncan ventured, not understanding what Arnold expected of him. He found himself watching the ladder, the skin on his back still crawling. A keeper would come soon, and the flogging they intended would leave him scarred for life—if he survived it. If the captain took the whip, Duncan would never leave the mast alive.

"But Providence has provided."

Duncan realized Arnold was staring at him, that the words were aimed at him. "Providence?"

"I personally selected every member of the Company," Arnold reminded him. Duncan had not understood why the stranger with the clerical collar had stood beside the judge's bench, not until the judge had declared his sentence commuted to transportation, then had turned and shaken Arnold's hand. "You had a European education. Before your lapse of morals, you were about to commence an honorable profession."

"That life is gone," Duncan said in a near-whisper, glancing at Woolford as he reminded himself of Frasier's discovery that Arnold had not been alone in selecting the men of the Company. "I am a convict now."

Arnold pushed the lanterns to the side of the parchment so its full text was uncovered. "The essential role of the Ramsey Company," he said with gravity, gesturing to the document, "is reshaping the destinies of men."

Duncan gazed at him uncertainly, then began to read. *On the ship* Anna Rose, *out of Glasgow,* it began. Printed on the first line, with large ornate letters, was his own name. He read the text, then looked up in confusion. It was an indenture, a document commuting his sentence of hard labor to seven years as indentured servant. There was a line for his signature beside that of Arnold, who had signed as agent for Lord Ramsey.

"There is no dishonor in such servitude. Many free men have

signed such papers to win passage to the New World," Arnold observed.

Duncan was beginning to remember his leap over the rail. This was how it had felt when the black waters had closed around him. "I have already won passage," he murmured, keeping his gaze on the table, watching as Arnold's hand clenched into a fist. Confusion still nagged him, even fear, but these emotions were overshadowed by his bitter resentment of the two men before him.

"We must replace Evering as tutor to his lordship's children," the vicar continued. "The king can be merciful. You were convicted for shielding an old highwayman. But your trial record mentioned he was an ailing relative. Perhaps you were simply honoring your duty to an aged family member without full knowledge of the circumstances," Arnold added in a tentative tone, as if he had been authorized not only to rewrite Duncan's sentence but the very record of his trial. "Sign, and the lieutenant will witness." The vicar pushed the lump of black cloth toward Duncan. It was a cap, Duncan saw, one of the black-and-grey caps worn by scholars at colleges, probably the one Evering had worn at formal Company gatherings.

Duncan suddenly recalled that young Frasier, fresh from schooling, was sometimes used by Arnold as a secretary. Frasier had known about the parchment when he had claimed that Duncan was being favored, though Duncan still could not entirely fathom the favors being suggested. "You are offering me freedom?"

"Of a kind, once off the ship. Freedom to serve Lord Ramsey in a more meaningful capacity. It is within my power to sign for the Ramsey family. You will remain a member of the Company, bound by the terms of your transportation. You will offer lessons to the men of the Company each seventh day, after services."

"You cause me to wonder, Reverend," Duncan said, with studied confusion in his voice. "Do you speak for God, or the king, or Lord Ramsey?"

"A man in your position," Woolford interjected icily, "should not consider the distinction meaningful."

Arnold folded his hands together in front of him and leaned forward, as if grateful for the opportunity to explain. "The Ramsey family has graciously appointed Arnolds to the local rectory in Kent for nearly three centuries. It is a small flock, dependent on the Ramsey estates. My elder brother tends to the spiritual needs of the tenants who remain there. I minister to the needs of the Ramsey family elsewhere, in as many ways as I am able. I am vicar of Edentown, new home of the Ramsey Company. I have the honor of also serving as a proctor to Lord Ramsey, and am empowered to conduct business in his name. Men of vision recognize that the hand of God is never confined to spiritual matters."

Duncan's confusion mounted. "The patron resides in the New World?" He met Woolford's stare. The officer was studying Duncan intensely, running his finger along a long scar on his own neck, the most recent of several that marked his neck and jaw. Though not far from Duncan's own age, Woolford had the hard, weary look of a man much older, and the cool eyes of a predator. The officer had caused Adam's death, Lister had insisted, by telling him they were bound for Lord Ramsey's town in the New York colony.

"In addition to his estates in England," Arnold continued, "Lord Ramsey owns a great house in the city of New York as well as lands in the west of the colony. He enjoys the vigor of life in America, knows he can better serve the interests of his cousin the king in the colonies. But he desires his children to be instructed by someone versed in the curricula of Europe."

Duncan searched Arnold's narrow, impassive face. The vicar's words were impossible. Surely he had misunderstood.

"Instructed for seven years," Arnold added with a thin smile. He lifted a quill and handed it to Duncan.

"A tutor?" Duncan asked in disbelief. "To an English lord's children?"

Arnold clenched his jaw, then pointed a long, bony finger toward the corridor behind Duncan. "Alternatively, you may have been an active participant in your uncle's traitorous acts and an active saboteur on this ship. Deserving of the most severe punishments, like those in these cells, bound for Jamaica." Arnold stood and pushed open the door to the cell corridor, then planted himself at the entrance. "Have you any notion what these wretched creatures face? What *you* may face should you not lift that goose feather?" he demanded, raising his voice as if wanting to be certain those in the cells heard. "Years of labor on the sugar plantations, if you are unlucky enough to survive so long. Insects so thick they are sucked into your lungs with every breath. Serpents. Yellow jack. Malaria. Hurricanes. Half don't live past their second year. Buried in a shallow grave without a marker, your bones mixed with all the other slaves who die." The soft-spoken Anglican priest had his own unique form of fire and brimstone.

Duncan glanced toward the cells, hating Arnold for so bloodlessly recounting Flora's fate within her earshot, then looked back at the soldier. He had seen the cool anticipation on Woolford's face before, in the courtroom crowd when his uncle had been sentenced. It was a moment when a life hung in the balance. He longed for the bleak hours in the cell when he had nothing to keep him alive but the insane notion of being clan chief. He had once seen a man, nearly buried alive, awaken from a coma as the gravediggers' dirt hit his shroud, a grey shell of a man with no human spark left. That was what Arnold and Woolford had hoped to drag out of Duncan's cell.

The quill seemed as heavy as granite when he raised it.

"When we disembark, you will be serving in the household of the Ramsey family," Arnold declared with an approving nod. "We shall abide no foolishness, no sedition. No reckless disregard for your own life, which belongs to Lord Ramsey for the next seven years. You are beloved of God."

Duncan stared at the vicar as Woolford lifted a second quill to witness. Had he heard the last words from any other man he would have considered them mockery. As he looked back at the parchment, he recalled the questioning, lightless eyes of Evering when they had pulled his body onto the deck. "How do I know," he asked, his quill pausing in midair, "that by signing I am not condemning myself to the same fate suffered by Evering?" He spoke slowly, searching the face of each man in turn.

Woolford lowered his quill, his eyes round with question. Arnold's thin lips pressed into a cold frown.

"Surely," Duncan declared, "you understand the last Ramsey tutor was murdered."

Woolford leaned forward, fixing Duncan with an intense, disbelieving stare.

Arnold's eyes turned to ice. "The professor drowned."

"With a rope around his neck?" Duncan asked.

"We have thoroughly reviewed the tragic circumstances," Arnold replied in a level voice. "Evering was despondent from the loss of his wife to fever last year. He has relatives back home. It does his family no favor to tell them it was suicide."

"Suicides on ship might throw themselves over the rail," Duncan observed, lowering the quill to the table, "or they might hang themselves. They don't do both."

"He simply intended his body to be recovered for Christian burial," the vicar asserted as he closed the door and returned to the table, leaning over Duncan. "The noose made certain his death was quick. The captain's log is complete, with my signature as witness. We have already reported that Evering slipped over the rail in the storm. I have written an obituary, to be published in London at Company expense. He is no less a hero for dying before we begin our destined work in America. The captain expects to hail an eastbound ship soon. The body and the death notice will be sent back."

"Had he been alive when the rope was placed around his neck," Duncan explained, speaking toward his cupped hands, "it would have bruised his flesh. There was no bruising."

In the silence that followed, a long, agonized groan rose from the cells.

Arnold's eyes narrowed. "You know nothing of such things."

"I seem to recall you once sought out my medical advice."

"You were never formally qualified as a physician or surgeon," Arnold rejoined. He raised a corner of the parchment as though in warning.

"You both heard in court that I had three years of medical study. For most of those years I stood in a surgical hall and examined bodies brought by the magistrates, organ by organ, limb by limb. I may not be sufficiently qualified to heal the living," Duncan admitted, "but I am quite expert at explaining the dead. Show me the body and I will show you the truth."

The words brought a puzzled twist to Woolford's mouth.

Arnold closed his hands together as if in prayer. "Such reckless allegations will only harm Lord Ramsey," he said, and exchanged a somber look with Woolford. "Evering was attached to the Company."

"On the first day of the voyage I heard you tell the assembled prisoners that the Company stands for honesty and true belief," Duncan pointed out.

The comment quieted Arnold. "And more," the vicar agreed. "It is an experiment under a royal warrant. When we succeed, twenty such companies will be chartered, and twenty new communities established to block the French and their savage allies. We will not fail. And we will not be distracted or disgraced. You, sir, are mistaken."

Duncan looked up. Had Arnold just offered an answer to why the army was so interested in the convicts?

"If the ritual was not a sign of a suicide," Duncan said, "then it is a message for the living, not the dead."

"The bloody heart was meant for us?" Woolford's voice had lost all its confidence. He leaned forward, suddenly and intensely interested.

Arnold slowly turned to stare at Woolford, whose reaction seemed to have taken him by surprise.

"How many in the Company have been in the New World before?" Duncan asked. Arnold pulled Duncan's quill from his reach, as if reconsidering his offer.

"Why?" the army officer asked.

"The ritual. Some of it was from the Old World. Some of it, I believe, was not. How many, other than Adam Munroe?"

Woolford studied Duncan intently, but did not reply.

"Surely it would have occurred to you, Lieutenant," Duncan continued, "that Adam Munroe's death, Professor Evering's death, the ritual, even the plunge of that poor girl into the sea, all of these events happened only after your trunk was looted. It became the Pandora's box of the Company. What did it have in it from America?" Duncan saw not anger but deep surprise flash in Woolford's eyes, quickly replaced by something that may have been worry. The officer stood, circled the table once, then gestured Duncan toward the ladder.

Five minutes later they were in a forward hold, a dim narrow space where the dank air carried the pungent, almost overwhelming scents of bilge water, spices, mildew, pitch, and spoiling meat. Arnold and Woolford stood by with lanterns as three keepers, led by Lister, pulled a canvas sheet from a long wooden box, then pried up the nails that secured the top. They lifted away the top and then quickly retreated, casting suspicious glances toward Duncan as they disappeared. Only Lister remained in sight, lingering uneasily near the entrance.

Professor Evering had been salted. His corpse had been cleaned before being laid in a bed of salt, his clothes neatly arranged, a worn silver timepiece added to his waistcoat. His flesh was drawn and puckered, his bloodless lips stretched in a grotesque grin. The professor's eyes were covered with large penny coins.

Arnold stepped forward and with his fingernails pushed the pennies away, letting them fall into the salt. "Pagans," he muttered in a disdainful tone.

"We always placed our cadavers in barrels of brine," Duncan said in an absent tone as he studied the body, his medical training taking over. "Preserves them quite lifelike."

"So the cook suggested," Woolford replied. "But a barrel of brine lowered into a grave somehow seemed less than heroic. And this way we avoid the risk that twelve stone of pickled pork gets buried instead." His words seemed to hint at amusement, but there was only challenge in his eyes when Duncan looked up.

Duncan worked quickly, unbuttoning the collar of the dead man. Rigor mortis had long since left the body, and he pushed the head from side to side between his hands while Arnold stood back with disgust on his face. "The most valuable benefit of the office of hangman," he explained as he worked, "is the privilege of selling his victims to the medical schools. I have examined over a score of men from the gibbet. Each one bore terrible contusions around the throat, because the rope always crushes the living tissue. See for yourself. The professor shows no such marks." He pointed at the pale skin of the man's neck.

"Surely this is a job for a magistrate," Arnold protested. "Some respect is due—"

Arnold was cut off by Woolford's raised hand. "There is no magistrate here," the lieutenant interjected, "and soon the body will be on its way home. Surely we owe the esteemed Evering an opportunity to teach his successor."

Duncan glanced at the doorway, where Lister lingered, looking strangely pained, then proceeded to probe Evering's remains, starting with his hands. They were soft, unblemished, showing no sign of a struggle. The professor's right hand clutched the small Bible Duncan had sometimes seen him reading on deck.

"I read from his own scripture at the service we held for him on deck," Arnold explained. "He kept to his books," he said in a louder, poised voice, as if he had decided to begin a eulogy. "When his wife died of fever a year ago he sought a new beginning. But he always seemed so lonely."

Duncan bent, studying the book in the scholar's hand. "Why is it damaged?" he asked. "He loved his books, he would never do that."

"Do what?" Woolford asked.

"The last pages are torn out." Evering's fingers did not resist as with his own fingertip Duncan pried up the back cover far enough to glance at the last page. "Revelations. Revelations has been ripped out of his Bible."

Arnold's mouth opened and shut as if for an explanation, but no words came out. Someone had removed the pages about the end of the world.

Duncan began examining Evering's attire. "Are these not the clothes he wore when pulled from the sea?"

"Dried and brushed, yes," Arnold confirmed. "We added the waistcoat and the watch."

His waistcoat. Duncan did not recall ever seeing Evering without his waistcoat, the pockets of which were always bulging, filled with slips of paper, even sea biscuits to share with the prisoners, who had slowly warmed to the quiet, gentle scholar. But when they had pulled him from the water, Evering had not been wearing the sleeveless garment. As if he had died before fully dressing. As if he had died in his own quarters.

"This is his everyday waistcoat," Duncan observed. "He had a black one, for Sunday services. And this is his ordinary watch. He had a gold watch with a fob shaped like a book."

"Gone," Arnold replied. "The thieves are as thick as rats on this ship."

"And his shoes?" Duncan asked.

"One of the keepers polished them," Arnold said.

"And repaired this?" Duncan asked, pointing to the buckle on the left shoe, which was smaller and shinier than that of the right.

"I suppose," Woolford said impatiently. "Why would we possibly—" he began, but the words died in his throat as understanding lit his eyes.

"What," Duncan asked, "was the professor's buckle doing by the blood-soaked compass?"

Arnold bent over the shoe as Woolford stared at it with a dark expression. Neither offered an answer.

Duncan paused again over Evering's left knee, where the britches seemed somehow to adhere to the flesh. He rolled up the fabric, having to pry it from the skin at the knee. "He knelt on something before he died," Duncan observed, squatting to study the chalky skin of the knee. Numerous small punctures radiated out from the patella, the skin slightly discolored around each. Several held tiny shards that glistened in the light. Duncan studied them a moment, holding a lantern close. Glass. Small, sharp pieces of green glass. They would have made it impossible for Evering to walk without incredible pain. Which meant the professor had not knelt on the glass before he died, but as he died.

Duncan moved to the pockets, discovering a slip of paper in the waistcoat. Hoping his companions did not mark his moment's hesitation, Duncan used his other hand to open a second pocket as he palmed the paper. From the britches he extracted a handkerchief, wrapped around a ball of leaves and stems, which Duncan smelled before extending toward the others.

"Seaweed?" Woolford inquired.

"Tea," Duncan replied. "Does a man contemplate a pot of tea and suicide at the same time?" He gazed into Evering's lifeless face, feeling a strange connection with the man, realizing how much they had had in common, remembering the quiet conversations he and Adam and Evering had sometimes shared. Evering had spoken passionately about the calculations he had made that predicted a comet that would be visible in North America by mid-autumn. Duncan sensed that he and Evering would have become close friends had the professor lived. And now, for the first time, Duncan realized that even in his death Evering might provide the key to Adam's mystery.

"A despondent gentleman, still in anguish over the loss of his wife, might do just that. Suicides are irrational," Arnold countered. "The death wish can seize them without notice. And we have only the word of a convict that he died before entering the sea."

Duncan sighed and circled the coffin, then quickly opened Evering's jaw, lowering his ear toward the dead lips as he firmly pressed on the man's diaphragm. A wheeze of air rushed up the throat, sounding so much like a cough that Woolford leapt back with a gasp of alarm.

Duncan stayed bent, close to Evering's mouth. "What say you,

Professor?" he asked in a solemn voice, gazing at Arnold as he spoke. He pushed again and a sound like a groan came from the body. "Exactly," Duncan said. "That is what I have been telling them."

The color had vanished from Woolford's face. He seemed to expect Evering to rise up from his coffin at any moment.

"Desecration!" Arnold hissed.

Duncan fixed him with a somber gaze. "I assumed we were after the truth. You still doubted my words," he declared. "So I thought you might believe the professor if he told you himself."

"This is blasphemy!" Arnold barked. "I shall never allow—"

"His lungs were full of air." Woolford's declaration silenced the vicar, who stared at the lieutenant, jaw open, his anger slowly fading, replaced with shocked dismay. "You have heard it yourself, Reverend. No water in the lungs," Woolford continued. "Air. This man did not drown."

The vicar stared at the dead man. "Then he died preparing his suicide. A fall. The ship was rolling in the rising storm."

Duncan lifted the dead man's head again, probing, and discovered a soft spot behind the left ear where there should have been hard bone. "Someone hit him from behind," he explained, pointing to the discolored, split tissue under the hair. "There is bruising, so it was done before death. The blood that would have clotted in the hair should have made it obvious, but the sea washed it away. It is a circle, nearly an inch wide. This was the end of a pole or spike. Perhaps the butt of a pistol. A hammer even," he added.

"He was preparing for his suicide," Arnold pressed, "planning to throw himself overboard after tying the rope to the rail, when a roll of the vessel knocked him backward, hitting his head so that he died before finishing his task. The top of a belaying pin could have made such a mark. He fell against the barrels and was hidden until that huge wave washed him over."

Duncan probed further, pushing back the professor's long hair, and paused again. "There's another," he said, and pointed to a second discolored circle, above the ear on the opposite side of the head. "He fell from the first blow, probably to his knees, and was finished with a second blow. This was no accident."

Arnold's face seemed to sag, then he turned toward the dead man. "Evering," he declared in a mournful whisper, then stepped closer. "When Jehovah calls, not even the noblest of mortals may resist," he added, his voice cracking. "God wills it so."

They stood in silence, gazing upon the dead man as if at a wake. In Duncan's youth, a man's friends would have kissed his bloodless face.

"He never spoke with the sailors," Woolford finally said in a slow, studied voice. "He acted as if the crew were invisible."

Arnold began a whispered prayer, his palm now on Evering's head.

"But he would often read to the prisoners," Woolford continued. "And write letters for them."

"In the evening," Duncan agreed, recalling how Evering stayed with the Company prisoners when they were allowed evening exercise, sitting on a barrel, writing as this or that prisoner whispered to him. Even the keepers sometimes asked the scholar to help with a letter. "And the barrel that hid the line on his neck. The knots that bound it were those of a landsman."

The vicar ended his prayer in midsentence. "What are you saying?"

"I asked the captain," Woolford explained. "The chaos that day started at dawn, when the new watch passed through the compass room. Evering died in the night. All the earlier watch crew save the helmsman were below, out of the weather. There was a terrible fog before dawn, so thick the helmsman could not see the midship lantern. But the crew were all together below, no one unaccounted for. His murderer," Woolford said, his voice fading to a whisper, "was someone in the Company."

The announcement seemed to take the strength out of Arnold. He lowered himself onto a nearby crate, then stared into his folded hands a long time.

When Arnold finally spoke, he had found his pulpit voice. "We will not have our noble experiment destroyed by scandal." He slowly raised his head toward the ceiling. "It must be resolved. One versed in the ways of death could do so."

Duncan looked at Woolford. The officer did not react to Arnold's apparent invitation.

"You have not yet signed the indenture, McCallum," Arnold observed.

Duncan felt his chest tighten, his mouth go dry.

"I believe," Woolford offered with a thin grin, "the good reverend has proposed an amendment to your terms."

"I cannot. I will not inform against the men."

"Of course the choice is yours," Arnold said, his prayer-like tone raising gooseflesh down Duncan's spine. "You can find our murderer. Or we can give you to the captain, who will lash you all the way to Jamaica. By the time you arrive, the flies will be burying eggs in your flesh as you lay dying."

Chapter Three

ARNOLD GAINED ENERGY AS HE paced around Evering's coffin. "You can have your indenture, have the freedom offered the Company tutor," he continued. "But you will provide an answer to this horrible crime."

Duncan's heart began rising into his throat. "I have nothing to do with this," he said.

"Your duty is to the Company, in all things. This must be addressed quickly," Arnold said, then circuited the coffin again as he collected his thoughts. "You will speak to no one about your work. You will assemble the facts, identify the killer, and report your answer to us."

"Surely you are mistaken," Duncan said. "I am a—" He struggled for a moment, no longer sure who or what he was.

"You are highly educated, a doctor in all but name. You have demonstrated your power of deduction. You will still be part of the Company. As tutor you will have sufficient latitude to observe its workings. The prisoners will speak to you as one of their own. And you will have ample opportunity to obtain my counsel to assure the proper direction. Or," Arnold said, his tone sharper, "I can burn the indenture." He punctuated his statement with a pointed glance toward the cells. "The captain is paid by the head for his deliveries to the sugar plantations. No one will object if he delivers one more than he started with. No one will notice if you disappear at sea."

Duncan did not reply.

"The Reverend and I will collect the letters the professor wrote for the prisoners," Woolford suggested.

"They were confidences," Duncan protested.

"Exactly," Arnold shot back. "It is but a fine line between the secrets of convicts and outright conspiracy. We shall collect all the Company letters still on board."

"They are part of the royal mails."

"Which is why we must review them before we land."

"You are asking me to be a spy, an informer. I cannot."

Arnold breathed deeply. He seemed to take strength from Duncan's protests. "I am asking only for the Company to be released from the threat of scandal. Prove your loyalty to Lord Ramsey. Sign our contract and find us an answer. A bargain any other man on this ship would leap at."

"*An* answer or *the* answer?" Duncan stared at the unhearing Evering, then flushed as he realized he had spoken aloud the question that had leapt to his tongue. He looked up to see Arnold's eyes flare.

"Practice none of your sophistry on us, McCallum," the vicar snapped. "The truth is a sacred thing. You have a duty to it. I bind you to it. If you sign and disobey, you will join the prisoners assigned to the Ramsey forests and confront the two- and four-legged beasts that dwell there. The members of the Company will not die of tropical diseases. But some will die of arrows and axes, I assure you. And worse."

Duncan decided it was safest to address the dead man again. "So justice is a private affair in America." He fought a temptation to take the dead man's hand as he would a friend's. In death the professor had become more a part of Duncan's destiny than ever he had been in life.

"Truly you have found a man for all seasons," Woolford observed, cool amusement entering his voice. "A doctor. A sailor, judging by his ease in the rigging. A tutor. Now a lawyer."

"It was my honor on this journey," Arnold reported in a chill tone, "to take delivery of his majesty's appointment of Lord Ramsey as a magistrate. Every man in the Company signed its articles, agreeing to submit to his judicial power."

"I was given the choice of signing the Company rolls or returning to prison. I was shown no articles."

"When we arrive at the appropriate answer," Arnold continued, ignoring his protest, "Lord Ramsey will close the matter officially. You will find he does not cower from difficult decisions."

Duncan was not sure what hurt worse, Arnold's threat to consign him to the prisoners bound for Jamaica or the reminder that to gain his freedom Duncan must become a lapdog for the aristocracy he despised so much.

As they left the chamber Woolford gestured Lister back inside to close the coffin. The old Scot moved stiffly, acknowledging Duncan with only a quick, empty nod as he passed. Duncan paused, sensing something had changed in the keeper. He watched as Lister silently set the pennies back over Evering's eyes, then lifted a mallet from a nearby crate and began sealing the professor into his box for the last time.

Five minutes later they were back on the prison deck. Duncan signed the indenture in silence, staring at the table as Woolford witnessed and Arnold rolled up the document. "The clothes," the vicar declared impatiently, gesturing toward Duncan's sleeve, "belong to the family Ramsey. We will not have them befouled in a cell. You may retain the smallclothes and shoes."

Duncan stared at the man in disbelief, but the protest on his tongue died as he heard another anguished moan from one of the cells. Slowly he began to unbutton his waistcoat.

Arnold climbed up the ladder without a word of parting, the clothing carefully folded over one arm, the indenture tucked under an elbow. Woolford sighed and extinguished one lantern, seemed about to climb up when he hesitated. "I could find a blanket," he offered.

Duncan had been working hard to hate the officer. Now Woolford's words had a tone of apology.

"I need nothing from you but an answer. Is Mr. Lister ill?"

The jagged scar on Woolford's neck went white as he clenched his jaw. "When prisoners flee confinement, a flogging must follow."

Duncan closed his eyes a moment. As the keeper who had brought Duncan back from his escape, Lister was supposed to be the one to bind Duncan to the mast and begin the flogging.

"But Lister announced that your disappearance had been his fault, that he had given you permission to linger another minute on deck after breakfast, that he had forgotten you, that you had not actually escaped."

"A lie!" Duncan gasped. "My God! The captain's fury—"

"Lister took your flogging."

The words ripped at Duncan like a hot blade.

Woolford raised the lantern and studied Duncan's face. "The captain himself administered the cat. Forty strokes. He acted as if cheated of a greater pleasure. Lister broke three splints of wood placed between his teeth but never cried out."

Duncan felt the blood drain from his face as he sank against the wall. He had doubted Lister, had questioned what it meant for the old Scot to bind himself to Duncan and the clan. So Lister had shown him.

The brittle silence was broken by the sound of movement on the ladder. In the shadows at its base stood Cameron, the tall, ox-like leader of the keepers, holding a bucket of worm-ridden biscuits.

Woolford had lingered, and seemed about to say something until he spotted the keeper. "Is she safe?" Duncan asked the officer.

The officer seemed to have a hard time finding an answer. "She lives. I can't decide whether what you did was incomparable bravery or incomparable stupidity."

"I thought her dead for certain."

"It was the first time she had been left alone on the voyage. Everyone had thought her sleeping." Woolford gestured him toward his cell.

"Who is she?"

The question brought a hard glint to Woolford's eyes. "Difficult to say exactly. She has been abed, too weak for speech, the entire voyage."

But not too weak to climb up the mast and out on the spar, Duncan nearly said. "Lieutenant, you have helped nurse her all these weeks," he pointed out instead. "Surely you know her name."

"I have heard many," Woolford's tone made it clear he would speak no more on the subject.

They stood silently staring at each other as Cameron distributed the biscuits down the line of cells.

"I have a brother, Lieutenant," Duncan ventured as he reached the cell door. "Somewhere in the army. When we arrive in New York, could you find where he is stationed?"

"It's a large colony."

"His name is James. James McCallum. A captain of the Forty-second Regiment of Foot."

Woolford gazed at him with an odd mixture of anger and worry. "Captain McCallum of the Forty-second," he recited in a tight voice, then spun about and marched toward the ladder as Cameron approached, brandishing the key to lock Duncan's cell.

By the time the lock snapped shut, the slip he had taken from Evering's pocket was back in his hand, held in the dim light of the hatch. He gazed at it with a sinking heart. It was nothing but a small star chart, with a trajectory shown in dotted lines through constellations and a single word: *October.* But Lister had been very clear in relaying Adam's words. *Heed how Evering explains his comet,* as if the comet might explain the threat to Duncan. His confusion seemed a palpable thing, a weight that was slowly crushing him. But Lister had shown him otherwise. The McCallum clan would not be crushed. He had to live—for Lister, for Jamie, for the Scots in the prisoners' hold, for the nameless woman he had saved.

With new, intense effort Duncan tried to understand the ritual at the compass, etching each of the bloody objects into his memory. He would ask Arnold for the objects, he decided, he would arrange them as they had been in the compass room so he could study each in turn, and together. There had to be a logic, however distorted, and if he failed to find it, he and others could pay with their lives.

Bone, buckle, eye, claw, feather, salt, heart. In his youth such an eye had appeared on a post in an island village, and even though his grandfather had named it as coming from a great shark, the villagers had abandoned their homes until a priest could be brought to purify the grounds. The devil's eye, they had called it. Eye from a great beast, bones from small ones. They had been from several different small birds, some with tiny, disconnected vertebrae, even the fragile bones of the wings. The eye and the bones. A great god and his mortals.

He lifted Evering's paper again, this time trying to create in his mind a dialogue with the scholar about his comet, like those Duncan had conducted with his medical professors in his prior life. Evering had been a man of science, and Duncan probably had more scientific training than any other man on board. The professor would open his journal and show the other pages of notes and maps; he would speak of the old records he had found that supported his predictions about the comet; he would—

Duncan suddenly closed his hand around the paper and grinned. It wasn't the comet. *Heed how Evering explains his comet,* Adam had said. *The journal.* Adam would know Evering would inevitably show him the journal. And in the journal would lie other secrets. It wasn't what the comet meant that mattered, but what was with the comet, the other pages inscribed during the past few weeks.

Food came twice a day, consisting each time of one of the small loaves, hard as planks, or a square of the worm-pocked ship's biscuit, sometimes with a spoiled apple or scrap of salt pork. Duncan slept, warm and dry thanks to the blanket Lister had provided, futilely trying every few hours to engage Flora in conversation. The mad-woman acknowledged him only with her unintelligible chants. "Take the skin you are," she blurted out once, like a cry of pain, the only English words she had uttered since Duncan's first hours in the cell. Her speech had become hollow and slow, sometimes slurred, as if she were distracted, even drunk, all proof that if she were not already mad, she was quickly progressing to madness. Sometimes, without speaking, she thrust her arm out and flailed the air, clutching his fingertips when he responded with his own hand. Each time, they stayed locked in the strange intimacy for several minutes, listening to each other breathe, never seeing each other's face. The few times Duncan tried to speak while holding her fingers she always withdrew. Flora had killed her child, and whether she had known before, Arnold had made it clear that she was going to a certain, agonizing death. Duncan recognized the symptoms even through the darkness. She had already started her dying, the gradual, agonizing way that Adam Munroe had died.

He was sleeping when they came for him again. Arnold left his cell door open as he walked back to the table in the entryway. As Duncan warily approached the table, Woolford appeared from the shadows. The officer absently gestured to a pewter plate at the edge of the table bearing slices of bread and mutton, his gaze locked on two letters in the center of the table. Duncan stared at the plate. He had eaten no fresh meat, no real bread, for months.

"There were more than twenty letters from the prisoners, several written by Evering over another's name," Arnold explained as Duncan stuffed a piece of meat into his mouth. "Mostly the ramblings of lonely men, asking for forgiveness, offering harmless lies to convince family not to worry. Some pleas to fund barristers for appeals. These two," he said, pointing to the center of the table, "cannot be so easily dismissed." He spread the open envelopes over the table. Evering had affixed wax seals to them, which had been opened by a clumsy trick, slicing away the seal with a hot blade, to be later closed with a larger dollop of hot wax over the original seal.

As Duncan stared at the papers, he recalled that he, too, had written a letter, addressed to his brother, cursing the king. He picked up the first and began to read. It was from the moody young keeper, Frasier, addressed to his aunt, the old maiden who had raised him when his family had been taken from him after Culloden. The letter spoke of an uneventful voyage, woven with bitter comments about his arrest and trial. *I know the secret of why the English went all the way to Auld Reekie when there were wagonloads of prisoners to be had in Ayrshire, Lanarkshire, and Argyll. We know what oozes out of Lothian barracks. We know how to treat the dog who stands over corpses. We know how to cut out the rot. Payment will be made before you lay out the Beltane fires.*

"It could mean many things," Duncan suggested as he read again the confusing words. What had the Company brought from Auld Reekie, the age-old nickname of Edinburgh, that they could not find in the western counties? And what was Frasier expecting from the army barracks near the eastern city? He read the words again with growing unease. In Highland lore a dog that stepped over a corpse had to be killed.

"It could mean this man from Glasgow intended to kill an Englishman," Arnold declared. "He has free range of the ship as a keeper. Convicted of striking a tax collector. He speaks of a pagan ritual."

"Many English children celebrate May Day," Duncan countered.

"Not by laying out circles of fire and leaping through them," Arnold shot back.

At the end of the letter was a postscript. *Before he was summoned by a witch, a man from Argyll traded these six buttons for a white deerskin pouch I found, stained with blood. Use them for one of the young nephews.* Inside the folded paper envelope were six familiar discs of wood.

Duncan stared at the page, not focusing on the words, then looked up at Woolford. "Why," he asked the officer, "would Adam Munroe trade perfectly good buttons for a bloodstained pouch?"

Woolford frowned. "Let's put to rest one troubled soul at a time, shall we?"

"You have not reclaimed your buttons," Duncan pressed.

"It seemed miserly," Woolford replied in a brittle tone, "to interfere with a gift to a child."

The officer pushed the second letter across the table. "I keep reading it, trying to make sense of the words."

It was from Cameron, the senior keeper who always showed the most enthusiasm when flogging his fellow prisoners—a four-page letter addressed to D. Camshron, care of a priest in Strontian. It began *Dear Doilidh,* and what followed was a rambling narrative of the voyage, boasting of riches to come in the New World, then speaking of Evering's death. *We know why men get fetched in the night. The darker the secret a man hides, the quicker he kills.* Woolford pointed to the closing passage, which read like a cryptic verse. *Three times up for your new one, three times* deiseal *kirkside,* it said, *hot coal behind. Three times over flame, salt against sins. Three times over iron so the devils gnaw their own bones.*

"He speaks of salt, of devils and bones," Woolford observed. "Black arts. And Cameron was in the colonies before."

Duncan read the words again and glanced at each man's face. Each seemed to be nominating his own candidate for the noose. "Surely only a letter to a loved one."

"You can't know that."

But Duncan did know, without a doubt. Lister was not the only one hiding something about his family. *Doilidh* was the Gaelic form of Dolly, just as the English translation for *Camshron* was Cameron. The words were about a newborn, but could only be understood by one from the Highlands. *Deiseal* meant sunwise in the old tongue— walking from east to west. A new mother on the first outing with her child was supposed to carry the baby up three steps to assure prosperity, then walk three times sunwise or clockwise around the *kirk,* the church, to avoid begin trapped by the spirits who craved newborns, tossing a hot coal behind to assure they were not following her. Passing the baby three times over flames was an old charm to protect a newborn, as was touching salt to a newborn's mouth. And a secret, second baptism at the smithy's forge, passing the infant over the iron anvil, was frowned on by the church but was a tradition steeped in time, from long before priests arrived in Scotland. It would deny the devils a chance to eat the newborn, making them chew their own bones instead. Cameron had left a pregnant woman, a wife or perhaps a sister, and wanted to be sure the off-spring was blessed in all the traditions of the Highlands.

Duncan eyed Woolford uncertainly. "I don't know that," he replied, then froze as terrible realization swept over him. He glanced at his companions again. Had they made the connection? Cameron spoke of a man fetched in the night. Frasier spoke of what the Company brought from Edinburgh. Arnold and Woolford had made but one trip to Edinburgh, to bring Duncan. And they had brought him onto the ship in the night.

"Nothing here explains what happened in the compass room," he observed, fighting to keep his voice level.

"Evering himself made the ritual," Arnold proclaimed. "He placed his own buckle there, stole into the gallery for salt and blood and the heart, even that horrible eye, which the cook says came from a shark they had boarded the day before. The claw must be from one of his own collections."

"Why would he do such a thing?" Duncan asked.

"He was deranged. Delirious. His grief erupted anew. Perhaps he saw something that set off a powerful memory. He was sending a final message to his wife before he took his own life."

"He was murdered. Not a suicide," Woolford reminded Arnold.

"He planned to commit suicide, McCallum may take that as certain," the vicar replied. "He was deeply troubled. I am unable to divulge the secrets of prayer, but suffice it to say we often knelt together. He must have gathered the objects in the compass room as one last expression of his anguish. Nothing more than the work of a highly literate man whose emotions overwhelmed his intellect. Bones means death. Two stacks of bones means two deaths. His and his wife's. The buckle signifies himself, a token from his own person. The eye is the evil that had stared down at him since his wife's passing. The claw symbolizes the agony he has felt, the feather his plan to join his wife in the ranks of angels. The heart is his own broken heart, the salt the earth that he is about to leave." Arnold's words, tentative at first, finished with a triumphant flourish.

"Evering," the vicar concluded in a superior tone, "was a romantic. The ritual at the compass proved it."

"Salt is also used to purify," Duncan suggested. "And metal, even in a buckle, can be used to fight demons."

Arnold gave an impatient, warning sound. "Not by any Christian."

"The church I knew as a boy," Duncan continued, "kept one foot in the old ways."

"At last we get to the truth of it," Arnold said in a smug voice. "I have explained why it had to be Evering who began the ritual. You have given us proof of the origin of the one who interrupted him. You shall record it so, McCallum. The killer committed his heinous deed, then rearranged the objects in a way that would have meaning only to an illiterate whose priests were little more than Druids."

Duncan fought down the bile that rose with Arnold's words. But he had to concede one germ of truth in what Arnold said, that the ritual seemed to have been prepared by two very different people, from two different worlds. "If it was not Evering who completed the ritual," he pressed, watching Woolford carefully, "then perhaps that part not made by the professor was meant to be read by a mortal."

"Meaning what?" asked the lieutenant.

"Meaning perhaps you will accept that it was a message for someone on board."

Woolford buried his head in his hands. When he looked up, his jaw was set in grim determination, as if he were about to do battle. "Half," he said. "Half the men."

Duncan did not miss the way Arnold's knuckles whitened. "I'm sorry?"

"You asked me how many had been in the New World before."

"Half would seem more than coincidence. It would take some effort to find so many who had both fallen out with the law and been in America."

"A credential much to be desired," Arnold interjected. "We had several weeks to fill the Company ranks, time to be selective.

Experience in the colonies told us they were strong, that they would require little time to adjust to the rigors of their new life."

Duncan had never known a man of the cloth who was an outright liar, but indeed had known many who chose to focus on pieces of the truth rather than the whole of it, when it served to make the point of their homilies. "The objects used that night," he said. "I would like to see them. Perhaps a closer examination would—"

Woolford raised a hand to cut Duncan off. "The crew was terrified of them. Mr. Lister and I wrapped everything in a canvas weighted with rocks from the ballast and tossed it over the stern."

Duncan stared at him in disbelief. "They would have told us more." It was as if Woolford, too, was interested in only fragments of the truth.

Woolford stroked the long scar on his neck again. It seemed to have become a nervous habit, one Duncan had not noticed before the storm. "Your pipe," he said abruptly, remembering now the clay pipe Woolford had often carried during the voyage. "You are no longer smoking. It affects your nerves."

Woolford grimaced. "Someone stole my tobacco," he admitted.

"And burnt it in the compass room," Duncan concluded. "I have never heard of such a ritual in the Old World," he added after a moment.

"There are other people," the officer observed in a hesitant voice, "people who burn the leaf to attract spirits."

"What kind of people?" Duncan pressed. "Who prays to spirits with tobacco?"

Arnold's glance of warning was quick but obvious. Woolford looked away from the vicar, into the shadows. He seemed to struggle to get the words out. "The people of the forest." Woolford's haunted expression as he spoke toward the darkness caused Duncan to twist about to study the shadows. It seemed Woolford's meaning was grasped first by something in his gut, turning it cold, sending an icy tentacle up his spine until it touched his brain. The savages. Woolford was speaking of the dreaded aborigines of the American woodlands.

No one spoke for a long moment.

"So tobacco was burned to gain the attention of Mrs. Evering in the next world," Duncan suggested in a careful tone, feeling Arnold's withering glance.

"Most of the men partake of tobacco when they can," Arnold interjected. "One of them stole it from the lieutenant, who was well known for having fine twists of Virginia leaf." He paused, taking note, as Duncan already had, of the sudden melancholy that had overtaken Woolford. "Evering brought the brazier for warmth. The tobacco fell as the murderer struggled with him."

"I must see the professor's quarters," Duncan finally stated. He dared not openly express interest in Evering's journal.

"The captain gave his orders," Arnold said. "You'll not be leaving the cell deck."

"I must see the other letters at least."

"Equally impossible," Arnold said. "You will not be permitted to tamper with the royal mails."

Duncan gazed at the letters in front of him. "Then surely you will return these to the mails."

"They have become evidence."

"There is but one killer. Even were it one of these men, the other is innocent." He searched Arnold's unyielding face. "Bring me paper and ink. I shall transcribe them. You can witness them as true copies. Surely," he entreated, "we will not punish the innocent. When will word reach their loved ones again? A child needs his buttons."

Arnold cast a disappointed glance at Duncan. "Innocent, Mr. McCallum?" he asked, as if unfamiliar with the term.

Woolford rose. "I shall make it so," the officer said, and hurried up the ladder.

Arnold paced around the table. "Paper and ink will provide an opportunity to commence your report," he observed. "Lord Ramsey is fastidious about records. He will desire a quick conclusion, but a complete written account. Flavor it with your science. The army will soon know of a killing in the Company," he added, with a glance toward the gangway where Woolford had disappeared. "Lord Ramsey will not desire a military inquiry to be opened."

"It could be useful to one writing such a report, Reverend," Duncan pointed out, "to know why the military would be interested."

Arnold considered the question for a long moment. "The Ramsey Company and the army share many of the same goals, but we are oceans apart in how to achieve them." The vicar gazed toward the cells. "Your report. It shall point out the sins committed along the way, with the truth shining like the light of the Almighty at its conclusion."

"You make it sound as if I am writing a sermon," Duncan replied. "And you forget I have been locked in a cell," he added.

"Your isolation but heightens your objectivity. You will record a simple and tragic tale. Evering was possessed by the demon of grief, compelling him to the unnatural act in the compass room. His lapse of faith gave the killer an opportunity. Amen."

Arnold was indeed interested in a sermon. "Perhaps," Duncan suggested with a solemn air, "there should be lightning. Evering could have been struck by a bolt that burned away his reason."

"Excellent," Arnold said, in the voice he used in the pulpit. "Poetic. A call from God. Worthy of the Ramsey scholar. You encourage me, McCallum."

"Then a mermaid rose up and killed him."

Arnold sighed, then answered by pushing open the door to the cell corridor. The smell of unwashed men and women, of mildew and human excrement, wafted into their chamber, mingled with the sound of weeping. The vicar paused, as if for effect, then approached the table again. "The killer will hang, whatever reason for the crime. Perhaps one of them stole something of value from Evering. His gold watch is missing. Linking the killing to a robbery would offer a strong moral lesson," he suggested. "The Company will witness the punishment after we arrive at Edentown. A perfect ceremony for setting the proper tone of the prisoners' new life. The path of righteousness," he added in a suddenly contemplative tone, "can be as slender as a thread. Do your work correctly, and there will be no need to raise the specter of sedition."

Suddenly Woolford was back in the pool of light cast by the lanterns, with a writing box holding paper, ink, and a quill. As Duncan arranged them on the table, Arnold climbed back up the ladder. Woolford paused at the dark corridor of cells, then ascended the ladder, leaving Duncan alone, staring at the white empty paper. He paced about the table, considering the threat against Scots in Arnold's parting words, fighting to dam up the unnatural fear that had surged through him when Woolford had mentioned the savages of the forest. British papers frequently reported on the cannibalism, the compulsive violence, the unquenchable blood thirst of the American natives. Animals in human form, they were often called.

When he finally lifted the quill, Duncan did not begin with the transcription of the letters, but with a list of names, sixteen names in a column, including his great-uncle, his father, and his grandfather. The name of every chieftain of Clan McCallum for the past four hundred years, names that had been burned into his memory as a young boy, an unbroken chain of names he and his grandfather had often shouted into the wind as they had sailed and rowed among the Hebrides. Angus McCallum, was the earliest, then Ian McCallum, Lame Rob, Alastair, Crooked James, and Blind William. When he was done he ripped away the long column and wrapped the paper strip around Adam's amulet, close against his skin; then he pulled the silver button from his pocket, examining it for the first time in direct light. It was intricately worked on the top, and though its dome had been smashed inward, the violence had not obliterated what was obviously, as Lister had reported, a map. The surface of the button had held a tiny rendering in relief of eastern America and Europe, exquisitely worked in silver.

The ship's beams creaked in the silence, and the table slightly canted as the vessel heeled in the wind. Duncan glanced toward the ladder and paused as something pawed at his memory. Woolford. Duncan had grown accustomed to the sounds made as those leaving the cell deck climbed toward the top decks, the creaking of certain ladder boards, the progressive opening and closing of hatches. Woolford's egress had not been followed by the same sounds. Duncan rose and warily approached the ladder.

He climbed one step at a time, pausing at each to listen, finally gaining the next deck, a series of cargo holds packed with crates, barrels, and trunks. His heart pounding, knowing if he were caught he would pay with skin and flesh, he pushed on the hatch door leading to the first bay. The door swung open on its iron pintels without a sound.

The second bay was separated from the first not with a door but with a hanging sailcloth, which he silently brushed aside. Thirty feet in front of him, Woolford moved along the stacks of crates and trunks with a hooded lantern, in his hand one of the iron bars used to pry up the lids. As Duncan watched, the officer paused, drank from a flask he pulled from a pocket, then opened a crate and began sifting through the contents.

Duncan inched forward, suddenly desperate to see at least the label on the crate, watching for variations in the blackness that might mean a hiding place. He had found it, a gap between two crates, when a quick, furry creature leapt onto his shoulder. The rat's transit across his back was silent, but not the creature's jump onto a stack of kegs, where it slipped, its claws scratching at the wood as it sought purchase on the round sides.

Woolford spun about, lantern in one hand, iron bar in the other, raised for throwing. "At this distance I can put this into your spleen before you make it to cover," he declared in a low, lethal voice.

"As a military art, I thought spear throwing went out with the Crusades." Duncan fought to keep his voice level.

"You'd be quite astonished at the arts of the modern American officer," Woolford growled, and lifted the pointed bar higher.

"I prefer you do it, here and now, Lieutenant, if you will not permit me to find the truth about the killings."

"Killing. There was but one murder."

"That's your dilemma, Lieutenant. You and I both know I cannot find the truth about Evering without finding the truth about Adam Munroe. You might have an interest in Evering's killer, but you cannot abide anyone knowing your secret about Adam."

"Do you have any notion what the captain is going to do to you?"

Duncan did not doubt Woolford was capable of killing him. But it was time to test Adam's words. Before the army used him it was going to protect him. He advanced, his hands held out at his sides. "We can stand here for half an hour, Lieutenant," he said when the pool of light reached his face, "as you recount all the ways you and the captain can end my life in unimaginable misery. I'll consider the point taken, provided you accept that when you take me before the captain and Reverend Arnold I will raise a dozen possibilities as to why you were creeping about searching boxes"—he glanced at the now-visible label—"holding the private belongings of the Ramsey family."

Woolford lowered his makeshift weapon. "Inventory," he muttered. "With so many thieves on board, we must watch every possession."

"Fine. Let us go explain that. If you prefer I will go alone."

"And receive a few dozen lashes for leaving the cell deck?"

"I will savor every stroke if your true colors be exposed."

"Are all Scots as self-destructive, McCallum, as you and Munroe?"

"Consider it a study in what men do when the king lances the bubble of their hope."

Woolford looked as if he had bitten into something sour. He leaned on a crate, setting the lantern beside him. "My preference in playing to a stalemate is to sweep the board and start anew. Shall we inspect the work that precedes us?" he said, aiming a thumb at a nearby trunk. The lock, Duncan saw, had already been forced, as had those of several others nearby, all bearing an ornate *R*, the Ramsey mark.

"What did you do to Adam last week?"

"I deeply regret to say I did nothing."

"What is so important about the Ramsey tutor to you, just a soldier with no ties to the Company?"

Woolford ignored the question, probed the contents of the trunk before him.

"Then why," Duncan pressed, "did Adam Munroe consider it such a catastrophe that we are going to the New York frontier?"

Woolford paused, stared into the shadows of the trunk. He seemed strangely wounded by the question. "The wilderness works in many different ways on men's souls."

"Many different kinds of fear, you mean."

Wooford slowly lifted his head, fixing Duncan with a sober stare. "You have no notion, McCallum, how right you are."

Duncan leaned forward to glimpse inside the trunk. With a chill he recognized the contents. Long bags of canvas, with laces at the top. The ever-efficient managers of the Ramsey Company had packed an entire trunk of burial shrouds.

"A ghostwalker," Duncan said as he gazed at the shrouds. "Does it mean one fixed on suicide?"

Woolford gripped the iron bar in both hands. "Not a word easily explained." His tone turned oddly melancholy. "The opposite of suicide perhaps. In America the dead can walk again."

"You took custody of Adam in the courts. You knew his record. Why did he kill himself?"

Woolford stared at the bar, twisting his hands, twisting his face, speaking toward the shadows. "Adam Munroe was the only one who was not arrested. He told Arnold that if he needed to be arrested to join the Company, he would gladly assault me and every soldier in Argyll."

"Impossible. He would not willingly give himself to slavery."

"I suspect you and I did not know him as well as we thought."

Duncan saw something in Woolford's eyes that frightened him, and for a moment the officer gripped the bar like a weapon again, but then he exhaled heavily, tossed it into the darkness, and moved down the line of forced trunks. Duncan followed a step behind. The first three contained fine clothes, which appeared disheveled but undamaged. The next, marked *Hand Implements,* held a top layer of blankets. But under the blankets at the top were at least two score bayonets, of a style for plugging into the barrels of heavy muskets, then hand axes and heavy knives nearly the size of swords. The next trunk held heavy woolen waistcoats, red with long sleeves—some with blue facing, others with buff. Though tattered from long use, they would still have had years of service left in them had not someone poured tar over them, soaking through the fabric.

"You brought these from a barracks?" Duncan asked.

"Not I. But all were made under the king's warrant. They were uniform coats, made for the army.

"But none is new."

"I daresay most are twenty years old and more. Quartermasters sometimes sell old equipment to pay for new. I know of a theater in Chelsea," Woolford observed, "that regularly buys trunks of it, for playacting." He paused and with a rueful grin tipped back his flask again. "My father's country estate had a huge courtyard. He called it his Roman amphitheater. We held plays there, great pageants where we praised kings and celebrated the ascendancy of England as the queen of civilization."

A second son, Duncan realized. Woolford had an aristocratic father and only a junior post. It could only mean he was unable to inherit. Woolford's voice grew distant. "'This sceptered isle, this precious stone set in the silver sea,'" he offered, irony thick in his words. "Shakespeare was my favorite. 'Conscience,'" he recited, now in a stage voice, "'is but a word that cowards use to keep the strong in awe.'"

"'Nothing in his life became him like the leaving of it,'" Duncan countered. "'He died as one that had been studied in his death. To throw away the dearest thing he owned.'"

"MacBeth."

"A Scottish king, on a Scottish death. Why did Adam insist on being on this ship?" Duncan pressed. "What did you do to drive him to his death?"

Woolford stared at his engraved flask a moment, then raised it with a salute to Duncan and drained it. "'Heat not a furnace for your foe so hot that it do singe yourself,'" he offered. He closed the trunk and then silently gestured Duncan forward, into the shadows. They walked past another canvas partition until they reached the thick, curving planks of the hull, where the sound of the coursing sea was unusually loud through the wood.

"I discovered it the day after Adam's death," the officer declared as he pulled away a small crate from the hull and extended his lantern.

An unnatural fear gripped Duncan. He steadied himself on the crate as he stared at a ten-inch-wide hole chipped into the hull beside one of the heavy support timbers. Someone was trying to sink the ship. "How thick—" he began.

"The hull planks are eight inches, if the ship's carpenter's to be believed. By my calculation less than an inch separates us from the brine."

"Are you saying Adam did this?"

"So I assumed. But when I came back again after he died, I found fresh chips on the deck."

"You did not tell the captain?"

"The captain has no imagination. He is like an artilleryman, all about hasty aim and loud explosions. He would rail about the Scots, then steer the ship for Halifax."

Duncan knelt, studying the size of the chips. The hole was immediately to the left of the large timber, hidden in its shadow. It would have been hard to spot on a casual inspection, as would have been the bayonet he pulled from behind the nearest trunk. "Surely you should tell the ship's carpenter," he enjoined.

"And scare away the culprit?" Woolford said. "Officially no one knows about this." He pushed the trunk against the hole.

"Officially?"

"In the army we have official files which go to the public, to the king. The unofficial ones have more texture, more interesting details."

"Like the truth."

"Usually enough material for any number of truths. Rather like Shakespeare."

"Like the letters we opened."

Woolford gestured him back toward the ladder. "I thought you reacted quite evenly. Splendid performance." He turned, and a cool grin returned to his face as he saw Duncan's bewildered expression. "Surely you understood Frasier's letter even if Reverend Arnold did not."

"Frasier has a troubled spirit."

"Frasier," Woolford declared, "has told the Company that they have a spy from the army within their ranks. Be grateful for your cell. Be grateful for the protection of Reverend Arnold. The other prisoners and the captain have similar intentions for you. But there is a big difference. The captain wants to throw you to the sharks. The men in the Company would prefer to find an ax and do it piece by piece as you watch."

Duncan, suddenly very weak, leaned against the hatch as he watched Woolford's lantern moving upward, a dying star on a bleak night. In the Highlands, one who openly stood at the side of the English might be an enemy, but at least one with whom honest battle could be done. But a secret turncoat was the lowest form of life, best dealt with by a blade in the spine on a foggy night. Duncan was the rot Frasier meant to slice away.

He found his way to the candlelit table in a daze and stared at the flame, trying to calm himself before returning to his work. He had transcribed one letter when he became aware of a presence behind him.

A thickset man stepped from the shadows. "I have these," Cameron said, extending a folded scrap of sailcloth. "The vicar asked me to clean the professor's shoes, to help brush his clothes, get the body ready."

Duncan laid the cloth on the table and opened it. It contained glass, small shards of green glass.

"When I went back for his shoes, these pieces were on his cabin floor. Should have thrown them over. But I shoved them in a corner under his bed."

Duncan pushed at the shards with the end of his quill. They matched those he had seen embedded in Evering's knee. The larger pieces were slightly curved. "What was it, Cameron?"

"A man in cheer may take a shot of whiskey and smash the glass," the keeper suggested.

"Too small for a dram cup. More like a vial," Duncan said, and suddenly realized exactly what the shards were from. It had been a dosing cup, one of the small columns used for administering medicines to the sick. He lifted the biggest shard to his nose. It offered a faintly acrid scent. "Was the professor ill?"

"Never a sign of it."

But there had been someone ill, Duncan realized. The woman who had jumped off the ship.

Duncan studied the big man. During their long voyage Cameron had shown nothing but contempt for Duncan. "Why do you tell me this?"

"I watch the post box for the Company, log in the letters, give them to the ship's clerk. That bastard Woolford, he took a letter of mine. The men in the hold know what is happening. We know when we get to the colonies one of us is to be hanged." Cameron stepped closer, reaching into his pocket to extract a folded paper. "But there be another letter I haven't shown them."

With a wrench of his heart Duncan saw it was his own letter, in which he had cursed the king and all things English. The dollop of candle wax he had used to seal it was broken. "Everyone knows ye were free that morning Evering's body was found."

"I was the one who discovered him," Duncan pointed out.

"Just the kind of clever trick a killer with a gentleman's education might use, to divert attention."

"I didn't kill him."

Cameron feigned a look of disappointment. "Let's not waste our time, McCallum. You and I both know all they want is a nice story for one of Reverend Arnold's sermons, then a proper hanging to make certain the men heed their new master. So you keep my name out of it and I'll keep yours out." Cameron waved the letter before Duncan's face, then returned it to his pocket. "Do we have an understanding?"

"It's only a letter."

Cameron seemed pleased with Duncan's resistance. "There was another piece of paper, a fragment which Mr. Lister took. Only he don't know I saw it first. I might write out a statement, all legal-like, attesting to what I saw. All about the professor's appointment with McCallum at the hour of his death."

Duncan buried his head in his hands a moment before looking up and nodding.

"But I have questions to be answered, Cameron."

The keeper shrugged. "I wish it over as much as ye."

"You were in charge of the prisoners scrubbing the forward deck the day before Adam died."

"Aye. Frasier and myself."

"Someone on that work party picked the lock on Lieutenant Woolford's chest."

Cameron's body seemed to tense. "Why would you say such a thing?"

"I saw some of your gleanings when they first appeared. Some were still wet. Because someone had placed them in a wash bucket to hide them. The trunk had foodstuffs from England. Cones of sugar that could be slipped into a pocket. An irresistible temptation to some."

The keeper's face clouded. "Young Frasier has a terrible sweet tooth."

"Young Frasier," Duncan agreed, "was sucking on a piece of sugar an hour later. And you were suddenly brimming over with trinkets for wagering. It was you who started the betting contests that day. Reverend Arnold would be disappointed to learn his keepers were involved in the thefts on the ship."

The keeper's face hardened. His hand went to the letter, as if to remind Duncan.

"Why then? Why force the trunk on the day Woolford announced the Company's destination? Like you said," Duncan added when Cameron did not reply, "we have a bargain, you and I."

"Wasn't my idea. I just helped the lad. Frasier allowed how he couldn't do it without help."

Help indeed, Duncan told himself. Frasier not only could not have achieved such a clever theft alone, he could not have conjured up the idea of seeking out the trunk packed with Woolford's deliveries for America. "You were there before. In America. What was it like?"

For a moment the big man seemed to shrink. "It was a fine farm, in the north of Pennsylvania, the Wyoming Valley they call it. But I still have nightmares. They killed my wife and two young children in front of me, left me for dead when the militia came running." He turned his head and lifted the locks that hung over the side of his face, revealing a knot of scar tissue at his hairline.

"And that is why you came to be Reverend Arnold's top keeper?"

"I was one of the first on board. I asked for prayers. The vicar heard my story and took pity. I know the way of things in America."

The way of things in America, Duncan decided, was already ripping the Company apart. He studied the shards on the table. "Evering had a good black waistcoat and a gold watch. Where are they?"

"Stolen, like the chart pinned over his bunk."

"What kind of chart?"

"I used to see it when I cleaned his cabin. Calculations and such. Things a tutor might be planning for his wee pupils, I suspect."

"What else was in the professor's chamber?"

"Usual things. Books. Clothing. A locked trunk. Boxes of things."

"What things exactly?"

"He had collections. Bits of nature. He was a natural philosopher."

"You mean like bones. And feathers."

Cameron nodded.

"Do you ever see the sick woman?"

"Only that day she tried to fly. She stays abed. Food goes in on trays. They watch her close as a newborn."

"Who watches?"

"The vicar. The lieutenant. The captain's wife sometimes. The professor did, before."

"Tell me something about the savages, Cameron. Do they have witches?"

The question seemed to shake the big Scot. He looked into the shadows before answering. "Aye. Terrible demon men, and women too, who can take the shape of animals. Fly like a bird. Swim like a fish. Wizards. Shamans, they call them."

"And these witches, these shamans who can fly out over oceans, do they use rituals with blood and bone?"

Cameron's eyes flared for a moment, but as he gazed into the shadows his anger changed to worry.

Duncan lifted a quill to continue his work. "You'll need to lock me back in my cell in an hour, Cameron. Meanwhile, ask the ship's carpenter if he is missing a hammer. And bring the log of Company letters submitted for the mails."

When the keeper returned, Duncan handed him the bundle of folded papers to convey to Arnold and quickly scanned the mail log. There were two lists of letters, labeled *Eastbound* and *Westbound*, with the names of the passing ships that had slowed to retrieve them. The few westbound letters included half a dozen addressed to William Ramsey, Esq., all from Arnold. Adam Munroe had written two letters addressed to an inn in New York town, both to the same man, a name that Duncan stared at in confusion. Socrates Moon. The mysterious Greek who had gone to England with their suicidal passenger six months earlier.

But most curious of all was another, also addressed to Socrates Moon, entered for the mails the day after Adam's death. It had no return name, only the words *Tutor, Ramsey Company.*

As the keeper escorted Duncan to his cell, he produced the stub of a candle, lit it, and handed it to Duncan. "Carpenter lost his best hammer," Cameron reported as he locked the cell door. "Was in the hold with the timber stores, but when he went for repairs after the storm it was gone."

"Tell me this, Mr. Cameron, in your log do you record the names exactly as written on the letters?"

"Aye. 'Tis an official thing."

A dark foreboding seized Duncan. Evering had sent a letter to the mysterious Greek but identified himself only as the tutor, as if it would mean something to the man, as if this Socrates Moon expected something of the tutor, whether it be Evering or his successor.

"I must have the letter sent by Evering," he said through the hatch. "Above all, I must have that letter."

"Gone. Posted on a passing fishing schooner these three days past."

Duncan's heart sank. He dropped to the floor as Cameron's steps receded in the darkness. After several minutes he extracted his list of ancestors and stared at it, whispering the names, until the little hatch on his door was pulled open and a large tin of steaming liquid passed through. Tea, sweetened with honey. He whispered his thanks and sat back in a corner with the mug just as the candle sputtered out. In the darkness that followed he found himself wishing for Flora's chants, which had grown strangely comforting to him. But she had been silent for hours, and the sounds Duncan heard most often from her cell were those of weeping. He tried to pass the time thinking of happier days as a youth in the Highlands and the Hebrides, but always his thoughts returned to Adam's haunting legacy and Evering's dead, questioning eyes, to the bloody compass and the fateful hour when the sea had closed around him. His foreboding was so real, so intense, he could taste it, like some salty, bitter thing in his mouth. Duncan had sought a final escape in the black water, had become certain the storm would be his ending. Everything had changed in the span of a quarter hour, when Lister had given him a reason to live, and Duncan had gone into the sea for a different reason.

But his life had indeed ended that day, Duncan began to realize. The man the storm had given back was not the same man who had gone into the water. He had fancied for a few hours that he might become the clan chief Lister wanted him to be, that he could indeed protect the Scots on board. But the Company had made him something else, something worse than a prisoner, something no clan chief could ever be. He had become an informer, a servant, a pawn to an English lord. Arnold and Woolford had given a terrible truth to Frasier's suspicions. Was Arnold truly so clever to understand he had found the perfect way to break Duncan?

No, a voice argued from some dim part of his mind; no, there is hope, for the indenture meant he had lost his chains, gave him a chance to act like a clan chief, if only in secret. But the weak voice soon died as Duncan began a new nightmare, a recurring one of two men on a gibbet. One was a man with a tartan cloth covering his face, his skin being flayed away with a whip wielded by Reverend Arnold. The other was his dead father, cursing him for failing to see what suffering Duncan was causing the Company. The English expected him to deliver a political parable. Now that Duncan had convinced them the professor had been murdered, they expected him to give them a Scot, any Scot, to hang for the crime. And the Scots, whom he had vowed to protect, wanted Duncan dead.

Chapter Four

HE WAS CHASING A LAMB in the kitchen dooryard as his mother watched from the granite step, laughing as he and the lamb tumbled together into a bed of flowers. Then the joyful bleats turned to snarls as the lambs grew long, sharp teeth and began scratching at his flesh.

Duncan exploded into wakefulness, gasping and groping in the dark for something to swing against the rats. Suddenly the cover of a lantern lifted an inch, an arm's length away. There were no rats, only strong, callused fingers wrapped around his leg, shaking him awake.

"Y'er scarletback fled," a raspy voice declared. "Like a brigade of French were at his heels."

As Duncan rubbed his eyes, squinting at Lister's dim shape, his hand went to his throat. There was an unfamiliar bitter taste in his mouth, a soreness in his windpipe. He glanced at the tin tankard that had been handed through the door in the night, filled with sweet hot tea. "Woolford's gone? How?"

"A fishing schooner overtook us," Lister said as he squatted beside Duncan, handing him a lump of gray meat wrapped in a limp cabbage leaf. "Smaller, more spry than this old bucket. As soon as the lookout called out, Woolford dashed below, then when she drew close, he hailed her, offered a reward for their trouble. She can close haul in this wind and make the harbor in a few hours. We'll be a day and more."

"Alone?"

Lister reached behind him and produced a stained, tattered sea bag, the one Duncan had used to carry his only earthly possessions on board. "Woolford, two sailors, and a man in a cloak went over in the ship's boat. With two trunks. Two sailors came back, no trunks."

"Who was the other?"

"I was below until they were clear of the ship. But Frasier's missing."

Duncan retrieved the crock of water in the corner of his cell and drained it. Still the acrid taste lingered. "The tea you brought," he said. "What was in it?"

"I brought no tea."

He had been drugged. Someone had dosed him, disguising it with the sweet tea, which he had ravenously consumed. But why, why would someone want him drugged in his cell? With a stab of worry he touched the stone in his pocket, the medallion on his neck, even examined the linen holding the button. Nothing had been disturbed.

"I heard what you did for me, Mr. Lister," he said. "You lied. You took the beating meant for me."

Lister forced a grin. "Ye were in no shape, lad. 'Twas far from the first time fer me. Once ye grow good scars on y'er back, 'tain't so bad. Like scratching an old itch."

"You brought me back from the dead that day on the mast, then took my punishment. Never in my life have I owed so much to one man."

"Tell me something, Clan McCallum," Lister said. "Do ye ken what the New World means?" The question seemed strangely urgent, somehow difficult for the old mate to express.

A different kind of prison, Duncan was tempted to say. "So far it seems to have a lot to do with dying."

"I've been there before. New York, Boston, Philadelphia. What I know is that ye can breathe there. It's about what is in front of ye, 'tain't about where ye were born, or what ye were born. The present don't have to compromise with the past." The old man eyes flashed. "I am going to trot down that gangway, dance a jig, and pick a blossom for the first lass I see."

Duncan's long hours in the darkness had left two burning impressions of the New World, a vague but fearful sense of something deadly lurking there with its eyes on him and the Company, and the demeaning way Arnold had stared at him when he was attired in the Ramsey clothes, his uniform for America. "For me it seems the New World will mean yes sir and no sir and wipe the mud from the young master's shoes."

Lister seemed uninterested in his wit. "I will tell ye how to repay me, Clan McCallum. Me, and the souls of y'er blessed parents."

Duncan's eyes narrowed.

"Go with the good reverend and take Evering's place. He be a harsh master but means ye well. Do y'er duty to the Ramsey Company and to the clan. Give the New World a chance. Preserve y'erself. What ye did for that lass in the storm, 'twas the work of a clan chief. If a killer be seeking to thin our ranks, ye be the man who can stop him."

Surprised at the emotion that flushed the man's face, Duncan hesitated, then soberly spat into his own palm and for the second time that week took Lister's rough, callused hand in his own. As Duncan returned Lister's gaze, it seemed he was looking into the eyes of his father and grandfather, it seemed he was making a vow not just to Lister but to all of them, to all the old Scots.

Down the corridor Duncan heard the scurrying of tiny feet. It was the middle of the night. "Take me to Evering's chamber," he abruptly asked.

"With the captain ready to have y'er tripe for stew? Not likely."

"You know Arnold demands an answer to Evering's murder," Duncan said. "I will not lie to satisfy him. You know what he will do if I do not find the truth."

The words seemed to take the protest out of Lister's eyes. He sighed, then stood, covering the lamp again.

"Give me something to act as a weapon. Your baton. If we are noticed, I shall make it clear I forced you."

"Be quick and keep y'er head down," the keeper whispered after handing Duncan the short, thick stick the keepers used to enforce discipline.

Lister took Duncan through a maze of small holds on the cargo deck, then up a ladder that opened into the forecabins, pausing every few moments to listen for sounds of men moving in the night, then creeping along a dim corridor, unlatching a cabin door, and gesturing Duncan inside. As Lister closed the door behind them and lifted the lantern cover, Duncan saw that the cabin was not much larger than his cell. It had been stripped, the long, swinging bed box hanging empty on its gimbals, the shelves behind it bare. The journal he had so desperately hoped to find was gone.

"His books?" Duncan whispered.

"Packed up by the keepers. Marked for Ramsey House in the port of New York."

The answers Adam had expected him to find had been boxed and sealed, and Duncan would somehow have to track them in America. He swallowed his disappointment and surveyed the tiny chamber. Above the bed were two ribbons, one faded pink, the other willow green. Stains of candle wax spotted the floor beside the bed. While Lister kept watch at the entrance, Duncan tilted the bed and lay in it as the dead man would have, his longer legs hanging over the end. He could touch the ribbons above, and knew from their discolored appearance that Evering must have often done so, dozens of times, as he must have long studied the missing chart that had hung on the four small nails still protruding from the planks above. This had been Evering's life on board, lying in the coffin-like box, reading by candlelight despite the captain's stern orders against open flames, gazing at his chart and the once-delicate ribbons. Dreaming about the comet he hoped to put his name to. Writing letters for the prisoners. And tending to the diseased banshee in the front cabin.

The shadows above the bed were so thick Duncan almost missed the slip of paper stuck into a joint overhead. A drawing of an arrow, he saw as he raised the paper into the light. A very particular arrow, for the shaft was shaded along its length, perhaps indicating paint, and the fletching likewise held four segments in different shades, giving the effect of stripes. Underneath, in the small, precise hand Evering used for his scientific notes, were two words—*Wolf Clan*—then short phrases that made his skin crawl. *Small bones speaking. Truth beads. Fishspeaker on the river. False faces.* With a trembling hand, he tucked the paper into his pocket.

Climbing out of the bed, he knelt and studied the shadows underneath, quickly spotting not just a few more shards of glass where Cameron had thrown them in the corner, but several others, much smaller, in a tight circle on the deck beyond the edge of the bed, pressed into the wood. "A cloth, Mr. Lister," Duncan asked as he scraped a few shards from the planks. "Something to put these in."

The old mate futilely searched his pockets, shook his head, and turned his nervous gaze back out the door.

In the shadows was a chipped ceramic pot, for Evering's convenience in the night, in which lay ashes of burned paper. Duncan looked back at the circle of glass particles. Here was where Evering had dropped a dosing vial perhaps only moments before his death, not just dropped it but smashed it deliberately, perhaps angrily. Duncan considered the scene. Evering had smashed the vial, then not long after been knocked to his knee, probably by the first blow of the stolen hammer, then received the second blow while on the floor. And at about the same time, someone—whether Evering or his killer, Duncan had no way of knowing—had burned papers in the night pot.

Duncan gestured for Lister to hold the lantern closer as he studied the ashes in the pot. He saw curved lines on a charred scrap, then at the very bottom words untouched by the flame, in Evering's hand. *The old fishspeaker will know,* it said. *Stag's Head. Show him the medallion.*

As they returned to the cell corridor, Duncan paused and put a hand on the sailor's arm. "After Woolford's chest was pilfered, had you seen Adam with Evering?"

Lister rubbed his grizzled chin a moment. "Aye. On the deck the eve before young Munroe died. A Sunday eve. The Reverend held vespers for the prisoners, and Evering and Adam sat nigh each other. Afterwards, the professor was writing a letter for Adam."

"But Adam," Duncan pointed out, "could write his own letters." Lister's brow knitted. "So 'e could."

Evering had not been writing a letter, Duncan knew, but recording notes of something Adam had confided to him. Adam and Evering had shared a secret, and both had died within days of doing so. A secret about the New World. "What do you know of this place Edentown where they take us?"

"On the frontier, a few days from port. Being built by the great laird. Some of the men know of it, say the road to it is lined with graves," Lister added, then hurried Duncan toward the ship's ladder that led below.

But Duncan paused when they reached the door to the cell corridor. "Are the pumps still manned?" he asked.

"Finished. Only a foot or so of water in the—" Lister broke off and muttered a low curse as realization lit his eyes.

"You must go to my cell," Duncan said. "Pull the door shut behind you. If someone comes, pretend to be unconscious. It must look as though I overpowered you." He lifted the hooded lantern from the peg where they had left it.

"Ye'll be dead five minutes after the captain finds ye."

"There are questions to be answered."

"Don't do this," Lister pleaded. "There's others who won't take so long as the captain."

"Like you said," Duncan rejoined, "a clan chief dies on his own terms. *Redeat.*" He stole back into the darkness, working his way down the row of cells to a small floor hatch at the end of the corridor. It was the work of less than a minute to pry open the hatch, releasing the garbage-midden stench of the bilges. He clenched his jaw, fighting a tremor of nausea, then dropped into the low, cramped space and, stooping, began moving along the keel, the dimmed lantern in front of him.

The captain of the *Anna Rose* fancied that the Company prisoners stayed closely confined in their hold except for their hours of daylight exercise. But by the end of the first month they had found a loose plank in the head, at the opposite end of the prisoners deck. Within a week they had loosened two more, discovering access not to freedom but to a secret though fetid retreat. While they seldom had to fight for the pleasure of sitting in the foul, near-suffocating compartment, certain prisoners regularly descended into the bilge in the middle of the night, for the pleasure of cursing the king in private.

Wading through the calf-high muck, Duncan reached the large crib of ballast bricks over the center of the keel, awkwardly crawling forward with the muted lantern held high. Something scurried on the stones beside him. The rats might dine on the decks above, but here is where they nested.

He had taken only a few cramped steps past the ballast bricks when a strong arm reached out of the shadows, clamping around his throat, and the lantern was snatched from his hand. He did not struggle but let himself be half led, half dragged through the bilge water until suddenly his lantern, and a second, were fully uncovered. Eight men stared at him with fierce, angry expressions. His assailant held a long, sharpened nail to his neck, against his artery.

"Pleased to see ye, y'er highness," the man sneered. "We saved some Company tea for ye."

"Rats won't have to go hunting tonight," another crowed.

"I only—" Duncan's protest was choked away by the metal pressing deeper into his flesh. He met the gaze of the filthy, unshaven men, the hardest of the Company. Each brandished a jagged fragment of ballast stone, a weapon sufficient to do murder. Behind them someone moaned in the dark.

A red-bearded man in remnants of what had been a coachman's greatcoat appeared from the gloom and bent over Duncan's face. "Who gave ye the right to pick one of us to die?" he snarled.

"McGregor, I never—"

"Serv' 'im 'is tea," McGregor snarled.

Duncan's head was slammed downward, submerged into the fes-
tering soup of seawater, urine, mildew, dead rats, and pitch. He did
not struggle at first, thinking they sought only to frighten him. But
they kept pushing, pressing him down, until his lungs were on fire,
and he flailed out, fighting for breath, clearing the water and gasping
for only an instant before being pressed into it again, the filthy spume
biting his mouth and nostrils. The dunking was repeated a third
time, until finally his assailant jerked him upright, gasping, retching.

"There was no murder on this ship until you named it so," the
bearded man growled. "Now the only murder that worries us be the
one you be committing against one of us." On McGregor's knuckles
were drops of fresh blood.

Duncan, gaining his breath, spat more filth from his mouth.
"Until another man is taken by the true killer," he shot back,
pushing the arm away from his neck.

"Ye name one of us, McCallum, and every jack one of us will
name ye. A pretty boy raised below the borders, just another English lapdog, we thought at first. Nay a Scot at all. Now we see ye're
worse, a slimeworm sent to consume us from the inside out. Poor
Evering sniffed y'er true scent and ye had to silence him." McGregor
leaned closer, his crooked yellow teeth inches from Duncan's face.
"Ye made it easy, boy, paying us a call. We won't even have to kill ye.
We'll just knock the senses from ye and cut a few slices on y'er
limbs. By the time ye wake, the rats will have eaten half y'er flesh."
The arm began to close around his neck again.

Duncan did not remember all the oaths of the Hebrides fishermen he had learned as a boy, but he recalled enough of them to
practice on McGregor, in the coarse Gaelic of the islands. He was
invoking the *glaistig,* the *uruisg,* and the one-eyed *direach,* vile
supernatural creatures all, when the ragged old Scot, eyes round
with surprise and dread, clamped a hand over his mouth and pulled
him from his assailant's arms.

Duncan pushed the hand away. "The English don't conquer us
by killing us. All they have to do is play to the fears and suspicions

that have kept Scots killing one another for centuries," he said in a simmering voice. He reached into his pocket, extracting the piece of folded newsprint Lister had found in Evering's cabin. "I came from no barracks," he stated as he handed the paper to McGregor.

The old Scot bared his teeth like an angry dog, but took the paper and leaned into a lantern.

"Whatever you may think about me," Duncan said, "you know Adam was one of you. He told something to Evering and Evering died for it. A secret about the Company. Perhaps Adam himself died for it."

"Death to spies!" came an unsteady, boyish voice from the shadows.

McGregor, ignoring the cry, stroked his red beard. "What are ye saying, McCallum?"

Duncan spat more of the filth from his mouth and lowered himself onto a low pile of ballast bricks. "How many of you were taken out of court together?"

The nail, moving toward his throat again, was halted by McGregor's outstretched arm. "I was alone, the only one taken from me town," the red-bearded man said.

"I think everyone was," Duncan said. No one refuted him. "They sought only certain types. Not just those with backs strong enough for seven years' labor."

"To what end?"

"To an end Adam glimpsed. We are not going there just to build some rich man's town. Where were you taken?" Duncan asked. "Where were each of you ordered into the Company?"

"Dunkeld," McGregor grunted, and nudged the man beside him.

"Oban," the man said, followed by quick answers from the others. Fort William. Girvan, Kilmarnock, Ballantrae, Fairlie, Culross.

"All recruited from different places, so the men did not know one another. To make it easier to tame us but also to make it more difficult to know what we all shared. What is it we don't see?" Duncan pressed. "Half have been in America before. What of the rest? If we cannot understand, we are doomed to suffer the consequences."

McGregor, giving up for now on his plans for Duncan, wasted little time in prying answers from the men in the bilges. Half of those present had served in the army or navy. He held the lantern to the faces of the remaining four in turn. "McPhee?" he barked.

"I allowed gravediggers to earn their pay twice," the man muttered.

"I pinched a few stags off me laird's hills," the second admitted with a grin.

"I fed my family for ten years off Lord Dundee's estate 'afore they nabbed me," declared the next.

"I kept the tables at Saint Luke's Infirmary filled for the teachers," confessed the last, a gaunt man named McSween.

McGregor threw Duncan a perplexed glance and muttered a curse. "Glory be. If we ain't soldiers, we be poachers and body snatchers."

Moans came from the dark again, and Duncan spotted a rivulet of blood flowing on the bilge water from behind the prisoners. "What have you done?" he demanded.

"He's been trying to kill us. Day by day carving a hole below the waterline."

Duncan pushed past the men. Frasier, the young keeper, lay sprawled against the hull, his lip swollen and bleeding, one hand grasped around the other, its index finger bloody and jutting at an unnatural angle. Duncan pulled the tail of his shirt from his pants and began ripping away a strip. "That nail!" he barked. "Give me the nail."

The man who had assaulted him made a growling noise.

"You've broken his finger! It must be set and splinted."

McGregor grabbed the nail, handing it to Duncan. The prisoners silently watched as Duncan ministered to the broken bone, then guffawed as Frasier regained his senses and began swinging at Duncan.

"Traitor! Spy!" the youth hissed then, hammering his injured hand into Duncan's thigh, and recoiled in pain. He gazed at the gathered men uncertainly, probably more bewildered than Duncan at the silence that had descended over them. Tears began streaking down his cheeks.

"An odd use of a spy," Duncan suggested, "to put him alone in a cell for the rats to nibble on." He bent and pulled Frasier out of the filth, onto a low ledge of ballast rocks. "If I were what you say, I would have reported your slicing of the hull."

"You never knew."

"I knew who did it a minute after I saw it. The hole was chipped out by someone left-handed, since the beam beside it prevented a right-handed stroke. It took many hours. No prisoner from the hold has been missing so long. The captain may be a tyrant, but he always accounts for his men. That leaves the keepers. And of them you are the only *corrach,*" Duncan explained, using the old word for a left-handed person. He looked about the rough faces before him. Certainly McGregor and his men would not have known about the sabotage on the cargo deck. There was only one possible explanation. But why would Woolford have told McGregor, then left the ship?

Frasier seemed to shrink. "My cousin understood," he said in an absent tone. "Play the odds, he said, that's how we beat the English. When he was pressed into the navy, he told me how he was going to drug the marine guards one night and walk into the magazine with a lighted taper. Three months later his ship exploded. Two hundred Englishmen, one Highlander."

Even the most brutal of McGregor's gang could find no response to the startling confession.

"Many of us might summon enough anger to chip away the first few inches," Duncan declared as some of the men bent toward Frasier, vengefulness in their eyes. "It's only the last inch of the hull that matters. He was never going to do it. What he did do was sabotage a trunk of Ramsey supplies."

The heat seemed to sap from several of the men. But as Duncan studied them, a rock thudded against his shin and he bent in sudden pain.

"Liar! I know how to kill English!" As Frasier lifted a second stone to throw at him, Duncan leaned over and clamped a hand around his arm.

"I came from the assizes like every man here," Duncan said in a level voice.

"Look at him!" Frasier cried. "He hides army secrets around his neck!" The top buttons of Duncan's shirt had opened in their scuffle, exposing a glimpse of what lay underneath.

Duncan did not move as McGregor pulled out the medallion, now with the dried thistle pressed into its leather seams and wrapped with his precious long strip of paper. The old Scot unrolled the list with a suspicious eye. "By God, McCallum," he spat, "'tis the work of an informer for certain! Who be these names?"

"The men of my clan," Duncan shot back, using Gaelic again. "My clan lairds. Now I am the oldest to survive, all those elder cut down by the king. Would you prefer I name for you the things they did to the bodies of my mother and sisters and six-year-old brother? Or how many weeks it took for my father's bones to fall from the gibbet after Culloden?" A new tone had entered his voice unbidden—the coarse, wild edge that erupted when rival clans parried before a fight.

McGregor grew very quiet. As the old Scot gazed silently at the list, Duncan watched the last of his venom drain away, replaced by a weary melancholy. He returned the paper and lifted first one, then the other of Duncan's hands, studying the many gashes left by small teeth. "Why do they do this to you?"

"Why do they do this to any of us? If we do not find out, we may as well go finish that hole in the hull."

"This one is still dangerous," McGregor said, indicating Frasier. "There be those who say he was with Evering the night before his death. The last to see him alive. If he confesses to you now, it saves the rest of us."

"I told them nothing happened that night," the young keeper said in a small voice, tears streaking the grime on his cheeks.

"What I want to hear, Frasier," Duncan said, "is why Adam invited you to rob Woolford's trunk."

"I never—" the young keeper began, then seemed to sense

something in Duncan's eyes that made him start over. It was why the prisoners felt no fear of assaulting the keeper. They all knew what Frasier had done with Woolford's trunk, and a word from any one of them would mean the loss of his keeper status. "He said he was certain there would be sugar in such a gentleman's chest, that there would be trinkets for the games, which I could give to Cameron to buy his silence. All he wanted was one thing."

"Brandy," someone suggested with a guffaw.

"Tobacco," Frasier said. "He wanted the tobacco. Except he said not to give it to him. I was to get it to Professor Evering."

"But Evering did not smoke," Duncan pointed out.

Frasier's face darkened. "Sometimes I think maybe I was the one, the one who did kill the professor. As well as done." Duncan sensed the men behind him shift, tensing again, and he shifted to place himself between them and the young keeper. "I saw Evering twice that last night, before the storm," Frasier continued in a hollow voice. "First on deck, speaking of the heavens, but then past midnight in the passage outside his cabin, though he did not see me. He was waving a piece of lit tobacco, letting the passage fill with the fragrance, then going into the sick room with it. He did something terrible with it, and I made it possible. Adam could never have intended it."

"Did what, lad?" McGregor demanded.

"Don't you see? Evering revived the *beanshith,* the banshee. I gave him the tobacco and the medallion like Adam asked, and he used the tobacco to revive the banshee. He didn't know she would kill him."

Duncan surveyed the rough assembly. Their hate had totally burned away, replaced with a dim confusion, even fear.

"Why did you ask Woolford about being at all our trials?" Duncan asked the young keeper.

"If the Company is to be used by the army, we should know it."

"But why now, why ask when you did?"

All the fight had gone out of Frasier. He spoke toward his hands. "Adam had died."

"I don't understand."

"Adam used to sing in the night."

"You're making no sense."

Strangely, it wasn't pain in Frasier's eyes when he looked up at Duncan, but embarrassment. "I asked him once," the young Scot said. "I missed my home so. There was a song my mother used to sing, about the sun setting over the loch with the heather in bloom. I asked him to sing it, and he did, every night when he knew I was in earshot."

"But why?" Duncan pressed. "If you were upset about Adam, why badger Woolford about the army?"

"Because of the lies they told, because of the way they treated him. Because I won't let it be forgotten. They put Adam in with the Company prisoners two days before sailing, as if he were just another one brought in from some village court. But he was the first prisoner, here before the keepers, before the murderers, kept by Woolford in a cell."

Duncan leaned closer. "How do you know it was Adam in the cell?"

"Because the captain's wife fed him when Woolford was away at the law courts. She was feeling ill one eve and told me to go down with the food. That was when I first heard him sing. I still hear him," Frasier added in a whisper. "I never saw him in the cell, and might have been taken into the deception like everyone else."

"Except he sang," Duncan concluded. "And you heard him later, in the prisoner hold."

Duncan tried to piece together Frasier's words with Woolford's revelation that Adam had volunteered to become a prisoner. "Sometimes," he said, "a man's crime can be knowing someone, or something."

"What secret could Adam have known that made him so dangerous to be locked in a cell?" Frasier asked in a rueful voice.

"What he knew was something about someone called a fish-speaker and an inn in America. And," Duncan said with conviction, "why the Company is going to need so many poachers and body snatchers." As well as, he almost added, a secret about Duncan that Duncan himself did not know.

When he returned to the cells, Lister had a bucket of seawater waiting for him, and Duncan gladly let the old mate dowse him repeatedly. But his dreadful foreboding could not be stripped away as easily as the stench. As Lister locked the cell door, Duncan leaned against the wall, feeling strangely weak. Confusion had become his new disease. Adam had condemned himself to the ship of his own accord, as if under some dark spell. Woolford's chest had indeed been the work of Pandora, its demons now preying on the ship. Woolford, he had slowly realized, must have told McGregor about the hole in an attempt to slow the ship's arrival in New York, as if he, like Adam, dreaded its arrival there. His legs gave way and he slowly sank to the floor, staring into the shadows. Much later he discovered that the black stone was in his lap, one hand clenched tightly around it, the other stroking the thing as if it needed comforting. He pressed the warm stone to his cheek, then to his heart, and then began wrapping it in the unused bandage, covering it in many layers. He stuffed the bundle into the bottom of his sea bag and settled into a corner of his cell, his hands clasped around Adam's mysterious amulet.

He awoke to shouts from above, sounds of celebration floating down from the main deck. An hour later his cell door opened and a dark bundle was tossed inside. His servant's clothes. Duncan glanced up to see Cameron's tall figure retreating toward the ladder.

"It's New York," Duncan said to Flora after he had dressed, awkwardly squared the tutor's cap on his head, and shouldered his bag. Her cell was as silent as death. Something moved inside. It could have been the despairing woman. It could have been a rat.

"I wish you good fortune, Flora," he whispered into the hatch of her locked door, then paused, knowing that luck had long ago abandoned the woman. In another time, another life, he would have tried to help her. But in this life he was powerless. He pushed his arm through the hatch, fingers extended, but she did not respond. "I wish you peace," he said in a cracking voice, then turned away.

He climbed warily into the sunlight, pausing with his head just over the rim of the deck—uncertain why he was not escorted, half expecting to be seized and chained again—then slowly approached the rail. The ship, docked at a wide timber wharf, was busily disgorging its cargo, human and otherwise. Cameron stood like a sentinel at the bottom of the gangway, forty feet from an elegant carriage attended by a broad-shouldered man whose skin was a rich chocolate brown, his waistcoat and britches a larger version of those worn by Duncan. Beyond the carriage were several heavy wagons with benches along their sides, guarded by the keepers and several brutish, thickset men armed with clubs and spontoons—the broadheaded spears sometimes used by the army—watching as the prisoners, wide-eyed, filed off the ship and climbed onto the wagon benches.

"Benign Providence continues to watch over you," an austere voice said at Duncan's side. Reverend Arnold was in his merchant's attire again and clutched a thin leather case, the kind Duncan knew was often used for military dispatches. "A short report now, and you will be done. There is a grand sermon here, about the pitfalls of forgiveness."

Duncan's mouth went dry. He searched the deck for an explanation, then studied the Company wagons again. In the first wagon two men with clubs sat behind the driver's seat, a crumpled shape on the floor between them. "What have you done?" he demanded.

"He was seen lurking about Evering's cabin last night, against our express command. As a keeper he had the run of the ship the night Evering died. He has condemned himself with his own traitorous ways. When we caught him he pulled a paper from his shirt and stuffed it into his mouth, obviously to destroy evidence against himself. The captain brought out the cat again, to loosen his tongue. He began pouring out curses in the Highland tongue, invoking the Jacobite prince. Lying from the start, betraying our trust in him as a keeper."

Duncan did not recall running down the gangway, did not remember touching the wharf, his first step in the New World. He was suddenly at the wagon's side, nearly retching from what he saw.

The pile of bloody rags was breathing, though only just. He leapt onto the wagon, parrying a keeper's raised club with a venomous glare. The old man's shirt was in ribbons, revealing crosshatches of raw flesh where the cat had done its work, partly healed and now reopened. His manacled hands were bloody and swollen, his battered face barely recognizable. Lister was not unconscious, but he did not seem to recognize Duncan.

"He wouldn't stay down, the old fool," Cameron said over Duncan's shoulder. "'Twere the sailors, with the captain urging them on. Lying about his Highland blood, to some it's as good as confessing a murder."

"Remove him, Mr. Cameron. He is in need of care."

"I cannot," the keeper said with a glance toward the ship.

As Duncan followed his gaze toward the captain, who now stood beside Arnold, a haze seemed to fall over his eyes. Cameron was not quick enough to stop him as he darted back up the gangway.

"He must have a doctor!" Duncan demanded. "You have no right!"

The captain seemed to take great pleasure in Duncan's protest. He signaled to someone behind him, and with a flurry of movement two sailors appeared, one tapping a belaying pin on his palm. "One more insult," the captain snarled, "and I shall appropriate you from the Company. There be no keepers on board to protect you now!"

"He did nothing last night but—"

The sailors seized Duncan, one on each arm, pressing him against the rail as they gazed expectantly at the captain, who stepped forward with a cold grin. The open hand that slapped Duncan felt like an oak plank.

"Reverend Arnold," the captain said in a satisfied tone, "I forego my demand for indemnity. I am taking this mongrel to—"

The captain finished his sentence with a terrified moan. With a strange hissing of air, a long, feathered shaft materialized in his upper arm.

Arnold uttered a panicked cry and dropped to the deck. The captain stood as if paralyzed, staring at the blood that flowed down his shirtsleeve, his ruddy face draining of color. Duncan's assailants released him and dragged their captain toward the cabins as the ship's bell began to ring frantically. Duncan slowly turned, not understanding, as a second arrow appeared, quivering in the wood of the rail directly below his heart.

The deck and the wharf burst into a chaos of fleeing figures, barking dogs, shouting sailors, and stevedores. Makeshift weapons appeared in the sailors' hands, and the captain, clutching his wound, barked orders as if preparing for boarders. But no more arrows came, no enemy charged the ship. The wharf gave no clue of attackers, no sign of a bowman. The panic seemed to affect all but a gang of boys perched excitedly on a pile of bales and an old man who hobbled away on a long stick. The arrows could have come from a dozen hiding places, from the shadows between the warehouses on the far side of the dock or perhaps from among the stacks of cargo on the wharf itself.

As Duncan slipped down the gangway, whips cracked and the Company wagons heaved forward, the teams urged to a trot by their panicked drivers. He stood at the bottom of the ramp watching helplessly as they disappeared. Lister, who had promised to dance a jig and pick a flower, had begun his new life in America.

After a moment Duncan felt a tug on his arm, and he turned to see the tall African, one hand on Duncan's bag. When Duncan refused to release it, the big man shrugged and stood aside to let Duncan set it inside the coach.

"I am Crispin," the big man announced in a deep baritone. "I will see you settled at Ramsey House. It is but a short ride from here." He cast a worried glance toward the shadows by the warehouses, then gestured Duncan inside.

"But the Company proceeds to the frontier," Duncan protested.

"The children's tutor must be with the children," Arnold said in a rushed, nervous voice over his shoulder. The vicar was guarded by two sailors. "The children reside here in the city except in the warm months. We will join the Company in two weeks' time."

Duncan was about to argue when he realized the big man meant they were going to the house where Evering's journal had been sent.

As Crispin gestured Duncan into the carriage, Arnold cast a worried glance up and down the wharf, then darted into a second, more ornate coach that waited behind a stack of tobacco bales. Crispin climbed into Duncan's coach, perching by a small wooden crate on the opposite seat as the driver called out to the team of matching chestnuts, and the carriage lurched forward. As he gazed at the *Anna Rose,* where muskets now bristled from the rail, Duncan fought a sinking feeling that somewhere on board he had missed the answers to the mysteries that beset the Company. But then he realized that here, in America, was where the Company was intended to be, here was where the unknowing players in this tragedy were finally entering their stage.

The waterfront adjoined a forest of masts, ships ranging from mighty square-rigged merchantmen like the one he had just left to sleek sloops and cutters, small sail-rigged dories, wide shallops made for river traffic, even two frigates and a troopship anchored in the harbor, streaming the Union Jack. Sturdy men unloaded glazed bricks from one ship, sacks of tea from another. The streets along the docks bustled with sailors, fishmongers, cats, street urchins, tinkers, and heavy wagons loaded with fresh-cut lumber. The boots of a dozen scarlet-coated soldiers pounded the cobblestones as they marched, double-time, toward the wharf. A girl in a tattered dress banged a tin cup, loudly proclaiming the price of her fresh goose quills. Laughing boys with soiled faces skirmished with mongrels. A stout woman hawked speckled hens in wicker cages. The morning breeze mixed the salt air of the bay with the pungent scents of old fish, horse manure, tea, rotting seaweed, sawdust, tobacco, and tar.

"I never expected Indians attacking the harbor," Duncan said. He found himself leaning hard against the seat, staying in the shadow.

"Nor would anyone else." Crispin studied Duncan a moment. "And it wasn't the harbor they were attacking," he said pointedly.

Duncan pressed even deeper into the seat.

They gazed outside in silence, until Crispin seemed to sense the questions forming on Duncan's tongue. "I am in service as the house butler," he explained. "Sent to retrieve the new set of porcelain," he added, tapping the box. "Painted with the Ramsey coat of arms by a craftsman with a warrant from the king himself." There was an edge in the man's voice. Was it sarcasm Duncan detected?

Duncan stared in the direction the Company wagons had gone, then found his gaze drifting back toward the strapping butler in front of him. Crispin's slightly undersized suit gave him the air of a powerful beast that had recently been tamed.

With a start Duncan realized Crispin was returning his stare. "There's so many ways people find to ask me the same question." His words were articulated with the slow precision of an educated man.

"I was just wondering how many men you've laid down with your left fist," Duncan said, motioning toward the scarred knuckles of Crispin's hand. "I was studying to be a doctor. For practice my professor sometimes sent me to the Saturday entertainments to treat the pugilists. I've seen many a hand like that in England."

"They never called me a pugilist where I fought," Crispin looked at Duncan with challenge in his eye.

"Yet you know the term."

Crispin cocked his head and raised his brow. "So that's how you're asking," he said with the hint of a grin. "I grew up working in the fields of Georgia, but my mama was a nursery maid. She listened to everything from the teachers. At night she taught me whatever the children in the big house had learned that day. Her lessons freed my mind. The prizes I won with my fists freed my body."

"When I was very young," Duncan said, "my grandfather was my only teacher. If I failed my lessons, he would take a cane to my backside." He realized he had removed his ridiculous scholar's cap and was twisting it in his hands.

"Bullies are not unknown in America as well."

"Not a bully. I loved him very much. At night we walked by the sea and he talked of life in the old century, of the stars, of our ancestors. When the moon was full, hanging over the ocean, he would keep me up 'til midnight at the water's edge, reciting poetry and old tales of heroes and magic, despite my mother's protests. I would have gladly taken two beatings a day for the chance to walk with him at night." He stuffed the cap inside his waistcoat.

Crispin fixed Duncan with an inquiring gaze, then offered a somber nod. After a moment he began explaining the sights outside the windows.

The town of New York was smaller than Duncan had expected, though it seemed more active than a community twice its size. The bloody war with the French and their Indian allies was largely being fought in the lands of the mighty Hudson River and its tributaries, Crispin reported, so the old Dutch settlement at the mouth of the river had become a vital depot for military supplies. The streets were choked with wagons from the surrounding countryside, bringing food and fodder to be sold to the army and shipped upriver to the garrisons at Albany and beyond. Hammers rattled in new construction to house the officials who conducted the business of war. Women in fine dresses walked on planks over the mud surrounding the worksites while men in tattered clothes hauled stones to the new structures, their feet sinking to the ankles in the moist grime.

"More homes are being taken for hospitals," Crispin said, his only pronouncement on the progress of the combat. He nodded toward a large brick house with several soldiers sitting on its wide porch, all wearing bandages on their heads or arms, most wearing absent, defeated expressions.

The three-story structure where the coach stopped was spacious, though of a far simpler design than one of the great houses of England. A tall clapboard building painted mustard yellow, with four dormer windows jutting from the shake roof, it reminded Duncan of many residences he had seen in Holland. As Crispin led Duncan up the brick walk, the box of porcelain perched on his hip, the big man leaned toward Duncan and paused. "The children most of all need to learn there's things other than grief and hate in this world," he declared in an oddly urgent tone, then straightened as he spied a stout woman in a black dress standing in the front doorway, arms akimbo. She began to loudly chastise him for the cavalier manner in which he conveyed the porcelain.

After surrendering the box to the woman, Crispin showed Duncan to a small, sparse bedroom on the third floor, under the slanting eaves, explaining that he had a similar room down the hall.

"There was to be a crate delivered to Professor Evering," Duncan ventured as he dropped his bag on the narrow rope bed.

Crispin nodded. "Carried to the teaching chamber. The Reverend spoke of the professor's tragic ending. Some people just don't travel well."

"I know not what Reverend Arnold told you. Professor Evering was murdered."

Alarm flashed in Crispin's eyes. "Surely he wasn't—" the big man began. "It couldn't have anything to do with—" he tried again, then grew silent and looked out the window, his brow knitted in worry.

A scullery maid entered, carrying a bucket of hot water that she emptied into the wash basin on the bedside table, and then hastened away without acknowledging Duncan.

"What became of the last teacher here?" Duncan asked to his back.

Crispin took a long time to answer. "Before, it was just gentlemen from Philadelphia or Boston who stayed a month or two. This is the first time all the children have been together. The two little ones will be sent to Europe for schooling in a few years. Meanwhile, Mr. Ramsey wants them to have a teacher from back home."

Duncan studied the man a moment. Crispin was employed by what must be one of the wealthiest families in the New World, but instead of boasting of its grandeur, he had pointed out its hate and grief; instead of using Ramsey's title, he was naming him with a common term of address. "I wasn't hired in England, Crispin," Duncan confessed. "I was a convict in the Company. I am a convict," he corrected himself. "A convict with indenture papers that can be revoked at any time."

The butler stiffened, responded with another worried stare, rubbing the back of his head as if suffering a sudden ache. He seemed about to fire back questions, but finally he only nodded. "I was once a slave, too," he offered with a shrug.

"You mentioned two young children. And the third?"

Crispin's face took on a pained, puzzled expression, as if Duncan's simple question were impossible to answer. "What did the Reverend tell you?"

"Just that I was to teach three children. What of the third?"

Crispin stepped toward the door with a reluctant expression, as if Duncan were forcing him from the chamber. "She needs the most . . . ." He sighed. "I don't have the words," he said, his voice overcome with a sudden melancholy.

Duncan stared after him, trying to fathom his abrupt change of mood, as Crispin retreated down the hall. He gazed out the window over the small, busy town for several minutes, fighting a terrible guilt for being in the comfortable mansion house while the Company moved toward the wilderness, gauging his chances of leaping on a horse and racing to find Lister without being stopped. He pulled himself away to quickly unpack and wash, then explored the house, encountering several servants who hurried past with hasty words of greeting and lowered heads. Wandering through an elegant dining room with an elaborate mural of the harbor painted on one wall, past a long mahogany table adorned with three matching brass candelabras, he found himself in a chamber lined with bookshelves. Duncan walked along the shelves in awe. Several were stacked with newspapers and periodicals: *The Spectator, The Gentleman's Magazine,* Dr. Johnson's *Rambler,* and something called *The Pennsylvania Gazette.* But there were also at least four hundred books, a veritable treasure, a collection worthy of the most learned men of England. The complete works of Hume were there, as well as Voltaire, Swift, Rousseau, Pope, Dante, Hobbes, and Defoe. One shelf held nothing but the works of the Greek philosophers.

Flanking the library's large central fireplace were four oil portraits in ornate gilded frames. On the right were one of the king and another of old King James II, the former regent who as the Duke of

York had taken the colony from the Dutch in the last century. On the opposite side of the mantel were two separate images, one of a beautiful woman whose vibrant face betrayed the austerity of her black dress and lace bonnet, her eyes as bright as the gold and ruby cross hanging from her neck. On a small table below her image was a vase of wilted spring flowers.

The man in the frame beside the woman had an impatient air and a wig of white curls too small for his large cranium. His was the only one of the four portraits that displayed the full body of its subject, seated in a throne-like chair. The man's closely set gray eyes burned not only with intelligence but with pride and ambition. In one hand he held an ornate compass. At his feet were hunting hounds, behind him a shadowy landscape with running horses over one shoulder and grazing stags over the other. Duncan's eyes went back to the hands, each of which bore heavy jeweled rings. It was the pose of a member of royalty, or of an explorer, a conqueror of lands. Duncan noticed something else in the shadows of the background, past the stags, at the edge of a dense forest. Stepping closer, he discerned a cabin of logs, with a woman sitting on the ground, cradling in her lap the head of what appeared to be a dying man stretched out beside her. He stared at the dim, unsettling image a long time, chilled by the memory of the attack in the harbor, admitting to himself for the first time that he had been caught up in the war with the savages before even setting foot in America.

Eventually Duncan's gaze settled on the carved and painted crest set in the top of the frame. On a blue field with gold stars stood a stone tower under a pair of crossed swords. Arched above them were three ornately painted words: *Audentes fortuna juvat.* Fortune favors the bold.

At the bottom right of the crest was a rearing black stallion; in the bottom center, a red rose; and at the left, a globe gripped in a hand. Duncan stared at the globe, then pulled from his pocket the button extracted from the bloody heart, studying it in the sunlight cast through the window. The globe of the button was identical to that of the crest, as intricately worked as the delicate carving on the frame. He examined the button's underside and saw many folds of metal. The crushed metal could have comprised such a wrist and hand, and he realized that the object could as easily have been a pendant as a button. Whatever its function, there was no doubt that the ornament that had been left in the bloody heart had borne the Ramsey family crest.

He paced slowly along the rows of books again, trying to comprehend this new riddle, noticing for the first time a narrow door in the corner of the room by the window. As he approached it he heard the muffled sound of a chair scraping the floor. The door flung open and an adolescent boy in the dark livery of the house servants emerged at a trot, holding a leather case on a strap—the case Arnold had carried from the ship. The youth was halfway across the room when, spying Duncan, he halted with a cry of surprise.

"What is it?" a harsh voice called from the chamber, and into the doorway stepped Reverend Arnold. He glared at Duncan a moment, motioned the boy away, then his eyes softened. "I have been remiss in not explaining the facilities to you, Mr. McCallum." The vicar quickly led him out of the library, then slowed as they reached the dining room. Outside, through the window, Duncan saw the youth hand the dispatch case to a thin, rough-looking man in a soiled leather shirt and a ragged fur cap, who hung the strap around his neck. The man's weathered, unshaven face bore several deep scars. The quick strides he took toward the horse tied at the gate were those of a wildcat. He reminded Duncan of the raw, feral men who inhabited the remotest parts of the Highlands.

"The arrows," Duncan said. "Did you discover who shot them?"

"A prank, no doubt. American children are notoriously unruly," the vicar replied hastily, though the uncertainty in his voice recalled for Duncan the panic that had seized the vicar when the first shaft had been fired. "I expect an early draft of your report," he abruptly added. "Lord Ramsey will require a full record. Your scientific details will please him. I have already written to him, summarizing how your science points to Lister, but no doubt you will want the opportunity to impress him directly with your skills of deduction."

"I said nothing about Lister."

"You proved that Evering died the night before he was discovered, when Lister was one of those unaccounted for. You proved that Evering was struck in the skull with a hard object. I discovered that Lister had offered to repair Woolford's broken chest, obviously a pretense to gain access to the carpenter's stores. You showed us how Evering had glass in his knee. Lister was seen hurrying from Evering's cabin in the small hours last night, trying to remove evidence. You already demonstrated that the one who finished the ritual at the compass had Highland roots. Do you forget that Lister stood in the hold while you examined Evering? He heard everything."

"Remove evidence? What evidence?"

"The glass on Evering's knee. Lister had a cloth of the same shards when he was stopped last night. Surely the glass shows Evering died in his cabin. Who but the murderer would want to remove the shards? And consuming the slip of paper when we caught him—not the act of an innocent man."

Duncan closed his eyes a moment. Lister had gone back for the glass, after Duncan had asked for a cloth to gather it in. And the paper would have been the slip in Evering's hand indicating a meeting with Duncan. Lister had eaten it to protect Duncan.

"I have every confidence that you will understand the situation after reflection. Let us meet tonight. Shall we say, in the library after the children retire? I shall bring the Old Testament." The vicar stepped toward the end of the long table. "There," he said in a louder voice, pointing to the kitchen. "You will find a room off the kitchen that we use for instruction. It is well lit and takes warmth from the kitchen fires. The large desk there is at your disposal, with writing implements and paper. Lord Ramsey has been so kind as to leave an atlas and other books there. The materials brought by Evering will be at your disposal. You are not permitted off the grounds, but you have free access to the kitchen, and on Sunday you will be invited to—"

Arnold's words were cut off by a peal of laughter. A boy of perhaps eight years and a girl who seemed about two years younger, both with light brown, curly hair, entered the room, a small spaniel romping at their feet. They did not see Arnold until they were halfway across the room. They halted abruptly, all joy draining from their eyes, and gazed nervously at the tall, stern figure in black. Arnold opened his mouth and seemed about to reprimand them, but then reconsidered as the children darted behind the skirts of a young woman who appeared with a vase of flowers.

She could be no more than eighteen, Duncan thought as he studied her, but there was something in her graceful countenance that spoke of sadness and wisdom far beyond her years. Her long brown hair, streaked with auburn, hung loose over the shoulders of her simple, hunter green dress. Her eyes, though quiet and intelligent, were remarkably shrunken, as if she had long been deprived of sleep. She wore no jewelry except a simple gold cross above the square bodice of her dress. Her unadorned face flushed with color as she looked into Duncan's eyes, and he struggled with the notion that he had seen her somewhere before. She was the third, the one Crispin had been scared to speak of.

"I had intended to make introductions at tea," Reverend Arnold said with a sigh, then stepped between Duncan and the newcomers, gesturing for the boy and girl to step forward. "Master Jonathan Ramsey, Miss Virginia Ramsey," he said with a quick motion to each of the small children. "And our Sarah," he concluded in a voice gone oddly still. "You may greet your new tutor, Mr. McCallum."

Sarah seemed to look for cues from her younger siblings, as if she did not understand what to say, then mouthed the words that Jonathan and Virginia spoke. "Good afternoon, Mr. McCallum. Welcome to our house." Jonathan gave a small, stiff bow; Virginia, a deep curtsy. Sarah, flushing again, made an awkward motion somewhere between a bow and a curtsy, the vase still in her hands.

Sarah seemed unwilling to look back into Duncan's eyes. She silently retreated around the table, walking along the far side, and stepped into the library alone to place the vase in front of the portrait of the woman, removing the old flowers. As Duncan watched from a distance, her left hand began trembling, and she quickly clamped her right around it.

Something new had entered the pastor's eyes, a sudden skittishness. As Duncan watched, Arnold pulled his own gaze from Sarah back to the children, who had not moved. His eyes flared and he stepped to Jonathan, prying something out of the boy's fingers. A long, narrow blade—a letter opener, held like a sword. Arnold dropped the blade into his own pocket and glared at the boy. Duncan watched in surprise as the boy braved the vicar's steely gaze for a moment before looking toward the floor.

"We must offer new prayers tonight," the boy said in a bold voice.

The comment seemed to unsettle Arnold. "Prayers for whom, son?"

"The one with the laughing eyes who carved me a beaver out of a stick," Jonathan said in an earnest tone. "He's gone to see Old Crooked Face at the crooked tree."

Arnold seemed to stop breathing for a moment. When he spoke his voice was hoarse. "Of course we shall pray." Duncan did not miss the alarmed glance he threw toward Sarah. "Meanwhile, should you not take your new tutor to his classroom?"

Jonathan, with an odd expression of triumph, took Duncan's hand and led him away. As they entered the kitchen, Duncan looked back to see Arnold hurrying out the front door, hat and coat in hand.

The boy scampered away after leading Duncan to the chamber Arnold had described, a cheerful, sunlit room with a large walnut desk and three small tables arranged in front of it, each bearing a slate but also sheets of precious paper, pewter inkwells, pencil leads, and quills. Duncan idly leafed through the expensive atlas on the desk, gazing at the vast, unmarked lands west of the American coast, then saw the open crate in the corner, its contents partially unpacked onto an adjacent bench.

Duncan quickly sorted through the items, more desperate than ever for a clue to Evering's murderer. A dozen thin books, primers for teaching young readers. An alphabet chart pressed inside a wood frame under a transparent layer of horn—a hornbook. Jars of pigment sealed with wax. Five identical wooden boxes, each crafted with small compartments inside, one containing minerals, another dried leaves, the others lenses, shells, and empty bird eggs. Large, rolled maps tied with yarn. Duncan's eyes drifted around the room as he realized the crate would have been packed before Evering had left England. His gaze came to rest on a chair by the door, holding a small, worn trunk.

More books were in the trunk, thicker volumes with dog-eared pages. Hume's controversial *Enquiry on the Principle of Morals.* A tattered edition of *Gulliver's Travels,* another of the essays of Berkeley, the great philosopher who had spent part of his life in the New World. Two collections of poetry, one in French. A volume on the flora and fauna of the Americas, which he spent several minutes perusing. Under the books lay three more of the wooden boxes Evering used for his collections. The first was filled with dried flowers, in small compartments made of stiff, interlocking sheets of wood. One of the compartments, labeled *Thistle,* was missing its specimen. The second box was nearly empty, its only occupied compartment containing the bones of a small mammal. One compartment of the third was untenanted, while the others were filled with lenses and faceted glass. As he lifted out the last box, he felt a thrill of discovery. At the very bottom lay Evering's journal.

Duncan's heart raced as he opened the worn leather binding. The first page bore a date nearly two years earlier, and all the early entries were long, dry descriptions of daily life in London. But then the following year's entries turned into poems, or efforts at poems, for many lines were crossed out. The verses he could decipher were stiff and heavy, strangely filled with science—the musings of an intelligent, though not passionate, man, an empiricist who for some reason had begun to speak in verse. After twenty pages these verses stopped, replaced by a several pages of lines strangled with emotion, most of them crossed out. Evering's wife had died abruptly, Duncan recalled, taken by a fever. There followed several pages more of cramped lines of poetry, some stained with what he guessed was wine. Several poems were about life aboard ship, with references to rigging like spider webs and sailors with lobster-claw hands and oyster-shell faces. Several more were about seabirds. The last half-dozen pages of writing were filled with verses about women, not typical of those before—romantic verses, sympathetic, soulful verses. Duncan would never have thought them from the same man had they had not been so obviously written in the same hand.

A beaver. He suddenly looked up at the doorway where Jonathan had disappeared. The boy had wanted prayers for the laughing man who had carved him a beaver. Duncan had known a joyful man who had carved a beaver into a mast. And Jonathan's friend, too, needed prayers. Because he had gone to see a crooked man. Not a crooked man, Duncan recalled, but Old Crooked Face. But it was impossible the boy could have known Adam, let alone learn the news of Adam's death so quickly.

Evering was on the desk in front of him, reduced to his essence. Duncan read the pages with the care he had learned in dissecting the dead, pausing over every word as if it were a symptom, gradually realizing all the recent poems were about not women but *one* woman. At first he thought they were reminiscences of Evering's dead wife, for the awkward lines were heavy with tragedy. But then two unconnected verses, a quartet and a couplet, described the subject:

> *Is this a goddess or god's own blunder*
> *She who, waking, opens a door for us*
> *I watch and weep, for how I wonder*
> *Stay she so sad in the arms of Morpheus*

then

> *Face so frail between long red tresses*
> *Belongs to the land of sleeping princesses*

Evering had watched his subject as she slept. Duncan read on. Evering had written about youth and age, about riches of gold and riches of the spirit, and how he thought the two incompatible. Throughout was a wrenching melancholy. The last lines he rested his eyes on were another couplet:

> *You claim all that beauty and wealth may yield*
> *Yet silent sadness be the power you wield*

Duncan found himself looking out the window, remembering the sick passenger, the nameless woman he had saved, the one Lister, too, had called a princess. So ill she had slept most of the time, Woolford had told him, usually watched over by Arnold, Woolford, Evering, and the captain's wife. But she had awakened in the storm, alone, and risen from her troubling dreams to act out a new nightmare. He recalled the two ribbons hanging above Evering's cot. He might have suspected a tragedy between lovers had Evering been younger. But in the poems Evering's affection was not one of passion, but of worship for the woman with the long tresses. And she could have grown attached to a man who might seem like a father to her. Had she learned of Evering's death, and been so stricken with grief she had wanted to die? Or, as Frasier insisted, had she been a witch who, once revived by Evering, had rewarded him with a hammer to the skull?

At the bottom of the penultimate page were notes for new compositions of a similar tone. With tiny cramped writing, no doubt to preserve his precious paper, Evering had written a series of disconnected words without punctuation. *Lost*, Duncan read, then *heart* and *stony run, oak*, then *bones*. He faltered at a word he could not fully decipher, written three times. *Tastgua*, it said, or *Tashgua*. It could have been *Teshqua*, Latin for *wastelands*—the kind of word Evering would use in his poems. At the end of the strange ciphers came two more words, written clearly though just as perplexing: *King Hendrick*.

He looked up, startled to see that without conscious thought he had lifted the black stone from his pocket onto the table. Lifting the book from the table, he studied the binding. The page after the last entry had been torn out, as had perhaps twenty pages at the back of the journal. The paper matched that which had been used for the prisoners' letters. Evering had sacrificed his precious paper so the prisoners might write home. But only one page was taken from the end of the text. He examined the next page, a blank one, noticing tiny indentations—faint embossing from the nib that had been pressed on the missing page before it. Duncan lifted a quill from the desk and slipped into the empty kitchen, where he dabbed the feather against the soot on the wall of the huge fireplace.

Back at the desk, he stroked the feather lightly across the empty page, turning the indentations into words, or fragments of words, white against the black. They were more notes, disconnected phrases that the professor must have memorized then decided to destroy. *The crow,* the faint first words said, *the crow will keep you alive.* Duncan touched the medallion under his shirt. Adam had given Evering the crow before Duncan had taken it from the bloody compass. *Show the fishspeaker,* he read next, followed by unintelligible scratches. *Keep McCallum from the army,* he read with a chill. The remainder of the marks offered remnants he could not connect in any logical sequence. *The ghostwalker at the ox wheel,* he read, then below that, *his tongue is in his heart.*

He studied the poems another quarter hour, then he tore the last four pages of writing from the book and folded them into his pocket with the stone. Tossing his scholar's cap onto the desk, he returned to the kitchen, found a small crockery bowl, filled it halfway with water from a bucket by the door, then carried the bowl back to the desk. Into it he dumped the contents of the cloth scrap Cameron had given him, the shards of glass from Evering's cabin.

He roamed back through the quiet house into the dining room, hoping to read some of the American journals he had seen on the shelves. He halted at the entrance to the library as he saw that Sarah still stood at the portrait of the woman, tears streaming down her cheeks, one hand trembling again as the other clenched it. He stepped into the shadows and watched her, flushed with shame for doing so but unable to look away. Her hair was loosened, sweeping over her shoulders, and she had a feverish appearance. She raised her arms slowly, extending them from her sides as if she were trying to embrace the woman on the canvas, a strand of russet hair falling across a cheek as she did so.

A chill shot down Duncan's spine. He had indeed seen Sarah before, had seen her with her arms thus extended, her hair tumbling, had seen her balance along the spar in the rising storm, then leap into the churning sea. His grieving angel. It had been Sarah he had saved that awful day; Sarah had been the sick, sleeping passenger. A banshee, the crew had called her. They had hurled belaying pins and curses at her. But, he knew now, Professor Evering had written poems about her. Evering's sad, frail princess. The eldest child of one of the most powerful families of the New World. The one Frasier had named as a witch, as the killer of Evering. The owner, no doubt, of the Ramsey pendant stuck in the pig's heart.

He suddenly realized he had uttered a gasp of surprise. Sarah's head slowly turned toward him, then she lowered her arms, scrubbed the tears from her cheeks and picked up the vase of old flowers as he awkwardly approached her.

"They keep flowers for her," Sarah whispered, forcing a small smile. She seemed so vulnerable, so frail. "Fresh ones, every day in spring and summer."

They. She spoke as if she were not part of the house, not part of the family.

"In the winter perhaps you could draw a flower on paper each day and leave it," Duncan suggested in his own whisper. She was a deer that might bolt at the slightest shift in the wind. "There are paints. We could add colors, paint entire bouquets."

The thought seemed to cheer Sarah, whose natural expression seemed to be one of melancholy. She offered another quick, tiny smile, self-consciously brushing a lock of hair from her face, her green eyes darting toward him, then away.

"There are three small desks in the back chamber, Miss Ramsey,"

Duncan observed. "Surely you will not need to sit through the same lessons as your brother and sister."

"But I must," Sarah said, speaking to the wilting flowers in her hands. "I have no arithmetic. I have little of writing." She gave him another skittish glance. "Please," she said in the voice of a small girl. "I desire to spend as much time as possible in the classroom." She made it sound as though she needed to escape from the rest of house.

What was the secret illness that had kept her bed-bound for the entire voyage across the Atlantic, Duncan wanted to ask. What had prevented Evering, the natural philosopher who seemed to have been so obsessed with her, from discussing her illness in his journal? Had she truly been so ill for so long that she had lost a decade of instruction, lost her adolescent years? He struggled to put a name to her malady, trying to connect her trembling hands and sunken eyes to any disorder he had studied.

When she looked up at him, her moist, nervous eyes were those of a child. He had never known such a creature. One moment she seemed to bear the weight of the world, the next she seemed so naïve, so innocent in the ways of the world; one moment so poised, the next, so awkward.

"I regret we were unable to get acquainted on board the ship," he ventured.

"I met so few of my fellow passengers," Sarah said. She seemed to struggle again to find words. "I was so fatigued, always fatigued. The professor would read to me, God bless him." She gazed at the ruby cross on her mother's bodice. "You were the one, they say. I never thanked you for taking me back from the sea," she said in a whisper. "A terrible accident. I was fortunate you were there."

But there had been no mistaking Sarah's action in the storm. She had deliberately, and with uncanny adroitness, climbed out on the spar, deliberately leapt into the sea. Was her illness killing her, was that why she had cast herself into the storm? With a shudder Duncan recalled how his fellow prisoners had been driven to suicide.

"A terrible accident," Duncan repeated with a slow nod. "The gale affected many people that day," he added. "My grandmother would lock the shutters tight in a storm, then bar the door and sit by it with an ax to keep guard. She said the earth spirits were fighting, and she would not let them enter in such anger." He offered the words with a small grin, but when Sarah turned back to him her eyes were sober and round, full of wonder.

"Did the professor read to you the night before?" he asked, hoping the softness of his tone might steady her. But her eyes grew still rounder and she pressed the vase close to her breast. She leaned toward the door, glanced at Duncan with sudden alarm, and then with a bound, the young doe bolted.

He watched the doorway for a long moment after she disappeared; then, remembering his experiment, he returned to the classroom. The bowl of water with the shards had acquired a faintly brown hue, and as he stirred it a dim odor wafted upward. He touched his finger to his tongue and grew cold. Though dilute, the acrid taste was unmistakable. The dosing vial had contained laudanum. Tincture of opium. Sufficient doses could put one into a coma-like state, and one who had become habituated to it could, when taken off the treatment, exhibit many disturbing symptoms, not the least of which would be trembling hands and sunken eyes. He remembered the bitter taste in the mysterious pot of tea given him in his cell. A strong dose of laudanum in a pot of tea could leave a man Duncan's size unconscious for hours, though he still could not imagine why anyone would have wanted him comatose in his cell. He gazed forlornly into the bowl, trying again to connect the cryptic evidence left by Adam and Evering. Somehow he had to wring enough truth out of it to save Lister.

Duncan found Crispin outside in the kitchen garden, pulling weeds from a bed of bean plants. "How did her mother die?" he asked as he knelt and began to help. "Their mother."

The walnut-skinned man took a long time to answer. "She was the one who hired me, when the other houses in town closed their doors to a freed black. Lady Ramsey was the only one who could soothe Mr. Ramsey's anger, the only one other than Sarah who could reach his heart. Two years ago Lady Ramsey was on a ship home, the navy mail packet, to visit her family and show them her new baby, a second son. A French frigate attacked as they entered the English Channel. No one survived."

They worked in silence for another few minutes before Crispin spoke again. "Mr. Ramsey, he disliked the French before, but since they killed his wife and son, his hatred has burned like a fire. He lives to ruin the French, to destroy their soldiers and those who help them." The late morning sun beat down on their backs and they fell into a languid rhythm as they worked. A scullery maid settled onto a back step and began peeling potatoes.

"Did she know him well?" Duncan asked suddenly. "Adam Munroe."

"He was here just the one time," Crispin said, then looked up in alarm.

"Jonathan revealed that he had visited," Duncan assured him. Not only had Adam visited Sarah, Crispin's expression told him it had been in secret. "I counted him as a particular friend. When was it, his visit?"

"Seven months ago," Crispin replied in a whisper, glancing at the maid.

"You mean just before Sarah fled." Sarah had gone to Scotland with the mysterious Greek, Socrates Moon. But shortly before that, Adam must have gone to Scotland, to his birthplace in Argyll. It must mean Sarah had followed him, after he had stopped at the Ramsey house to give her secret directions.

Crispin sighed and leaned toward Duncan. "You'll have to help me, McCallum. It's more than one man will be able to do, protecting the girl."

Duncan remembered little Jonathan, holding the letter opener at his sister's side. "Protect Sarah? From what?" Duncan's query was drowned out suddenly by the beat of a drum.

A child cried out in excitement, and Jonathan appeared at the side of the house, calling for Crispin, motioning them toward the street. As they reached the front of the house, Virginia emerged from the front door, pulling Sarah by the hand.

"Soldiers!" Jonathan exclaimed. "Our brave redcoats!"

"A patrol," Crispin explained. "Sometimes the general sends patrols out to make the people feel safe. There are terrible reports from the frontier."

"The Forty-second Regiment?" Duncan asked, suddenly very interested in the tight ranks of redcoats that appeared around the corner, five ranks of four men each, muskets on their shoulders, followed by a drummer and an officer on horseback. Across the street, men stopped and raised their hats in salute to the stern infantrymen.

"Hurry!" Jonathan cried, pulling Sarah toward the street. She seemed reluctant to approach the soldiers. "We'll miss them!"

But the patrol halted in front of Ramsey House. A sergeant in the front rank glanced back at the mounted officer, who nodded. To his surprise, Duncan recognized the man on horseback. But Lieutenant Woolford, stiff in a red brocaded jacket, gave no acknowledgment.

The glee of the children abruptly changed to fear as the drum stopped and four soldiers wheeled, then sternly marched through the gate, directly up the brick walk, halting beside Crispin and Duncan. The children retreated, trying to pull Sarah with them again, though now Sarah seemed to want to stay, even seemed about to say something to the soldiers. The sergeant looked at Woolford again, then nodded at the four men, two of whom lifted manacles from their belts. As Duncan saw anger enter Sarah's eyes, he stepped toward her, worried about what she might do. But as he did so, strong hands clamped around his upper arms on each side. Before he could utter a word, the manacles were on his feet and hands. He struggled a moment, about to lash out with his elbows, then saw the fear in the children's eyes and relented.

"Crispin!" Sarah cried. "Stop them! They have no right!" She grabbed Duncan's arm and pulled as the soldiers began to lead him down the brick path, holding him so tightly she was dragged several feet, her shoes scraping on the bricks as the soldiers led him by the chains.

"Patrick! Do not do this thing!" she shouted. It took a moment for Duncan to realize her plea was addressed to Woolford, who only stared straight ahead.

Crispin was suddenly at her side, prying Sarah's fingers from Duncan's arm, wrapping his thick arms around her from the back to restrain her. Tears welled in her eyes.

As the soldiers pulled him through the gate, Duncan turned for a last glimpse of Sarah. Jonathan stood in front of her now, his arms locked around his sister's legs, pushing as if to keep her from the soldiers. Amid his confusion he remembered his vow to Lister. He had given the New World a chance, and he had lasted four hours.

Chapter Five

*T*HE SUPREME ADVANTAGE OF BEING at war, Mr.
McCallum," declared the tall, well-fed man in the scarlet
coat, "is that our beloved King George entrusts his soldiers with such vast discretion in reducing our enemies." The officer,
who had been addressed as Major Pike by several nervous subordi-
nates, paused to play absently with a loose thread in the gold brocade of his cuff, then looked up at Duncan across the ornate table
that served as his desk. "There is no greater thrill than standing in
command of a battery and knowing the king desires you to evis-
cerate the vile creatures before you with good English lead." He
reached to pour himself a cup of tea. "Feel free," he mocked,
pointing to the tray that held the teapot and a plate of scones.

Duncan sat six feet in front of the desk, manacled tightly to the
chair. They were in a sprawling house that had been converted to
army offices, apparently the military headquarters of the city.

"I have done you no harm," Duncan protested for the fourth
time, twisting, futilely straining to see the faces of the men who
sometimes paused in the shadows beyond one of the room's open
doors to stare at him. They had left him alone in the chamber for at
least thirty minutes after chaining him to the chair. In the quarter
hour since Pike had arrived, the officer had stated no charges, given
no indication why Duncan had been dragged through the streets to

the headquarters. He seemed to be waiting for Duncan to confess something.

"I believe, McCallum, that some men act as the hand of God," the major said, his eyes like soiled ice. "I believe in the propensity of all other men to conspire and lie and cheat. I believe that although a sheep may be shorn, it will always grow the same wool."

"And *I* believe you must be more specific," Duncan replied evenly, returning Pike's glare.

Pike rose, lowering his teacup to the desk, and slowly walked to the corner, where he retrieved a well-worn horse crop. He bent it in his hand as if testing it, then approached Duncan, tapping the end in his palm. "I am a senior officer in His Majesty's army," he declared with smug anticipation. "Flaunt me and you flaunt the king."

When Duncan remained silent, Pike extracted an envelope from an inner pocket and dropped it on the front of the table, then stepped to the window and stared toward the Hudson, a hundred yards away. As Duncan's gaze shifted from the riding crop, still in the officer's hand, to the envelope, his mouth went bone dry. It was his letter to Jamie, the one he had left on his hammock the day of the storm, the one he had last seen in Cameron's hand.

"I am enamored of this bold, new land, McCallum," Pike said, speaking toward the window. "I will not let it be subverted by the likes of you."

"You speak in riddles, sir," Duncan said. Anger was beginning to burn through his fear. Here, personified before him, were all the men who had strung up his father and killed his mother, sisters, and young brother.

When Pike turned toward him, his eyes were cold slits, his mouth curled into something like a snarl. Duncan did not actually see the man move, just was suddenly aware of the officer looming over him and the crop slashing the air. The slap of the loose leather tip against Duncan's cheek was like a hot blade.

Pike's eyes were wild, his jaw open like that of an eager predator as Duncan reeled back and the officer raised his arm again. Then suddenly his gaze shifted to something behind Duncan, and the fire left his face. He straightened, lowering the crop to his side, and retreated a step.

"I understand he is bound to Lord Ramsey," a dry voice stated, in a casual, almost whimsical tone.

Duncan twisted to try to see who spoke. The man stood directly behind his chair.

"Surely that can be no excuse, sir," Pike muttered. He glanced at the crop in his hand, then tossed it into the shadows.

"Were you aware, Major," the refined voice continued, "that Lord Ramsey never visits London but that he lunches with the king? A few drops of common blood, they say." The speaker walked past Duncan to stand where Pike had been, facing the window. He was years older than the major, though his powdered wig and the fact that he did not show his full face made it difficult to be certain. The officer held his short, compact frame ramrod straight, the habit of a career soldier. "Let there be no misunderstanding." he said, still facing the window. "Enlighten our guest."

"General, surely it cannot be necessary. Obviously—" Pike began, but then the hand held behind the general's back tightened into a fist. Pike glared at Duncan, stepped to the table, and extracted a paper from a stack near the chair.

Duncan studied the man at the window, vaguely aware of something warm dripping down his cheek. The general seemed to bear a profound weight. He was studying the river, watching upstream as if expecting something from the north, where the bitter war with the French was being waged.

Suddenly Pike was hovering over Duncan again, extending a large paper, a broadside, dropping it into Duncan's lap. It was a bounty poster. An officer was wanted for desertion and sedition. A hundred pounds sterling was offered for the man or proof of his death—a princely sum, one that could buy a man a large farm.

As Duncan stared at the name, a fog seemed to form behind his eyes. He felt shrunken, and cold, and helpless.

"The name of the Forty-second Regiment of Foot is spoken with reverence among our troops." Pike's voice seemed to come from far away as Duncan still stared at the broadside. "The Black Watch, they call it, and to the French they are the black face of death. In battle there is no task they cannot be trusted with. If there is a hole in the bloodiest part of the line, the Black Watch goes to fill it. No need to order them. They will demand the privilege." A fierce and angry pride had entered the major's words. "They are the granite upon which our army stands."

It took a long time for the major's words to register. Duncan could not take his eyes from the name printed twice the size of the font on the rest of the poster. *Captain James McCallum.* The army was seeking his brother Jamie, so they could hang him.

"In July of last year," Pike continued. "Nothing was preventing us from marching straight to Quebec but four thousand French soldiers at the fortress we call Ticonderoga. We outnumbered them four to one. We sent in the rangers, we sent in troops of infantry. The great guns of the French made short work of them. Then we unleashed the Forty-second. The brave lads were chewed up but kept advancing over the bodies of their own dead. We would have taken the breastworks and sent General Montcalm fleeing home to King Louie, except a Black Watch officer deliberately disobeyed orders. By the time we knew of Captain McCallum's treachery it was too late. The bastard cost us the battle, then fled like a coward. We now believe he works in the aid of the enemy, was probably doing so that very day."

Duncan did not know how long he stared at the broadside. But when he finally looked up, Pike was pacing around his chair. "When were you going to meet him?" the officer demanded, Duncan's letter in his fist. "Where is the traitor?"

"I knew nothing of this." Duncan's voice cracked as he spoke.

Pike's eyes flared again. He glanced in the direction he had thrown the crop, then charged at Duncan's chair with an open hand raised. Three feet away he halted with a look of surprise and stared spitefully over Duncan's shoulder.

"I thought we had established that he is with the Ramsey Company," a new voice interjected. Duncan became aware of someone bending toward the manacles, then recognized the voice. Woolford.

"Then damn the Ramsey Company," Pike shot back. "He is the source of our problem, and therefore the cause of our defeat."

"As I have explained, Major, this particular McCallum has never been in the colonies until a few hours ago," Woolford said in a cautious tone. The general, still at the window, shifted his head slightly to the side, but otherwise did nothing.

"Obviously, Woolford, you are incapable of fully assessing his letter," Pike proclaimed. "It implies there were earlier letters. We can assume they were equally full of sedition. This man is no doubt the one who turned Captain McCallum against his king."

The words cut deeper than the crop. "Impossible!" Duncan protested. But the denial came out in a hoarse croak. He had indeed beseeched Jamie to remember the clan, and for the first year after he heard the news of his brother's commission, he had not written at all, so reviled had he been at the thought that Jamie had joined the very army that had destroyed the Highland way of life.

As Duncan heard the click of a key behind him, Pike's lips curled into a spiteful grin. "The Ramsey Company is doomed before it even sets foot in the wilderness," he growled, then cast another wary glance toward the window. "In three month's time there won't be enough of it left to bury."

Woolford said nothing, but released the manacles and stood. Pike watched not Woolford, but the man at the window. When the general did not react, Pike seemed to deflate. By the time Duncan staggered to his feet, rubbing his wrists, Woolford had retreated out one of the side doors.

"It matters not," Pike declared in a frigid whisper, leaning over Duncan. "Lift a finger to help your brother, and you will hang at his side when we find him. Make no mistake, McCallum, we will find him. Our custom with traitors is to leave them hanging for a month or two, as a reminder. They are familiar with the practice in Scotland, are they not?" he added harshly. "I hear the magpies in forty-six were too plump to fly." The major turned for a moment toward the man at the window, who continued to stare out the window. When he turned back, there was an odd expression of defeat on his face.

The general paced the length of the window, then turned to Duncan. "What say you of the murder of Lord Ramsey's scholar?" He had an open, honest countenance, though crows' feet of worry had grown around his eyes.

Duncan glanced at the nearest door. "The death of a learned man is a loss to all the world."

The officer offered Duncan a sad smile. His dark, intelligent eyes fixed him with something like deep curiosity. "To our world, yes," he said, as if another world had been at work in Evering's death. Pike withdrew into the shadows, then left through a side door. The new turn of conversation seemed to have frightened him.

"You are the one guiding the Ramsey Company to its painful truth," the officer observed. "What does that make you, Mr. McCallum? High sheriff of the Company?"

"It makes me the dog they all want to kick. To save one of their own I must fight through ranks of clansmen."

The general seemed amused at his answer. "A murder on the high seas. An investigator who is little more than a convict himself. Tedious legal questions could be raised. The Ramsey Company was allowed to be formed because of the war."

"You think Evering a casualty of war? I can't imagine a man further removed from it."

The officer fixed Duncan with an intense stare, then responded by retrieving something from the shadows and dropping it on the table, an arrow with brown and white fletching and bars of brown on the shaft.

"Someone involved in the war sought to kill the Ramsey tutor today."

Duncan drew a shuddering breath. "I was under the impression," he said, "that the savages fought in the forests. I did not expect the army to permit an attack in the city."

The general smiled at this taunt. "Why would an Indian want you dead?"

Duncan sank back into his chair.

"Two arrows, aimed so precisely," the general continued. "Your assailant wasn't satisfied with the captain taking you away—he had to be sure you were dead. The first to stop the captain, the second aimed right at your heart. But for the ship's rail you would have died before you hit the deck."

"Impossible. No one even knows me. . . ." The protest on Duncan's lips faded. The cap. No one knew him, but the cap had identified him as the Ramsey tutor.

The general stepped to the front of the desk and leaned on it, studying Duncan. "How was Professor Evering connected to the savages?"

"Evering? He had never even been to America." But even as the words came out Duncan recalled the drawing of the arrow in Evering's cabin. He studied the projectile on the desk with new interest. It was a perfect match. The striping, the careful painting was too intricate for it to be a coincidence. Someone had drawn such an arrow for Evering on the high seas, and then one had been aimed at Duncan's heart. It was as if someone had been toying with the tutor, warning of his destiny when he landed in America.

"You'd be surprised how far these arrows can fly," the general mused. "We are searching. We are very interested in the man who sought to kill a second Ramsey tutor." He stepped closer, studying Duncan, as if waiting for a reply. "He is unlikely to give up, now that you are arrived in his homeland."

"Why?" The question came out in a hoarse whisper.

"You tell me. The Company seems overflowing with secrets."

"Secrets worth dying for?"

"Secrets worth killing for."

Duncan stood and stepped to the desk, his hand trembling as he lifted the arrow, running his finger along its smooth shaft, putting a finger to its sleek flint point, then suddenly looked out the window, up the river. "If they thought Evering held a secret that was vital to them," he said, the thought bursting on him like a cannon shell, "then learned he was murdered, they would assume his killer had it, too."

The general said nothing, but offered another cool smile.

Lister. The old man, marked as Evering's murderer, faced the same danger from the savages as Duncan, and he was headed toward the frontier, which teemed with natives. There had been horses outside, mounts for dragoons. If he stole one, how quickly could the army pursue?

"The tutor is part of the Ramsey Company," the general said in a more insistent voice. "If the tutor must die, it is because of the Company. Something the Company did or is going to do."

"I am hardly privy to Company secrets, General."

"You are not trying hard enough, McCallum."

Duncan looked back at the door where Pike had disappeared. Pike had wanted Duncan because of his brother. The general wanted him for something else. "Are you trying to stop the Company?"

"The Company has been authorized by the king himself," the general replied. "Surely I would be powerless to stop it."

The two men stared warily at each other.

"Who was Adam Munroe?" Duncan abruptly asked.

The general gave a nod of grudging respect. "A militia officer. A former prisoner whose terror drove him across the Atlantic when he was released."

"Prisoner of the French?"

The general sighed. "I am certain we can work this out like gentlemen."

He was offering some kind of bargain, and Duncan did not even know what was being negotiated. "Are you suggesting the army does not want Evering's killer identified?"

"In war, the victor is the one who always keeps his eyes on the flame."

The man was speaking in some code Duncan could not decipher. Duncan stepped to the window. In the distance he could see the square earthen slopes of batteries along the river. "If you believe the death is connected to the war," he asked, "why not conduct your own investigation?"

"I would not tamper with Lord Ramsey's secret weapon."

Duncan fought to keep his voice steady. "You mistake me, sir. I am but a bound servant."

"Surely a man of your capacity cannot be so beguiled by coincidence."

As he grappled with the words, Duncan looked not at the nameless general but at the bounty broadside lying on the table. Lord Ramsey would have known about his brother. Reverend Arnold and Woolford would have known when they traveled halfway across Scotland to retrieve Duncan, and only Duncan, from the prison in Edinburgh. Duncan found himself backing away as the general watched him with a narrow smile.

"We shall not decline your gratitude," the general declared, "when you have reflected on what we have done for you today." He made no effort to stop Duncan's withdrawal toward an open door but lifted a hand and pointed to different door ten feet away.

Duncan hesitated then complied with the gesture. On the corridor wall opposite the door, a hand-drawn map had been pinned, marked at the top with two words that halted Duncan's retreat. *Stony Run.*

September 1758, it said under the caption. A small, irregular shape near the center apparently represented a fortification along a river. Two rows of crudely drawn trees flanked it. To the southeast along the same meandering river was an open space marked *German Flats.* Below the map was written *King Hendrick's band. Seneca. Mohawk. Onondaga.* Then a table that was headed *Rangers Killed,* with the names of half a dozen men and, finally, *three ghostwalkers.* Ghostwalkers. He read the words twice, in desperate confusion, then glanced back at the general. The officer had followed, was only six feet behind him, studying him with a dangerous smile.

No one confronted Duncan as he retreated down the hallway, looking for the door to the street. He had paid little attention when the soldiers had hauled him inside and dragged him to the office.

Passing a room where three officers examined a map on a table, he paused, gazing at the man on the left. Over his chest was the red tunic of an officer, but below was a kilt. The officer turned and examined Duncan with a disdainful stare. He wore the plaid of a Scot but the steely countenance of a British officer.

Duncan headed for the pool of sunlight on the floor that must mean an open door, and was moving at a near trot when he rounded the corner and collided with a half-naked figure. In an instant Duncan forgot his furor at Pike, his pain over the news of Jamie. He reeled, stumbling backward, his heart pounding, his knuckles pressed to his mouth to stifle a cry of alarm.

The man's rich, copper skin glistened as if oiled. He wore nothing above his waist but a folded brown blanket thrown over one shoulder and tied about his middle with a braided leather strap. His skull was shaven clean save for a small patch of black hair at his crown, from which hung several narrow, foot-long braids, with red and blue glass beads strung at the tips. Triangles of silver dangled from his pierced ears, a chain of bone and shell from his neck. Over the blanket hung a powder horn, in the leather strap of which hung two small knives. His leather leggings bore long fringes along the seams, as did the edge of the soft leather slippers on his feet. From the hair at his crown, down the man's fierce countenance, ran evenly spread rivulets of blood. No, not blood, Duncan realized, but rust-colored paint applied so that the man appeared to have just emerged from battle.

Duncan's jaw opened and shut as he stared at the savage, who did not move, did not change his proud, disdainful expression even as his eyes focused on Duncan, studying him as he might some animal he was about to butcher and consume. For a moment Duncan thought of shouting for the soldiers, then he recalled that it was not only the French who had aboriginal allies in the great war.

As Duncan inched toward the door, the Indian's hard black eyes flickered, as if he recognized something about Duncan. He made a soft clicking sound with his tongue and was answered with a movement in the shadows of the corridor beyond. A second savage appeared, dressed much as the first, and studied Duncan with an intense curiosity, pointing to the blood that now dripped down Duncan's face. With a stunningly quick motion his finger touched Duncan's cheek, wiping blood onto his finger, gesturing with it toward the offices from which Duncan had come, his eyes lit with an intense emotion that seemed part amusement, part hunger. He muttered something to the first Indian, then drew a line with Duncan's blood on his own cheek.

Something in Duncan wanted to protest, to fight back, but his tongue would not work. As the Indian touched his finger to his companion's cheek, leaving a second stripe of his blood, Duncan summoned enough strength to back away several steps, then he bolted through the front door.

When a hand clamped around his arm as he reached the sunlight, Duncan lashed out, pounding the man's wrist several times before he noticed the scarred brown knuckles.

"Crispin!" he gasped.

The big man reacted to neither Duncan's blows nor his words, but silently led him forward, down the steps, past the stern sentries and onto the cobblestone street. They moved to a heavy open wagon pulled by two large grey horses, Crispin urgently motioning Duncan to the plank seat as he stepped to the team. The butler had traded his elegant clothes for plainer dress, covered with a brown greatcoat. Crispin checked the harness and then paused, speaking softly to each of the animals before joining Duncan on the seat and, with a tap of the reins, urging the team forward.

As Duncan turned to watch the army headquarters fade into the distance, he felt a dark, hollow thing growing inside. He did not hate Major Pike for his instinctive cruelty, nor for putting chains on him, nor even for striking him. He hated Pike for extinguishing the spark of hope that had kindled inside him since the day on the mast with Lister. He had begun to think that he could endure years of bondage, because afterward he and Jamie and Lister would build a future together, construct a farm, rebuild the clan. But now his brother was lost forever to him. Both Jamie and Lister, the sum total of those he was blood-bound to protect, were destined to become gallows ballast long before Duncan's servitude was up, if an arrow did not take Lister first.

Between the pangs of hatred and hopelessness, the general's words echoed. They had been important not only for what they had revealed—the reason why Duncan had been worth the trip to Edinburgh by Arnold and Woolford—but also for what they had not. The general had not been interested in Jamie, he had been interested in the Company. He recalled Arnold's worry that the army would open its own investigation. The Company was competing with the general in some strange quest. And Duncan was Ramsey's secret weapon.

"What did they desire from you?" Crispin asked.

"I do not know," Duncan admitted after a moment's reflection. "I am being played on a hook and I cannot see who holds the line. But I must get to Edentown," he added in an urgent tone. "I need a horse. Just a horse and a map."

Instead of answering, Crispin extended a rag to him.

"The blood," the big man said.

Suddenly Duncan saw the stains on the front of his shirt. Blood was dripping from his jaw.

"We'll put honey on that tonight," Crispin said. "Ease the pain, help the healing." He clucked at the horses to urge them around a man guiding a loaded oxcart.

"I cannot return to Ramsey House," Duncan pressed. He found himself watching the trees, the rocks. With a mixture of shame and fear, he realized that he was watching for savages.

Crispin pointed ahead, toward the brilliant fields of ripening wheat that were coming into view. Duncan was about to renew his plea for a horse, then hesitated and examined the bed of the wagon. Although a canvas was tied over its contents, he recognized the outlines of trunks. He saw, too, that a coach was steadily gaining on them, steered by the same man who had driven them from the harbor.

"With luck," Crispin said, "we'll make the ferry with enough light to reach the inn on the far side of the river."

"And then?"

"Miss Sarah decided she could not wait to reunite with her father."

Duncan's heart leapt at the news. "Edentown? Sarah is in the coach?"

"And Miss Virginia and Master Jonathan," Crispin said in an oddly defensive tone, then chirruped to the horses again and fixed his eyes on the road.

Duncan looked back at the wagon's cargo and the coach. He had been in the custody of the army two hours at most, but in that time Sarah Ramsey, still obviously suffering from her sickness, had decided to flee the comfort of Ramsey House.

"You neglected to bring Reverend Arnold," he observed, "and these trunks mean no brief visit. She is planning to stay."

The comment caused a shudder in his companion.

"Have you been there, Crispin? The frontier?"

"I've been there, and I vowed to myself never to return." The butler clenched his jaw and looked toward the far side of the Hudson, which seemed lined with cliffs capped by an impenetrable wall of trees.

Crispin jerked his thumb over his shoulder, explaining that in the front corner of the wagon was a pile of rolled pallets where Duncan could rest. Duncan readily accepted the suggestion and stretched out on the soft mound. Before shutting his eyes, he extracted the pages he had torn from Evering's journal, turning to the tiny cramped words at the bottom of the last page—Evering's last entry. The professor's lack of punctuation had caused him to misread the words. Duncan had taken the notes to mean Evering was planning to compose another of his poems, one about a heart which was like a stony creek or about someone with a heart of oak withering to bones. But in his hastily scrawled notes, Evering, who had never been to the New World, had been alluding to Stony Run, where a battle had taken place the year before. It could only mean that Evering had learned it from Adam, who had been in America, who had fought in the militia there. The army's map had included other words. *Ghostwalkers.* And why would the army write of the ancient Roman Seneca, he asked himself as his eyelids grew heavy, and he folded the paper back inside his shirt. And why, he wondered as he surrendered to his exhaustion, with all of his knowledge of history, would Duncan not know of King Hendrick?

When he awoke two hours later, they were moving through rich green hills populated with grazing cows, interspersed with rolling fields where sturdy men and women bent over rows of maize with long cutting knives. Jonathan sat beside the driver of the coach behind them, and eagerly returned Duncan's wave. Virginia leaned out of the coach window, pointing out birds and butterflies.

"Do you know Lieutenant Woolford?" Duncan asked as he climbed to Crispin's side.

"Everyone in the colony is acquainted with Lieutenant Woolford, if not in person, then from accounts in the newspapers."

"You mean he is famous?"

Crispin hesitated. "What do you know about this war?"

"English kill French. French kill English. It's been going on for centuries."

"Mr. Ramsey says this war is different from any ever fought. He says this is the first time war is being fought all over the world. North America, Europe, India. The coasts of Africa and South America." The big man grew silent again. The discussion seemed to bring him pain. "My mother used to teach me about war," he continued after a moment. "Armies are supposed to face each other in lines and shoot bows or muskets or crossbows at each other."

"If wars were always so pretty," Duncan said, absently touching the long gouge on his cheek, "I'd still have my family."

"Here," Crispin continued, "the war is waged in the forest mostly, in the unmapped wilderness. Soldiers go into the forest and are never seen again. Settlers go in, entire families, and disappear. Sometimes it's French troops, but mostly it's the red savages raiding from the north, Huron and Abenaki, the French allies. The lucky ones are killed. You can read the stories of what the Indians do to prisoners, and hear more in the markets. Men hung over fires and roasted alive, fathers butchered alive in front of their children. They cut away scalps. Some say when a man loses his scalp, his spirit just spills out into the dirt and dries up," he added in a hollow tone.

"What does this have to do with Woolford?"

"The only way the Indians can be beaten back is to meet them in the forest on their terms. That is what the rangers do."

"Rangers?"

"Wilderness fighters. Frontiersmen mostly, trappers and farmers who were burnt out, looking to even the score, others trying to keep the fight away from their homesteads. Many of them are nigh savages themselves. Led by army officers. Captain Rogers in New England, he's the best known. But Lieutenant Woolford does the same in the lands west of here, in the New York and Pennsylvania colonies. Most of the victories in the war have been delivered by rangers."

"Woolford fights Indians?" Even as he asked the question something acrid seemed to settle on his tongue. With a shudder he remembered the two savages in the army headquarters. They had adorned themselves with his blood. He could not connect the glib officer he had known on the ship to such creatures.

"Been doing it so long they say he's half Indian himself. He disappears into the forest, too, but he always comes back."

Duncan fought another shudder. The savages he had encountered seemed not so much human as wild animals in the shapes of humans. "You're a butler in a great house, Crispin," Duncan observed, sensing his companion's dread of the Indians. "Surely you need not be going into the wilderness."

"Someone had to come to drive this wagon. . . ." Crispin's voice faded. "But I won't go into the wilderness. Don't ever go into the wilderness. There are farms between here and there, and a few villages. Rough country, sure enough, but Edentown, that marks the edge of the world. As far as anyone can go and still be safe."

It was Sarah. Crispin had come, against his better judgment, against all his fears, to protect Sarah. "She was drugged, Crispin," Duncan said after a moment. "She was kept unconscious by opium, all the way across the Atlantic."

Crispin's eyes welled with moisture and he looked away. When he finally spoke, it was toward the horizon. "I used to bounce her on my knee and she would laugh, how she would laugh. Everyone in the room couldn't help but join in. She and her mother spread joy like birds in spring. I haven't heard her laugh for more than a dozen years," he added in a voice gone desolate. "Maybe that's all I want, just to hear her laugh." He glanced at Duncan. "She goes into her spells and doesn't seem to see any of us. It's a disease of the spirit, the Reverend says."

A disease of the spirit. But Sarah had not only fled the city, she had fled Reverend Arnold, her spiritual keeper. She had tried to put an ocean between herself and Arnold.

"She found one of her old porcelain dolls when she first arrived off the ship, and carried it around for hours, speaking to it. Then last night in the moonlight I found her burying it in the garden." The words hung in the air a long time, seemed to follow the wagon like a cold fog.

Suddenly Duncan remembered that Woolford had left the ship early, with a cloaked companion. Sarah.

The sun was still two hours above the horizon when Crispin pulled the wagon to a halt by the edge of the wide river, onto a ramp of mud and clay strengthened with mats of dried reeds. A rail-thin man with a ragged beard slept against a huge willow tree, before a decaying platform of logs floating in the water.

Duncan scanned the opposite bank, over a mile distant. "When is the ferry due then?" he asked. The driver of the coach, already on the ground beside them, uttered a low laugh. Crispin, too, grinned, then jumped out of the wagon, pausing to toss a pebble at the napping figure before stepping to the coach. The sleeping man sat up in alarm, lifting from his side an old musket that looked as if it had lain in the grass for years. He rubbed his eyes and moaned. Beside him a duck stirred in the grass, bending its neck to watch him. It was tied to a stake, a strap tight around its neck.

"Finished for the day," the bearded man warned as he began picking at his teeth with a twig. "Done took over enough wagons for three days' work already. Come back on the morrow."

"The Ramsey Company's business today is not completed," Crispin observed in a stern voice.

The ferryman looked as if he had bit into something sour. "The Ramsey Company," he sighed, "be multiplying like rabbits." He rose, leaning on the musket.

Duncan saw the fresh, muddy ruts of wagon wheels leading down the bank and, with a flutter of hope, surveyed the opposite shore. They were on the same path as the prisoner wagons, though many hours behind.

A large woman, at least six feet tall and twice the circumference of the man, appeared at the head of a path. She turned toward the trees, emitted a whistle so loud the horses started, then grabbed up a handful of her mud-stained dress and made an ungainly stooping motion that Duncan took to be her imitation of a curtsy. "A fine eve to be on the waters, y'er honors," she declared with a grin. The few teeth in her mouth were yellow and crooked.

As Duncan watched in disbelief, two strapping boys appeared and began laying planks from the ramp to the decrepit wooden platform and arranging long oars along its sides. "Surely you do not mean to convey us on that pile of sticks?" he asked as he climbed down from the wagon.

"She's given good service these twenty years, and before that was a grand Dutch coaster," the man said with a hurt expression. "Generals have used her, and great lords, too," He straightened, smoothing his clothes with a nervous expression as the young Ramsey children descended from the coach.

Duncan now saw that the top platform of logs was built over a sturdy, broad hull, probably built in the prior century, its railings and deck furniture now cut away.

Two more youths emerged from behind the tree and began arranging long sweeps into brackets at the side of the ferry.

"Only one vehicle each crossing, y'er honor," the ferryman announced. "Ease y'er team onto—" The man's words died and his jaw hung open as he stared in alarm over Duncan's shoulder. "Bloody Christ!" he moaned and jerked on his wife's arm. Her face darkened.

"When did that happen?" Duncan heard the woman ask the man as she snatched up the old gun.

Duncan turned in alarm. Nothing had changed, except that Sarah had emerged from the coach. Her chin was up, but her eyes were filling with pain. She silently stepped to the ferryman's wife and put her hand on the barrel of the weapon. The woman's face drained of color. As everyone watched, strangely paralyzed, Sarah lifted the heavy gun from the woman's hands and set it against a tree, then silently bent, rested her hand on the back of the duck, which cowered, as stricken by her presence as the humans, and released the strap from its neck. She nudged the bird toward the water, and in an explosion of movement it burst into the air. With a whistle of wings it disappeared down the river. The spell broke.

"She had no right," the woman muttered as if Sarah were not six feet in front of her. The only one of her company not subdued by Sarah's strange actions was the tallest of the oarsmen, a lanky youth who advanced on her with anger in his eyes, a hand uplifted as though to strike her. His foray was cut off as a furious figure materialized on his back, a small fist pounding his shoulder, a thin arm ensnaring his neck. In an instant Duncan and Crispin were beside the pair, Duncan trying to pull the boy away, Crispin restraining the ferryman, who seemed ready to pound the boy with a fist.

"Jonathan Ramsey!" Sarah's voice cracked like a whip, stilling both her brother and the young oarsman, who suddenly seemed frightened.

"I never meant . . ." the oarsman sputtered. "Dear Jesus, I wouldn't have . . . ." His face dropped. "Only we was going to roast it for Sunday dinner."

The coachman hurried to the ferryman's side and stuffed a coin in the man's palm, which revived his spirits sufficiently for him to turn and begin barking orders to his crew. A moment later, the vessel ready, he turned and gestured toward it. The four boys each had one of the sweeps in their hands. "My wife be pleased to make tea for them that's waitin'," he added, with an uncertain glance toward Sarah.

Crispin leaned toward Duncan's ear. "You'll have to take the wagon across yourself."

Duncan was about to protest when he saw the worried way the big man studied Sarah. "Of course," he said, then stepped to the first team and guided them onto the vessel.

"You took three wagons across, loaded with men?" he inquired as the ferry glided away from the bank.

"Aye," the ferryman replied. "Each poor soul looking more scared than the one before. Lord Ramsey's folly, they're calling that Company of his."

"And later," Duncan ventured, "a rider, a thin man with a dispatch case?"

"Hawkins." The man pronounced the name like an epithet. "Hell-bent, he was, clutching that case like it was gold. Mounted his horse and leapt off before we was proper docked. Ramseys," the ferryman spat in a crestfallen voice as they pulled into the river. "The day be more than full of Ramseys and their flocks. A punishing crew, eh?" He studied the shallow waves a moment, then barked out an order. Two of the youths began fitting a spar into a hole in the deck, onto which a small, much-patched sail was rigged.

"I am but recently employed," Duncan replied, reluctant to admit that he had been in the New World less than twelve hours. "It seems a rigid household," he offered.

"The musket!" the ferryman suddenly shouted, and began frantically yelling for his wife to toss the weapon to him. When she refused, glancing toward Sarah, the man turned, crestfallen, and studied the western shore with worried eyes.

"What frightens you so?" Duncan asked.

"The savages, boy. They want to kill you."

Not for the first time that day, Duncan's mouth went suddenly dry. "Me?"

"You. Me. All of us. Neighbor of ours packed up to take free land in the west. Indians wouldn't have it. Burnt his cabin. Gave him to the squaws. They took three days to kill him, with pointed sticks and such."

"But there are settlements on the western shore. Edentown."

"You don't know them tribes. They appear quick as spit and are gone just as fast. This very morning there was an attack in the city itself. An arrow right into a man's heart, blood everywhere, the savages casting a spell so's no one sees them."

Duncan opened his mouth to correct the ferryman, but no words came out. But for a few inches of wood the man would have been speaking the truth.

The ferryman busied himself with the sail for several minutes, returned to Duncan's side in front of the team, then frowned, studying the sky, and reset the sail. "Used to be, I had a hand who could read the wind like words on a page." The farther they moved from shore, the more relaxed the man became. "Y'er Ramseys cost me my best mate ever. Worked for me for nigh twenty years. One bad crossing and he's under the tyrant's thumb."

"Lord Ramsey took one of your men?" Duncan stroked the nose of one of the big grey horses.

"Jacob the Fish, we called him. He never spoke much, but we fed and clothed him, and he returned an honest labor. He could catch fish by calling them with squeaks and grunts—the damnedest thing."

Duncan froze a moment and looked up. *The old fishspeaker will know,* Evering had recorded. *Show him the medallion.* "How many ferries might someone bound for Edentown take?" he asked.

"Naught but this, if ye seek the quickest road to Edentown."

The words had been Adam's, and he had known for certain that Evering would eventually meet the man he called the fishspeaker. "Where is he, this Jacob?" Duncan asked, trying to keep the excitement out of his voice.

"That be what I was saying. Lord Ramsey came through a month ago and arrested him, declaring him an enemy of England. When I said he was an enemy of no one, Ramsey asked if I should be arrested for harboring an enemy. I asked by what authority, and he raised a hand to strike me, then after a moment just said I should consider him a magistrate of the king. When we got him across, he dropped the fee in my palm and as quickly snatched it away, saying it be my fine. Ramsey must have crossed twenty times in the last five years, seen Old Jacob every time and never said a word."

Duncan clenched his jaw, trying to hide his disappointment. He touched the medallion under his shirt. "Then surely something was different that day," he suggested, suddenly sensing that there was nothing more important than finding this man Jacob and showing him Adam's amulet.

"I've thought on that, many a night I have thought on that. A farming family with children was taking passage. That trapper Hawkins was with Ramsey."

"Jacob must have given offense somehow."

"Not at all. He knew to stay away from Ramsey, just showed the children what he could do with the fish, like he did with all the children who cross, telling them to learn to see the beauty beneath the surface of the world. Never spoke much, but sometimes he had words about the natural world that made him sound like a preacher man." The ferryman scratched his beard. "He almost fell in that day. Was leaning too far over the edge to point out a great sturgeon. I caught him, but he went in head first, nigh to his waist. He came up spurting and laughing. The children laughed—everyone laughed but Ramsey and Hawkins. He took off his shirt and wrung it out." The ferryman shrugged. "When we reached the shore Ramsey ordered the local militia captain to seize him."

The two men fell into a deep silence as the wind began tugging at the sail and the little ferry surged forward. The fear and foreboding that had seized Duncan began to subside as he surveyed the rugged landscape, replaced by an unexpected thrill of freedom. He found himself looking for the escaped duck. A warm breeze blew, carrying the scent of fresh-cut hay. Fish jumped. A skein of geese flew over the broad, wild river.

"This is the real earth circling about." The words leapt from his tongue without forethought, the haunting words of Flora, who lingered at the edge of his consciousness. He glanced awkwardly at his companion, but the man seemed strangely moved by Duncan's declaration.

The ferryman stared at Duncan, then nodded, rubbing his grizzled jaw, and turned his own gaze over the water. "On the wind it walks," the boatman said in a sober tone.

"I'm sorry?" Duncan asked.

"On the wind it walks, come to restore the beauty," the man added, then turned away as one of the youths called him to the tiller. As Duncan gazed after him in wonder, a solitary duck flew over the ferry, so low he could hear the whistle of its wings.

The inn on the far side of the river proved to be a tidy, spacious Dutch farmhouse with asters blooming along its long, wide front porch, and a whitewashed plank by its door proclaiming in black letters *The Stag's Head Inn* under the image of a bounding deer. Several outbuildings of stone and white planks flanked the inn, with a broad oak giving shade to the barnyard. A freshly killed pig hung from one of its limbs, and a small live one rooted among the green acorns on the ground. He glanced at the retreating ferry returning to the opposite shore, then looked back at the sign. Evering had never been there, but had secretly recorded the inn's name. Duncan was on the path meant for the murdered Ramsey tutor, with a killer stalking him, and the only way to save Lister was to stay on the path, facing the murderer to come.

The innkeeper, a sturdy ruddy-faced Dutchman with a German wife, jovially assisted Duncan with the team, leading them to a water trough carved from a single long slab of stone, its edge worn from long use. The New World, Duncan had begun to realize, was not as new as he had imagined. He probed his memory, reminding himself that the Dutch had settled the lower reaches of the Hudson more than a century before.

The Dutchman brought Duncan a pewter mug of strong apple-jack, then pointed out the stable where he could unhitch and feed the horses.

"What became of the old man named Jacob who was arrested last month?" Duncan inquired as they walked to the barn. "Is there a jail? I'd value a word with him."

The Dutchman only frowned, then fidgeted with the knife on his belt and glanced toward the forest.

"Do you fear a raid?" Duncan asked.

The innkeeper glanced into the shadows. "Don't speak of such things," he said, "bad for business. Most of us keep dories hidden away, filled with supplies. If the alarm is raised, we will flee. No hope in fighting." He pulled the bridle from one of the big grays, then fixed Duncan with a sober gaze. "Had to fill those Company guards with drink to halt their wagging tongues this afternoon. Scared the girls in the kitchen half to death with all their talk about Indians in New York harbor."

"But the war is north of here."

The Dutchman shrugged. "The French move faster than our army, stealthy as their Indians. They have small raiding parties roaming the lands west of the Hudson, all the way to Pennsylvania. Homesteaders west of here are being scalped every week, their killers disappearing like phantoms. If the French triumph over our army, every house north of the city will be burned. And if they take the Hudson, they take the continent. The only thing that keeps the French from my door is the fact that the Iroquois tribes don't support them, and the French raiders have to come through Iroquois country. This war, it's all about the Iroquois. Biggest mistake the Frenchies made was recruiting all those Hurons and Abenakis first, without considering how they were traditional enemies of the Iroquois. If they had had the sense to court the Iroquois, we'd all be dead by now. Even so, most of the Iroquois stay out of the fight, other than the Mohawk and a few Seneca."

Duncan's mug stopped in midair. "Seneca?"

"One of the six tribes of the Iroquois federation. The western-most. You got to be careful with those Seneca. Too many married into the French."

It had been one more thing he had not understood about Evering's cryptic message, because he had not understood the New World. Impossibly, Evering had not been referring to the ancient Roman but to one of the Indian tribes, when, just as impossibly, he had described an obscure American battle despite having never set foot in the colonies. "The ferryman seemed confused about why Old Jacob was arrested," Duncan observed.

The Dutchman shot a glance over his shoulder as if to see who was listening. "Old Jacob is just a hermit. His people are almost all dead. Goes for days without speaking. But always smiling. He would carve little wooden creatures for the children. Every time an animal was born here, he would come and say a prayer over it. The great lord left him in the custody of the local militia. Old Jacob was dispatched by their captain."

"Killed?" Duncan asked in sudden alarm.

"Sent into the mountains where he can trap and call fish in the lakes the rest of his days. Lord Ramsey didn't know that Jacob the Fish had once saved the captain's daughter from drowning, or that folks around here thought of him as an old uncle to all the little ones." The man looked at Duncan with a twinkle in his eye. "This isn't the old country. Great lords may know they are gods in the Old World. But here we know they are not."

Spoken in the Old World, Duncan told himself, the words would have been sedition.

The Dutchman waved toward an ox-drawn cart bearing a man and half a dozen children that approached on the road along the river's western shore. As the innkeeper jogged toward the cart, the man at the cart called to him with a single word in greeting. *Captain.*

Duncan settled onto a small stack of hay along the stable wall and drained the mug as he watched the ferry, now a speck near the far side of the Hudson. As he studied the evening sky, his thoughts returned to Jamie. There were places like Holland where Scottish fugitives congregated, helping one another. But no matter where he fled, Pike would eventually find him, Duncan knew. And once again Duncan would likely learn about the death of another family member, the last of them, by reading it in a newspaper. Damn the army, damn the meddling Woolford. At least he would not have to see the officer again.

Duncan yawned, threw his arm over his eyes, and fell into a deep slumber, broken by a vision of a witch holding his grandfather over a cliff. "Black snake wind!" she cackled toward the sea, as if calling in a storm.

A shadow fell over him and he shot upright, looking into Crispin's broad countenance. The sun was gone, its last rays streaking through the trees of the dense forest beyond the inn. A group of men sat on the porch, holding mugs out as the innkeeper filled them from a pitcher.

"You made a hasty crossing," Duncan observed as he rose and began helping Crispin with the horses of the second team.

"Two riders arrived. We all helped with the sweeps," Crispin said, a hint of foreboding in his voice. "Miss Sarah had one of her spells. Jonathan sat with her in the coach, singing to her. She's better now, with the children inside taking supper."

"And we'll be at Edentown tomorrow?"

"Three or four days at least. Depends on the roads. Depends on the rivers. Depends on the war." Crispin sketched a rough map in the dirt, explaining how they would be skirting the highest of the Catskill Mountains to a point beyond, to a land drained by the headwaters of mighty rivers called the Delaware and Susquehanna, after the names of two native tribes.

By the time they finished with the animals, the first stars were blinking in a deep purple sky and the men on the porch had retreated into the front chamber that was used as the inn's public room, lit with candles arrayed on an iron wheel suspended from a ceiling beam. The innkeeper stood behind a long wooden bar cabinet filling more mugs, glancing frequently into the adjoining room where his wife sang out instructions in German to several girls serving hot meals.

Duncan and Crispin lingered in the open doorway for several minutes, enjoying the fine spring evening. Then, as most of the room's occupants began filing toward dining tables, Crispin excused himself to join Sarah and the children in the dining room. Duncan, fighting a powerful thirst, stepped toward the innkeeper. The only two men left in the room leaned against the bar—a compact man with shaggy, graying hair and a much taller, younger one, both dressed in identical long, dark green waistcoats over brown britches tucked into high brown stockings. The attire had the appearance of a uniform, though like none Duncan had ever seen. Hanging from the leather belt each man wore over his jacket were a large knife and a cartridge pouch.

Though the men kept their backs to him as Duncan approached, the moment the taller of the two spoke, Duncan froze. With a burst of speed he reached the man's side, spun him about, and slammed a fist into his jaw.

Lieutenant Woolford staggered backward, landing in a sprawl by the fireplace. Duncan did not wait for him to rise, launching himself through the air to land on the officer. But as he raised his fist again, a blade materialized at his neck, its edge pricking his throat, strong fingers seizing the locks at the back of Duncan's head.

"Excuse my manners," Woolford said in a steady voice, not moving. "You have not been introduced to Sergeant Fitch. His appearance of age has fooled many men no longer breathing today. He is the very best at what he does." As his assailant relaxed his grip, Duncan twisted to meet the gaze of Woolford's sinewy companion. A treacherous grin split the man's grizzled, leathery face.

Woolford rubbed his jaw as he stood, then surveyed the room. The innkeeper was studiously ignoring them. "If you had done that with a roomful of witnesses, McCallum, I would have been forced to arrest you."

"Again," Duncan shot back.

Woolford frowned, then shrugged as if conceding a point and rubbed his jaw again. "I deserved this one perhaps. Just the one, mind."

Fitch offered an amused snort and belted his knife.

"You stole my private correspondence to my brother," Duncan growled. "You had me dragged through the streets in chains."

"If you search your dim memory, McCallum, you will find that you yourself were the cause of your trouble. You may recall how you told the world about your connection to the infamous Captain McCallum of the Forty-second. You gave me no choice but to send official word. I know nothing about your letter. And as for the arrest, that was an order from Major Pike. If I had not gone to the house, there would have been only his bullies to fetch you. For many in the army, your brother is more reviled than the French."

Duncan's anger began to ebb. "I never knew about Jamie," he said in a hollow voice.

"No," Woolford agreed. "That was clear to me on the ship, and clear to General Calder when you saw that broadside. Pike wronged you." He studied the wound on Duncan's cheek, which had broken open again and was weeping blood. "For that I am—I am sorry," he said, seeming surprised at his own words. "And I shall buy us all a round of that excellent applejack," he hastened with more cheer. "I am fair parched from our journey."

The innkeeper set out and filled three heavy mugs. By the time Duncan reached the bar, Fitch had drained his and disappeared out the front door into the night. Duncan drank slowly, in silence, letting the cider dilute his anger as he pondered Woolford's words and how Adam Munroe had secretly carried the newspaper story of Duncan's trial. "The brother of such a notorious fugitive might offer a means of finding him," he ventured at last. "Adam used his knowledge of how to find me to bargain his way into the Company."

Woolford replied with only a frown.

"But how could Adam have known I was Jamie's brother?"

"That was what you might call private information."

Duncan's mind raced. "You mean Adam knew Jamie?"

"Their paths had crossed. I wasn't sure of the truth about your connection to him until the moment I saw your face."

Duncan looked up at the ranger. "Meaning you also knew my brother."

Woolford drained his cup before answering. "We served a few weeks together."

Duncan considered the words a moment. "So you struck a bargain with Adam Munroe, and without a by your leave, you change my life forever."

"I seem to recall," Woolford shot back, "that you were rotting away in some mildewed cell. And it was Arnold's bargain to strike, not mine."

It was Duncan's turn to drain his mug. "If I search my memory as you suggest," he observed after a moment, "I didn't tell the world about my brother. I told you, with Cameron ten feet away."

"Even the biggest of birds sometimes sings."

"The letter. I last saw the letter with Cameron."

"Cameron's papers show he started life as a merchant. Perhaps for him everything is still about striking bargains."

Duncan glanced out the door to the porch, where Fitch had disappeared. "You were going to bring me to America and not tell the general or Pike? Why?" he demanded. "Your duty is to this man you call Calder."

"My duty," Woolford said, as if correcting him, "is to bring peace to this land." He fixed Duncan with a dangerous gaze, then lifted the pitcher again.

Duncan gave up trying to break the strange cipher in which Woolford spoke. "My brother was no coward."

"I daresay he was a hero to his men," Woolford turned to Duncan. "Pike did not convey the fullness of the story. Captain McCallum did not flee. He ordered his men to retreat and regroup. By that time the tripe-skulled fool who—" Woolford paused. "By then," he said in a more judicious tone, "the esteemed commander of our troops, General Abercromby, had already sent a dozen companies into the French guns. A frontal charge against cannon and

mortar, when every officer advised against it. We could have cut
them off and starved them out. We could have brought in our own
artillery in a few days time. But Abercromby was hungry for glory,
desperate for a quick victory. At every turn of the battle, mistakes
were made. After six hundred of our brave lads had fallen, your
brother said it was no longer the bastards in front of them who were
killing his men but the ones behind. He called back his soldiers, said
he would no longer send more Scots to useless deaths. Pike may call
it cowardice. Most just call it mutiny. If your brother had stopped
there, the general would not have had the spine to bring charges."

"Scots?" Duncan asked in surprise, then remembered the kilted
officer he had seen in New York.

"The Forty-second Regiment," Woolford said. "The Black
Watch. It's a Scottish troop, mostly Highlanders. The king permits
them to wear kilts. For their bravery, they are even allowed a few
pipers despite the laws against them at home."

Duncan turned away to gaze into the fire, struggling with a pang
of guilt, a feeling that he had somehow wronged his brother. Until
that morning at the army's headquarters, while he had not entirely
forgotten that the army had allowed a few Scottish troops to be
formed, he had always assumed them to be lowlanders living in English ways. Duncan had never considered that his brother might have
found a means to come back to the old ways. "Pike said he deserted,"
Duncan recalled as he fixed the ranger with another suspicious stare.

"He all but said your brother caused the defeat at Ticonderoga—
a strained interpretation of events. Your brother ripped away the
insignia from his coat and threw off his gorget, knowing he would
be broken, then said he was going to collect the wounded. He had
saved another hundred from death by his order to withdraw, then
he and a few of those most loyal to him saved another score lying
bleeding on the field. But on his last trip carrying the wounded to
safety, the survivors say they saw him point to a surrounding hillside, then run into the trees with a dozen of his men. Another
artillery barrage from the French prevented anyone from following."

"Then he could have been killed."

"He was glimpsed a week later in the forest, with a handful of Highlanders who had been listed as missing. When a patrol followed, they were ambushed at night. Every man was knocked unconscious and woke up tied to a tree, having never glimpsed their attackers. But not one soldier was seriously harmed. On each of their packs was a small bone. Some said it was forest phantoms who'd attacked the patrol."

"Where would he go?"

"People say he is in Canada. Nova Scotia perhaps," Woolford said, referring to the colony that had adopted the Latin name meaning *New Scotland.* "Or in France. Pike has sent letters to every garrison commander in the army, especially in Europe, every commander in the fleets. He insists your brother has betrayed us and is helping plan the next French campaign."

"Why is Pike so rabid about him?"

"Pike was a senior aide to General Abercromby that day. A victory would have guaranteed him a colonelship. Instead he is assigned to duties behind the front with no hope of promotion."

"What kind of duties, pray tell, provide for chaining a man to a chair and whipping his face?"

"Gathering information for planning." Woolford looked up with a sardonic grin. "They call themselves Military Intelligence, to keep us from using the true description. Now he thinks he will rewrite the battle by proving your brother was in league with the French that day."

There was movement at the outer door, and Sergeant Fitch appeared, nodding at Woolford, then hastened to the bar as the innkeeper refilled his mug. Where had the sergeant gone, Duncan asked himself, remembering the warnings he had received that day. The savages could be anywhere.

"I need to find Jacob the Fish," Woolford said to the innkeeper. "Tonight."

Duncan slowly turned toward the officer, not sure he had heard correctly.

"He was arrested, Lieutenant," the Dutchman replied.

"Captain, if you please," Sergeant Fitch interjected. "He's got hisself anointed."

"Promoted since this morning?" Duncan asked, suddenly suspicious again.

"Since three months ago, apparently," Woolford replied. "But word did not catch up until I landed."

Duncan studied Woolford as the officer pressed the innkeeper about the missing Jacob, realizing how little he understood about the man. He did not trust Woolford, but did not hate him as he once had. Woolford was not simply another brandy-swilling bluestocking prig who had purchased a commission and passed his time carousing in garrison towns. He was a brandy-swilling bluestocking who willingly entered the dark hell of the wilderness so he could confront the savages, risking a horrible death again and again—and who, just as strangely, seemed more committed to finding peace than to obeying his own senior officers. But why, in the middle of the war that was so important to him, had he sailed to England? And why, once there, had he decided to accompany, even assist, the pious Reverend Arnold and the Ramsey Company?

Woolford leaned toward the innkeeper. "I must speak with Old Jacob."

"Gone, sir," came the reply. Duncan heard the Dutchman say, "He had been planning to leave, told me he had business with old friends. He won't be back. In the mountains, I daresay, building a hut for winter. He was no threat."

"Damn you, old man, I know he was no threat." Woolford's mouth twisted in frustration. He gazed outside, into the night, for a long moment, before turning back to the Dutchman. "Then I must know what he said when he was leaving. What happened that day?"

"Lord Ramsey," came the innkeeper's hesitant reply.

Woolford's knuckles whitened as he wrapped his fingers around his mug. "Where exactly in the mountains?"

"I cannot say for sure. North and west, I daresay. He won't be found unless he wants to be."

Woolford closed his eyes a moment, then cast a pointed glance at Fitch, who quickly reached for his own mug, as if suddenly in great need of the potent liquor.

They drank in silence, stabbing with wooden splints at the slices of hot sausage volunteered by the proprietor. Duncan became aware of a soft, lyrical sound from the dining chamber, gradually growing in volume, that he recognized as the strains of a violin. As patrons in the room lifted chairs, turning them in the direction of the music, Sarah came into sight, standing against the wall, flanked by her siblings. Beside them on a window seat rested Crispin, alternately watching the night and the Ramsey children.

"What Shakespeare do you have, Captain," Duncan asked after a moment, "for a tutor to an old family come to a New World?"

When Woolford did not respond, he noticed the intense way the officer stared at Sarah.

"You spent much of your voyage with Miss Ramsey," Duncan observed.

"Not exactly with her. She was sleeping most of the time, like she was in a coma. I would take my turn watching her. Sometimes I would read aloud, though she seldom gave sign of hearing."

"I would have thought her father would have wanted a doctor to escort her. Instead she had you and the vicar."

Woolford's gaze was full of challenge but Duncan did not look away. "The Reverend received instructions from a great physician in London before embarking."

"It was he who prescribed the laudanum?"

Woolford stared into his cup. "I took no pleasure in assisting with that. She was judged mentally unfit for a voyage. We had no choice. The doctor said otherwise we would have to tie her to her bed. Mix it with tea, he said, every cup of tea, so soon she would not notice the bitter taste."

It was Duncan's turn to gaze into his mug, so as not to reveal the flash of discovery in his eyes. Before he died, Evering had been making tea for Sarah and had smashed the dosing vial. Before he died, Duncan realized, Evering had been reviving her. They must have sat in the night, speaking secretly, just as Adam and Evering had done. He had been wrong to think the disasters on the ship had started with the opening of Woolford's trunk. There had been another event, perhaps just as important. Sarah Ramsey had awakened.

Duncan fixed the officer with a sober gaze. "You lied to Adam Munroe about the destination of the Company, about it going to a Ramsey plantation in the south. What else?"

"That," Woolford said with a sigh, "was the only lie that was necessary. You would think it a small thing."

"But you knew it wasn't. Not for him. Not for you. For his sake, you owe me the truth. I had thought the key to Evering's death lay in the connection between Adam and the professor. But perhaps that is not the connection that was important. How did Adam Munroe know Sarah?"

"They lived in worlds apart."

"You mean one in chains, one chained by opium."

"I mean no one would ever expect such two to be acquainted. The Pennsylvania dirt farmer and the silk-gowned heiress."

The truth, in the hands of a man like Woolford, was not necessarily a helpful thing. "I take it they met in the New World. Why were they both on the *Anna Rose*?" But Duncan needed no answer, not after considering what he had learned about Adam. Adam had been on board because of Sarah Ramsey, had been so desperate to sail on the prison ship with Sarah that he had threatened to assault soldiers, and had ultimately bought his passage with news about Duncan.

The scars on Woolford's neck blanched again as he clenched his jaw. "No one," he said slowly, "expected Sarah to stir from her cabin."

"No one," Duncan shot back, "expected Evering to become a channel between them."

"No one expected the *Anna Rose* to become a death ship," Woolford countered. Sarah abruptly rose, pulling Jonathan onto the dance floor, swinging his arm in time to the unseen fiddle. "She only survived because of you," he added after a moment. "That water was certain death. In England people would say it puts her forever in your debt."

"And here?"

The ranger shrugged. "I know Indians who would say it makes you forever responsible for her. That because you interfered with the spirits' plans for her, there is no spirit to watch over her now."

"Were they lovers?"

"Of course not. She is . . . ." Woolford struggled for words, then gave up. "Adam was married."

"Impossible. He would have told me." Duncan's mind swirled. Pursuing Adam, even in death, was like chasing a ship in a changing wind.

"In my experience, McCallum, the secrets of the heart are always the most difficult to put into words. I met his bride. A wild but gentle beauty. You would never find two who adored each other more."

"What happened to her?"

"They were driven apart," Woolford said in a tight voice.

"If it was not passion that drove Sarah to Adam in Argyll, then what? Her family is here."

The ranger offered only a small, ironic frown, as if to say Duncan had answered his own question.

"Did you know Evering wrote about her in his journal?"

Woolford's brow knitted. "What journal? Where is it?" he demanded.

"At the house in New York," Duncan said. "Why would he write about Stony Run? What happened at Stony Run? How could he know?"

Woolford seemed to shudder. He turned to gaze out the darkened window. "It's a place in the forest nearly a hundred miles north of Edentown. There was a council of Iroquois tribes led by a great priest, a powerful shaman. Something happened when the shaman met the other chiefs. Many died. At headquarters they listed it as a battle. But I believe there were no enemy there." Woolford grew very still. When he spoke again it was in a near-whisper. "Sergeant Fitch and I arrived a few hours later. It was no battle. It was a series of murders, a massacre first of friendly Indians, then of my rangers when they followed the killers." Woolford turned away to stare at the crackling fire.

"God's breath!" Duncan gasped as realization flooded over him. "You're trying to find the murderers."

The ranger kept his gaze on the flames. "They were good men. Each one like a brother to me." He could not conceal the pain in his eyes when he looked up at Duncan. "Evering couldn't have known about Stony Run," he said. "It was not something the army wished to publicize."

"He knew," Duncan said, "because he spoke with Adam."

The ranger lowered his head into his hands a moment. "Guilt can often loosen a man's tongue. Sad cases, Munroe and Evering. If it is possible to die of confusion, then perhaps they died of the same cause." Woolford poured himself another applejack and drained it in one gulp.

"And where does King Hendrick fit into the tragedy you are scripting?" Duncan asked. "Evering connected him to Stony Run."

"An old Mohawk chief. Teyonhehkwen was his tribal name. Visited England nearly fifty years ago, when they labeled him a king to ease his introductions in court. One of our strongest allies. Died fighting the French in 'fifty-five at Lake George. Over eighty years old. He stood up with bullets flying around him, shouted out, 'Who wants to live forever,' and charged a line of French infantry with a war club."

"You speak of him as of a friend."

"I am proud to name him so. If he had been a soldier, he'd have been in the Black Watch. If he had been a king of old, he would have been a pillar of chivalry."

"Evering wrote of him, yet he's been dead these four years."

"He had a band of zealous warriors, mostly related to him by blood, who still fight in his name. Good men, brave men, who perform rituals to keep pure, like knights of old. Half were killed at Stony Run without their weapons at hand. Hendrick was tossing in his grave that day."

The pieces of this puzzle were not fitting together, but at least they were coming into better focus. Duncan fell into a deep silence, working over each fragment again in his mind. He found himself looking out the window into the darkness. He had not forgotten Adam's warning about the army. His resentment of Woolford, built over weeks at sea, lingered like a bitter taste in his throat. He poured himself another drink. "They took Lister for the murder," he said. "They beat him within an inch of his life."

The ranger offered a grim nod. "Arnold made sure I knew. For now your friend is safer than any man in the Company, I daresay. The guards know they must preserve him," Woolford declared in a sober voice. "He is to be the star of Ramsey's first pageant of justice."

The words tore at Duncan's heart. Somewhere ahead, along a frontier road, Lister lay beaten and bound in the night, probably convinced that Duncan had abandoned him.

Eventually he became aware that they were both watching Sarah. She had begun a waltz with her little brother, whose face shone bright as a candle.

"Do you have intentions with respect to Miss Ramsey?" Duncan asked.

The question made his companion wince again and break his gaze from Sarah. "In my life I have known a handful of women who had the power to disturb my sleep. I will admit to you she is one of them. But she is different. It is not the beauty of Sarah Ramsey that disturbs my rest, it is the enigma."

They watched in silence for several minutes. Woolford stepped behind the bar a moment, found a writing lead and a scrap of paper and quickly scrawled something, then leaned on the bar and gazed into the dining room again. Several dancers began staring at Sarah, and pointed at her. They began to separate, leaving a wide space around her as if she held some kind of contagion. She kept dancing, her smile more strained. It would be impossible for her not to sense that the others were shunning her.

Woolford cursed under his breath, tossed the paper across the bar, and stepped into the dining chamber, sweeping little Virginia into his arms and taking to the dance floor at Sarah's side. Duncan sat listening to the crackle of the logs in the huge stone fireplace, watching uneasily as Sergeant Fitch appeared outside the window and sat on the porch, studying the darkness. His gaze drifted toward the paper left by Woolford. The ranger had heard his request for Shakespeare after all. His quote for the New World was from Hamlet. *A man may fish with the worm that hath eat of a king,* Woolford had written, *and eat of the fish that fed of that worm.*

The strains of the fiddle cut through the voices in the dining chamber, and several diners began clapping the beat of a new, livelier tune as tables were pushed back with Woolford's encouragement and others joined in the dancing. Duncan stepped to the open door and stared out over the broad Hudson, lit by a quarter moon. The river was a divider of sorts, between civilization and the beginnings of something that was the opposite. Strangely, he remembered the scene set in the corner of Lord Ramsey's portrait, the simple cabin with the dying man cradled by a woman. In his mind, the scene had become the central feature of the painting, as if the aristocrat were there just to give it context.

His apprehension began to fade as the fire crackling behind him and the moonlit water glistening outside transported him to the evenings of his youth. Drifting into a fatigued reverie, he could almost hear the old songs that his uncles would play on fiddle and pipes.

No. The sound was real. He turned toward the dining room. The clapping had stopped as a sad, stirring song played, then the fiddler sang without accompaniment. In disbelief Duncan stepped to the entrance of the dining chamber. *Mo Ghile Mear,* the song was called. Our Hero. Its words might have applied to the brave defeated heroes of any people. But anyone from the Highlands knew it was not a song about any hero, for it had been written to honor Bonnie Prince Charlie, the leader of Duncan's father and the other Scottish rebels who had so valiantly stood at Culloden. As Duncan strode into the chamber, the red-haired fiddler began the next verse in the original Gaelic. After a moment, Duncan joined him in the Highland tongue as the two stared at each other with fire in their eyes. Duncan found his heart hammering. In Scotland they could have been arrested for such a display.

The others in the room stared, some grinning, some with their eyes misting, until suddenly there were heavy footsteps behind him, and Duncan turned to see Woolford standing at his shoulder, fixing him with a smoldering gaze. The musician immediately raised the fiddle to his shoulder and began to play an energetic reel, walking among the tables, gesturing more dancers onto the floor.

"You have no idea of the dangers you touch upon, McCallum," Woolford warned. "I don't know where you're bound in the end, but you'll not get there by walking backward."

"It's just a simple song."

"Don't take me for a fool. And don't be so reckless with your own life. Or do you need ask which of the great lords you wish to serve, Ramsey or Calder?"

"I don't understand."

Woolford eyes narrowed. "You think for a second that Calder would have released you if it did not serve him?"

"I owe nothing to the army."

The officer shot him an impatient glare and pushed him back into the dark, unoccupied barroom. "The Romans wrote about how the legions would trap wolves that were preying on their camps," he declared when they reached the shadows. "They would tie a goat out in the forest and lie in wait."

Duncan knitted his brow in confusion.

"Calder can't take a chance that Pike is wrong in believing Jamie and his Scots are aiding the French in a new campaign. He has to snatch Jamie or risk another season of defeats. And you, McCallum, are his goat."

The words fell heavier than the chains the army had put on Duncan. It seemed the fitting conclusion to his first day in America.

The New World was a sham after all. The oppressors and aristocrats of the Old World had found their way across the Atlantic.

"Of course," Woolford added in a harsh voice, with an inclination of his head toward the Scottish bard, "if the wolves became wise to the ways of the Romans, they would just kill the goat before it could be used against them."

Duncan turned away, about to flee outside, more desperate than ever to find the old ferryman Jacob, whose message for the Ramsey tutor would finally put sense around the chaos of the day. But suddenly Sergeant Fitch was in front of them, leaning toward Woolford. The sergeant had his hand on his blade and was watching the night through the open door as he spoke to his captain.

"Our Indian, sir," Fitch announced in a low, urgent voice. "Dead in the summer kitchen."

Chapter Six

WOOLFORD DARTED OUT THE FRONT door. Duncan ran into the dining chamber, frantically looking for the children among the small crowd of dancers. He found Crispin in a chair in the corner, each of the small children on a knee, each sleeping on a broad shoulder. Sarah was nowhere to be seen. Crispin himself was leaning against the wall, his eyelids heavy until Duncan conveyed Fitch's news.

The butler shot up, clutching the children to his shoulders. "She's gone!" he gasped. "Went into the kitchen several minutes ago."

Duncan lifted Jonathan into his own arms and followed Crispin through the throng into the adjoining kitchen. The chamber was empty except for a sturdy girl swabbing dishes in a wooden tub. Fitch and Woolford had not chosen to spread the alarm, Duncan realized, though the proprietor and his wife had also vanished.

They searched the other downstairs chambers of the inn to no avail, then carried the children to the upstairs bedroom where their traveling trunks awaited. The two men laid the children side by side under a coverlet. "One of us must stay," Duncan observed, looking out the window at the moonlit grounds. Someone moved along the edge of the forest with a torch.

Crispin said nothing but lifted a ladder-back chair from the peg where it hung on the wall, set it sideways by the window, where he could survey both the barnyard and the door, and then sat.

Moments later Duncan stood at the front door, working to contain the unnatural fear that had seized him. The savages were indeed outside, and Fitch had found one dead. He lifted a splint of wood from the stack by the door, raising it like a weapon, then stepped into the shadows, studying the farm buildings in the moonlight. He selected a squat structure with a broad chimney, thirty feet from the rear door of the inn, connected to it by worn stone flags. It seemed empty as he approached; then he saw that its walls held no windows. When he opened the iron latch there was shuffling inside, and as he stepped into the candle-lit chamber he found Woolford standing against the wall, hand on the hilt of his knife.

The ranger captain gave a silent grimace but did not interfere as Duncan approached the heavy plank table in front of the huge, cold fireplace. The proprietor stood on the opposite side of the table, one arm around his wife, who cried on his shoulder. A younger woman sat on a stool, a blanket draped over her head, which was bowed so low the shadow of the blanket hid her face.

He had expected a certain satisfaction at seeing one of the savages laid out for burial, had painted in his mind's eye one of the fearful creatures he had seen at the army headquarters humbled by death. But he found no satisfaction, no sense of retribution, only a deepening confusion.

The wrinkles on the man's countenance and the spots on his hands told Duncan that he had been of considerable age, though intertwined in his black shoulder-length locks were but a few strands of grey. He was dressed in the simple homespun clothes of a working man, his trousers worn and frequently patched, though torn and muddy at the knees. A small leather pouch hung from his neck, a larger one from his belt. The man still had a hint of color in his face, Duncan saw. He had been dead less than an hour.

As Woolford replaced a guttering candle on the mantel, Duncan noticed a discoloration on the dead man's left cheek. Not a bruise, he saw on closer inspection, but a tattoo. An image of a spotted fish had been intricately inked into the skin. The tattoo gave a strange power to the man's still countenance, and Duncan stared at it as he rounded the table, stared at it until out of the corner of his eye he saw the ravaged flesh on the opposite side of the man's head. A deep, ragged gash ran from his temple along the side of his skull, ending behind his ear. His scalp hung loose.

Duncan found his medical training asserting itself. "This wound didn't kill him, at least not right away," he said after a hasty examination. "It was made four or five hours ago. He was beaten on the head and ribs. His eyes are dilated. A bad concussion to the brain." On the man's right side, his shirt clung to the skin, and its long, wet stain ran down the side of his trousers. Duncan lifted the tail of the shirt and studied the discolored flesh below the man's ribs—a treacherous stab wound, though it showed no signs of being lethal in itself. "He could have lived had he but stayed still."

"He made it back, crawling," the innkeeper explained. "We found him lying on a ledge out back, gazing at the stars, a stone's throw from the barn. He always slept in the barn when the ferry stayed overnight."

Duncan's tongue seemed to grow impossibly heavy as he saw the forlorn way the Dutchman and his wife looked at the man, and glanced back at the fish on the cheek. He started, "He's not . . . he can't be . . ." and tried no more. There was no need to ask the question that rang like an alarm in his mind. The man was Jacob the Fish. The one man in all the world who could explain the mysteries surrounding the Company was an Indian, and that Indian was dead. Not the one man, he chided himself, the next man. First there had been Adam, then Evering. At each step along his path, the man who could best explain the violent mystery surrounding the Ramsey Company had been killed.

The woman in the blanket looked up, tears streaming down her face. It was Sarah.

"You said he was going into the mountains." A strange remorse entered Woolford's voice as he spoke to the Dutchman. "You said he was safe." Duncan glanced at the ranger in confusion. Woolford was famous for killing Indians; his job was to destroy Indians. But there had been at least one, he recalled, who had been a friend of Woolford, whose name had sounded like a king of Europe.

"He was. I told him never to come back, at risk of his life," the innkeeper replied grimly. "But he had no family except us these past few years, the ferryman's clan and ourselves. He was here before any of us came. About the last of his tribe. He helped my father build the house here more than sixty years ago. He was always here, as long as anyone can remember. He belonged to the land here, and to the river. He was part of the land. The first name of the river, the Indian name, came from his tribe."

"Then my father came through." Sarah's voice was steady, and she spoke to the dead man's face. "When I was a little girl, every time we came across, he would carry me on his shoulders. He would catch fish for us, lure them into his hands to show us their beautiful colors." She reached out and squeezed the dead man's hand. "I thought he was a wizard of some kind, but my father said he was just a filthy red Indian and told me to keep away. He secretly made a doll for me out of cornhusks."

"Why now?" Duncan heard himself say. "Why did he come back when he was safe in the mountains?" He understood nothing of what he saw, certainly not the respectful way Sarah treated the dead Indian. This was not a savage like those he had encountered at the army offices, or like the bloodthirsty creatures Crispin spoke of. This was just an old man with a sad, wise face. The last of his tribe. Duncan had known other wise old men who wandered the Highlands, the last of their tribes.

Woolford lifted the pouch at the dead man's belt, loosened the thong that bound it, and looked inside. "Empty," he announced, then turned it upside down, over his palm. A small, solitary purple bead fell out. As he gazed at it the officer's face tightened. After a long moment he sighed, then futilely searched the trousers pockets. When he reached the small pouch at Old Jacob's neck, bound with a strip of white fur, Woolford did not open it, only arranged it neatly over the dead man's heart.

"I sent militiamen into the forest," the innkeeper reported.

"They will find nothing," Woolford said.

"How could he have received that terrible gash?" Duncan asked. "It is no bullet wound. It is like that given by a sword."

"The work of the war," Woolford said.

"But what—" Duncan struggled to understand. Who were the militia looking for? Indians were the enemy, but this one was an honored friend. Then he reminded himself again that Indians fought on both sides of the war, and raiding parties had been reported. "What Indians use swords?"

"Someone tried to lift his hair," the innkeeper muttered.

Duncan looked around the room in confusion.

"Someone," Woolford explained in a barely tolerant tone, "expressed an interest in his scalp. He fought back."

Duncan suddenly felt very cold. "Surely you are mistaken," he whispered.

"*Mein Goot.*" The innkeeper's German wife cast him a peeved glance. "How long have you been in the colonies, *junge?*" she asked in a harsh tone.

Duncan and Sarah exchanged a quick glance. "Long enough to know it's Europeans who get scalped," he replied.

"You know nothing," the woman declared, and began washing the dried blood from the old Indian's face.

"He died a warrior's death," Woolford said, then moved to help the innkeeper straighten a blanket over the corpse.

Duncan placed a hand on Woolford's arm, stopping him. "I must understand better what happened." He pushed back the blanket and lifted the tail of Old Jacob's shirt.

"No!" the ranger protested, grabbing his hand. "Some respect—"

"The last time Ramseys came through, he was arrested. This time," Duncan said in a perplexed tone, "he died." Woolford slowly relaxed his grip. "There were two things different the day he crossed

the river with Lord Ramsey," he continued, opening the buttons.
"An extra traveler, a trapper, and an accidental dunking." Duncan
quickly explained what the ferryman had told him. Woolford
stepped back as Sarah silently helped Duncan unbutton the dead
man's shirt, exposing the old Indian's chest. It bore another tattoo,
unlike any Duncan had ever seen—a large, expertly rendered image
of a spreading tree over his heart, encircled by small animals. A wolf
at the bottom, in the most prominent position. A squirrel. A hare.
Something that looked like a hedgehog, and others Duncan did not
recognize.

No one made a sound, except for Woolford, who gave a deep sigh
and settled onto a stool.

"What does it signify?" Duncan asked.

"The wolf is a clan mark," Woolford said. "I told you about King
Hendrick. The wolf was his mark, the mark of his clan, given when
a youth becomes a warrior. Hendrick and Jacob had the same
Mohawk grandmother, and when his parents were killed, Jacob
spent most of his boyhood with Hendrick's people. When Hendrick
went to Europe, Jacob decided to honor the dying tribe of his parents and took up their ways, the Mahican ways."

Duncan pointed to the tree on the dead man's chest. "The rest
of it?"

"Among Hendrick's people the sign of the tree is very rare. Perhaps five men alive today bear such an image over their heart. A
powerful emblem. If it was used in an organized church, it might be
the mark of a cardinal, one of great spiritual power. The animals
would have been earned later, one at a time, badges of honor."

"My father would never recognize such things," Sarah said in a
hollow, puzzled voice.

The Dutchman gave the answer, pronouncing the name like a
curse. "Hawkins."

The air went dead for a moment.

Woolford grimly buttoned up the shirt. When he had finished,
he placed one of the Indian's hands under the little neck pouch, the

second hand on top. He produced a leather strap from his pocket and tied the hands tightly together. When he finished, he looked up at Duncan. "You say he was attacked four or five hours ago?" When Duncan nodded, the ranger turned to the innkeeper. "When did the Company leave here?"

"Six, maybe seven hours ago."

The door opened and two of the innkeeper's boys appeared, each carrying an armful of cedar boughs, which their parents began arranging around the body. Sarah, scrubbing the tears from her cheeks, stepped outside, toward the house. A moment later Fitch appeared at the door, and Woolford joined him, moving silently into the night. The boys left, backing away from the corpse, then one returned moments later carrying a large Bible closed with leather latches. Their mother arranged a stool at the head of the table, with two candles at her side, and began softly reading in German. Duncan also retreated, but not outside, only to a corner, into the dark behind the door, where he leaned against the cold stone wall. He was bone tired but strangely transfixed by the scene. The reason the old Mahican had come to the inn was so important, it had been worth dying for. Another thought, uninvited, overtook him as he stared at the dead man. Jacob must have been in his eighties, been born in the seventh decade of the prior century. Which made him roughly the same age as his grandfather. His grandfather, too, had once called a fish and ridden on its back.

Duncan stared at the body in weary confusion. It was some time later when he realized he was stroking the stone bear in his pocket.

He was about to leave when someone entered and stepped to the side of the dead Indian. Duncan pushed himself back against the wall. Woolford had returned. As Duncan watched, the ranger handed the woman something, then pulled from his jacket a large feather, streaked in two places with vermilion, and set it under Old Jacob's hands, alongside the little leather bundle.

The woman took the object Woolford had given her, held it over a candle flame for a moment, then dropped it into a bowl.

"I've seen that feather before," Duncan declared as he stepped out of the shadows.

Woolford frowned at him and glanced at the woman, who had taken up her German prayers again.

"You said you discarded everything from the compass room." A wisp of smoke drifted out of the bowl. It was tobacco. Woolford had given the woman some of his precious Virginia leaf to burn.

"Everything but this," the officer said. "It didn't belong in the sea."

"What does it signify?"

"The sign of a warrior, someone who has drawn blood from an enemy," the ranger said in a near-whisper, his eyes on the dead man. He reached into the pouch at his belt and extracted a needle and thread, then bent over the old man's head, pierced the flap of loose skin with his needle, and began sewing the scalp back in place. "People don't understand the war. And it's well they don't. They think it will be won in palaces in Europe. They're wrong. It will be won and lost at Indian campfires in New York and Pennsylvania. With so many of our troops needed in Europe, a handful of chiefs have our fate in their hands. And if everyone knew how precarious is the balance, the harbors would be mobbed with people fleeing for Europe. Make those chiefs upset with us, and the war is lost. The continent is lost."

Duncan stepped to the officer's side and extended his hand.

Woolford hesitated, then handed Duncan the needle. "I forgot. You are a doctor to the dead."

"Sarah mourned for this man like an old friend," Duncan ventured. Another tattoo became evident as Duncan reconnected the skin, a three-quarters circle, centered on the ear, with slim red tapering lines radiating outward.

Woolford seemed to consider the words a long time. "You heard her. He had shown her kindness years ago."

An enigma, Woolford had called her half an hour earlier. Not only was Sarah an enigma, but so, too, was every conversation about her. "She is like a child," Duncan said. "Why are so many terrified of her? What has she done to them?"

A long moment passed before Duncan realized the prayers had stopped.

"That which we cannot understand, we try to take on faith," the German woman whispered. "But where our faith is not wide enough, we turn to fear."

Duncan glanced at Woolford, who was nodding, his jaw clamped shut. It was all the answer he would receive. He finished sewing up the scalp, reconnecting the pieces of the tattoo over the ear. "A sun," he concluded.

"Mark of the dawn catchers," Woolford explained. "An old rite, almost forgotten. You have to run from one dawn to the next, pausing only at certain sacred places."

"The badge of a pilgrim," Duncan suggested, though he still could not connect the spiritual notions Woolford described with the savages he had seen earlier that day, or the terrifying tales of the heathens told elsewhere.

Woolford settled onto one of the chairs by the body, turning away from Duncan as the woman took up her prayers again. Duncan watched a few minutes in silence, then stepped outside with one of the candles. He paced slowly around the barn, peering into dark places between the posts and beams, and found a lean-to built against the barn and filled with split firewood, then a second matching structure with a plank door on leather hinges. Inside he found a space perhaps twice the size of his cell on the ship, lined with slabs of bark and animal skins, a pallet of sackcloth and moss at one end. He knelt, extending the candle, and quickly found several drops of fresh blood on the earthen floor. Jacob had made it back to his home after all.

The sparse chamber offered few clues about its inhabitant except for some small mottled feathers stuck into the bark, a long peg on which hung several bird skulls, and a worn pair of leather slippers hanging from one of the beams. As Duncan stretched the candle toward the roof, a silent figure stepped behind him.

Duncan pointed to the blood on the floor. "Why would he come in here and not stay on his pallet, why go back outside?" he asked Woolford.

The ranger knelt and examined the crimson drops before answering. "So he would die under the open sky."

"Why the skulls?"

"Alive or dead, the birds of the forest are considered by the tribes to be messengers."

"Messengers?"

"To the gods. They whisper in the gods' ears, report back what they see."

What, Duncan asked himself, would the skulls at the bloody compass have reported? He knelt by the pallet and turned over a flat slab of bark lying beside it. Underneath, etched in the dirt, were two curving lines, parallel except where they connected at top and bottom. He had seen it before, drawn on the mast by Adam before he died. Duncan pried up the slab of bark on the wall at the head of the pallet, revealing perhaps forty more sets of curving lines drawn on the side of the barn with a charred stick. It was as if Jacob drew the symbols before he slept at night.

"The messengers can carry words beyond. But the snake," Woolford explained in a near-whisper, "is especially sacred, the bringer of dreams, the guide to the other world." He cast a self-conscious glance toward Duncan. "I mean it is what they believe. The snake lies on the edge of this world and the next. You visit the other world, where the spirits live, the real world, through dreams. Dreams are sober business to the Indians. They will entirely change their lives based on one dream. In many tribes those who lead in battle may achieve great power. But the greatest power of all is reserved for those who can explain dreams."

"His shoes," Duncan said, pointing to where the line of blood led, toward the hanging slippers.

"Moccasins," Woolford said, then stepped to the beam, where the red, still-moist trail led.

"Why would he come inside to change his moccasins?" Duncan asked. He handed the candle to Woolford, then lifted them from the peg, probing them with his fingers. "Not to change them," he corrected himself. "To leave something in them." Duncan extracted two small pieces of paper. "Could he read?"

"Passably well, though he never took to writing. For each one of us who trouble to speak their tongue, ten of the Iroquois speak a European language." Woolford extended the candle toward the paper on Duncan's palm, and uttered a small gasp as the words came into focus. *Anna Rose,* said the first line. *First acorns, bloom of the asters,* said the next. Duncan recalled the green acorns in the barnyard, and the flowers along the front of the house, which would have begun opening not many days earlier. It was a way of conveying a date to one who used only a natural calendar, a way to convey a message about the arrival of their ship.

The second paper held an effort at only one word, written in a crude hand. *Tshqa.* The word and the stick-figure animal beside it—a bear, Duncan guessed—were surrounded on all sides by stick men bearing axes and bows. At the very bottom were two rows of what appeared to be ornamentations—lines of ovals, some filled in, some hollow.

Woolford seemed to have stopped breathing. The sudden desolation on his face seemed to make him a smaller, older man.

"What is it?" Duncan asked.

Woolford offered no reply, only looked at the empty pallet, as if trying to see the man who had slept and dreamt there.

"He had no ink," Duncan observed.

"What are you saying?"

Duncan bent to retrieve a small feather from the pallet and held it close to the candle, showing the hue at the end of its shaft, then pushed the candle closer to the paper. "He drew this in his own blood."

Woolford closed his eyes a moment, then spoke the words Duncan struggled to avoid. "This is why he died," the ranger said, "to bring this message."

Duncan stared at the earthen floor. Another man had died on the path of the Ramsey tutor. "Adam spoke of Tashgua," he said after a long moment.

"Impossible," the ranger rejoined. "Why would he speak to you of such things?"

"Not to me. To Evering, who wrote the name in his journal. At General Calder's office, the army's chart of Stony Run bears the same name."

Woolford paced along the wall of the lean-to. "Tashgua is an aged priest," he said in a reluctant tone. "A shaman. One of the fifty chiefs who govern the Iroquois nation, though unlike any of the others. They say he is from an unbroken line of shamans dating back centuries. They say he speaks languages no man alive understands. They say he is the one who connects them to the way things used to be, before the Europeans came, to the old spirits who always protected the tribes. A sage. A sorcerer. A prophet. Take your pick. Most hated by some in the tribes, most beloved by others. A small band of warriors protect him, including what's left of Hendrick's men. They call him guardian of the gods. Tashgua complains that his people are moving away from their ancient roots, that being a tool for either side in a European war will spell destruction for his people. But most in his tribe are more interested in muskets and brass kettles." The ranger stared intensely at Duncan now, as if seeing something new in him.

"Tashgua was there, wasn't he?" Duncan ventured. "At Stony Run. He was the reason for the massacre."

Woolford stepped to the door, pausing to look back at Duncan. "In England, pretending to know more than you do is a national pastime. Here it can get you killed."

"How many have to die," Duncan retorted, "before you tell me why the Ramsey Company is in such danger?"

"The Ramsey Company?" Woolford asked in a bitter tone. "Look to yourself, McCallum."

"I don't understand?"

"You said Jacob was attacked four or five hours ago. Fitch found his trail nearby, marked by drops of blood."

"I still don't—"

"It was someone in the Company, someone you told about Old Jacob."

"No!" Duncan protested, then with a terrible stab of guilt understood Woolford's words. The Ramsey tutor was meant to meet the Mahican, who would explain everything. Duncan had spoken of the fishspeaker when in the bilges with McGregor and his men, which would have been as good as telling the entire Company. Jacob had come back from his safe exile to meet the Ramsey tutor, and he had died for it.

"Damned your eyes, McCallum, I will know what Evering told you!" Woolford growled, suddenly full of wrath.

"Can't you see, Captain?" Duncan said in a tormented voice. "Evering was killed to prevent him from passing his secrets on." Duncan knelt by the pallet as though in prayer, as if to beg the old Indian for forgiveness. Now Jacob had died for the same reason.

When he looked up, Woolford was gone.

He sat very still, overcome with grief for a moment, as he began to accept the truth. Jacob may have known he was on a path where death lurked, but it had been Duncan who had sealed his fate. He lifted the stone bear from his pocket, comparing it to the animal in the drawing Jacob had left. As he bent toward the light, the bear dropped from his palm, rolling on the dirt floor to settle beside another large piece of bark leaning against the wall. *Let the old one take you where she needs to go.* With a cautious, tentative finger he lifted it, then jerked backward with a twitch of fear. Drawn on the smooth back of the bark were scores of snakes, at least a hundred. Jacob may have belonged to the adjoining land. But he had also belonged to the world of the spirits.

Duncan studied the message in blood again before stuffing the two papers into his pocket, desperate to understand. Was this truly the message Jacob had died for, the message Evering had expected? The lines of ovals were not decorative, he decided, but part of the message. The first of the two rows had six short lines preceding its row of six ovals—two filled in, then one hollow, then two filled in and one hollow again. The second row had four short lines, then eight ovals—two solid, two hollow, then the pattern repeated. His gaze drifted back to the bear drawing, a man and a bear surrounded by men who seemed to want them dead. It could have been an image of Duncan and his stone.

Angry shouts from the barnyard woke Duncan at dawn. He leaned out the open window to see Captain Woolford berating the proprietor as Fitch led a saddled horse out of the barn. Duncan quickly dressed and found Crispin standing on the porch, gazing forlornly toward the river. The ferry was approaching, a single horse and rider its only tenants.

"She's gone," Crispin announced in a dismal tone.

Duncan's heart leapt into his throat. "Sarah?"

"The innkeeper found her saddling one of the coach horses before dawn." Woolford explained as Duncan reached him. "She promised him Crispin would pay him double the value of the saddle, then galloped down the road."

"Alone?" Duncan gasped, and gazed toward the shadowed trail that led west.

Woolford checked the saddle girth of his horse, then conferred briefly with Fitch, gesturing toward the ferry. Fitch bolted inside, returning with a scrap of paper on which Woolford hastily scrawled a note, handing the paper to Crispin as he swung onto the horse. "You must take the children to their father," he said. "The sergeant will stay with you to Edentown."

"Where is she bound?" Duncan asked no one in particular as Woolford took his rifle from Fitch, pressed his heels to the flanks of his mount, and galloped down the narrow road. "Why would she go alone?"

"The body is gone," the innkeeper announced, as if in answer.

"The girls in the kitchen," his wife declared, "told her of the Indians in the harbor. She must be wild with fear."

"The ferry," Fitch muttered.

Crispin made a rumbling sound in his throat. "Let us take a hearty breakfast," he said with a glance toward the river. "It shall be an arduous hour ahead."

Duncan studied the ferry again and finally recognized the tall, lean figure in black.

Reverend Arnold was dark and brooding as he strode into the tavern. He surveyed the dining chamber in silence, then seemed to relax as he saw the trunks of Sarah and her siblings stacked by the door, where Crispin had conspicuously left them. He called for the proprietor to have the dirt brushed from his coat, then joined the two men at their table.

"Servants of the Ramsey house may not," Arnold declared in a simmering tone, "simply decide to load the family into wagons and relocate. You had no permission to leave New York."

Crispin assumed a meek, apologetic expression. "Miss Ramsey explained that she had turned eighteen and that made her old enough to decide family business in the absence of her father," he explained in a flat voice, as if reading a script. "She said she had urgent messages for her father, and instructed me to take her and the children. She said you had meetings with the army that could not be disturbed." He glanced at Duncan. "She said she would not be so disrespectful to you and her father as to leave their new tutor behind."

The announcement seemed to confuse Arnold. "This shall be discussed with Lord Ramsey," he said after a moment's reflection, though his voice held more resentment than anger now. The vicar sighed, glanced back at the trunks, and pulled out a chair as the innkeeper's wife set a third cup and saucer on the table. Crispin started to rise but was motioned back into his chair by a weary wave of Arnold's hand. The vicar reached for the pot of tea and drank deeply before turning to Duncan. "I protested most vigorously your treatment by Major Pike. They had no right to restrain a member of our household."

Duncan offered the grateful nod he knew Arnold expected, then ate quickly and hurried out the rear door to the summer kitchen. The chamber was indeed empty, with no sign left of the dead man but a few cones from the cedar boughs and the stubs of the candles used in the vigil. He found the proprietor in the barnyard, speaking with Sergeant Fitch, who was wiping down Reverend Arnold's horse. "Jacob's body," Duncan said, "you must have seen what happened to it."

"I collapsed onto my pallet at midnight," the Dutchman replied. "Perhaps Fitch saw. He and the captain never slept in their beds."

Arnold appeared on the porch, calling the innkeeper, who muttered under his breath and trotted to the clergyman as Duncan stepped deeper into the shadows. A moment after Arnold followed the innkeeper into the building, his voice was raised in shrill outrage. The vicar's anger upon discovering that Sarah was missing built like a tempest. Scullery girls spilled out of the rear door, the proprietor's wife out the front. Crispin finally emerged onto the porch, Arnold at his side, gesturing toward the barn. As the vicar's commands for his horse to be saddled echoed into the yard, Fitch appeared, calmly explaining that the mare was now needed to pull the coach since Sarah had taken one of the team.

"Which of the Ramsey vehicles shall we leave behind?" the sergeant asked when Arnold protested. "The grand coach or the wagon with the family belongings?" Arnold answered with a scowl, then accepted from Fitch the note written by Woolford, which the vicar read, frowning, and stuffed into his pocket.

It was but the work of a few minutes for Duncan to steal away as the others readied the teams, entering through the empty kitchen into the silent barroom. On a shelf under the bar he quickly found the journal used by the innkeeper and scanned the column of names and payments made in the last ten days. Three nights earlier, before the *Anna Rose* had docked, Socrates Moon had stayed at the inn. The mysterious Greek who had accompanied Sarah to England— Adam's secret correspondent—had crossed their path. Duncan studied the ornate handwriting, the odd way the double *O*'s in the signature overlapped, then with a shiver of excitement compared them to the writing on the first message from Jacob's moccasin. The double *O*'s were identical. Socrates Moon had left the note for the old Mahican.

A horse neighed outside. Duncan quickly scanned the rest of the ledger. Two nights before, a day after Moon, another man had stayed at the inn, as if he had been following Moon—a man Duncan knew had next gone on to the Ramsey house in New York town, to collect a dispatch case from Arnold. He had signed one scribbled name, without a Christian prefix. Hawkins.

It was nearly noon of the fifth day of travel when they reached the first of the neat, cleared fields that marked Edentown, the Ramsey estate. Duncan had passed much of the time walking with the sergeant and Crispin, learning about the rugged geography they traversed and about the New World generally. They named for him unfamiliar trees like sugar maple, sassafras, hackberry, butternut, tulip poplar, and hickory, and sketched crude maps of the region with sticks in the earth as they sat at campfires. Their little caravan passed through small crossroads villages, where mills were often being constructed, past old houses of stone and newer ones of logs, where children in ragtag clothes peered shyly at the grand coach as it rolled by. Crispin pointed out birds that were unknown to Duncan and spoke of the native animals, like the porcupine whose elastic quills covered the medallion the butler had seen hanging from Duncan's neck.

When out of earshot of the children, Fitch spoke of the native peoples and taught Duncan the meaning of Indian words like tomahawk, canoe, and succotash, describing how, as with nations in Europe, tribes rose and fell from dominance in their regions, how the Mahican, then the Lenni Lenape—called the Delaware by Europeans—had once been the powerful masters of the eastern lands, and in time were overshadowed by the Iroquois. The Iroquois themselves, whom Fitch often referred to as the Six, for the six nations that comprised them, were held together in a confederation that was doomed to failure, the sergeant insisted, since they foolishly acted like ancient Greeks, giving a vote to every warrior, even allowing women to choose their chieftains.

"You make it sound as though they have a civilization," Duncan observed.

The grizzled ranger gave an amused grunt. "Last time I wasted time trying to figure who was civilized in this world and who weren't, I had only fuzz on my cheeks," Fitch said, and spat a dollop of tobacco juice between his feet.

On the fourth day, as they had lunched at the edge of a high, open ledge, Duncan had stood alone, surveying the blue-hazed ridges that rolled toward the west. "She's there by now," a voice had suddenly observed. Fitch knelt at his side, looking at the ranges.

"You mean she's safe?"

"I mean she's at her father's town." The sergeant extracted a musket flint from his pouch and began freshening it with a stone, a habit that had begun to worry Duncan, for it meant Fitch wanted to be ready to use his weapon at any moment. Just as he had learned about the plants and animals of the new land, so, too, had Duncan learned more about the odd ways people spoke about Sarah. More than once when they had stopped at settlements and farms, he had heard the inhabitants ask Jonathan or Virginia if their older sister traveled with them and had seen the relief in their faces when the children replied. The prior night, at a huge trestle table populated with a family of twelve, a girl had completed Arnold's blessing by adding, "and keep their witch from our door." Jonathan had responded by rising and taking his meal outdoors, then sleeping in the coach.

"Where did you go that night at the inn?" Duncan asked the soldier, who was showing signs of a grudging friendship after Duncan repeatedly rescued him from the evangelical ardor of Reverend Arnold. "Did you see what became of Old Jacob's body?"

Fitch paused and rubbed the gray stubble on his jaw. "He took his own skin and kept it all those years. Sorry few can claim that, red or white."

For a moment Duncan's spine crawled. He had heard the words

before, on the ship, spoken by the murderess Flora. *Take the skin you are,* she had said. "His own skin?"

"It's an Indian way of speaking. He did only true things. His true things." Fitch shrugged. "I don't know the words, McCallum. I'm just an old soldier. He was totally his own man, knew who he was and never let anyone change that, even as his clan died around him. He knew things about the workings of the earth that you and I couldn't even guess at."

Duncan stared at the man, unable to fathom how Flora could have acquired such words, but wanting more desperately than ever to understand. "What are the true things, Sergeant?"

Fitch considered the question a long time as he kept working the flints. "I s'pose if you could speak them, they wouldn't be true," he said at last. "It was like when Jacob would call a trout, and the fish would come and kiss his hand, never afraid. Ain't no words to describe the watching of that, or the way that fish and Jacob would look each other square in the eye and know what the other was thinking."

Duncan gazed back over the mountains. "Are you saying you and the captain buried Old Jacob?"

"We did the right thing," he said. Fitch looked up and searched Duncan's face, then reached into the pouch at his belt.

"You mean you—" Duncan began, but the words choked away as he saw what lay in Fitch's outstretched palm. It was a length of cloth, a tartan plaid, a brown field with stripes of dark green and red.

"An odd thing, lad," Fitch offered with a meaningful gaze. "We lifted this from the belt of a dead man at Stony Run."

Duncan squatted and took the cloth from the sergeant, stretching it between his fingers. It was a sash, a belt cloth of the kind a *Gaidheil,* a Highlander, would wear. "There were Scots at that battle, with the Indians?"

"I'd nay say a battle. More like murder on a grand scale. Half a dozen Iroquois were dead in the brush, including the one with this sash. Sixteen more were lined up and shot. Major Pike and the captain arrived not long after, from different directions, and exchanged harsh words. Pike wanted to burn the bodies and be gone. The captain posted rangers around the bodies to keep them from Pike and sent me to the towns for men to carry the dead back."

"Towns?"

"The Six have settlements same as white folk. They have ways about their dead, too. They wash 'em and dress 'em and say words over 'em."

"And place cedar boughs on them," Duncan asserted.

Fitch nodded. "Some of the old tribes, like the Mahicans, they would place 'em on a scaffold in a likely spot, overlooking a valley or close to where two rivers join. Seven, eight feet in the air, with food and fixings for travel. Takes a year, the Indians say, for a spirit to find its way to heaven."

Sergeant Fitch, Duncan realized, had finally told him what they had done with Jacob the Fish. He looked back at the plaid in his hand. "Were there fair-skinned men among the dead?"

"No, but if a man were to shave his head as some warriors do, and dye his skin with walnut juice, might be difficult to say."

"Did you know my brother?"

"He ran with us a spell."

"Ran?"

"Run the woods. That's what rangers do. You have to be like a deer. Quiet. Fast. Always watchful. Forget that for a minute, and be ye deer or soldier ye can die. Officers from the regular army get assigned to run with us, sometimes to punish them, sometimes so they can understand the enemy. Most don't last. They die. They get sick with nerves. One shot himself in the foot so he would be sent home. But some understand."

"You mean," Duncan said in an inquiring tone, "some change."

When Fitch looked up, there was a glint of surprise in his eyes.

"Because," Duncan continued, not certain where the words came from, "they glimpse true things."

Fitch said nothing but stopped his work and followed Duncan's gaze over the rolling, forested hills below them.

"Why didn't my brother join you and Captain Woolford then?"

"The Forty-second wouldn't have it. He was too valuable." Fitch eyed Duncan again. "He had a quick hand and a good heart, y'er brother, but he would not suffer mule-headed officers."

Duncan offered a nod of gratitude. He had been ashamed of his brother for joining the army, but now, his brother a target of public condemnation, he felt no shame at all. "And Adam Munroe, did he run with you as well?" he asked.

Fitch needed a long time to compose his answer. "Munroe was a Pennsylvania man," he said at last. "Our work be in New York territory."

"But you knew him. And Adam knew Old Jacob, who died not long after he did."

The observation seemed to worry Fitch. He busied himself with his stone again. "Not everyone who runs in the woods is a ranger," he said in a nervous, low voice.

Duncan gazed out over the hills, watched one of the great white-hooded eagles that sailed the currents above the ridges. After a moment Duncan squatted beside the grizzled soldier. "Did Jacob speak with bears as he did with fish?"

Fitch's chipping stone lost its direction, slicing into the back of his hand. He gazed at the oozing blood a moment, then returned the flint and stone to his pouch. When he rose, a look of wonder had entered his eyes. "There was a settler who took a huge bear a few years ago. He boasted about it, told how he would make a fine bear blanket and mittens from its paws. But that bearskin disappeared from his barn, along with the skull and paws and claws he had cut out. His maize crop failed that year. Since then I've heard of three or four other bears shot in these parts. Each time the skin disappeared. Folks say those skins got up and walked away to some bear paradise deep in the woods."

"Do you believe that, Sergeant?" Duncan asked, sensing in his empty hand the cold touch of the bear stone.

"There's old ones among the Six who won't speak openly about bears, because they are the most sacred of all creatures, like gods walking on earth, the spirits that anchor people to this world. There's a great shaman who can take the shape of a bear whenever he wishes."

"Do you believe it?" Duncan asked again.

"What I believe is that I won't be shooting any bears," the soldier had replied, and had walked back to the coach.

The fields of Edentown radiated outward from a compound of nearly twenty structures, including one large, two-story house of stone and a huge, elegant, English-style barn, four times the size of the house. The barn was made of stone, squared logs, and a shake roof, and stood on the eastern banks of a wide, shallow river. In the fields, teams of oxen with plows broke the earth for winter wheat. In one pasture, enclosed with a zigzag snake-rail fence, a dozen milk cows nibbled at high clover; in another, two score sheep grazed. In a field of golden hay, men labored with scythes. To the north, others were felling trees along the edge of the tall, dense forest that surrounded the estate to the north, south, and beyond the river to the west. Logs were being dragged by heavy horses toward new cabins, and a palisade wall was being erected along the north side.

"The Lord be praised," Crispin sighed. Duncan followed his gaze to a solitary figure in a green dress, waiting on the steps of the house. Sarah Ramsey had indeed found her father's town.

As they drew to a halt by the barn, Jonathan and Virginia Ramsey erupted from the coach with an exclamation of joy, running toward their older sister, who swept them up in a wide embrace. On the steps behind Sarah a solemn, bewigged figure appeared, dressed like a country squire. He waited for Jonathan to bow and Virginia to curtsy before kneeling and taking them both into his arms. Lord Ramsey had lost weight since the portrait in the New York house, but Duncan could not mistake the close-set, steely grey eyes that turned to him as Crispin led the children into the house.

"Mr. McCallum," Lord Ramsey said in greeting, "we have so anticipated your arrival." Duncan recognized his careful, clipped tones as the product of England's elite schools.

Duncan's uncertain nod of acknowledgement froze as he met the gaze of the older Ramsey daughter. Sarah looked like a thin porcelain statuette, but her countenance seemed free of the effects of opium. Although melancholy still ruled her features, there was also a fire in her eyes that he had not seen before. Her father, noting Duncan's distraction, stepped in front of Sarah as she offered him a shy smile.

"Mr. McCallum," she announced, "has reached the edge of the woods." The unexpected words seemed to mean more to her father than to Duncan. Ramsey's eyes flared and he turned to his daughter with a censuring stare. Sarah retreated up the stairs.

"Professor Evering was ready to move heaven and earth to reshape the Ramsey heirs," Ramsey proclaimed, addressing Duncan again. "We have equally profound hopes for you," he added, then pointed to a broad-shouldered man in a brown waistcoat waiting at the corner of the house, and marched back inside the house.

"Consider yourself well and truly blessed," the man in brown said as he approached. "We had to stand for an hour's speech when we arrived." It was Cameron, only changed in appearance: scrubbed, clipped, and neatly attired. "I'm to see you to your manor," he said, pointing to a compact log structure across the stretch of drying mud that served as the main street of Ramsey's town. Duncan pulled his bag from the wagon and followed the keeper, who explained that the Company had been divided into parties of wood clearers, builders, and farmworkers, joining a dozen craftsmen already employed at the town. Cameron recited the function of each of the buildings as they walked. A summer kitchen, a smokehouse and butcher's works, a springhouse, a carpenter's shop, a milking stable, a forge, a cooper's shop being used temporarily as a chapel, a spinning shed, a kennel with huge hunting hounds, and finally several long log structures, the newest of the buildings, that served to house the men of the Company.

"He will send for you when tea is ready," Cameron announced as he opened the door to the schoolhouse.

Duncan paused on the threshold, glancing back at the house as he wondered why Ramsey would consider his heirs in need of reshaping, then stepped into an austere room with a large fireplace, lit by a single window and furnished with one table in front of a piece of slate on the wall, facing three smaller tables. Through a narrow doorway he spied a bed and a chest of drawers in a smaller chamber. "What happened after you crossed on the ferry that first day?" Duncan asked abruptly. "Another man was murdered. An old man with a fish on his cheek."

"You mean an Indian then. Beg pardon, sir. I think Indians just die. Never heard that one could be murdered. May as well call a farmer a murderer for turning a pig to bacon."

Duncan gripped his emotions and pressed on. "Did you see him?"

"Heathens have their own strange ways," was Cameron's only reply.

Duncan stepped to the window and gazed out.

"There's a crib in the forge for charcoal," Cameron declared to his back. "The smith put a lock on the door."

"And who keeps the key to this dungeon?"

"In the main house." As Duncan turned to confront Cameron, a grimace creased the keeper's face. "Lord Ramsey says if any man disobeys the law, he has the authority to punish. He says those who survive the full seven years will be given fifty acres of good bottomland."

"Those who survive?"

"We're in a war, His Honor reminded us that first day," Cameron continued in a stiff tone, "and the way we win is by cutting down trees, building cabins, and obeying his commands."

"You had a letter of mine, Cameron," Duncan said as the keeper withdrew. "Who did you give it to?"

"Didn't need it anymore. Murder's been solved. We know who is going to hang."

"We had a bargain," Duncan pressed. "You keep the letter, I steer suspicion away from you."

The keeper's face darkened. "Like I said, the murder is solved."

"Not until the trial."

"There's another piece of paper, my certificate about seeing your name on Evering's body. I have that in a safe place, McCallum."

"Excellent. You understand my point. We still need each other. Is there a guard on his cell?"

"I need you for nothing."

"You misunderstand. I know you gave the letter to the army. Captain Woolford knows. How do you think Reverend Arnold and Lord Ramsey will react when they learn you had contact with the army?"

A silent snarl formed on Cameron's face.

"Is there a guard on the cell?"

"Most times," Cameron spat.

"Then call him away, now."

Duncan watched as Cameron left the building, calling out to the men carrying rocks from the fields, retrieving a stick where it leaned on the side of the barn and twitching it on the backside of old McGregor for moving too slow.

Five minutes later Duncan circled the barn until out of sight of the main house, quickly locating a smoke-stained stone structure beyond the milking shed. The furnace was cold, the bellows idle. Beyond the anvil was a sooty structure of heavy vertical slats spaced a few inches apart, filled waist-high with charcoal, its door kept shut with a length of chain connected with a padlock.

"Mr. Lister," Duncan said, pressing his face close to the planks. "Are you in pain? Can I get you something?" A scrap of cloth extended through a gap in the planks. It was stained with dried blood.

"Just before dawn comes a great chorus of birds." The voice that came from the shadows was dry as sticks. "You've never heard such singing. A little taste of heaven."

"I beg you not to be contemplating heaven just yet."

"I've heard only gulls these past thirty years. 'Tis a sweet choir to awaken to."

On the ground Duncan noticed a piece of birch bark shaped into a cone, fastened with a splinter of wood. He filled it with water from the smith's bucket and passed it through a gap in the slats.

"The day you crossed the river," Duncan said after Lister had drained the cup and passed it back, "a man was killed. Did you see anything?"

Lister scooped away charcoal, making a hollow where he could sit close enough that Duncan could see the dim glow of his face. "Don't know about a killing. But there was a phantom lurking about. He weren't meeting the Company, he was just studying it, following close as a shadow, cool as a fox. We were an hour past that Dutch inn. Young Frasier had tended my wounds and left me with a crock of water. Most of the men were out of the wagons, walking, herded on by the keepers and those guards. I was inconvenienced in the wagon, nothing to do but enjoy the day. A bird sang then, too. I thought nothing of it at first, but it persisted, a short, questioning song that seemed to want an answer, but none ever came. The bird followed, then I saw a dark shape close by, a stone's throw away. At first I thought it a stump, but then it moved, and the bird song moved. The shadow would disappear, then appear a quarter mile up the road as we passed. It went on for two or three miles, the song and the shadow, the song getting more and more lonely."

"And then?"

"A rider galloped up behind us. A man all in leather with a face like a shard of flint. Had words with some of the keepers. Frasier and Cameron. Showed them a piece of paper in his pocket. Took a drink from the water barrel tied to the back of my wagon, still on his horse, studying me with eyes like two black pebbles. Then he heard the bird, too, and he froze and turned toward the woods, his hand on his big skinning knife. He grinned, chewed off a cheekful of tobacco, and galloped on."

"The shadow in the woods?"

"Never saw it again. Never heard the bird again."

"Nothing else happened?"

"The road was full of bends, and crossed through many boulder fields that made it difficult to see the last wagon and those walking behind. I did not see Cameron, nor Frasier, for nigh an hour. But after another hour came the thing in the tree."

Duncan filled the cup and Lister drained it once more. When he started again his voice was low and wary. "At first I thought it was a child in a blanket, and I was going to be sick. But it was a bear, a baby bear, recently hung from a tree on a noose over the road, blood dripping from its mouth. Its little paws were caught on the rope like it had struggled to escape before dying. I didn't like it. No one liked it. Spooked the horses, even the guards. We made a ring of big fires that night and kept them burning 'til dawn. After that first night we drove straight through, sleeping in the wagons, driving in the moonlight."

"What have they told you?" Duncan asked. "About what will happen here."

"There's to be a trial. There's to be a hanging."

Duncan fought to keep his voice steady. "Do you need something? A blanket?"

"At night I burrow down into the coal. Cameron jokes about it, says get used to it since where I am going all there is is burning coals."

"Food?"

"Mostly what I need is a bath," Lister said with a hoarse croak, his effort at a laugh. "Get me a bath and a bottle and they can do their worst."

"I know you did not kill Evering." Duncan declared.

Lister took a long time to answer. "If I told ye I did, we would both be shamed and y'er new American clan will be for naught. If I say nay, ye'll try something foolish."

"The history of my days," Duncan said in a slow voice, "can be traced from one foolish act to another."

"And the most foolish would be to throw away y'er new life for a dried-up sack of bones."

"I seem to recall a day on a mast," Duncan replied, "I seem to remember gripping hands. A pledge was made. It works both ways, you know. You brought me back to life. We must both endure the consequences of that bargain."

In the silence that followed, Duncan could hear the wheeze of Lister's leathery lungs. A lamb bleated. A milk cow bellowed. "The

Ramsey lass arrived a few hours after we did," Lister said at last. "I can see the side of the house from here. She stands at an upstairs window and just stares at the forest. She weeps for hours, she's so scared. Frasier works in the kitchen sometimes, helping with the meals for the men."

"That man in leather," Duncan asked. "Was he here when you arrived?"

"Aye. Hawkins be his name, I ken. Five more looking just like him walked out of the woods a few hours later, carrying muskets. Axes and heavy knives in their belts. Empty eyes. Hawkins got a keg of rum from the great house. Got drunk in the barn, carousing all night, must have slept on hay in the empty stalls. Cameron announced that Hawkins is now a keeper. Six of the Company left with him this morning, new weapons in their belts. McGregor, plus McPhee. McSween. Ross."

As Lister related the other three names something cold seemed to scrape across Duncan's spine. The body snatchers. Hawkins had taken all the body snatchers. "Did Lord Ramsey speak with them?"

Lister sighed but did not answer the question. "Surely ye ken why we Scots have survived so many centuries against the English?" he asked. "We know when to retreat. We be masters at knowing when to retreat."

"If you always retreat, eventually there is no ground left behind you."

Lister muttered a low curse and grew silent again. A soot-covered finger appeared through a gap in the planks, pointing across the river. "Do you understand where we be?" he asked.

"The frontier."

"Do ye ken the old maps that warned how boats fell off the edge of the world if they sailed too far? They had the right of it, they just mixed up land and sea. On the other side of that river ye fall off the world."

"Some men go inside and return."

"Then they be different men when they return, emptied out by the blackness. Makes me feel like a cowering boy just to watch it.

The darkness there is like nothing I've ever seen. Worse than the blackest sea in the blackest storm. Ye can read the sea, but ye can't read that. There is no bottom to it, there is just black behind the black." There was an unsettling edge of fear in the old sailor's voice. "It stretches without roads for hundreds of miles. Thousands. There is no soul alive who's been from one side to the other, who knows where the far side lies. Go into it," the old sailor warned in a voice that began to frighten Duncan, "and the clan dies."

"Why would you say such a thing?" Duncan asked. "Why would you think I would be so foolish as to cross the river?"

Lister responded by extending a long, bony finger toward a wooded island in the river. "Find Frasier. Go meet Professor Evering. Even the dead are not safe over there."

Duncan looked back, knowing he could not have heard correctly. "Who?"

"The real Professor Evering. He came out of the western forest yesterday."

Chapter Seven

"THERE BE OLD WOMEN IN Scotland who would know how to send it back," the young keeper said as he gestured Duncan toward the island. Frasier had hatred in his eyes when Duncan approached him in the kitchen garden beside the house, but something seemed to compel him to share the thing he had discovered. "We should have buried him proper, at sea. It was wrong to let him linger, force him to cross the sea twice without touching land." He rose from the upturned earth, his eyes still sullen and resentful, and motioned Duncan to join him at the riverbank.

Pausing across from the island, Frasier stepped into the water up to his knees. He did not speak, though his lips seemed to be moving in a silent prayer. The fear in his eyes told Duncan he meant to go no farther. Even from a hundred feet away, his hand shook when he pointed toward a tall hemlock at the south end of the island.

Duncan chided himself for not bringing a shovel, an ax, something from the forge for a weapon, then retrieved a short limb from the ground and entered the water. He waded slowly until the water was up to his thighs, remembering Lister's intense fear and his warning never to venture to the far side of the river, where the black forest began. The island was thick with small alders, and Duncan walked with his club upraised, recoiling as a long-beaked bird burst from some reeds, then moving warily toward the small knoll. At last he reached the clearing around the tall hemlock, and froze. A demon stood in front of the tree, staring at him.

The left half of its hideous head was relatively benign, but the right was twisted and bent so that the haunting smile of the left turned into a grotesque open frown, showing bright white teeth below a six-inch misshapen nose.

He raised his club and ventured closer. The demon wore a black sleeveless waistcoat, out of which arms made of sticks extended. In the twigs of one hand hung a gold watch, its chain linked through a buttonhole to a familiar gold fob, in the shape of a tiny book. In the other twig hand was the skull of a small bird; a paper had been rolled through its eyes. Around the thing's shoulder hung the skin of a snake.

"One of the scullery maids said I'd find berries over here," came a thin, fearful voice behind him. "I brought a basket, had nearly backed up to the thing before I saw it. It's Evering. His watch, his fob, his waistcoat."

Duncan fought to keep his voice steady. "You and I both know, Frasier, that his body was sent back to England."

"It's what Evering became, his punishment for defying something that lives in the forest." Frasier's matter-of-fact tone was as unsettling as the gruesome thing in front of Duncan. "It drew out his spirit from the ship and withered it and sent it back to watch."

It's what Evering became, according to Frasier, for taking the path that Duncan was now on. "Watch what?" he asked, taking a step toward the thing.

"Us. The town . . . God's life!" Frasier cried as Duncan advanced toward the tree. "Don't touch it!"

Instead of touching the thing, Duncan stepped to the side, studying it. The head, he saw, was a mask, expertly carved of wood and stained dark red, with horsehair fastened to the top. The teeth in the sinister mouth were made of bits of shell. It had been hung with a leather strap on a limb that jutted from the tree, with the waistcoat and arms braced in a crosspiece tied with vines.

He pried open the pockets with a twig, finding nothing. This was Evering's good waistcoat, the one stolen along with his watch from his cabin. Directly below the effigy was a small pile of ashes. He knelt and stirred them. Tobacco had been burned.

"Who have you told?" he asked.

"No one. Lister, since he can tell no one. Lister understands these things. We're all going to end up like this."

Duncan turned to him, for a moment as frightened by Frasier as by the effigy.

"We should have known," Frasier added, "after what happened to that bear."

But as little as Duncan understood about the New World, of one thing he was certain. Whoever had made the effigy was not one who killed bears. He looked back up at the twisted countenance. What had happened here was like the ritual on the ship—part European, part not. Part Indian, he forced himself to admit. A new realization struck him as he gazed at the twisted mouth. He was looking at Old Crooked Face. Adam had gone to Old Crooked Face, and so, apparently, had Evering. With trembling fingers, he reached for the roll of paper in the bird skull and was about to read it when the cries began—the terrified screams of a child.

He burst out of the brush at the edge of the island to see Virginia standing on the bank fifty yards upstream. By the time he reached her, the screams had become silent, her jaw moving up and down, her face white as a sheet, her eyes wild with terror. Caught in the rocks midstream were bodies, mutilated bodies that had clearly been in the water several days. Suddenly Crispin was there, gathering the girl into his arms, running toward the house with her as Cameron began directing men into the water.

"Settlers, drifted down from the north," the keeper said as the first corpse was pulled ashore, a man without hands, without eyes, without a scalp.

Duncan realized he was still clutching the paper from the bird skull. It was a page torn from a Bible, the same size that Evering had carried. It was from Revelations. *Go*, Duncan read, *and pour out the seven bowls of God's wrath on the earth.*

Wigs. Wigs were Ramsey's lifeline on a stormy sea.

When Duncan found Crispin at the rear of the summer kitchen, the butler was addressing what at a quick glance might have appeared to be a group of seated gentlemen. On a trestle-and-plank table were half a dozen hairpieces supported on rounded, wooden pedestals specially designed to store them. Crispin was extracting a skillet of buckles, cylinders of baked red clay, from the oven built into the wall, which with skillful and patient wrapping would restore the drooping curls.

A gentleman of modest means might have but one wig which, depending on whether it was human, goat, horse, or calf in origin, could represent a significant investment. But the Ramsey head was versatile, and wealthy to the point of opulence. An old-fashioned periwig, a grizzle wig, a campaign wig, a ramillies—the odd-looking bob wig made popular by Dr. Johnson—and even an informal bag wig were all on the table, marking Ramsey's connection to the brocaded, lavender-scented courtesans of his habitat across the ocean.

From the shadows Duncan watched his new friend, his hands coated with powder, clad in a starched white shirt buttoned too tightly at his neck under a sleeveless brown waistcoat. He had never seen Crispin in the performance of his household duties, and the sight made Duncan so uncomfortable he was about to retreat, when Crispin spoke to him.

"These hairpieces redeemed us," the big man reported with a glance toward Duncan. "Reverend Arnold was complaining about our abrupt departure from the city when Mr. Ramsey silenced him and announced that he had been about to send for me, because his curls were in such disarray." A kitchen maid appeared from inside the building, wiping soot from her hands. As she began arranging the buckles in front of the periwig, a bell sounded from the kitchen door. A look of relief shot across Crispin's features. He straightened and gestured Duncan toward the house. "Tea," was all he said.

"She made it safely here," Duncan observed as they walked toward the house.

"The captain rode hard all that first day," Crispin replied. "She kept always ahead of him, so he had never a glimpse of her. He kept riding west, toward Edentown, thinking she was still in front. But then she came trotting up behind him, not far from here, her horse worn to a shadow. Won't breathe a word about where she had been."

They still had no answer to the questions that had hovered over them, unspoken but conspicuous, during their journey together. Had Sarah been driven by horror at the old Indian's murder or by fear of the report of the attack in the harbor? Or had it been something else she had seen in Jacob's death, something that Duncan had been blind to?

Crispin led Duncan into the library in the northeast corner of the great stone house, where windows looked to the west and north. Lord Ramsey, sitting in a high-backed Windsor chair with a large tray constructed into the right arm, acknowledged him with a nod but continued reading the book perched on the tray. Behind him were shelves containing perhaps five dozen books and a large number of periodicals. Against the wall to the right was a heavy secretary desk of cherry wood, its hinged top closed. An elegant, engraved fowling piece hung on the fireplace mantel. On the north wall by the window hung a large drawing, a map of a town and the river along its edge, with buildings drawn in great detail, each labeled in an ornate hand. Another map, of the New York colony, hung on the adjacent wall, bearing notes in several hands. Several muskets leaned in one corner, beside a rack containing a dozen heavy swords and two old-style metal breastplates. The room had the air of another military office.

Studying the compound through the window, Duncan compared it to the map. Though it was labeled *Palace of Husbandry*, the barn was located as shown on the map, as were the summer kitchen, the forge, the spinning shed, and all the other existing structures, though the map held three times the number of buildings that currently stood outside, including a church, a courthouse, and a jail. But the house was different. The house they stood in was much smaller than the three-winged mansion on the map.

When Duncan turned, Reverend Arnold was standing by the window, staring toward a plot of land beyond the barn, where whitewashed stakes outlined a broad rectangle. Duncan glanced at the map again. It was the site of the yet-unbuilt church.

"The vicar has informed me of your good service on the ship. You brought my daughter back from the dead." Ramsey seemed to struggle to keep emotion out of his voice, and Duncan understood why he had chosen not to have the conversation in public upon his arrival. "She is so much like her mother. Uncannily like her mother. I will not forget how well you performed that day. You shall be repaid." He stepped to a silver tray on a low table by the window and poured a cup of tea from a delicate porcelain pot painted with violets, handing it to Duncan.

Ramsey seemed to think that Duncan had saved Sarah for him, that in leaping into the black, churning sea, he had merely been performing his duty to his patron. "Miss Ramsey and I were not meant for the sea that day," he ventured.

"Truly God has marked her," Ramsey said, regaining the poise in his voice. "The first lady of Edentown will be needed for many tasks. The church choir must be organized, a flag for the courthouse designed and sewn. Naming of babies. The kitchens. The cellars. The gardens. The seasonal festivals. All the families will look to her. There are things only a Ramsey woman can do." In his mind, Duncan realized, Ramsey was running not the town that existed outside but the one in the drawing. His gaze drifted back to the map. The current house wasn't wrong, he saw now, it was merely the base. The wings still had to be constructed, on either side. The only thing not on the map was the palisade wall being built along the northern woods.

"Miss Ramsey seemed most anxious for her reunion," Duncan

observed. He glanced out the window toward the little island. Though he could not see it, he knew the Evering effigy was staring right at the house. Before he had left the hemlock, he had paced around the tree and had found small, wrapped bundles of fur and a strange arrangement of deer antlers, more than a dozen of them, tied with vines in a circle. Now that his fear had subsided, he realized they could have been offerings, that perhaps in the world of those who had made it, the effigy wasn't meant to frighten but to serve as a shrine.

"She was sorely missed. She is a builder of empire."

Duncan sipped his tea, replaying the words in his mind. Just as Ramsey spoke of the Edentown in his mind, not the muddy reality outside his door, the patron seemed to be speaking of a different Sarah. "Should she not take time to recover from her illness before she embarks on carving up continents?"

"Fortunately," Arnold interrupted, "she is in better health than we've seen in a year. Destiny waits for no one."

Ramsey stepped to the window and surveyed his budding empire. "But first we must eliminate all shadows from our midst."

Duncan's belly tightened as Ramsey fixed him with a meaningful gaze.

"Lord Ramsey desires your report," Reverend Arnold explained. "The record must be completed. The first case for Edentown's magistrate must present an intellectual and moral pillar, a pristine example of logic and science."

"Surely you understand I have had no opportunity for inquiries."

"What possible need is there for further inquiries?" the vicar pointed out. "The evidence has all been assembled, the killer apprehended. All that is needed is the proper organization of your thoughts and the lifting of a quill."

"My logic and science have not pointed to Mr. Lister," Duncan said, swallowing hard. "As you say, the record must be complete. There are questions I might ask the army," Duncan suggested, trying not to look conspicuous as he watched for Ramsey's reaction. "There was a general who asked about the death of Evering. He seemed to think that his death had some connection to military matters."

Ramsey withdrew into himself a moment, then helped himself to snuff from a silver box on the side table and paced in front of the window facing the river. "You told General Calder it was none of his concern," he said without breaking stride. Duncan thought it was an invitation, but Ramsey continued in his imperious tone. "You told him the Company is an enterprise of Edentown. You reminded him Edentown is mine, by royal charter. You vowed to yourself that the Company would emerge victorious."

Duncan could see an ox team working the field closest to the barn. He had an overwhelming desire to be among the prisoners, plowing the earth, hauling stones, cleaning stalls ankle-deep in manure, anywhere but playing the rag puppet to such a man. "The killer is still at large among us," Duncan said. "I think he or an accomplice killed an old Indian at the ferry inn."

"Impossible," Ramsey said. "As I told Captain Woolford when he mentioned it, Indians are always dying. It is a sign of our victorious God. Do not be distracted from your duties."

"General Calder," Duncan said, "believed I should be interested in a battle where many of our Indian allies died. At Stony Run."

It was not exactly alarm Duncan saw in the look that passed from Ramsey to Arnold, but something like a wary resentment, as if Calder had just stolen a point in some game between them. And Calder had used Duncan to make the score.

"The Indian who died at the inn had the name of our ship," Duncan continued. "He was trying to pass a secret to someone in the Company. Or someone he expected to be with the Company. A man who would kill Evering over a secret would have little hesitation in killing an old Indian. It could not have been Mr. Lister, for he was in chains." Ramsey and Arnold grew very quiet, Arnold staring out the window, Ramsey at his map. "You say you will repay me for saving your daughter, sir. I ask that you release him on his parole."

"Impossible."

"On *my* own covenant then. He is an old man who will not stray far."

"And what recompense will you offer when he kills again?" Arnold inquired.

"I pledge my indenture. If you find me mistaken, then put me in chains mucking out the horse stalls for seven years."

Ramsey replied with a silent frown, then stepped closer to his map. "In England," he offered with a gesture toward the drawing, "towns and their populations have become such random, disheveled things. Here we have the opportunity to correct all mistakes." He fixed Duncan with a sober gaze. "Our century stands at the culmination of civilization. We are its ambassadors."

The lord's library, Duncan decided, was the most treacherous terrain he had yet encountered in the New World. He noticed small numbers in the lower right corner of each building sketch, the house bearing the numeral 3. Examining the numbers of each sketch and the status of the new construction, he recognized the sequence. "The very last structure to be built in your utopia is the courthouse," he observed.

Reverend Arnold seemed to welcome the comment. "Next is the house of God. What need hath man for the courts and legislation when he has a church and the Decalogue?" he asked, using the High Church reference for the Ten Commandments.

"I am writing a commentary on Plato," Ramsey announced, abruptly changing the subject. "Where else but in the New World do we have an opportunity to shape an entire society according to his esteemed principles?" The patron fixed Duncan with a level gaze. "Each of us is born to a destined duty. The ancient sage teaches that the highest reward is the fulfillment of that duty." Ramsey had not changed the subject after all.

Duncan dared to return Ramsey's stare for a moment, then lowered his gaze. Lister was right. He was going to have to master the skills of retreat. "I shall tirelessly strive toward my just rewards," Duncan said in a taut voice. He placed his cup on the tray and offered a slight bow as he maneuvered toward the door.

Ramsey raised his cup toward Duncan as if in salute.

Duncan wandered about the compound, admiring the huge barn, more English than the house itself—its mortised beams joined like those of a mighty ship, with thirty stalls and central grain storage chambers and tool rooms under a cavernous hayloft—but soon found himself back in the classroom, staring at the blank slate on the wall. Checking that the door was latched, he extracted tattered pieces of paper from his pocket and arrayed them in front of him on the teacher's table. His list of the McCallum clan chiefs. Evering's poetry. The two messages from Jacob's lean-to. He found a sheet of paper and began writing, one line for each event in the mystery that lay before him, then tore the list of events into slips, one line per slip, and arranged them in a row, top to bottom. *Evering breaks vial of laudanum. Compass ritual,* said the next. Then *Evering murdered* and *Sarah awakens.* He studied them for several minutes, then shifted the last paper to the top. *Sarah awakens, Compass ritual, Evering murdered.* After a moment he wrote and tore more slips. *Frasier and Cameron loot Woolford's chest. Adam barters with McGregor for the bear stone from Woolford's chest. Woolford flees the ship with Sarah to be in port a day before the others. Adam commits suicide. Jacob the Fish receives message about ship from Socrates Moon. Old Jacob murdered. Duncan attacked in New York harbor. Woolford secretly writes Moon. Moon leaves message for Jacob.* He arranged the papers in an arc before him, as he once had done with the names of the bones when memorizing the sequence of the human skeleton. As he stared at the slips, convinced that if he could only place them in the right sequence he would glimpse the truth, a terrible weight seemed to close around his shoulders. The skeleton before him was that of the monster responsible for the violence and mystery that simmered below the surface of the Ramsey Company. Here before him, in his hands, hung the life of Lister. He wrote a last slip and put it in front of all the others. *Massacre at Stony Run.*

He turned to his list of clan chieftains and recited each name out loud, then retrieved and unwrapped the bear stone, placing it before him, facing the paper slips, as if it might help him translate the events and the dialogue in his patron's library. It had not been Ramsey's words about Lister that had made Duncan's skin crawl. There had been something else, when he had described the death of Old Jacob. Indians are always dying, Ramsey had said. *It is a sign of our victorious God.* In his youth, Duncan had been forced to listen to the same words spoken from English pulpits, about the destruction of the Highland Scots. He stared at the clan names again, then pushed the slips aside, unfolded the message Jacob had made in his own blood, and stared at it. It was meant for a man who understood more than Duncan did, meant for a man more conversant with the violent truths of the New World. He buried his head in his hands.

Flora is alone, with no hand to hold. The thought pounced upon him from nowhere. The guilt he felt for leaving the mad, faceless murderess on the ship would not be shaken. She was gone, condemned to slow death in the tropics, and for the rest of his life he would feel the helplessness, the pain of not being able to help her, the doubt over whether she had, like him, been unfairly convicted. He was a clan chief and was supposed to help Scots in peril. But he had failed her. Her strange words, the soft, desperate touch of her hand during the long, dark hours, had moved him more than he cared to admit. Flora, too, had been touched by the New World, he knew now, for her words had been echoed on the river and the frontier road, had been the seed of a strange, unnamable awareness that seemed to be building inside him. At night, at the edge of sleep, he sometimes sensed a warmth in his fingers, as if she were still there. She had become an invisible member of his clan, more real in a way than Sarah, who had proven an imposter. The night before, he had dreamt he had stayed with Flora, gone to Jamaica and escaped with her in a small, swift sloop on a warm, dark sea.

He became aware of a small, round face peering through the window at him and hurried to the door. "I am in need of a guide, Master Jonathan," he declared, "Will you show me your town?"

They moved along the perimeter of the little community, past the dog kennels and pens where rotund sows suckled piglets. Some of the workers, men not of the Company, called out greetings to the boy, who answered with awkward waves. Others, familiar from the *Anna Rose,* glanced nervously at Duncan and looked away without speaking.

Duncan had to admire the planning that had gone into the construction of Ramsey's town. The nucleus he was creating would have sustained a much larger community. They passed saw pits where logs were being cut into planks, a mason's yard where large stones dragged in on ox sledges were being shaped for lintels and sills. He studied the men with the oxen, remembering Evering's cryptic words on the sheet torn from his journal. *The ghostwalker at the ox wheel, his tongue is in his heart.* But Duncan saw no ox cart, no wheel of any kind among the great beasts.

Jonathan pointed out a lime kiln built into the knoll beside the northernmost pasture, even a potter's shed where rust-colored bowls were lined up on a bench to dry in the sun. Ramsey's fields were laid in careful squares, divided by walls of stone collected in the clearing of the fields, except for a flat acre of thicket and small trees that extended like a tongue into the fields from the south, disrupting the neat sequence.

"Where are the other children?" Duncan inquired as they watched three men hew beams to use as roof rafters, beside others spudding bark from chestnut logs.

"Virginia is at the butcher's with Reverend Arnold, where he goes to plan the week's meals. There are no others."

Duncan's gaze settled on two of the workers, not of the Company, laboring at a stump. They wore iron collars around their necks. "What sin," he inquired in a taut voice, "did those men commit?"

Jonathan followed his gaze. "Escaped. Father sometimes goes to Philadelphia and brings back bondsmen from those arriving on the ships. They sign papers to stay. When they flee, Mr. Hawkins brings them back. He uses father's bear dogs," the boy declared, nodding toward the kennels. "Father says we must always keep them a little hungry in case there's work to be done. Such men must be reminded of their sin," he added in a flat tone. "God wills it so." Duncan did not need to ask the origin of that particular script.

Duncan clenched his jaw and kept moving. It wasn't so much a Greek utopia Ramsey was building as a Roman circus. "Some of these men must have families," he said. He tried to steer toward the thicket that jutted into the fields, but Jonathan pulled him in the opposite direction, carefully avoiding looking at the thicket.

"Not here," the boy replied. "Not yet. Father will tell them when they may bring their families from the settlements."

"When did they start building the palisade wall?" Duncan asked after a few silent paces. He spotted another group of workers, a dozen men in two columns, walking with Cameron at the lead, holding barrel staves like muskets.

"Last autumn. Eventually it will protect the entire town."

Last autumn, Duncan reminded himself, would have been after the incident at Stony Run, after Sarah Ramsey had fled.

They paused at a stone-walled well and sat on its side to drink from the wooden ladle hung on its timbers, speaking of the geese migrating overhead. Duncan showed the boy how to turn a blade of grass into a whistle between his thumbs, and to Jonathan's delight, a jay answered from the forest.

"Jonathan, why did your sister go to England?" Duncan abruptly asked.

The boy looked at the earth at his feet, his muscles visibly tensing.

"Father says she was sick. She needed doctors there."

"But where was she before that?"

Jonathan clamped his hands together and began wringing his fingers. "If mother had not gone away, it would have been different. We said prayers for Sarah's tortured soul, for all those years. Mother said when we met Sarah, it would be in heaven. But then mother went to heaven. And Sarah . . . .When at last she could see us, we were not allowed to speak with her. Not allowed to touch her." Tears welled in his eyes. As Duncan put a hand on his shoulder, the boy recoiled as if he had been struck, then sprang up. Duncan was certain he would run to the house, but instead the boy took five quick steps and turned, waiting. Duncan rose and followed the boy back toward the riverbank, where he stopped at a clump of alder bushes only a hundred feet beyond the house.

At Jonathan's feet were pebbles, scores of pebbles arranged in a shape from Duncan's boyhood. It was a Scottish cross—a cross of equal arms, each a foot long, overlaying a circle. It was a symbol discouraged by the modern church, for the shape harkened back to the sacred circles of the blue-painted Picts and the Druids. Men like Arnold were loathe to admit how much Christianity had borrowed from the pagans. In the remote lands of Duncan's youth, such a device had often been used as a charm, a powerful device for banishing demons.

Two inches from the bottom and top of the cross were straps of iron, probably the most precious commodity in the town. The bottom iron appeared to be the handle of a long kitchen spoon, bent and rebent until it had snapped away. At the top was a narrow, six-inch piece of strap iron. Duncan lifted each in turn. As a charm against demons, many Highlanders considered iron even more potent than a cross.

Duncan studied the position of the cross. "Are there more?" he asked the boy.

Jonathan seemed troubled by the question. "They break the eggshells, too," he blurted out.

"Eggshells?"

"Every morning on the pile where the cook leaves the pot scrapings, the eggshells are all lined up, each with a hole cut in the bottom."

Duncan nodded somberly. "Show me the other crosses."

Jonathan led him along the bank to two more crosses made of pebbles, with iron arranged as at the first, one of the pieces the bowl from the broken spoon. But when the boy paused a third time, he did not gesture toward the ground. Duncan followed the boy's shifting gaze toward the far bank, the barn, the fields, then realized the boy was simply looking everywhere but the one place he could not bear to see.

Duncan saw the ants first, a line of them leading under the shadows of a clump of alders, then stepped closer and froze. The ants were devouring a dead fish beside another cross. The fish was in the middle of a vertical row of objects and signs. The first set was the skull of a small bird with lines drawn in the earth beside it. The skull and lines had been stomped on with a heavy boot, crushing the bone and nearly obliterating the lines. Next came two sets of curving lines side by side, then the fish, then a yellow feather, then two stick figures that caused Duncan's breath to catch—a beaver and the curving lines of the snake. Then came another feather and another skull, this one with a piece of iron jammed into its eye socket, pinning it to the ground. Finally there was a small cloth pouch, no more than two inches long, drawn with a string at the top. Beyond the signs in an arc around the top were handprints in the moist soil, of two different sizes. Past the hands, encircling the cross and objects, were lines of bootprints, all walking in the same direction around the cross and the adjacent objects. Someone had walked three times around, a *deiseal* or sunwise circuit, used for admonishing demons.

Duncan's gaze drifted back to the fish. Its mouth had been forced open with a small twig. The fish had been speaking and was now dead.

The boy, still not looking at the objects, was trembling. Duncan put a hand on his arm. "When did you discover this?"

"This morning," Jonathan replied in a quivering voice as he dared a glance toward the ground. "I was gathering stones. I thought maybe I should cover it all with dirt. Should I tell Reverend Arnold? I don't know what he would do." The boy leapt back, the color leaving his face. "It's coming to life!" he gasped.

Duncan followed his stricken gaze to the little sack. It was moving.

"I think," Duncan said, working hard to keep foreboding out of his voice, "we should just leave this the way it is."

"Because it is a curse to keep them on the other side?"

Duncan weighed the boy's words, gauging the position of the design, on the upside of a small swale, facing the house. The cross was not aimed at the western forest, or the island. "Because it is a curse," he repeated. But he knew the row beside the cross was no curse, nor a ritual. They were looking at a dialogue. The cross had been made first, by a Highlander. Then the first skull of a messenger had been added, with lines of a message. Someone had then answered with the curving lines, four facing right, four left, like parentheses. They could have been claws, the number of claws on a wolf's front paws. Then the feather, the stick men, the beaver and snake signs, the fish, the signs of Adam and Jacob, then a feather as if in acknowledgment. Finally the skull and the small, moving pouch. Duncan picked up the little bag and opened it. A large bee crawled out onto his thumb, gazed at him, then flew straight up into the sky. He stared after it a long time. Birds might be messengers to the spirits in the Iroquois world. But in the world of the Highlands, it was the bee who carried messages to the dead.

He stepped backward, taking in the entire scene. There had been a dialogue between two parties who could not, or would not, meet face to face. But a third had also participated, coming back, interrupting with a boot, a strap of iron in the skull of a messenger, and a *deiseal* circuit. And Duncan knew who at least one of the three was. He looked up at the boy, who stared in silent fear at the river, then with his pencil lead on a flat white stone added one more sign to the row, where the bee had been. A drawing of Adam's she-bear.

"When I found it, I couldn't find you. I went to tell Sergeant Fitch," Jonathan explained. "But I changed my mind."

Duncan pulled the boy away to the sunlight at the edge of the garden. "Why?"

"I saw Mr. Frasier lead the sergeant into the kitchen and I followed. I was in the entry and they had not seen me when I heard Mr. Frasier tell Sergeant Fitch that he would keep Cameron away while he went below, into father's cellar. No one is to go below.

Father would have them both lashed if he knew. Mr. Frasier was ordered out of the house yesterday, removed from his house duties, for going onto the second floor where none of the Company is allowed. I should tell Father. But—" Jonathan bit his lip for a moment. "Sergeant Fitch carved me a toy horse. I like the way he laughs. He taught me the songs of some birds." The boy searched Duncan's face. When Duncan offered no reply, he ran away, not to the house, but to the white-staked rectangle beyond the barn, where Reverend Arnold was pacing off his church.

Duncan lingered at the cross, uneasily circling it, crouching by it again, placing his own hand over one of the prints as if to assure himself that its source was human. Finally he stepped around the front of the house, searching the nearby trees and the rough-scratched, struggling flowerbeds at its foundation, and found what he had expected. He leaned against a tree, studying the town, then with grim determination moved into the shadows along the edge of the fields until he reached the thicket that interrupted the fields. A knot formed in his belly as he gazed into it, then he pushed through the mountain laurel toward the center, where young oaks and chestnuts grew over a field of boulders. He advanced warily, starting at the screech of a squirrel, tripping over a log on the ground. As he heaved himself up he saw that it was not a log but a hand-hewn timber, a charred and rotting timber. He spotted another timber, and one resting on another, then, his breath catching, he discovered why Ramsey had not cleared this patch of forest.

The boulders were rough-hewn tombstones, a dozen of them, for eight men and women and four children, all dead the same year, 1746. Duncan rested his hand on the largest of the stones, onto which a flying cherub had been carved.

1740–1746, he read under the angel, then his heart lurched and he sank to his knees. The name carved on the stone was Sarah Ramsey.

He did not know how long he wrestled with the despair that seized him. He watched his fingers moving across the stone as if of their own accord, trembling, peeling away the lichen growing in the carving. He scrubbed at the stone with his fingertips, then slumped against it, head in his hands, wondering at his pain. Was it just the weight of the terrible foreboding bearing down on him, he wondered, or was it also the year? It was the same year, 1746, that his parents had been taken from him—the year of Culloden.

An hour later he was back at the schoolhouse table, studying his slips of paper, fighting a new desperation that had seized him, rearranging the slips again and again, pausing for minutes at a time to stare at his quill and the blank papers before him, pausing later to gaze out the window toward the great house, seeing, as Lister had, the woman using Sarah's name staring at the forest from the second floor. He could not escape the sense that he was being asked to strike a fire in a powder magazine.

Eventually he became aware of a presence and looked up to see Crispin holding a plate of cold beef and potatoes.

"Look like you've seen a ghost," the big man said as he shoved the plate across the table.

"I did. I stepped into that thicket that juts into the fields."

Crispin's face sagged. "No one goes there. The ground is cursed."

"They were the first settlers, weren't they?"

Crispin looked longingly toward the door, as if he were thinking of retreating, then pulled up a stool and sat opposite Duncan, but spoke toward the window. "There had been a little settlement, a few cabins long abandoned when Mr. Ramsey bought the land. He hired six families to clear the first fields and came in that autumn for a month, mostly to hunt. It was warm. Indian summer they call it, because that's a favorite time for the tribes to raid, to get plunder for their winter camps. He went out hunting stags for three days, downriver in Pennsylvania, took half the men with him. When they came back everything was burnt, all the people hacked to pieces. It was Iroquois, folks say, back when they were not all our allies."

"You mean he left his daughter here while he hunted," Duncan ventured. The way Cripsin broke away to stare into his folded hands was answer enough.

"I will not go near the place. Lord Ramsey has ordered briar thorns planted all around it. If he saw you there—"

"Sarah Ramsey is there."

The houseman buried his head in his hands a moment. "'Tis wrong to be digging up old graves. With Lady Ramsey gone, there's no one else," he added in a voice gone hollow.

"Why can no one speak a straight word about her?" Duncan demanded. Crispin was not trying to bait Duncan, he knew, or deceive him. He was just trying to protect the strange woman whom Duncan had pulled from the Atlantic.

"Stay out of the woods," Crispin said with sudden pleading in his voice. "No good for anyone."

"They want to condemn Lister to hang, Crispin," Duncan said. "And I believe the truth of it to be bound up around this woman using a dead girl's name. Without it, all I can do is point out possibilities, explanations that could be wrong. Innocent men have already died. Another will hang if all I can find is shadows."

"But your friend," Crispin declared with an uncertain grin. "They released him, reduced him to the ranks of the workers. He's in the river, singing like a boy."

Without another word, Duncan raced out the door and moments later halted beside an oak on the bank. Half a dozen prisoners were watching the jaunty old man in the river, some grinning, others wearing uneasy, nervous expressions. Lister had stripped to his waist and was sitting on a flat rock midstream, singing something bawdy about ladies in Spain as he scrubbed his arms with sand and rushes. Thirty feet upstream stood Frasier and another keeper, armed with clubs.

"The old fool's heart is as light as a leaf," said a voice at his shoulder. Duncan turned to see Cameron hovering close, the keeper's eyes full of worry and locked on Lister. "Mine would be, too, with so much brandy."

"What happened?"

Cameron shrugged. "Order came from His Lordship, with a pint of his finest French spirits. Release him into the Company, reduced to prisoner rank, but watch him close."

As Lister shifted on the rock, playfully skipping a pebble along the current, several of the onlookers paled and turned away. The old man's back was a latticework of scars, overlaid with long, ugly scabs from his most recent lashing.

Had Ramsey actually taken Duncan at his word, actually accepted that he owed Duncan a debt? But then Cameron handed Duncan a cloth-wrapped bundle.

"Greetings from our patron," the keeper declared and stepped away.

Inside were several sheets of fine white paper and four fresh-cut quills. He glanced back the house. Arnold stood on the rear porch, gazing at him expectantly. They weren't repaying a debt. They were forcing the bargain, increasing the stakes. Duncan had to finish his report. They didn't intend Lister to stay free for long. They were simply striking at Duncan with an invisible lash.

At midnight Duncan arrived at the door of the great house, the report folded inside a blank sheet of paper with Lord Ramsey's name on it. He paused and touched the iron thumb latch. The door was unlocked. With a quick survey of the yard to confirm no one watched, he stepped inside and laid the report on a side table under a flickering candle in a pewter holder. The house was still and silent. He lifted the candleholder and ventured over the wide plank floor into the kitchen in search of something to ease his mounting hunger. With guilty pleasure he discovered and quickly consumed the heel end of a loaf, dipping it in a tub of butter left on the windowsill, then saw the small door under the back stairway. He lifted its latch slowly, wary of making the slightest noise, then raised the candle and moved down the steps into Ramsey's forbidden cellar.

Rows of wooden crates and barrels lined the large, dirt-floored chamber. He ventured along the nearest wall, extending the candle to read the labels. Madeira, Port, Brandy. Sugar, salt, ale, and a dozen other consumables. Across the stone flags along the opposite wall were crates and trunks bearing the Ramsey name in the black letters he had seen on the ship. It took but a few moments to verify that they were the ones he and Woolford had seen in the hold, one still smelling of tar, though its ruined coats were gone. Beyond, under a heavy canvas cover, were more kegs of rum than he could quickly count. He raised the candle and discovered in the far corner a small chamber constructed of heavy timbers and planks. Its narrow door did not yield when he tested the latch.

Such safe rooms had been used at his medical college to store habituating doses, where doctors were so numerous it was impractical to provide them all with keys. He held the candle close to the door, saw through its crack the dim shape of a wooden bar blocking the door near the top, and began exploring the planks, pushing, probing the cracks in the wall with fingers and toes. The first plank around the corner groaned as he pushed at its bottom, its top swinging out on a pin concealed at its center. The locking bar, attached to the top of the plank, pulled clear of the door, and he stepped inside.

Kegs of rum lined the front wall of the chamber. In the nearest corner stood a low bench with a rack holding four heavy horse pistols, newly flinted, each loaded and primed, ready for use, several more flints under the rack, with gun cleaning cloths. A small table against the back stone wall held a bound ledger, a house account, with records of household purchases in the front. But in the rear of the book was another list, a record of payments over several months to perhaps two dozen different men, most of the names repeating, the most frequent entry being that of Hawkins, each entry bearing a number of hashmarks beside it. They could have indicated pelts, or game for the kitchen. The most recent entries, for Hawkins and five other men, had been made three days earlier, in a different handwriting.

Beside the book was a hand-drawn map that showed the country north of Edentown, following the river north as it meandered through rough-drawn ranges. Halfway up the river was a sketch of rock formations with tall columns of stone, marked *Chimney Rocks.*

The only other features were farther north and slightly west, two places separated by half an inch, marked in a cramped hand and underlined. *German Flats* and *Stony Run*. Below, at the bottom of the map, was a single word: *Okewa*.

He was about to leave when his gaze fell on two flour sacks, each with lumpish contents. Upending the first on the table, he discovered an ornate red-peaked cap, tall and military with a large *49* embroidered in gold brocade. He studied it in the dim light, putting his hand inside it, not understanding why it should be kept so secret. He stretched it over the candle. There were four small holes in its side, each big enough to insert a writing lead, spaced in two pairs four inches apart. They were too small for bullet holes, too regular to be the work of wool-eating insects. At the bottom of the flour sack was a brass cylinder, perhaps five inches long, perforated with holes and tapered at the base, topped with a hinged, domed cap.

He absently opened the second sack, upending it onto the table, then with a moan backed away. Inside were skulls, perhaps twenty skulls of birds, messengers to the gods. His hand trembling, he returned the bones to the sack, then dropped the cylinder into his pocket. He lifted the cap to return it to its sack, then paused and quickly tucked it inside his belt, pocketed the map, and jammed several of the guncloths into the empty sack.

A minute later he was out of the house, calming himself with gulps of the cool night air, heading across the plowed fields in the moonlight. He sat against a huge stump that had been too big for the oxen to extract, trying to lose himself in the deep night sky.

He turned the red cap over in his hand, uncertain why he had taken it, uncertain why it would be important to Ramsey. But somehow it seemed to be a start, a tiny step toward becoming the chieftain that Lister wanted him to be. As he studied the stars he began to sing, in quiet Gaelic, an old ballad about a Highlands warrior who battled the gods to save his clan.

Chapter Eight

*L*ORD RAMSEY SENT FOR HIM before noon the next day.

"I have read your report," the patron announced from his desk chair. Duncan's papers lay under one jeweled hand. "You confuse me, McCallum. What was it you did not understand about your task? In my experience, Reverend Arnold expresses himself more than adequately." Arnold stood behind Ramsey, arms folded across his sleeveless waistcoat.

Duncan returned the vicar's smoldering gaze, then addressed Ramsey. "I gave you precisely what you need, sir. A way out, a means to avoid scandal while also avoiding the harm to the Company that would come from condemning an innocent man."

Ramsey frowned and waved the papers in front of him. "You say it is a pattern, that the same forces are at work in the deaths of Evering and some old savage, that it is connected to the battle at Stony Run. You offer a detailed scientific review of Evering's corpse, but you decline to adopt the vicar's view of the puzzle in the compass room. I fail to see how this restores the balance in the Company." The patron's gaze drifted out the window to the settlement's newest structure, a threadbare tent, and he frowned again.

In the early morning new travelers, unwelcome to Ramsey, had arrived. A tall, gray-bearded man had stopped Duncan, asking for Reverend Arnold. After five minutes of conversation, he had introduced himself as Reverend Zettlemeyer, a Moravian missionary who had brought in survivors of raids on a dozen homesteads. Ramsey had offered them the tent, which he had ordered to be erected at the far side of the fields. With the battered settlers had come half a dozen red-coated soldiers, fresh from New York, who to Ramsey had been even less welcome than the settlers.

"The ritual at the compass," Duncan explained, "was capable of many interpretations. The Reverend saw it as the work of a London professor, but the Reverend himself is the product of a proper English education, like Evering. He gave," Duncan said, struggling for words, acutely aware that if pushed too far they would shut him out and decree their own solution, "the proper interpretation for a learned and moral man." Arnold appeared confused for a moment, then offered an uncertain nod. "But what if the killer had not been blessed with such a refined education?" The ritual, he had begun to realize, hung over Arnold and Ramsey more heavily than the actual murder of Evering.

"You suggest the killer had already taken Evering's life before performing the ghastly ritual?"

"I am suggesting the bones could represent those who died at Stony Run, the salt a sign of the salt lick near the battle site. The claw and eye could say that something powerful is still watching, still at work, set on determining the outcome. The buckle might indicate the soldiers who fell. The feather was that of a warrior, representing the Indians who died. Someone was saying the battle for Stony Run is not over. Someone was warning of retribution. Someone," he suggested, "who had been there, at Stony Run."

Lord Ramsey, strangely, closed his eyes for a moment, clutching the arms of his chair. "You can't know that. You don't know that. The feather could not have been from an Indian. The ship was coming from England, not America. And you fail to mention the bloody heart."

"I thought it prudent not to dwell on the heart. It was a different kind of statement, against the Ramsey Company."

"Ridiculous!" snapped Arnold.

Duncan reached into his pocket and dropped the smashed pendant on the papers in front of Ramsey. "This was stuffed in an artery."

Arnold seemed about to protest when Ramsey picked up the piece of mangled silver and dropped it into his palm, staring at it forlornly.

"Captain Woolford would confirm it," Duncan added, "and my words about the feather."

The statement seemed to snap Ramsey out of his sudden melancholy. "Surely you did not tell Woolford all this."

"Not yet. But Reverend Arnold did request that I report to both him and the captain."

"That was when we were still on board ship," Arnold quickly amended. "The troubles began with the death of Professor Evering," he observed. "He had no possible connection to the events at Stony Run."

"You're mistaken. He knew about it, knew of its secrets."

"Impossible."

Ramsey, pacing again, stopped at the north-facing window, gazing resentfully at the red-jacketed men now walking along his street as if on patrol.

"He wrote about it," Duncan explained. "There was a journal."

Arnold's face went as stiff as his starched collar, and he advanced on Duncan, leaning so close Duncan could feel the vicar's breath. "What journal?"

"It was not just scientific notes he kept."

"I must have it!" Arnold demanded.

"It was left in the city," Duncan said. "But I shall append a statement to the report. I will sign a witness oath, attesting that Professor Evering had an informant. A member of the Company gave him a secret about the army at Stony Run, then not long afterwards the professor was killed. We would be remiss not to recall that half the men in the Company served in the army."

"We will need your real report," Arnold interjected. "We cannot embark onto this dangerous ground on such a capricious basis. And you have neglected to reference the seditious statements of the Scottish prisoners."

"But this is the report that serves the Company best," Duncan urged, "one that above all you want the military to glimpse. It concludes the murders relate to military intrigue, not a concern of the Company. It allows the Company to avoid a scandal. The army has failed to explain what happened that day at Stony Run. There was a battle, but they failed to report any traces of the enemy. One could suggest they have obscured the truth. The Company is victim as much as those who have died. Someone seeks revenge for what was done there, or to correct a wrong committed there, someone with secret knowledge of what happened that day. Someone," Duncan added, "with cause to seek out the shaman Tashgua."

In the stillness that suddenly seized the room, Duncan heard the distant bellow of an ox. Ramsey rose, stepped to the window, staring at the forest a moment, then turned toward Duncan with an expectant look.

"We will direct the report only to the governor," Duncan continued. "If you sent it directly to the general he would be suspicious. The governor will want Calder to secretly see it, both to put the general in obligation for the favor and to gauge his reaction to it. They must both be aware that what happened at Stony Run is unresolved. We will suggest the murderers' work is not complete, that the intrigue begun at Stony Run has not run its course, that someone apparently seeks to stop the Ramsey Company's work on the frontier, and that the only reason must be that they do not want an English victory in the war. The governor will have to thank you for bringing this to his attention. The general will have to volunteer that the army will address the matter. The military has its own courts, private courts. The weight of a hanging is lifted from the Company."

"What if Lister is the killer after all?" Ramsey asked in a tentative voice. "You have directed attention away from him. Yet you have not proven he is innocent."

"It is not the role of a court to prove the innocence of every man, only the guilt of one. Mr. Lister had no real evidence against him except his unexplained appearance in Evering's cabin. A sworn statement with the report explains he was there at someone else's request."

"Your statement. Your request," Arnold pointed out.

"The statement of your scientific expert, saying he was there to assist with the science of Evering's death. You cannot accept my statements for one purpose and reject them for another. I would pledge my life on his innocence."

"Or at least your liberty," Arnold rejoined in a smoldering tone. The vicar turned to Ramsey. "Surely this is too inflammatory, my lord. To incite the army unnecessarily serves no purpose."

But Ramsey was staring again at the red-coated trespassers past his barn. "Why would the army dance to your song?" he asked. His eyes were working fast now, studying Duncan one moment, Arnold the next.

"The proposal only succeeds," Duncan said, silently thanking the patron for providing the opening he had been longing for, "if the general does indeed know a black deed was hidden at Stony Run. Then he knows that continuing to obscure it will cloud his political aspirations. Calder thought he would intimidate the Ramsey Company by suggesting that I would trip over the events at Stony Run, as if we, too, had something to hide. But we are not so frightened by the truth as he should be. He will never expect the Company to be so bold as to shift the play back to him. As the ancient Greeks showed us," Duncan declared, his sober gaze on Ramsey, "in war, surprise is everything. This is a shrewd and defiant move declaring to those who matter in this colony that the Ramsey Company shall be neither subordinate nor beholden to the army."

Ramsey leaned back into his chair with a distant expression as he gazed out the window toward the dark forest beyond the river. Arnold stepped to the tea tray and hastily poured himself a cup.

"You have reason to resent the army, if I am not mistaken," Ramsey observed in a tentative tone. He rose and slowly paced along his bookshelves.

"I will not shy from embarrassing them."

"But what you suggest could be construed as practicing trickery on the army." A dangerous smile grew on Ramsey's face. "The governor may wonder about our motives."

"You will provide proof of the army's motive by pointing out that the war hinges on the loyalty of the Iroquois, that the death of so many of them at Stony Run needs to be resolved. The obvious conclusion is that secret French agents were at work. It would not be exaggeration to suggest a traitor is at work. It would be motive enough for the army to lie, to keep their actions in shadow, clearly motive enough for more lives to be taken.

"You will prove your loyalty," Duncan continued, "by pledging that you will not speak publicly of this embarrassment to His Majesty's government, by assuring him that you would never openly suggest someone in Calder's command is capable of hiding traitorous activity. It takes a powerful man to keep a powerful secret."

Ramsey stopped his pacing and turned to face Duncan again, his eyes lit with a new energy. "If I were Calder learning of this report, what would I do?"

"I would end my preoccupation with the Ramsey Company," Duncan said. "Because any act against the Company's interest only strengthens our allegations. I would take steps to assure the governor that the king's enemies are the sole focus of my efforts, lest anyone suspect that personal ambition was afoot."

Ramsey absently ran his fingers along the spines of his leather-bound books. "To call upon you to teach my children," he said in a contemplative tone, "that is the greatest test of your own loyalty."

"Sir?" Something in the atmosphere had shifted. There was a scent of invitation in Ramsey's words.

Ramsey faced Duncan. "We do the work of empire here. We are the empire here. Great things shall be done, great rewards bestowed. The world I give to my children will be vastly different from what you see here. England the way it should be, without any of its faults or ambiguities. I will share with you a secret few understand. The name of Ramsey will soon ring throughout the land. The Ramseys and those who stood by them shall be celebrated in histories read by generations to come."

Duncan glanced at Arnold, half expecting the vicar to utter an *Amen.* "We shall provide answers about human nature," Arnold said instead.

"The savages must be driven from the land, must they not?" Ramsey demanded.

The question hung in the air as Duncan tried to make sense of the abrupt shifts in their conversation. "Yes, sir," he said at last.

"The science of man must be brought to the land," Ramsey said.

"Yes, sir," Duncan repeated in a tight voice.

"And the rule of God and his laws."

"Yes, sir," Duncan echoed, grasping his part in Ramsey's liturgy.

"I asked Reverend Arnold to explain every detail of that day in the storm. You were surely a dead man when you leapt into the sea. But you reappeared, with the eldest of my children in your arms. What did you see, what did you feel in that dark water? Did you not sense the fingers of God cradling you?" Ramsey asked with an odd glint of hope in his voice.

"All I remember," Duncan said, "is waking in a prison cell, cold and shivering."

Ramsey seemed to relish the answer. "Job, too, had to endure great suffering to appreciate the role the Almighty had granted him. Eventually you shall recall what happened to you in the water, when destiny put its hand upon you, and you must record it for the Company archives."

Duncan found his gaze drifting out the window, toward the men laboring in the muddy fields. He would never feel so unclean as he did now, standing there in Lord Ramsey's library. There were two other new arrivals, for that morning McGregor had appeared, escorting one of the Company men who had also gone with Hawkins into the forest, a younger man wearing a crazed, hollow expression. The man had become useless in the forest, his sensibilities in some kind of shock. Duncan clenched his jaw and fixed the patron with a level stare. He may not know his role in the drama that was unfolding, but he certainly knew what Ramsey wanted to hear, and it was no struggle to speak ill of the army. "We will not allow mere generals the upper hand in the events of the day," he declared.

Ramsey's eyes narrowed. Arnold, seeming to sense a cue, rose and shut the library door.

"When you issue your report to the governor, you will show him that one company of Ramsey men is more effective than ten companies of soldiers," Duncan concluded, beating down his shame.

Ramsey stepped to the big desk, gesturing Duncan to turn away as he opened its hinged top. Duncan heard a series of drawers slide open. The patron was accessing a locked compartment, he knew, a paper safe often built into such desks and opened by positioning the small interior drawers in a designated arrangement. After a moment Ramsey cleared his throat, and Duncan turned to see him holding a rolled sheet of vellum. With a triumphant look, he motioned Duncan closer and unrolled the document on the desk. Its script was elegant, the scrollwork along its borders intricate and colored with rich hues, like an illuminated manuscript. But Duncan's gaze quickly settled on the huge ribboned seal at the bottom, beside a date only three months earlier.

"The king himself," Ramsey declared with a conspiratorial air, lifting a map from the desktop and laying it on the arm of his desk chair. A massive tract was outlined in red. "Ten thousand square miles. Much of the colony to the west, all the way to the great inland seas that feed the Saint Lawrence. The king wants it to be ours."

Duncan's heart seemed to wither as he watched the thin smile form on Ramsey's face.

"I am impressed with your usages of death," the English lord declared to him, then stepped back to the tray and poured another cup. "Would you prefer sugar in your tea, Professor McCallum?"

"Carolina." It was the first word Lister spoke when Duncan found him working at one of the new cabins. "It is our answer," the old sailor said, gesturing Duncan out of earshot of his companions. "Hundreds of Scots are there, in the mountains. I hear there are even towns where they speak only the old tongue. Sometimes the smith talks as he works. Last year some Scots in thrall to Ramsey fled south and made it, out of the reach of his dogs. Scots go there to be free, far from the law. Cameron's been collecting canoes on the river above town. We can take one, get to the Delaware, and follow it to Philadelphia, work a ship to Charleston."

"You mean us to flee?"

"I mean for us to live. Yesterday a wagon arrived at the carpenter's shed. I watched them unload fifty muskets. Bars of lead, powder horns, bullet molds, all stowed and locked in the shed. Lord Ramsey, he is taking us into the war somehow."

Duncan studied the great house. There was movement in an upstairs window. The woman using Sarah Ramsey's name was staring into the forest again. He had begun to feel somehow victimized by her. He had saved an impostor. "Woolford's pack is on a bench in the barn," he said. The ranger had disappeared two days earlier. "I must speak with him."

"He ate by the south well with Fitch, then walked into the woods near there."

Duncan followed the perimeter of the fields below the house, pausing frequently to peer uneasily into the forest. This was not the western bank, he kept telling himself, this was a thinned, tamed forest. Lifting a heavy stick for a weapon, he ventured slowly under the trees, turning frequently to assure he kept the huge barn in sight. It took nearly an hour of nervous forays into the shadows for him to discover the clearing, three hundred yards beyond the fields. Under the boughs of several huge beech trees, four logs had been arranged in a square, in the center of which was not a fire pit, as Duncan expected, but a three-foot-high platform made of long, flat stones stacked on top of one another. The scene had been set many years earlier. The benches showed signs of rot; the stones of the cairn were covered with lichen. Seedlings sprouted in the square around the cairn.

A solitary figure in green sat on one of the logs, his rifle beside him, staring at the stacked stones as if waiting for something to climb out of them. Woolford, looking exhausted, did not glance up until Duncan was a few feet away, then reacted with a small frown and gazed back at the cairn.

"They say that in the last century, the tribes and early settlers made places like this near every settlement." The ranger's voice seemed drained of emotion. "They say old Penn and the Quakers visited them often, to speak with the chiefs. Few could speak both English and the tongues of the tribes, but there was far less bloodshed. Now that we can speak with one another, all we want to do is kill one another."

"It is a meeting place, then?" Duncan asked as he sat beside Woolford.

"The Edge of the Woods place is what the tribes call it. Old Jacob and Hendrick used to tell of such ceremonies they joined as young warriors. It is where those who came out of the woods met those not of the woods. Those who came from afar would talk about the difficulties of their journey, to show the sacrifice made for the sake of discourse among peoples, speaking loudly so the messengers in the trees would hear.

"Each chief would hold a wampum belt to underscore the importance, to show the truth of his words. It was also done between tribes, before Europeans came. The host would symbolically wipe the sweat from the traveler's limbs and pretend to pull thorns from his feet, then clean the eyes and ears and mouth, to be certain all would be clearly understood. Sometimes evil spirits would follow from deep in the woods, and words had to be said to drive them away."

Duncan looked about again. He had arrived at the edge of the woods, Sarah had said when Duncan had arrived, and earned the unspoken censure of her father for using the words. "A wampum belt?" he asked, not sure why he was whispering. He gazed upward, into the dense, glittering canopy supported by the broad grey columns of the beeches. It was as if they were in a cathedral.

Woolford replied by standing and stepping to the stone platform. With both hands he pushed back the heavy stone on top, and Duncan joined to help lean it against the stack. The long, narrow stones underneath had been crisscrossed to form a hollow in the center. From the compartment Woolford lifted a bundle of leather, unfolded it, and extracted a four-inch-wide belt of small beads, strung in intricate patterns. As he unfolded it to its full three-foot length, Duncan saw that the background of one half was made of white beads, its many figures depicted in purple, and the other half was of purple background, with white figures. Between the two squares at either end were the shapes of men and women, houses, deer, and axes, with a tree at the center.

"It is their way of saying important things, of sending important messages," the ranger explained. "When they hold such a belt, they can only speak the truth."

"What does this one say?" Duncan realized he had seen such beads before, or one such bead, in the empty sack on Old Jacob's belt, and recalled the alarmed way Woolford had stared at the single purple bead.

"I don't know. I've never seen one like it." Woolford seemed shaken, more worried than Duncan had seen him yet.

In the silence that followed, Duncan recalled the reason he had sought Woolford. "Hawkins took several of the men. Where did they go?"

For once, the ranger offered a direct answer. "We followed their tracks ten miles upriver. They joined others, with three canoes. Not far north, one man climbed out on the opposite bank. Fitch started to follow him, but then two more bodies came floating down the river. Settlers, dead several days. We dug graves instead."

Duncan found himself looking toward the river. It was like wilderness kept coughing up the dead. "They call Hawkins a trapper."

"He started making his living by taking fur pelts, years ago. Mink, otter, beaver, marten. He would boast about how he devised traps that did not kill right away, that would only pin them, sometimes for days, until he had the time to personally cut their throats. Now he sells his finely honed skills to the highest bidder."

"Including the army?"

"The highest bidder," Woolford repeated.

"Is he going to Stony Run?"

Woolford offered no reply.

"If you seek the murderers from Stony Run, Captain, tell me why you keep coming back to Edentown?"

"This belt," Woolford replied in a voice gone melancholy, "may be the closest I've come to an answer. The tribes are very wary of words, and whom they give them to. They believe in showing, not telling," he added as he studied the belt again.

"Last night in my classroom I made two lists on my slateboard," Duncan revealed after a long silence. "On the one side it said *salt, evil eye, bee, iron, Scottish cross, deiseal circuit.*"

"*Deiseal?*"

Duncan paused to explain the meaning of each in Highland tradition. "Beside that list I wrote another: *bird skulls, wolf clan arrow, beaver, crooked man, crooked tree, painted feather, bear.* I could add *wampum beads.*" He explained what Jonathan had shown him that morning.

Woolford grew very quiet.

"Since the day Evering died, a dialogue has been under way, using mystical signs of the Highlands and the Iroquois. It isn't so much the pattern of violence that holds the key, it is the pattern of that conversation."

Woolford had closed his eyes. "A bear," he said. "Why did you list a bear?"

Duncan was not ready to speak about the stone bear that had been rescued by Adam from Woolford's trunk, or the nightmare he had suffered the night before, of Adam tossing the stone bear between blood-soaked hands. "On the road past the inn," he said instead, "a baby bear was executed on a rope, the day Jacob died."

Woolford looked as if he had been struck. "Why did you not tell me this?"

"Why," Duncan rejoined, "would I think you needed to know?

What is it about a bear that frightens those who have fought in the wilderness?"

Duncan watched with unsettling confusion as the ranger closed his hand into a fist, tapped his heart, then, with two fingers pointed up, made a spiraling motion toward the sky. "What it is about a bear," Woolford whispered, "can never be spoken."

Duncan pulled out the brass cylinder he had taken from Ramsey's safe room and dangled it before Woolford. "Then speak about this."

"A case for slow match," the ranger said absently, his gaze back on the wampum belt. "Grenadiers carry them, usually on their chest straps. Not many grenade bombs are used over here, but grenadiers still carry the cases. It's part of their tradition, part of their official uniform." Duncan's inquiry finally seemed to register with him, and he looked up. "Where did you find it?"

"In the forest," Duncan lied. "One of those soldiers must have dropped it."

Woolford frowned, then took the metal case, staring at it. "They're infantry sent from New York town, not grenadiers," he said with a puzzled expression, then pocketed the case. He stood and carried the belt back to the stone pillar, pausing before setting it back inside.

"Is it a call to war?" Duncan asked.

"They send what they call a black belt for war. All purple." The ranger seemed to reconsider. "I don't know. Fitch says Iroquois camps are being systematically raided, small groups are being killed in secret. The raiders use canoes so we can't track them. The tribes may be calling a war council, keeping it secret from the army. But this belt, it has the messages all mixed. War, death, women, prisoners, celebration. Fitch met some warriors north of here. They were excited, on edge. They used words he had never heard before. He says they seemed to be speaking about miracles, or signs from spirits that had been long sleeping. A miracle of the water, one of the earth, one of the sky. Nothing makes sense."

Duncan pointed to the tree in the center of the belt. "It looks like it has a stick man at the top."

"A man in a tree." The tension in the ranger's voice seemed to say it was the sign that worried him most of all. "Some in the Six use it to indicate a prophet. A man in a tree. A crown of antlers."

"Antlers?"

"Deer antlers, tied in a circle with vines. A tribute paid to prophets."

Duncan studied the belt, and Woolford's troubled gaze. "It could have been here for years."

"No," the officer said. "I always check when I arrive here. I don't really know why." When he turned to Duncan, his face was clouded with worry. "The cairn was empty three days ago." He set the belt inside and covered it. "Go back to town, McCallum. You'll never understand this."

"I've seen a crown of antlers," Duncan confessed to the ranger's back as Woolford lifted his rifle to leave. The officer turned, leaning on his gun, as Duncan began explaining about Evering the dead prophet.

Duncan stared at the blank slate in the schoolhouse for an hour, knowing he must plan lessons for the Ramsey children, unable to think of anything but his strange conversation with Woolford. Giving up, he found Frasier sitting on a shaving horse in the shade of the barn, working with a drawknife to make trunnels, wooden nails, while the men prepared for the evening meal. The sullen young keeper took no notice of Duncan as he finished rounding a trunnel out of a narrow split of ash, offered no thanks when Duncan handed him another splint to clamp and trim.

"Iron's hard to come by in Edentown," Duncan observed in an even voice. "At the rate you're using it, you'll be pulling up the floors of the great house for their nails."

Frasier missed the placement of a stroke and sliced away a quarter of the split, ruining the trunnel. He still said nothing as he tossed it aside and accepted another from Duncan.

"My grandmother and I used to make the old crosses with pebbles when I was a boy," Duncan offered. "And she always cut holes in her eggshells."

"It's all been a lie," the youth declared suddenly. "All the evils of the old country were going to be left behind, they told us. But here is where the demons of the world all are born."

"Who told you that?"

"One who knows. One who's seen them roast men alive and eat their flesh."

"Hawkins? When did you speak with him?" Duncan asked.

"I should have finished that hole on the ship," Frasier declared in a chilling tone. "Here we just wait between the demons and the English."

"Where is Hawkins?"

"Fighting the demons. He at least understands the job before us, Cameron says."

"Cameron?"

"Aye. Mr. Cameron brought rum out for Hawkins and his men. They shared stories."

"What kind of stories?"

"About the responsibility of Christian men when they meet the heathen."

A shiver ran down Duncan's back. He had never asked Cameron what he had done after his family had been slain. A man like Cameron was not one to turn the other cheek.

"When you see Hawkins next, pose him some riddles," Duncan suggested. "Ask when was the last time the army paid him money, Frasier. Ask him what he did with our body snatchers. Ask if bears ever follow him in the forest."

Frasier's face clouded, but he remained silent, working the drawknife.

They worked without speaking, Duncan extending the splits when the young keeper reached for them.

"Did you see who made those other signs by the house?" Duncan finally asked. "Beside your cross."

Frasier clamped his jaw as tight as the bench vise and kept working.

"A house spoon broken into pieces. There is only one member of the Company who has worked in the kitchen. One who knows the wisdom of the eggshells." It was a very old practice, nearly forgotten by the time his grandmother was a girl, but there were still those who believed witches could magically turn eggshells into vessels that would transport them through air and water.

"I care not if I am stripped of my rank as a keeper," Frasier proclaimed.

Duncan took a moment to understand. "I have no reason to speak to Lord Ramsey of this. All I wish is that you be sure of your demons before acting against them. The boy found the crosses. He thinks they are to keep the savages away. But I searched the front of the house. There's iron in two trees and hidden in the piles of dirt along the porch. You weren't aiming them at the Indians. You were trying to contain something inside the house."

"My aunt used to explain things to me and my cousins, in a small room sealed with a ring of salt. She said people like us, we are blessed with vision that others never find. When we see the evil, we must fight it, one demon at a time." Frasier kept working but glanced toward the great house. He wasn't worried about being reported to Ramsey but about whether his iron would stay in place. "They say you are responsible for freeing Lister," the youth offered in a grudging tone.

"He did not kill the professor." Frasier had always preferred his own theory, Duncan recalled. And his banshee had moved into the great house.

"When you stole onto the second floor, what did you see?"

"Witches owe their powers to charms. My aunt told me of one who had a blue bone, another with a black hen that was the source of her powers. Destroy them and the witch shrivels to dust."

"She's little more than a girl, Frasier."

"You would protect her? You did not know her true color the day you pulled her from the sea. But now—"

"I still do not know," Duncan confessed. Though he had begun to resent the way the truth seemed to be bent around Sarah, he also could not put out of his mind the frightened, wounded way she looked at the forest. He had not forgotten the words spoken by Woolford at the tavern. Because he had saved her, he was responsible for her. "You still have not said what you found in the house."

When Frasier did not reply, Duncan leaned closer to his ear. "Ox shoes. In the far north stall of the barn. All the oxen here have been shod. There is a box with old ox shoes. Good iron. No one will miss them. But lift no hand against the lass," he warned.

Frasier studied him solemnly for a moment before speaking. "Cameron. What I found was Cameron going through things in Reverend Arnold's private chamber."

"What things?"

"At the vicar's bedside table. Lifting his hairbrush. Going through his pockets."

"For what?"

"Surely ye know the way of those creatures. She must have him in thrall, by some enchantment. He was helping her. He was collecting hairs and threads."

Duncan closed his eyes a moment. A person's hairs, like threads from their clothes, were used by witches to cast spells upon them. "You think Cameron is working against the Company?"

Frasier lowered his drawknife. "Cameron has his secrets. He tells everyone he was in the militia. He never mentions that afterwards he was in the regular army. But Sergeant Fitch remembers him, says he fought at Ticonderoga."

"But he went back to Scotland, started a new life."

"A tinker came through yesterday. Cameron was asking him about ships sailing to England, whether there were more in Philadelphia or New York."

The young Scot kept working the knife along the wood. "The professor was going to show me his comet this summer, below the Big Dipper," he said after making two more trunnels, his voice now melancholy. "Adam was going to show me how to tan a deer hide. He said slippers of soft buckskin would be an admirable gift to send my aunt." Frasier cast an awkward glance at Duncan.

"I miss them also," Duncan offered.

"That last night before he died, I let him linger at the rail to watch the sunset," the young keeper explained. "He watched the dusk like he had never seen one before. When darkness fell, I touched his arm to go below. He didn't move at first, but he spoke toward the waves. 'I have seen things no man ever should have to see,' he said, then he looked at me. 'There are promises made,' he told me, 'which if broken will end all good things ever again. 'Tis a rare great thing to be honored with such a bond,' he said, and should I ever be so fortunate, I was not to shy from the blessing." Frasier was not only the youngest of the keepers, he was the youngest of all the prisoners, and never before had he seemed so like a lost boy. His voice trembled when he spoke again. "I made a promise, too, the night after Adam died. I promised to the stars that I would find revenge. Because he saved my life, with his singing." Frasier seemed unable to look into Duncan's face. "The English mean for all of us to die. But I know how to slice open Ramsey's hull now. And I know better than to stop this time."

A chill ran down Duncan's back.

A bell started ringing, signaling the evening meal. Without another word, Frasier rose from the bench and was gone.

The next morning before dawn, after a night of restless, uneven sleep, Duncan discovered a note pinned to his door, folded and fastened with a wax seal. *The children will be here six weeks,* it said. *I require a plan of instruction. Geography. Mathematics. Classical history. Much of philosophy and, of course, the biblical lessons. Aristotle. Aquinas. None of the atheist Hume, nor of the traitorous Swift. Prepare for us to review tomorrow at tea. R.* Under the note was a dog-eared volume of Plato's *Republic,* in which Ramsey's cherished philosopher described the perfect state as one run by an educated elite, supported by professional functionaries.

Duncan crumbled the paper in his hand, squeezed it into a ball, and hurled it into the cold fireplace.

He had provided for Ramsey a carefully worded version of the deaths of Evering and Old Jacob, which the great lord could exaggerate to gain leverage over the army. But Duncan was no closer to understanding what had happened to the two dead men, only more certain that the threat continued, that Ramsey was capable of turning it into a nightmare for all of them, and that even if he had been able to stop Lister's hanging, Duncan could never serve such a man as Ramsey for seven years. He gazed out the window toward the forge, Lister's empty cage. He had freed the old Scot, as his grandfather would have done. And now Lister had given him a way for them both to be free. Carolina. The frail hope that had entered Lister's voice when he had mentioned the place made Duncan's heart ache. Lister was right. They had to flee. If ever there was to be a new clan, they had to run, and elude Hawkins and the hounds.

His gaze drifted back to the crumpled note. Why would Ramsey say the children were staying for six weeks? Crispin had said they would stay through summer, twelve weeks at least. He leafed through the Plato, fighting the emotion that boiled under his skin. The Ramsey shackles could not have felt more real if there had been iron around his feet. He slammed the book shut, gazed emptily into the cold fireplace, then rose and left the building, walking away from the town, toward the open fields. He sat on a stump for several minutes, watching frolicking lambs, then absently strolled along the animal pens, pausing to gaze at the young pigs as he chewed again on Frasier's words. *The English mean for all of us to die.* In freeing Lister he may have begun to act like a clan chief, but the Company of Scots still faced some unknown doom if he could not resolve its mysteries.

"Men say ye be like a doctor or such." The words came like a frigid blade along his spine. He looked up into a gaunt scarecrow face over soiled buckskins.

Duncan did not move as Hawkins stepped to his side, in front of the pigs. Strangely, he held a young rabbit, small enough to fit in his palm. Duncan recalled seeing a nest under a log at the edge of the wheat field.

"I've had training in—" he began, before realizing the trapper was not interested in a reply. Duncan put a step between them, placing himself out of the range of the man's sinewy arms.

"It be truly amazin', the things that spill out when ye gut a man." Hawkins spoke in a level, casual voice, his narrow eyes aimed like gun barrels at Duncan. "There's some in the tribes that collects parts, string up a necklace of ears or such. Must be of the medical persuasion, too. Onc't I saw a string of men's privates." Hawkins raised the terrified rabbit and stared into its eyes. "Hell," he said with a cold laugh, "onc't I saw a savage cut open a prisoner's belly, pull out his breakfast, and feed it to his dog as the man watched." He stroked the rabbit's neck with a finger. The creature quieted, settling into his palm.

"What do you collect, Mr. Hawkins?" Duncan asked in a brittle voice.

"Prayers," Hawkins replied in a whisper, grinning, "the last sounds the dying make." With that, the rabbit uttered a shuddering cry, cut off by a snap of bone.

Duncan looked down to see the little rabbit limp, its neck broken between two of the trapper's fingers. Hawkins tossed the body into the pen. Instantly three pigs began a tug of war with the still warm creature, ripping it into pieces and devouring them. Duncan stared numbly at the little patch of blood on the dirt before looking up. Hawkins was gone.

Shaken, he found his way back to the schoolhouse, reviewing the events of the past days. He had done nothing to provoke Hawkins. Except tell Frasier to ask certain questions. Opening the book he had left on the table, he read again, read until the hairs on his neck rose and he snapped his head up. Captain Woolford had materialized ten feet away.

"Do you have any idea of the damage you have caused?" Woolford demanded. The odor of brandy reached Duncan even before the ranger advanced a step, leaning forward as if about to pounce.

Duncan had never seen such wildness in the officer's eyes. "Major Pike only considered you a nuisance before, a possible link to your brother. Now he will revile you as much as your brother. Calder will have no choice but to send more men west. You have forced him to move the regular troops, to make a show for the governor."

"I did not expect your reaction so quickly. How did you discover what I wrote?"

"The original was dispatched yesterday on a swift horse. Before it left a copy was transcribed."

Duncan had seen a figure at the dining table, with quill and paper. Crispin. "Before, there was a chance of finding answers. Now you have unleashed a pack of mad dogs, banishing every chance of a ranger having a quiet dialogue with any Indian within two hundred miles. And it will take them but a few moments to realize that if the army was responsible for Evering's death, there was only one member of the army on board the ship. If Calder decides to look for a quick solution, it will be my head he offers."

"I am pleased to have finally gotten your attention, Captain. Perhaps you will finally admit that the paths you and I follow are the same? The murders of Evering and Jacob, the death of Adam Munroe, are all rooted in what happened at Stony Run. You are trying to find justice for the massacre at Stony Run. My mystery and yours have the same answer. And finding it is now as urgent for you as for myself."

Woolford, suddenly unsteady, dropped onto one of the students' stools. "You will never understand. You cannot understand."

"I understand more than when I arrived a few days ago. I understand not to touch a bear or a snake. I understand the army and the Ramsey Company are rivals somehow. I understand that a woman pretending to be a dead girl is at the eye of the storm. I understand what it means to have your people destroyed by an oppressor."

Woolford, elbows on the table, buried his face in his hands. "When the army first sent me to America eight years ago, no one dared go into the forests. Everyone had heard stories of savages who ripped out your liver and ate it as you died. I was ordered to join a militia scouting party in the winter. Our leader and half the others drowned when our canoe went over a waterfall. We were lost and starving and it began to snow. One man froze to death. A Mohawk family found us more dead than alive. Two of their men lost toes to frostbite while carrying us back to their village. King Hendrick's village. More snow came, eight or nine feet of it. We spent two months with them. They taught me their language, taught me the ways of the forest. I watched as they prayed to their spirit world. I played with their children, helped with their dead. When I came back to the settlements, I signed on as a ranger."

"What really happened at Stony Run?"

Woolford took a long time to answer. When he finally spoke, he faced the fireplace. "The leaders of the tribes see the future hurling at them, forcing them to new ways, and they don't know what path to take. Tashgua was arguing that the Iroquois should end their involvement in the war, that the tribes needed to go back to the old ways, before muskets and silver coins and whiskey. Ten of the most important chiefs agreed to meet him, to take part in his ceremony to reach the mother spirit. Where they went, no one was allowed to take weapons."

Woolford fell silent, and rose to face the window before continuing. "I discovered the bodies, every chief but Tashgua, and many of those who travel with Tashgua as his guard."

"Pike was there?"

"Came in behind me, hours later."

"Fitch showed me a piece of tartan."

"At least three of the dead were deserted soldiers."

"From the Black Watch?"

Woolford nodded. "They had taken up new lives with Tashgua's band. I saw to it they were taken back with their fellow warriors."

"Without telling Pike," Duncan said.

"He would have strung them up for the crows. That's when I sent a squad out for reconnaissance. They never returned. Two days later I found them dead, every man. General Calder's report said they were killed by French Indians, Huron or Abenaki. But each of their guns still held its priming. My men would not have faced the enemy without firing a shot."

"But why, if you were trying to find the killers, would you suddenly leave for England?"

Resentment filled Woolford's eyes. "I took leave because there was a surviving witness."

Duncan grew very still. The realization came out in a hoarse whisper. "Adam Munroe." *I have seen things no man ever should have to see,* Adam had told Frasier. He gazed back into the cold fireplace, the haunting words of Frasier echoing in his mind. He had to find the young keeper, had to make him reveal what he knew that could destroy the Company, had to make him understand the danger he was in if he spoke about Adam to anyone else. A dozen more questions for the ranger sprang to mind.

But when he looked up, Woolford was gone. A motion outside caught his eye. Cameron walked past the barn, carrying a heavy sack on his shoulder. No, Duncan saw, as he sprang to his feet, it was a limp man.

He found the big Scot in the open bay of the forge, locking the padlock of the crib. Blood stained the front of his shirt. "Will be no doubts this time," Cameron growled as he saw Duncan. "Every man in the Company will want to see him swing."

Duncan pushed past the keeper, struggling to see inside the makeshift cell. "Who—" Duncan began, then his tongue withered as he saw the checkerboard scars on the man's exposed shoulder.

"Mr. Lister. The bastard killed young Frasier."

Chapter Nine

RASIER'S FACE WAS FROZEN IN a twisted grin, as if the melancholy young Scot had thought his assailant had been offering a joke. But the prank had included a heavy, blunt object that had been slammed so hard into the side of his head that it had flattened the cartilage of his ear into his skull and knocked several teeth from his broken jaw.

"A commander," came a brittle voice over Duncan's shoulder. "That's what they call these big hammers." He turned to see Cameron holding one of the long-handled wooden mallets used to pound logs into place in the new cabins. Its head was a tattered cross-section of log ten inches wide.

"Look at him," Cameron spat. "The young fool treated Lister like an uncle. Wouldn't have suspected ill of him even when the commander was raised over his head."

"You can't know it was Lister."

"Not just me. It was four of us who found him, sitting there beside the boy, muttering in the old tongue, his hands shaking, trying to put the teeth back into the boy's jaw."

"An act of mercy, not the act of a killer." *I know how to slice open Ramsey's hull now,* the youth had said hours earlier.

"At his side was the great hammer, with his own bloody handprints upon its handle. And things taken from the young one's pockets lying at his knee. With Mr. Evering gone, you should be the one to write the letter to his family, McCallum."

Duncan's gaze lingered for a moment on the heavy tool. For a second time, murder had been done with a hammer.

"What things?" Duncan asked. An angry crowd of Company men was gathering, uttering indistinct oaths, spitting toward the forge, some facing the dead keeper and making the sign of the cross on their chests.

Cameron pointed to a flat rock six feet away that held a few coins, several nails, and a set of ox shoes.

"You moved the body?"

"Mr. Lister would not let go of the boy when we approached. There was a wee struggle."

For the first time Duncan noticed a pool of blood on the ground. Frasier had no open wound, only blood slowly oozing out of his mouth and nose. "Why was Lister away from the barracks in the night? He was under special watch."

"The work party came in late, by torchlight. Everyone washed up in the basins by the door, grabbed food on the way to bed. When I checked, Lister was on his pallet. So I thought. But he had stuffed sacks under his blanket."

Duncan surveyed the frightened faces before him, then fixed Cameron with a level stare. "Meet me with bandages at the forge," he said.

"Like hell," Cameron spat. "The murderer is proven and there's the end to it."

"I have not explained to Reverend Arnold who looted Woolford's chest on the ship, but he would still listen with rapt attention. They know at least one of their trunks was also sabotaged. No doubt Lord Ramsey, too, would find it of interest. He longs to assert his powers as magistrate. And then there is the matter of your communicating with the army."

Cameron pulled a plug of tobacco from his pocket, cut its end, and stuffed the piece into his mouth, all the while fixing Duncan with a cold, assessing stare. Without another word, he turned and walked toward the great house.

Lister was lying on his back in the coal bin, his eyes closed. From the quick irregular breathing Duncan knew he was not sleeping. "Where are your injuries?" he asked quietly.

The hoarse laughter that came from the shadows caused Duncan to shudder. "Cameron and I had a bit of a frolic. He took it unkindly when I tripped him, so he used that commander on me ankle. A few days of idleness will be just the thing."

"Why, Mr. Lister, why did you leave the Company quarters last night?" Duncan inquired.

"The birds. I told ye before, every day I've been here the birds have sung as the sun rises, and flowers open. I watched from here, all those days. 'Tis the hour the light penetrates deepest into the wall of the western forest. Yesterday, the birds there stopped singing."

"You violated Ramsey's orders so you could watch the sun rise?"

"'Tisn't poetry I refer to, Clan McCallum. The sun rose, the flowers opened. No birds sang."

Duncan's mouth went tinder dry. "You mean someone was in the woods, watching the town," he said in a low whisper.

"More than one, I'd say. There's raiding parties, Indians led by French, more settlers being scalped every day. If you open the door of the barn loft, you can see from the fields to the river in the moonlight. Those who run the Company are blind. They keep all those guns locked away at night, with nary a guard along the river. From the loft door I could slide down a rope when trouble comes."

"And do what?"

"To swing down and run to the schoolhouse would take but a moment. If we were quick about it, we could slip away in the confusion of battle, to the Delaware and Philadelphia. With luck they will think us killed in the fighting."

"Did someone from across the river attack Frasier?" Duncan looked back toward where the body lay, now surrounded by men. From the place he had died, it was a toss of a stone to the river.

"The river had mist over it, spilling up the banks. A shadow was moving at its edge, but it never came out past the alders."

"They found you kneeling beside him."

"Like I said, I was in the loft. I heard low voices in the gray light before dawn. Then there was the sound like a brick on a melon, and someone gave a laugh."

"A laugh?"

"Not exactly a laugh. More like a satisfied grunt. When I got there the lad was crumpled in the grass, his life's breath already gone from him."

"What did you seek in his pockets?"

Lister took a long moment to answer the question. "I told you I had been asked to prepare Evering's body when he died. I didn't do it alone. Frasier was with me."

"Frasier took something of Evering's?"

"Both of us. The professor had a box of dried flowers."

"I saw it. I was grateful for the thistle you took from it. And Frasier?"

"A pretty thing. I think he thought to save it for his aunt." Lister shifted, reaching into a pocket, then handed Duncan a three-inch-wide rectangular object through the slats of the crib. "The lad meant no harm. When a sailor dies on a ship, those who clean him for burial get to take some small thing from the man's kit. But the Ramsey Company is not so forgiving. I would not have him called a thief o'er his grave. The lad was nurtured on great fears, thrown out into a harsh world too early."

The object was covered with a yellow and red pattern of dyed porcupine quills, like Duncan's medallion, shaped into a sheath for a small blade, but the deerskin backing was stretched over a rigid metal object. Duncan looked up at Lister, wondering if he understood. "It was taken from Woolford's trunk," he explained.

"I supposed as much. But it was there in Evering's cabin, in a little hollow in the beam. I think Adam gave it to the professor."

The lacing on the back revealed brass. Duncan grabbed a small chisel from the anvil and worked at the leather thongs, releasing the metal into his palm. He stared at it in stunned silence. It was a brass buckle, with a *4* and a *2* set on its front. The Forty-second Regiment of Foot. Jamie's regiment.

"Who did Frasier see yesterday?"

"He was in a state, ye might say. Always so sad, always so frightened. Yesterday, when we broke for rest at the palisade, he said Reverend Arnold was right, the Indians are spawn of the devil, that the Company be on a crusade, that the answer was for Reverend Arnold and as many other clergymen that could be found to be sent with bars of iron to a place called Stony Run."

Duncan's head shot up and he strained to see Lister's face. "Why Stony Run?"

"Hawkins. Frasier spoke with him when he was here, got drunk with him in the barn that night. Hawkins told him Stony Run was where Satan himself waited. Frasier said Woolford was a ranger, which meant he had Indian friends. He said Woolford left the ship early to meet one, to arrange for Arnold and you to be murdered by that arrow. He said, saving Sergeant Fitch, every damned soldier and all the English could be butchered by the heathen and the world be better for it. He spoke with Fitch often, said Fitch was the only sane man in the army. He said the way to destroy a man like Ramsey was to destroy what he coveted most. Then at dusk last night he took a blade from the saw pit."

"A saw? And did what with it?"

"Hid it in the barn, as best I could tell. Came out of the barn without it, then he spied Hawkins by the cooper's shed, and the two of them argued. Why the burn?" Lister asked.

But Duncan had no answer.

Cameron appeared and unlocked the narrow crib door. Duncan made him stay to witness his work as he pulled away Lister's bloody shoe. The skin over the ankle was scraped and bloody. The bones were shattered. Lister would never walk the same again. "I'll need splints from the cooper's shed." Cameron, sensing the cold fury in Duncan's voice, did not protest. "And a crock of rum."

Crispin tried to stop Duncan when he approached the library an hour later, but then seemed to see something in Duncan's eyes and relented. "There's no need to hold him," Duncan declared to Ramsey's back. The manor lord was writing at his cherry desk, its folding top open, revealing its pigeonholes stuffed with papers.

"Plato. I have been giving this considerable thought," Ramsey said, his head rising but not turning. "We must dose them heavily with the father of all philosophers. A man who understood the practical aspects of power."

"Kneeling by a body does not make a man a killer. His bloody prints on the hammer mean nothing. The blood came from Lister, when Cameron struggled with him. You could not have Lister for the prior murders, so to ease your embarrassment you take him for this one."

"An uncharitable suggestion," a thin voice interjected. Arnold was sitting in the wing-backed chair by the window, reading a news journal. "Your term as administrator of murders lapsed yesterday. It is time to focus on your duties to the children."

"You said once you could have no cloud over the Company," Duncan said.

"Our duty to justice is unwavering," Ramsey said with a distracted air, then paused and scribbled on a paper as if to record the thought. "Our noble philosopher reminds us that the particular expertise of those in government lies in constantly adjusting the balance of social affairs, without being seen to do so."

"Plato wasn't living with a company of Scottish prisoners beside a wilderness of savages," Duncan observed in a taut voice.

Ramsey frowned. "Last week we had two challenges before us: how to keep the army out of our affairs and how to establish our moral authority over the Company. You gave us the perfect script for the first. Now young Frasier's death gives us the perfect opportunity for the second." Ramsey stood and paced in front of the window. "We still needed to confront the fact that Mr. Lister lied about his identity. No one would resort to such deception without a criminal motive. Whether he seeks to hurt our cause because of

Jacobite sedition or because he is paid by the French is all the same to us. In dealing with our enemies, we need look no further than the Old Testament."

"You know Evering sent letters for Lister as well," Arnold interjected, "though we never examined them closely."

"Because you never believed him to be a Scot."

"Exactly," Arnold said, as if Duncan had proven his point.

"He's just an old sailor." Duncan heard the helplessness in his own voice.

"Did you know the crime for which he was condemned in England?" Impatience was creeping into Arnold's tone. "He accosted an army officer trying to stop a barroom brawl. Left him unconscious and fled. But his former captain testified to his character, leaving him a candidate for a trusted position in the Company. Only now do we realize the larger deception. A pattern of violent conduct against British authority."

"We dispatched your excellent report," Ramsey said. "The governor will hear of Professor McCallum. Without you, that particular victory would not have been possible. Now, as Reverend Arnold suggests, you must move to the greater challenges of the Ramsey heirs."

The words pinched at something inside Duncan. He grew very still, and cold. "What will become of Mr. Lister?" he asked, staring toward his feet.

"A trial. First we must build a proper judge's bench and prisoner dock. I am sending for carpenters and joiners from Philadelphia. Unfortunately, we may not break in a new gibbet without a warrant from the governor," Ramsey noted with chagrin. "It could be two or three months before the trap door swings."

Duncan felt numb. "But there will be a trial?"

"An excellent trial, a grand event," Ramsey said, new enthusiasm in his voice. "Attended by all the Company, all the settlers on Ramsey lands. I shall issue a detailed judgment for publication in New York and Philadelphia. The good reverend has suggested that we open on a Sunday, after services, so the proper tone is set. I shall read from the Greeks in my opening, about the solemn responsibilities of all citizens to stay true to their destined duties. The general, of course, will have to abstain from interfering, thanks to your insightful report, McCallum. I commend you. None of this could have been possible without you."

Duncan was not aware of setting out for a destination, did not really understand why he went to his room and retrieved the stone bear, was so lost in his peculiar mix of shame and fury that he paid little attention to where his feet were taking him until he was passing through the thicket that walled the secret cemetery.

Strangely, for no reason he could articulate, the place had begun to take on the air of a sanctuary. He stood before the tombstone with Sarah's name on it, feeling an inexplicable urge to say something. Here lay the real Sarah. Here was the true starting place of the mysteries that swirled about the Ramsey Company. The men of the Company were in the path of a cyclone that had been building its fury for a dozen years. He knelt and began pulling weeds from the base of the stone. When he had cleared the grave, he noticed small white flowers blooming nearby, and with a stick he dug several up and planted them on the mound. Kneeling on the fresh earth, he stared at the dates and the little angel above, touching it, clearing out the remaining dirt accumulated in the carving. Here at least was something he understood. A child cut down by mindless savages. He had had a brother, barely six years old, lost in the bloodbath after Culloden. He felt he should pray, but knew not what to pray for. At last, fighting a trembling that abruptly seized his hands, he buried the bear at the base of the grave and rose, backing away.

His gaze was on the forge all the way back to town, until, a hundred feet away from it, he saw Reverend Arnold standing at the entry to the cooper's shed, his makeshift chapel. As he watched, Arnold took a step in, then out, and repeated the motions, an uncertain torment twisting his features.

The vicar blocked the door when Duncan tried to enter. "Lord Ramsey awaits your plan of instruction," Arnold asserted.

"Surely he would recognize the need for divine inspiration," Duncan shot back, and slipped through the doorway.

It was a small, dim chamber, which Duncan had visited only once before, barely large enough to hold thirty men tightly packed on the benches that lined the walls. The only light came from the narrow, rough-hewn table used as an altar, which held two candles and a small stack of prayer books. But the brass cross Duncan had seen earlier had been replaced.

"A prank," Arnold declared in an uncertain, worried voice. "A papist Highlander prank."

In the place of the brass cross were two long bones, joined together with a thin leather string, resting not directly on the table but on a lush animal pelt.

"I don't recall any Catholics," Duncan observed as he approached the table, "who use beaver fur and bone on their altars."

"We've seen these pagan rites before," Arnold said, his voice gathering strength now, "the first time a murder stained the Company."

"Before, you agreed it was not Mr. Lister."

Arnold turned his pale, hard face toward Duncan. "Before, I agreed it was better for the Ramsey Company to blame the army."

Arnold, Duncan recalled, had once said they were going to provide the answers to human nature. But he had never mentioned what the questions were. "The last time, they seemed to be calling on the devil. This time, they seem to be calling on God."

"They are mocking our God," Arnold said. He had not moved from the doorway. "There was a Bible. Who would steal a Bible?"

Duncan warily lifted the cross, surprised by the thought that there was a simple, natural beauty to it.

"I'd say 'twas more like they wanted two gods to get acquainted," a dry, raspy voice observed.

Duncan turned. In the corner, in the shadow behind the door, sat Sergeant Fitch. The grizzle-faced ranger looked bone tired, but his eyes were lit with a strange excitement.

"Who would do this?" Duncan asked as Fitch rose and approached.

"Like nothing I've ever seen before," the ranger said. "If two spirits were coming from different worlds to meet," he added in a contemplative tone, "I reckon this would be their Edge of the Woods place. Sometimes they seek to exchange hostages. They be offering to exchange gods as hostages."

The words seemed to stun Arnold as much as Duncan. The vicar, his face pale as a sheet, backed out of the building.

Fitch, a look of wonder on his face, seemed not to hear when Duncan asked him if he had seen Indians in the barnyard. He left the sergeant staring at the altar and returned to the forge.

> *Come on me brave seamen that plows on the main,*
> *Give ear to me story I'm true to maintain . . . .*

The dimly lit figure inside the coal crib kept singing until Duncan tapped a post.

"Edentown be paradise indeed," the old Scot said, leaning toward Duncan with the clink of chains. "I lay about all day out of the hot sun."

"You said Frasier and Hawkins argued. Could you hear about what?"

"The boy spoke softly, too low for me to hear. He was excited, seemed to want to tell Hawkins urgent news. But Hawkins cursed him, said the boy needed some rum. Frasier spoke again, something about treason. Hawkins slapped him like a misbehaving child, then left the lad staring at the ground. Later, when no one was about, the boy walked around the barn three times, sunwise." A *deiseal* circuit. Frasier was seeing demons everywhere. But Hawkins was the wrong demon to cross.

"I'll tell you a secret, Clan McCallum," Lister whispered after a moment's silence. "I got sent to the Company for a scrape with an army officer. But ten years ago I was ashore, back home visiting what was left of me family, when a lieutenant of the Royal Navy came to press me last two young cousins for service. When we argued, he drew his sword and slashed one of the boys on his arm, saying we were not permitted to decline the king's desire. I knocked the blade from his hand, but the fool pulled a pistol. I jumped him, the gun went off, and the ball pierced his heart. We threw his body in the sea. It were a noose for me for certain, but the boat his party came in capsized on the return with all hands lost. Everyone just assumed he was lost at sea. So I've been cheating the rope ever since. My account is overdue."

"You didn't kill Evering or Frasier. You didn't murder anyone."

"I see their faces in dreams, me father and those who died on Culloden moor. I never should have lied about me name, never turned me back on who I was," Lister said in a hollow voice. "Used to be once a month, but now the dreams come every night. I was meant to die by English hands at Culloden. I cheated them all by lying and running away to sea, and that be the plain way of it."

They had reached the truth of it, Duncan realized. It was why Lister had so readily revealed his secret Highland roots to Duncan, why he was ready to accept the noose, not for killing an English officer years earlier but for abandoning his clan and the Highland ways.

They sat in silence. Doves cooed in the barn next door.

"There's autumn flowers sprouting along the edge of the fields," Duncan said. "I saw thistles." Through the slats of the crib Duncan saw a sad grin form on Lister's lips. "One day we're going to build a cabin on the side of a mountain in Carolina, you and me and any Scot who wants to join us. We'll plant thistles for the joy of it and speak the old tongue all day, dance a jig all night."

Again Lister took a long time to answer. "It's the New World, lad," the old sailor said in a flat voice. "Find yourself a new kind of dream."

"I already have a dream," Duncan said. "You gave it to me. And now it's burnt too deep to walk away from. I vow you will not hang, Mr. Lister. You gave me my life that day on the mast. A sad wretch I would be if I did not return the favor." What was it Adam had told Frasier? *There are promises made which, if broken, will end all good things forever.*

From the shadows on the far side of the schoolhouse came the laugh of a young girl. Duncan rose. "What happened to them, your two cousins?" he asked before stepping away.

"Bonny lads, both of them. The only joy of their mother's vexed heart. A different press gang caught up with them a month later. They both died when their frigate was sunk by the French off Brest."

Duncan found Virginia sitting on a stump beyond the school-house, watching her brother throw pebbles at pieces of broken crockery lined up on a bench. Jonathan wore a sober air as he aimed his missiles, his younger sister calling out in amusement whenever he hit one of the targets. Duncan settled beside the girl, watching her brother. It wasn't just solemnity on the boy's counte-nance. There was fear, even anguish. He did not respond with glee when he hit the crockery, but with a flash of something that might have been called hatred.

After several minutes Duncan invited them to see their new class-room. Asking which of the small tables they would choose for their own, they each took a side table, leaving the center of the three empty, each glancing at it nervously.

"Where is Sarah today?" Duncan asked.

"Father and the vicar," Virginia offered in a grown-up voice. "They fret so about her. Reverend Arnold reads the Bible to her for an hour each day."

As she spoke, one of the housemaids called the children's names from the porch of the great house. "Father's giving us music lessons," the girl announced brightly, then gathered her skirt and skipped away, with Jonathan a few steps behind, marching like a soldier.

Duncan quickly stuffed a piece of paper and a stick of writing lead in his shirt, slipped into the barn to retrieve one of the spare ax handles leaning against the wall, and found his way to the ceremonial ground, the Edge of the Woods place. He lowered himself onto one of the log benches, his heart racing, and clutched his makeshift weapon. Never in his life had he been frightened of the wild, until now.

A twig snapped and he fought an urge to dart back to the fields, then saw it was one of the small, brown, spotted creatures Crispin called a chipmunk. He stared into the canopy, calming himself, then stepped to the stones in the center of the clearing. The Indians were

savages, but those same savages, at least some of them, held ceremonies like those of the church and seemed to have reverence for
the truth, had something about them that stirred a battle-hardened
man like Sergeant Fitch.

He paced about the stone platform and then, feeling like a violator
in a temple, slid the stone from the top. He stared inside the compartment, then studied the forest, his heart thumping again. The
wampum belt was there, but beside it someone had lain a bundle of
feathers and fur tied with a single string of beads. His heart rose up in
his throat as he surveyed the forest around him again. An Indian had
been there, half a mile from his own bed, in the past twenty-four
hours, and now he was intruding into that Indian's secrets.

Extracting the paper, Duncan began to carefully replicate on it
the shapes on the belt he had first examined with Woolford. A
square at either end; figures of men holding axes; a large tree
topped by a man in the center; several small *X* shapes with the top
of each *X* connected, alternating with animal shapes. The figures
were meaningless to him. But they meant something to someone
at the settlement. When he finished, he extracted from his waistcoat the pages he had taken from Evering's journal and read every
line again, attempting to decipher even the many lines that been
crossed out. The pages were mostly filled with Evering's maudlin
verses, some further describing Sarah as she slept, others reflecting
what seemed to be Evering's growing unease about landing in
America. Duncan kept returning to several lines that seemed to be
premises for poems never written. *If dreams transport you to the other
world and you dream two months without waking, would you not try to
stay on the other side forever?* the professor had asked. Then, under a
series of *X*s meant to obliterate the words, Evering's chilling version
of an old children's rhyme. *There was a crooked man who climbed a
crooked tree. He found a crooked promise and kissed the crooked sea.*

The thought of Evering caused him to lift his head toward the
river. He returned the belt to the cairn, then stepped toward the
water. Duncan kept learning from Evering, long after his death, as if

the scholar were speaking to him from the spirit world. He found himself on the riverbank, gripping his fear, and stepped into the water.

The crooked face of the effigy seemed to be staring directly at him when he arrived under the hemlock on the island. Almost nothing had changed since his first visit, except the crown of antlers was in front of Evering now, with several feathers leaning against it. In one of the professor's twig hands was a little stick, four inches long, with a single strand of beads attached to one end. Several notches had been cut into the stick. With mounting fear Duncan lifted the stick and its beads away. With a shudder he discovered what it was that was frightening him even more than on his first visit. Evering's watch was ticking.

He backed up several steps and examined the beads on the stick. They were white and purple, arranged in a pattern of two purple and one white, the same as in the strand around the new bundle in the cairn; the same, he suddenly realized, as one of the oval lines drawn by Jacob the Fish in his dying message. The old Mahican had been sending a wampum message, without the beads.

An hour later Duncan sat on the school steps, making notes in the late afternoon sun, when suddenly a figure erupted from behind the cooper's shed, stumbling, steadied by an older man who was pushing him forward. They walked along the wall of the building, disappearing around its far side. When they reappeared, Duncan put down his papers and stood, stealing along the shadows for a better look.

It was McGregor and the other Company prisoner who had been brought back, the man still wearing the same mindless, numb expression he had worn when he had appeared from the forest. On the third round, Duncan realized the two men were making a *deiseal* circuit around Arnold's makeshift church.

"What was his sin?" Duncan asked a Company man who watched the ritual uneasily.

"Killed a snake with an ax," the man replied in a perplexed tone. "Old Fitch had a fit. Broke off the ax head and tossed it in the forge to melt. McGregor said he knew a way to make things right."

Duncan waited for McGregor and his companion to finish their circuits, then reached the old Scot as the two men, finished, stepped to a drinking trough. "What happened out there with Hawkins?" he asked.

The old Scot swallowed hard before answering. "We came upon a farm where everyone had been killed, days earlier. Blood everywhere, the bodies in pieces, picked by the crows. That night we stayed with a Welshman who sold us rum, who told us tales of the heathen, said if we kept going upriver the Huron would take us home and hang us up alive for meat, slicing off pieces for their stew pots."

"But that was where Hawkins was taking you? Upriver?"

"I don't know. Yes. They're not coming back. Over there, in the forest, it's like being thrown into the ocean not knowing how to swim. For four days, this one," he said, indicating the younger convict with him, "never slept. 'Tain't right, McCallum, 'tain't for people like us to—" The Scot's voice trailed off as the younger man wandered away into the makeshift chapel. "Hawkins, he left the boy on the trail, weeping like a babe, so weak he couldn't walk. I told Hawkins the boy was Ramsey property, that he couldn't be wasted like that without accounting to the great laird." McGregor shook his head. "He sneaks into the chapel when e're he can. I'll have to drag him out again, a'fore Reverend Arnold hears."

"Hears what?"

"His prayer, always the same prayer. *May I die soon,* he says, *may I die quick.*" With a sigh McGregor stepped toward the chapel.

Duncan returned to the schoolhouse steps, keeping an eye on the men who walked along the muddy paths of the town until he spied a compact, sinewy figure in green. Fitch entered the barn and was sharpening his hand ax on a grindstone when Duncan approached and silently took over the turning of the handle. The sergeant nodded and continued working the blade with grim determination. A Company worker appeared with a spade to grind, and backed away as he saw Fitch. The men treated the sergeant like some kind of wild beast that sometimes prowled in their midst.

"The Indians use codes in their beads," Duncan said after a minute. He extended the strand of beads on the stick with his free hand. "Jacob used the same code."

Fitch paused, testing his blade with a callused thumb, glancing at the beads. "This used to be their land. Even if Ramsey offered to pay for it, which he didn't, they wouldn't understand. Their brains can't fit around the idea that men can own land."

"Who exactly uses such codes?"

"The Six," the sergeant said toward the trees, then turned to Duncan. "Each of the Six Nations has its own bead pattern, to identify it in messages. Four strands, with two purple and one white, that be Onondaga. They are the central tribe, the keepers of tradition, the ones charged with watching over sacred things. The ones with the most powerful shaman."

"Tashgua, you mean."

"He was born Onondaga. But he lives apart now, away from the Iroquois towns, with his own band, has for years. Like a band of roaming warrior priests, protecting the old ways."

"But there are soldiers here. Surely hostiles won't move about with the soldiers so close."

"Gone, with the last of the settlers, worn out by Ramsey hospitality. There was a farmer named William Wells, with a place not many miles north. Killed and scalped two days ago, but his place wasn't burnt, so those settlers went there. And the troops were just a small patrol, due to go back soon."

Duncan examined the stick again. "It has ten notches. What does that mean?"

"It's a council stick, lad. A religious council. An Indian shaman wants to talk. Ten notches means in ten days."

"Are you saying it's an invitation?"

"If 'twere given to an Indian, that's what it would be."

"Where? Where is this council?"

"If you have to ask that," Fitch replied, "then I reckon it ain't intended for you." He rose and pushed the tomahawk into his belt.

"Given recent events, I reckon 'tis the last place any sane Christian wants to be."

Duncan put a hand on his arm as the sergeant took a step away. "Adam Munroe was supposed to be with the Company. He would have known how to read the beads."

Fitch looked away. "Aye," he confirmed in a reluctant tone.

"Because he was a ghostwalker," Duncan ventured. "Because he was a prisoner of the Indians," he added in a questioning tone.

Fitch frowned. "Ghostwalker's just a name for the pitiful souls who are brought back, not Indian but no longer exactly European either. Most of them move about without purpose, having lost the way of themselves."

"How long was he a prisoner?"

"There was an expedition of Pennsylvania militia three years ago. He was one of those who did not come back," Fitch added, then hurried away.

Adam had trusted Duncan with the stone bear, he had said, because Duncan was becoming a ghostwalker. For a horrible instant he thought Adam meant he was to be captured by the savages, then he understood. Duncan was between worlds, too, able to see certain true things because his true people were lost. He looked down at the notched stick. *It ain't intended for you,* Fitch had said. But maybe it was. The old Ramsey tutor had given it to a new one.

It was dusk when Duncan returned to the schoolroom. Dropping the paper with the drawing of the belt onto the table with his other clues, he stared at them all, arms folded on the table, until his head dropped into his arms and he slept.

When he awoke, a nearly full moon had risen. He unlatched the door and sat on the stone step, watching the sky, his thoughts constantly drawn toward the old Scot in the makeshift cell. Finally he rose and stepped inside to his bedchamber. Pulling out the sea bag he had brought from the ship, he extracted the clothing and reached into the bottom, removing the tattered, stained muslin bag that held his most precious possession. Holding the bag tightly to his chest, he stepped outside. He studied the forge a moment, then stepped away from it, walking hurriedly over the open ground, slowly finding his way through the laurel thicket until he reached the overgrown cemetery. As he reached into the sack, his heart gave a sudden lurch, and he stood unmoving, overwhelmed with emotion. The intricately crafted pipes had been handed down through his family for at least two hundred years, but they had been lovingly cared for, left to him by the old uncle who had sought refuge with Duncan, secretly kept for him by one of his Scottish professors who had visited him in prison and then appeared in the courtroom when he had been sentenced to transportation.

Slowly, methodically, sitting on one of the ruined cabin walls, Duncan prepared the instrument, flooded with memories of his grandfather playing and teaching him with the same pipes. Finally, the bladder bulging with air, the reeds wetted and reset, the drones tuned as best he could manage, he clamped the blow-stick in his teeth and grasped the chanter. He was out of practice, but the fingering came back quickly. His grandfather had taught him many lonesome ballads of the Highlands and the seafaring island folk, and Duncan played all he could recall, each song releasing him further from the guilt and hopelessness he felt in the Ramsey compound. Long-dead scenes opened in his mind, of his mother dancing with him in the kitchen as his father played small music, of his grandfather offering a solemn *pibroch* to bless the fishermen each spring before they set out on the treacherous Hebrides waters. His heart thundered, and a new energy reached his piping. He was rowing with his grandfather on a calm sea as the old man piped to the whales and seals. He was at one of the joyful Highland weddings, where men who smelled of heather and peat piped all night by a bonfire and girls danced over swords.

Duncan did not know how long he played, how long he had been transported to the country, and clan, of his youth, but when

he had finished, he brimmed with unexpected tranquility, a light-
ness of heart he had not known for months, perhaps years. He
returned the pipes to their sack, then carefully laid the bag inside a
hollow log by Sarah's stone, stuffing the end with moss. He entered
the night-still paths of Edentown boldly, buoyed by his unexpected
contentment, and had begun to circle the barn, hoping to come up
on the back of the forge so he might whisper to Lister, when a
murmur abruptly stopped him.

His heart seemed to shudder. Impossible, he told himself. A trick of
the mind. The lack of sleep, or perhaps the lingering effect of the
piping affected his senses. He pushed a hand against his temple to drive
away the strange working of memory and guilt that had overtaken his
brain. The voice of mad Flora had entered his mind and would not
leave. He shook his head sharply once, twice, then drew in a deep
breath before taking another step. The voice faded but came back,
stronger, and unmistakable. Flora was speaking to him, using the alien,
sibilant language that had so mesmerized him on the ship. But Flora
was gone, hundreds of miles away, back on the high seas by now.

He moved through the shadows as if in a dream, until he saw a candle
lantern that had been hung from a peg in the center aisle of the barn.
Impossibly, the phantom was there, sitting cross-legged in the pool of
light with her back to him; the heads of the horses extended beyond
their stall doors, and the animals seemed to be listening attentively. It
was all a dream. He had to be dreaming. His consciousness had surrendered to his guilt. Her long, dark hair flowed down the blanket she had
wrapped around her shoulders. The way she spoke the strange syllables, which echoed in his memory every night, left no doubt. The
phantom was Flora, his murderess, whose hand he had held in the dark.

"*Haudenosaunee! Haudenosaunee!*" came the chant. "*Ohkwari!*"

She seemed to be addressing someone, though she spoke toward
the oak plank wall. Her head bent lower and lower, as if she were
falling into a trance, and Duncan ventured closer, fifteen feet away,
then ten, and still she spoke her strange tongue without seeming to
notice him. Finally the Flora of his nightmares would have a face.

But as he took another step, a hand closed around his arm. He turned to see Crispin beside him, wearing a haunted, frightened expression. The big man gripped him so tightly it hurt, pulling him backward, not making a sound. Suddenly the chanting stopped and the woman turned, shot upright, lifting the blanket over her head, and fled into the shadows. But in that instant Duncan had glimpsed her face.

"Sarah!" he gasped.

A shadow appeared at the opposite end of the barn and intercepted the girl, pulling her toward the fields. Duncan, too, felt himself led away, his mind roiling with contradiction. He found himself seated on a low stool in one of the oak-planked tool rooms at the back of the barn, lit by a solitary candle, and looked up into the tortured countenance of Crispin.

"I've been so blind," Duncan groaned, sinking his head into his hands. His slender certainties were in ashes. Everything he had concluded about the murders, everything he had done since the storm on the ship, had to be reconsidered, every piece of the puzzle dismantled. "It's her grave out there after all," he said. "But she didn't die."

"They thought so," Crispin whispered. "They truly thought so, for a dozen years, and her mother mourned her every day, had the children pray for her soul. The bodies had been mutilated, many burnt to the bone."

"Instead, she was taken."

"Sometimes they make slaves of children," Crispin's voice cracked as he spoke.

Duncan felt again the despair he had first experienced at the grave, only deeper now. He felt as if he would weep at any moment, as he thought of the beautiful, gentle girl Sarah must have been as a six-year-old, and the horror she must have suffered with the savages, wrenched away from the world, deprived of all mercy, love, and hope. "A ghostwalker," Duncan said with a chill, and the word had an odd, biting texture on his tongue. Sarah's sickness had a name after all. She was one of the wretched souls who had returned from the purgatory of captivity, having lost all connection to the civilized world.

The heavy door swung open and Woolford entered. "The sergeant has her," he assured Crispin. "She weeps."

"It's how it goes," Crispin said in a tormented voice. "She has one of her spells, then she cries, then she goes very still, as if paralyzed, nothing moving but her eyes and lips, whispering those words of hers. Usually at night, the hours before dawn. At first, last fall, she did it every night. Her father caned her until she stopped, shouting he would beat the savage out of her. Tonight I watched her door for three hours but drifted off. Then the piping started. She was at the bottom of the stairs already when I woke, disappeared into the night in the seconds it took me to reach the door."

"You're saying she went outside because of me?" Duncan asked. "That she . . . went into her spell," he said, borrowing Crispin's words for lack of better, "because of the pipes?"

"I will not say why she does anything, only that the pipes sounded and she slipped away to speak those words. But why the barn? Why here, with all the woods about?" Crispin asked Woolford, who only shook his head. "Too many already call her witch," Crispin added. "If the men find her like this . . . ." His voice grew too weak to finish the sentence.

Duncan searched the ranger's face. "You found her at Stony Run," he ventured.

Woolford sighed, glanced at Crispin, and nodded. "She was unconscious when Pike's men discovered her in the brush, tended by two other white captives who would not leave her. Some of the senior officers at the camp knew the Ramseys. She was the spitting image of her mother, and around her neck she still wore a Ramsey locket, wrapped in fur. She had lost nearly all her English, wouldn't sleep on a bed the first month."

"You should have told me."

"No!" Crispin insisted. "Lord Ramsey forbade anyone from speaking of it. At first I did not think he could bear the shame of it. How could one of the greatest families in all the empire have it known that their eldest had been a slave to the savages for a dozen years, that she had become little more than a savage herself? How could she inherit, how could she be respected by the landed families? How could she have a life of her own? I would not speak of it, even if Lord Ramsey had said nothing, for her sake. Nor should you, by all that's holy. God only knows the horrors they commited . . . . It's bad enough without more talk of it. You've seen the way the people in the settlements look at her."

"What happened after she was found?" Duncan's confusion was quickly giving way to shame. He had begun to think of her as an impostor, had clung to his memory of the faceless Flora while resenting Sarah, when in fact the woman who had touched him so deeply on the cell deck and the troubled Ramsey daughter were one and the same.

"Some of us won't speak of it for fear of what it will do to the girl," Woolford confessed. "All the others won't for fear of the girl herself."

"Surely there is nothing to fear from Sarah," Duncan said.

Crispin seemed surprised at Duncan's words. "When she was brought out of the woods, she carried a stick, a club really, with bear claws fastened into it like thorns, strips of fur hanging from it. She shook it at people and they grew ill. That's when people began calling her a witch."

"She had been taken from the one whom even the Indians fear," Woolford added in a low voice, fixing Duncan with a pointed gaze.

It took a moment for Duncan to understand. "Tashgua," he said with a shudder. Sarah may not be a witch, but she had been enslaved to one.

"The army left her at the Moravian mission in the north," Crispin explained. "She wouldn't leave, so we went there, taught her how to be English again. Sometimes she would call out in the night, make noises like animals. We stayed with her for weeks, then took her to the city. Even then I would have to sit and hold her hand, sometimes for hours."

Duncan remembered the way Crispin always quieted nervous

horses. "Adam Munroe was one of the others with her? He was at the mission?"

"Gone by the time we arrived. He had been in the militia, captured by Hurons who traded him to some Ohio Indians, who then traded him to the band that held Sarah. The army wanted to learn secrets from him, about the tribes, but he fled."

"And after another month in New York town, she ran away to Argyll to hide with Adam."

"We thought she had gone north," Crispin explained, "to be with the other Indian captive she had been rescued with, the one who had stayed at the German mission. Lord Ramsey and Reverend Arnold spent days with him, speaking about her, about their lives with the tribes, trying to understand her, to understand what she might be doing, then he had a mental collapse and stopped speaking. I stayed in New York, asking questions wherever I could. A boatman remembered rowing a woman in a cloak to a ship in the night, bound for Glasgow on a dawn tide, saying she was returning home after visiting relatives in Albany. Major Pike came to the house, demanding to know where Adam Munroe had gone. I didn't know, I told him. But I told Reverend Arnold that Adam said his home was in a place called Argyll."

"So Arnold went to look for her in Scotland," he said to Woolford. "Where you were already looking for Adam."

Woolford cracked open the door. "It is a dangerous night for such discussions," he observed in a voice heavy with warning.

"When exactly," Duncan asked, "did Lord Ramsey decide to recruit a company of prisoners?"

"Last autumn," Woolford replied.

"After Sarah fled," Duncan concluded, "after Ramsey spent time speaking with the other ghostwalker about her time with the tribes, after his hate for the Iroquois began burning as hot as his feeling for the French."

"You are dabbling in what some would consider affairs of state. Treacherous ground for an indentured servant."

"A danger I readily accept when others dabble with the life of an old man and an innocent girl. What is Ramsey going to do with an armed company of men?"

"Defend his land," Woolford said.

"Fifty men for ten thousand square miles?"

"Ridiculous. He has only ten thousand acres."

"Arnold did not only cross the Atlantic for Sarah," Duncan explained. "I have seen the charter he brought from the king. All the lands to the great lakes in the west."

Woolford eased the door shut and stepped to Duncan's side. "Impossible."

Duncan quickly explained what Ramsey had shown him.

The ranger reacted as if he had been kicked. "He and Calder both aspire to be governor," he said in a hollow voice. "With that land Ramsey would have by far the stronger claim." Woolford looked at Duncan. "But he can't take the land. It belongs to the tribes."

The chamber went deathly still. Somewhere in the distance an animal brayed.

It was Duncan who broke the silence. "Calder has his own means of taking the land, by building forts across the territory. Ramsey accomplishes things more subtly. By bargain and bribe."

"God preserve us," Woolford said with something like a moan. "The charter would be meaningless with the tribes still on the land. The king wants them to compete, and let the one who expands the colony westward be the victor." A darkness fell over his face, and his warrior's eyes returned. When the ranger spoke again it was in a worried whisper. "There was a new wampum belt this afternoon, another I had never seen before. Fitch was upset by it. He thinks it says the world is going to end at Stony Run in ten days." He spun about and disappeared into the night.

Duncan wanted to ask who would make such a prophesy, then knew it was not necessary. There was indeed a prophet they knew, who would speak with beads. Tashgua, Sarah's former tormenter.

Duncan stared into the darkness, recalling the map he had taken from Ramsey's secret cellar room. "What price would be put on ten thousand miles of virgin land, Crispin?" he asked after a moment.

"Not the lives of his children," Crispin replied in a hoarse voice. "Never the lives of his children."

Duncan stared in surprise at his friend, chilled that the thought would enter his mind. The big man's face swelled with emotion. As his eyes moistened, he stepped into the night.

Duncan followed a moment later, wandering alone across the barnyard in the moonlight. He leaned against a rail fence, drinking in the night air, trying to reconnect the pieces that had fallen apart that night as he stroked the nose of the plow horse that came to investigate him. There could be no denying that the Company had been created by Ramsey to help cement his land claim, though Duncan could not see how, or his own role in it, despite Calder calling him Ramsey's secret weapon. Adam and Sarah had apparently discovered their roles and flung themselves into the sea.

He had given Ramsey reason to divert his attention from the Scots in the Company, but Duncan was not so beguiled by his own words to think any of them safe. He had bought time, but seemed no closer to the truth about Jamie or Stony Run. Now his failure to find the truth had meant Frasier's death, and Lister's being prepared for the gallows. His emotions swirled, blocking any rational thought. Flora had been in the barn, was no longer a vague, helpless longing but a flesh-and-blood woman who lived in the great house.

The horse started and as Duncan turned to follow, shadowy forms closed about him. He ducked, twisted, and ran. As he reached the schoolhouse, hands closed on his shoulder, more hands than he could resist, and something slammed into his head. He collapsed, had a vague sense of being caught before hitting the ground, then of being carried. When he recovered his senses, he was in one of the sheds, his hands tied to a beam over his head. In his groggy state, he was not even aware of others present until a spike of pain on his spine jolted him awake.

"What are you—" His protest choked in his throat as the lash hit him again, like a red-hot poker pressed to his skin. Again it hit, and again, shredding his shirt. Five times, ten times.

"You are fortunate," came a slow, refined voice through the darkness, "that we could not bear to have our children's tutor the subject of a public flogging. And we understand how a man of deep feeling can become reckless with his own life. So let us explain what will happen if you demonstrate such seditious tendencies again. We shall select the oldest Highlander remaining among the prisoners, and we shall whip him to an inch of his life. I do not expect you to cease this insolence because you fear me. You will stop because you fear causing your precious Scots more harm." Ramsey's silhouette was barely visible against the moonlight that seeped between the logs. "Be assured, we shall find your wretched pipes, and we shall burn them. You will soon realize how merciful we have been, out of the debt we owed you. And did we mention your Mr. Lister shall be deprived of food for two days?" Ramsey spoke no more, just stood silently as Duncan received five more lashes. He clenched his teeth, determined not to cry out, remembering how Lister had broken three splints of wood when taking forty.

At last the searing stabs ceased, and in a blur of pain Duncan saw a flash of steel as the strap that bound him was cut, heard the shuffle of feet that meant his assailants were gone. He did not know how long he stayed slumped on the ground, fighting the agony, but eventually he staggered outside and dropped beside the barn's water trough, submerging his head, scooping water into his palm and sluicing it down his back. He sensed movement in the shadows, but did not care. If they came again he would resist, he would show Ramsey that not every Scot retreated. The thought reminded him of someone else. He found another ax handle, picked it up, and marched to the forge.

He approached stealthily, his club raised, but found no guard under the dim candle lantern. Tossing his club on the ground, he staggered onto the smith's stool.

"'Twas a bonny thing you did this night, lad," a hoarse voice said through the slats. "Men were listening in the barracks, be sure of it. I ain't felt such joy in years. I didn't think I would ever hear a pipe again."

"You knew it was me?"

"I gathered y'er things on the ship. I kept that brown sack hid away."

A shudder of pain wracked Duncan's body.

"First few hours be the worst, lad. Ye need liniment or grease. Don't let the wounds dry and crack." Duncan heard the sound of chains as Lister inched closer. "And listen to me, listen sharp. I told ye there be Scots, to the south, in the Carolinas. Good Highland men, living far from John Bull. The scars on y'er back will be y'er ticket. Ye must go there, lad. It's y'er only chance. Me bum foot will hold me up, so I'll just have to meet you there. Ye'll n'er survive seven years under this—"

Duncan jerked about as something cold touched his back. A hand closed around his shoulder. "I have liniment," Crispin said. "Hold still. I had prayed Mr. Ramsey had fallen asleep. He did not hear his daughter but he surely heard the music. He held his temper well with you."

"You can be in Charleston in six weeks' time," the old Scot continued.

"Mr. Lister, don't—" Duncan warned.

"This one slips pieces of bread between the logs in the rear," Lister interrupted. "He knows the Carolinas. Black slaves go north to be free. Scottish slaves go south."

"First time I entered one of those settlements, I was frightened," Crispin declared. "Most of the men had hair the color of fire, wore skirts, and spoke in a babble that hurt the ears. They drank hard and laughed a lot. When I came north, I passed through another such village, having a festival. Throwing logs end over end like giants in the hills." Duncan's back arched as the liniment touched it, then he slowly relaxed.

"He would need a pack, Crispin," a soft voice interjected from the shadows. "And food. As much food as he could carry, for he must not take time to stop for it."

"Miss Ramsey!" Crispin gasped.

"Keep quiet or you will alarm the house," Sarah said in a soft, weary voice. As she stepped forward, a pool of bright light appeared before her. She had opened the shade of a lantern in her hand. In her other hand she held a shirt. "I have brought Mr. McCallum a clean shirt from the laundry. Lord Ramsey's, but he owes as much." Her tone became matter-of-fact, all business, giving no evidence of the strange delirium Duncan had seen her in an hour before. Setting the lantern on the anvil, she took the tub of liniment from Crispin and began applying it to Duncan's wounds. "Also some coins, and a tomahawk for cutting firewood," Sarah said in her new, conspiratorial tone. "Not yet, of course. Your back must heal. A map should be made."

"You cannot," Duncan protested.

Sarah hesitated. From the corner of his eye, Duncan saw her lower the medicine tub. "I have heard of another Flora," she declared.

The words reached a place Duncan had not thought she could find, and the ache they brought made him forget for a moment the pain of his lashing. Flora McDonald had become a legend in Scotland for risking her own life to help Prince Charlie escape to a French boat off the Highland coast as his English pursuers closed on him.

Sarah lifted the tub and set to work again. "You forget how much I owe you."

Duncan gripped two slats of the coal crib as another wave of pain wracked his spine. His mind raced. This was the innocent, taciturn daughter of the man who had just flayed his back. No, this was the woman who had been turned into a savage by her Indian captors. No, this was Flora, the melancholy soul who had chanted in the cell next to his and touched his hand in the dark. But now she seemed none of these. The girl who applied the liniment to his torn flesh was a strong, spirited creature who was knowingly defying her father. Somehow he knew he would never understand the mysteries that were enveloping the Company, and threatening Lister with execution, unless he could understand how, and why, all these people seemed to live within Sarah.

"I will not leave Mr. Lister to hang," Duncan declared.

"A fleeing bond servant is sometimes easy to forget," Crispin said. "If Mr. Lister flees, however, they will say it proves his guilt—and an escaped murderer, they are sure to hound."

"He speaks true, Clan McCallum," the old Scot said through the shadows.

"Do you think Mr. Lister guilty?" Duncan asked Sarah, forgetting until the words left his mouth how she reacted to questioning.

Sarah stopped applying the liniment but did not bolt. "No," she said at last. "But if you stay, my father will use him against you."

"This lass is wise," Lister said. "Wait a few days, then disappear."

"I will report you ill," Crispin added, "so you will not be missed for a day or two. There is no war in the south. Scots go there, far from the law. Far from the army," he said in a pointed voice. "They will know about your brother. If Captain McCallum of the Forty-second has half the sense of his brother, he will already be there, with answers for your mysteries."

"I cannot leave," Duncan insisted.

"Then ye be a damned fool," Lister shot back.

"That," Duncan said in a falling voice, "we can take as proven." If he did find the truth in the Carolinas, he would return, even it guaranteed an iron collar for seven years.

Crispin began covering the last of Duncan's wounds. Sarah had melted back into the darkness without a word.

When he returned to the schoolhouse, his room had been ransacked. His pallet was thrown against the wall, and his few articles of clothing were strewn about the room and stepped on by muddy boots. The drawers of the chest all hung open. Duncan pulled the pallet onto the ropes of the bed frame and dropped onto it, belly first, and was instantly lost in slumber.

There was a half day of lessons slated for the morning, and Duncan was up at dawn, silently taking breakfast in the kitchen with the house staff, returning to stand on a wooden box to write the alphabet at the top of the large slate behind his table, pausing every few moments to fight the pain that shot across his back each time he stretched out his arm.

As he rang the bell at eight o'clock, the young Ramsey children bolted out of the great house, Sarah walking a few steps behind, wearing a plain grey dress, its lace collar buttoned tightly around her neck, her hair tied in a ribbon at the back. She offered Duncan a nervous smile and joined her siblings inside, sitting at the small table behind Jonathan and Virginia. They recited the alphabet together, then Duncan invited them to write a word that began with the letter *A*, to gauge how far the younger children had been instructed.

Jonathan and Virginia worked quickly but Sarah stared at the alphabet, pain in her eyes, before laboring over her own slate. After a moment Jonathan held up his board, showing the word *Albany* in careful letters. *Ax*, Virginia had written in a practiced hand. When Duncan stepped to Sarah, her hand trembled, and she pushed the slate away as if it scared her. She had written *Akrn* in crude, misshapen letters, but expertly sketched a tree beside them.

"Excellent," Duncan said, pushing the slate back so her siblings could not see.

He read aloud the remainder of the morning, relieving Sarah of the need to write again. When he dismissed school for the day, she lingered behind.

"My tongue can find the words, but not my fingers," she said, gazing awkwardly at the floor. "My mother taught me before. But it is difficult to bring those things back from so many seasons ago." Her gaze lifted toward the window. A little gray bird perched on the windowsill, looking inside. "I am ashamed."

"There is no shame in the lamb who stumbles at first step."

The hint of a smile flickered on Sarah's face, and she dared to meet Duncan's own gaze for a moment. "Could I learn the songs your mother would sing to us orphan lambs?"

"They were in Gorse, the old Gaelic," Duncan said, not daring to ask why she referred to herself as an orphan. "You have to have an ear for it, like the pipes."

"*Ceol Gaidhlig,*" she said. Gaelic music, in the old tongue.

He stared at her. A question is as good as a bludgeon to her, he reminded himself. She had, after all, spent months with Adam, himself a *Gaidheal,* a Highlander. "You are a never-ending source of mystery, Miss Ramsey. It reminds me of another word. *Haudenosaunee.*"

Sarah noticeably relaxed. "It means people of the longhouse. The Iroquois. The Six, the sergeant calls them."

"Longhouse?"

She picked up the chalk and drew a long structure with a curved roof, explaining how saplings were tied together for the ridge poles and covered with elm bark to make a house, with several hearths inside, one for each family.

"It would be a rare bargain," Duncan proposed, "if for each English word I taught you, you would give me one in Iroquois."

She offered a nervous nod, and he wrote the word *maple.* "The Haudenosaunee do not draw their words," she said, "but I can give you the saying of them." She drew a turtle. "*Anonwara,*" she pronounced, a hint of excitement in her voice.

They worked for another two hours, without lunch, and Sarah's table became covered with papers filled with the words she asked Duncan to spell. *Oak, hemlock, cedar,* and a dozen other trees. *Deer, beaver, eagle, owl, wolf,* beside drawings with his own makeshift spellings of the Indian words she gave him. *Erhar,* dog. *Anokie,* muskrat. *Kenreks,* lion. *Ohskenonton,* deer. As a learner, she was as fleet as a creature of the forest, and for the first time Duncan saw on her countenance something that, if not contentment, was at least satisfaction.

"And *bear?*" Duncan asked.

Sarah hesitated only a moment. "*Ohkwari.*"

It was what she had cried out that first night, in the cells, then again in the barn. *Haudenosaunee,* she had said, then *ohkwari.*

"Your father will have missed you at lunch, Miss Ramsey," he reminded her.

Sarah gave a sour smile. "He takes his lunch privately, at his desk." She looked up. "I am not practiced in the ways of etiquette. But we are not so many years apart. When we are together like this, are we allowed to use our Christian names? Duncan."

"I remember telling you stories of my childhood, Sarah," he ventured.

She stood, and he was sure he had frightened her away, but she stepped to the window. The view of the river and the deep woods seemed to quiet her. "When I left the spar that day, it seemed I was falling forever. I don't remember being in the water. I just awoke in the cell and thought I was in one of the places spirits go to. It was only later in New York that Captain Woolford told me you were the one who saved me." She searched his face as if for an explanation. "You cleaned my grave," she added in hollow whisper, as if it had been another way of saving her life. She leaned into the glow of the window and touched the glass with her fingertips. "I remember so little of my time on the ship. I was always sleeping, or felt as asleep even when awake."

"They dosed you with strong medicine."

"They gave me tea, always bitter teas. My stomach would turn over from it, but they would just give me more. Reverend Arnold explained I was going through a spiritual crisis, and I knew he was right from all the terrible visions I had. He said that it was the hand of Providence at work in me, that going across the ocean in my strange hibernation allowed me to be made anew. They said after you fished me from the water, that the captain insisted I be put in the cell. The vicar was very apologetic. Lord Ramsey said it was the right thing to do, to keep me safe." She stepped back to the desk and began sounding out each of Duncan's written words. *"Beaver . . . deer . . . wolf."*

She did not seem disturbed in the least by her strange confession, or her time in the ship's cell. She had already been a prisoner for twelve years, Duncan reminded himself. A dozen questions leapt to his tongue. When he approached, she glanced up, suddenly wary. He could sense her muscles tensing.

"I regret not getting to know the professor better," he offered. "A learned man of great natural curiosity, especially about the New World."

Sarah ran her fingers through her auburn hair, which at some point had lost its ribbon. In their time together, Duncan realized, a wild, almost ragged look had settled upon her. She had begun to make small twisting movements as if her tight-necked dress had become a straitjacket. "I would wake in my bed and he would be sitting there. There was always someone in the cabin with me, but he was the only one who kept to a chair beside the bed. The others always stayed away, at a table, reading to themselves. He was the only one to realize that in the small hours of the morning I was closest to wakefulness, and he arranged it so he was there in the middle of the night. He diminished my dose, so I would wake and we would talk, in whispers, and he never told the others. He had a daughter who had died of a fever years ago. She would have been my age. He said that God had smiled on him, to allow him the chance to be with me the next few years as I came of age."

Duncan began to get a measure of the fragile balance of their conversation and spoke of his own conversations with the professor, of his respect for the gentle ways of the scholar as much as for his intellect, of Evering's fascination with the night sky and his hoped-for comet. "The storm that day," he said at last, "it was unlike any I had ever seen. I was in the mast when it struck. I heard my grandfather's voice, though he's dead these twenty years."

Sarah gave one of her sad, wise nods, as if not at all surprised. "He brought me tea the night before. Real tea, not medicine tea, for the first time. He said I was well enough to stay up all night with him, that the day was his daughter's birthday and his way of celebrating would be to hear more secrets about my life."

"He had decided you had had enough medicine."

She shrugged. "I can't resent them for dosing me during the voyage."

"I thought it was because they brought you against your will."

"Young deer, unused to people, can take such a fright they run for miles."

"But you bolted across an entire ocean. What frightened you so much, Sarah?"

He had done it, had broken the balance. She grabbed the papers on her desk and slipped away, watching him like a cornered animal. But she paused at the door to answer. "The world," she whispered. "So many people without true skins." She took a step across the threshold, then halted so abruptly it seemed she had been struck, her eyes fixed on something beyond the entryway.

Duncan darted to her side. Jonathan was throwing stones at old pots again, this time not only hitting the old crockery but stomping the pieces into the dirt after he had broken them. Sarah's hand clutched her breast and she seemed to sag. She stepped backward as if to hide, seemed to sense Duncan's presence, and put a hand in his, not fully enclosed, but intertwining the fingertips the way they had from their cells. It was not a touch of affection, but of fear. After a moment came the sound of shattered crockery, and she turned, her eyes awash with tears. Without a word she fell against him, clutching his neck, and wept like a little girl.

His lack of sleep the night before drove Duncan to his bed in the afternoon. He collapsed onto his pallet and was aware of nothing until a hand shook his shoulder. It was past sunset, and Crispin stood at his side. Sarah hovered shyly in the doorway, holding a lantern. She had tied her hair into plaits that hung from either side of her face.

"We have brought you something," Crispin said as Duncan swung his feet onto the floor. Resting against the door frame was a small pack, made of canvas, with leather carrying straps, like those he had seen on the shoulders of Woolford and Fitch. "A blanket, a hand ax. A flour sack with dried meat and biscuit for two weeks. A loaf of bread wrapped tight in a cloth. A hand-drawn map to the Scottish settlements from Charleston, and another of the route to the Delaware from here. There is a downed tree at the edge of the old cemetery. I will place it there and cover it with bark. It will be there when the time comes. I knew men in the south who kept such things hidden, sometimes for months or years. Just having it kept their hope alive."

"Crispin says he will teach me after you leave," Sarah blurted out. She bit her lower lip and stared at the floor.

"At nighttime," Crispin said solemnly as he positioned himself at the door, like a sentry. "Like my mother did for me. Until a new teacher comes."

"I could believe you wish me gone," Duncan said.

The words seemed to hurt Sarah. "I wish you free, sir." Her voice, though strong, swirled with emotion. He had begun to understand something about her. Pushing against her emotion, her restless spirit, was what drew out her strength. "Free and safe, and in search of the truth. Crispin and I have both known what it means to be a slave. It is in our power to make it not so for you." She looked up and met his eyes. "I know of no other way to repay you. You must let me repay you or I will bear dishonor. A life for a life. Mr. Lister, too, insists you must go. Crispin and I have discussed things. When you arrive in the Carolinas, you must write to the name on the map. The name is a settler a few miles north of here, a kind man who will know what to do with the letter. I will have news to write you then. We can find ways to delay the trial. Perhaps Lord Ramsey will lose interest. No matter what happens, you must promise to leave."

Duncan looked up in alarm. "What is going to happen?"

"This is the edge of the woods. The place between worlds. I died here once before."

The casual way she spoke the words made the hairs stand on Duncan's neck. "You mean you were taken away before."

"My parents buried me," Sarah said, speaking very slowly now, as if English were again causing her difficulty. She looked into her hands and murmured to herself in her other language, the soft, swishing tongue of the forest people. "I existed only in their past. I was dead. It is the way of things for me. I die and become something else, like I did on the ship. I was once a little girl. I was once a prisoner. I was once a ghostwalker. I once lived only in dreams for two months. I lose mothers. I lose fathers. You are a *Gaidheal,* surely you understand what it is to be cut from your root." She cupped her hands, her fingers slowly rising, like something growing, then she collapsed them and made a sharp slicing action with her hand.

Duncan glanced at Crispin and saw the same unsettling confusion he himself felt. The fear he felt from her words was unlike anything he had ever known. Something deep inside him seemed to be trembling. She was out on the mast again, and this time he knew not how to save her.

"Promise me, Duncan McCallum." Her voice cracked, and she pressed her fist against her lips, her eyes closed for a moment. When she spoke again, her voice was somber and insistent, her cheeks were flushing. "In all my life, I have never asked a thing of a man. Do me this one honor. If you value your life, if you value my soul, do this. Wherever Lord Ramsey wants you, there you must not be. If you stay or cross into the forest, he will use you. He will use you and destroy you." He had heard almost the exact words before, from Adam. "Give me your oath you shall escape to the south."

When Duncan finally spoke, his own voice cracked. "I promise."

"There will be killing," she added in an absent, weary tone. "I want you out of the killing. For me it is just the way of things. I want you never to mourn me."

Duncan stared, so numbed by her matter-of-fact announcement that he did not resist as Sarah picked up his hand and with a sad, awkward smile shook it. "Do not lose your true skin," she whispered, then gathered her skirt and slipped away.

"In her room," Crispin said in a thin, frightened voice, "I found these, maybe twenty, spread out under her pillow and under the bed." He handed Duncan several familiar slips of paper, the slips he had written words on for Sarah. But she had used them again. On the backside of each she had drawn two squiggling lines, connected at the ends. Sarah had been retreating back into her spirit world. "She stopped and clamped my arm like a frightened kitten when we were coming here. She looked back at the great house with a tear rolling down her cheek and said they meant to cut her father into pieces and scatter them in the forest."

When sleep came again it was full of nightmares, jumbled images of his grandfather and Lister, of Sarah and the savages he had seen at the army headquarters, of screaming animals and arms reaching up out of graves. By the time the waking nightmare began, he did not at first trust his senses. The screams were distant, the frightened neighs of horses much like the cries of the creatures that inhabited his dreams. But then, through the black night, he saw the flames of the cabins at the far side of the fields and heard the first musket shot.

A spine-wrenching howl came from the woods as he opened his door. Much closer was a second cry, from a Company man cowering at the corner of the building. "Indians!" he moaned, shaking so hard he dropped the ax from his hand.

Chapter Ten

*I*N AN INSTANT DUNCAN THREW on his clothes and was out the door, running not toward the fires but toward the great house. The compound was in chaos. Men ran in every direction, some screaming in panic, some grabbing hayforks and shovels for weapons, others running with buckets to battle the fire. Ramsey appeared on the porch in nightshirt and cap, shouting for Woolford and Fitch, then another war screech from the woods caused Ramsey to clutch his heart and press against the wall.

As Duncan reached the porch Ramsey grabbed him, pulling Duncan in front of him as if he expected an arrow at any moment. More shouts came from the river, followed by victorious cries of men shouting that they had killed one, then another, of the attackers. At the door of the carpenter's shop, Duncan saw Cameron distributing muskets and powder horns. Ramsey had allowed his secret arsenal to be opened.

Some men fumbled with the heavy weapons, others quickly huddled in a group and fired volleys into the woods, then, as Cameron pointed out a dark shape behind them, turned and fired toward the open field past the barn. Sparks flew high in the sky. Terrified animals brayed from their stalls. Ramsey disappeared into the house. As Duncan stumbled from the porch, someone put a bucket in his hand and he headed toward the fires at a slow, dazed jog.

One new barracks cabin was consumed in flames, which now licked at the unfinished palisade wall. Twenty men with brooms and wet blankets beat at the flames that had reached the second cabin. Duncan ran fifty yards to the river and filled his bucket, returned and tossed it on the flames, then picked up a smoldering broom and began beating at a tongue of fire spreading toward the hay fields. The night became a blur of frenzied work against the sparks and flame and breathless runs to the river, punctuated by terrified moments when he and his companions lay on the earth as shots whistled over their heads.

At last a glimmer of dawn appeared in the east, and the shouts faded, then ceased. Duncan heard nothing but the tired calls of work parties running buckets of water to the smoldering foundations of the cabins. As he walked back, emotionally and physically drained, he was surprised to find no wounded men on the ground, no bodies strewn about the village. But then he passed the cooper's shed and with a groan of despair discovered a green-clad figure lying face down in a pool of blood. As he rolled the body over, the man's hand reached out as if to throttle Duncan. But the fingers that gripped his neck had no strength left. He looked into the desolate eyes of Sergeant Fitch. Blood oozed from a gaping wound in his chest, more from his mouth. Fitch opened and shut his jaw as if trying to speak, but only coughed, choking on the blood that now began to flow more heavily over his lips. The sturdy old Indian fighter had taken a tomahawk in the chest, and they both knew he was close to his last breath. As his eyes glazed over, he raised his trembling hands and made a series of motions. With what appeared to be great effort, he ran his open hand down the side of his head to his shoulder. As bubbles of blood appeared on his lips, he clenched a fist then under it stretched two fingers of his other hand, moving them back and forth, rapidly at first, then more slowly as the strength left them.

As Duncan watched with an aching heart, the old ranger closed his eyes and drifted away, then abruptly opened them and with a heave of his chest coughed up more blood. One hand, limp as a ragdoll's, gripped Duncan's as the other fumbled with something on a leather strap hanging from his neck. Fitch freed it from his tunic and closed his hand around it a moment before the light left his eyes. As Duncan hung his head in grief for the steadfast sergeant, the closed fist rolled off his chest. Fitch had been gripping the small metal badge used to identify Woolford's rangers, around which he had fastened a dozen little yellow feathers.

Suddenly Duncan became aware of weeping behind him, and he turned to see Crispin, his clothes torn and sooty, cradling Jonathan in one arm. The boy sobbed against the big man's shoulder.

"They've taken her," Crispin declared in a tormented, cracking voice. "They've taken our little girl again."

The sorrow that had overtaken Duncan transformed into something dark and angry and fearful. "Sarah?" His groan seemed to come from somewhere distant. "Which way?" he demanded.

Crispin stared at the black forest beyond the gray, dawn-lit river. "Gone," he said with such despair Duncan thought he, too, was about to cry.

Duncan battled an impulse to race into the forest himself, then he glanced back into the forge and looked at his hands, still covered with Fitch's blood. "Have them bring the wounded to the schoolhouse," he directed, and stepped to the nearest water trough to scrub his hands.

A quarter hour later, having covered the school desks with linens to take the wounded, Duncan was tying a strip of cloth tightly around the ankle of a man who had twisted it running in the dark fields, having already set the broken arm of a man struck by a falling timber, when Crispin entered.

"There is no one else," the big man announced in a puzzled tone, "only a few who need salve for their burns. No one wounded by the Indians. Only Fitch killed." He glanced wearily toward the great house. "I must see to the children."

At least ten men with muskets were guarding the house when Duncan entered it a few minutes later. No one stopped him at the entrance, nor at the door to the library. Ramsey sat at the edge of his desk chair, head in his hands, a half-empty glass of gin at his side.

"The soldiers found her before," Duncan said. "They can do it again."

"We never expected something so foolhardy," Ramsey said in a brittle voice. He drained the glass and slammed it into the empty fireplace, bits of glass exploding across the hearth. "We'll have guards with guns, every hour of the day."

"They have destroyed us." The words came from Arnold, in a bleak, hollow voice.

The younger children are safe, Duncan was about to say, the main compound is intact.

"The house seemed secure enough," Arnold said. "The attack was on the north side, at the cabins. We set men to watch at the south side of the house, the point nearest the forest, and I went to help at the fires. Lord Ramsey went to safety in the cellar. They came right into her bedroom, from the river. Wet footprints were all over the upstairs hall. They took wigs," he added in a confused whisper, "half His Lordship's hairpieces."

"Wigs?" The news seemed so odd that Duncan almost asked Arnold to repeat himself. But then he followed Arnold's gaze to the desk in the corner. It was in ruin. The top leaf had been levered open, splintering the wood around the lock, and the small drawers inside had been tossed on the floor, some crushed underfoot. The panel behind them—which, Duncan knew, had enclosed the paper safe—had been forced open, and bits of its wood lay strewn on the desktop.

"They stole the king's charter?" Duncan asked, not bothering to conceal the disbelief in his voice.

For the first time since Duncan had known him, Arnold was at a loss for words. He glanced at Duncan with a helpless expression. "Our sacred grant," he groaned.

"There must have been a hundred of the savages," Ramsey said. "They were everywhere. It would have been a massacre but for our valiant defense."

"No more than ten," a deep, fuming voice interjected. Woolford stepped into the room, his face soot-stained, his clothes spattered with mud, in his hand a red-painted club that ended in a large knob with an iron spike protruding from it. "And if they had come to kill, there would be damned few of us left standing right now."

Ramsey quickly closed the desk, then rose and stood to lean against it. "It was a pitched battle," he protested. "You heard the gunshots. Doubtless French troops as well. My brave lads kept them at bay."

"Every shot I heard came from an English Brown Bess. Only our guns were fired," the ranger said. "And if you wish to know the fettle of your brave lads, look to your pasture. There are two champion milk cows lying dead by the hands of your Company marksmen. And a chestnut stump with enough lead in it to sink a boat." When he met Duncan's gaze, he sighed. "They took her across the river. Their tracks lead northwest."

"My little Sarah," Ramsey moaned. Tears erupted on his cheeks. "Dear God, my Sarah. Enslaved again . . . . Thank God her mother is not here to relive the anguish."

"What did they take from here?" Woolford demanded.

Duncan watched Ramsey, who even in his weeping exchanged an uneasy glance with Arnold.

"They killed your sergeant," the vicar stated. "Destroyed our new barracks for the Company." He advanced on Woolford, as if trying to force a retreat. "We will collect the bodies of those we killed. At least we can tell the world the price they paid for their atrocity. If we are fortunate, we may have shot a French officer or two."

"There won't be any bodies," Woolford shot back. "Even if the Company bullets connected with any of them, which I doubt, they will have taken away their casualties. And you will certainly find no evidence of the French." The ranger studied Ramsey and Arnold a moment, then cursed under his breath. "Is it truly possible you could be at the center of this maelstrom and not comprehend it?"

"We do not need the army to explain our suffering," Ramsey rejoined icily, and turned his back on the ranger.

With a vengeful glare Woolford raised the lethal spiked club in his hand. Duncan leapt forward, for a terrible instant thinking the ranger meant to strike Ramsey. But with a blur of movement the ranger brought it down on Ramsey's delicate porcelain teapot, the spike embedding in the refined mahogany table. Ramsey spun about, a snarl on his mouth, but as he saw Woolford's face, white with rage, he shrank back and fixed his gaze on the shards of painted flowers that covered his carpet.

When Woolford spoke, the venom in his voice was a palpable thing. "These were no Huron, no Abenaki, no French Indians," he hissed. "They were our friends the Iroquois!" Woolford spun on his heel and was gone.

Duncan found Jonathan near the edge of the river, gathering stones into a pile under the eye of a guard fifty feet away. His cheeks were streaked where tears had fallen, his eyes sunken and absent. Duncan watched the boy in silence, then collected a handful of pebbles and added them to the boy's pile.

"If I had enough stones," Jonathan said. "I could have stopped them." His voice was halting, as if he were about to start sobbing again at any moment. "Next time I shall kill them all. I have learned to kill frogs and squirrels," he offered with hollow bravado.

"Did you see them, Jonathan?"

"I tried to stay awake, but. . . . If I had been awake I could have raised the alarm, I could have thrown stones while Sarah hid." The tears began again, and the boy collapsed to the ground, tucking his head into his folded knees as he sobbed. "When I awoke, I thought it was Crispin who held me. He was so large and strong, and he patted me on the back like Crispin." The boy seemed to have aged years since the day before. He scrubbed his cheeks and gazed fearfully toward the far bank.

A shadow flickered across them. Woolford was there, bending, dropping more stones onto Jonathan's pile. The boy pushed his chin out, acknowledging him with a solemn nod—the young recruit in his officer's presence. "When he stepped to Sarah's window, in the moonlight, I saw his hair," he continued, raising both hands and placing them on his crown, covering all but a center patch of hair, pushed up between his fingers.

"It's called a scalp lock," Woolford explained, kneeling at the boy's opposite side.

"He had stripes of paint on his face, and his eyes were big black circles. A witch, I am certain. On the side of his face was a crow. He must have cast a spell, because when I tried to scream, no sound came out. I hit him with my fists. That's when he did it."

"Did what?" Duncan asked in alarm. "Something to Sarah?"

Jonathan shook his head slowly. "He laughed." The words hung in the still afternoon air. "But savages can't laugh, can they? They kill. They scream. They invite terrible spirits to inhabit their bodies. That's what he was doing," the boy decided, looking back at a second-story window. "It was his way of calling a devil."

"Where was Sarah when this happened?" Duncan asked. "Was her tongue also bewitched?"

"I don't think she awoke until he made that sound. She leapt out of bed, calling my name, then someone else in the room spoke in the forest language and she spoke no more. I didn't see, didn't hear anything else. He put me on the windowsill and pointed to the moon. He meant to kill me if I didn't keep looking at the moon, I'm sure of it."

"Did you see her leave?"

"I think they beat her and carried her away in a blanket. I turned when I saw the cabins burning, and they were gone."

"It was all over before it started," Woolford concluded. "She was already in the woods by the time the cabins ignited. Just a distraction, to keep everyone here while her abductors raced away."

"Crispin and I cleaned Fitch's body," Woolford reported as the boy set off to collect more stones. "When we lifted it, there was something underneath. The key to the lock on Lister's cell."

"You're saying he was trying to release Lister?"

Woolford took out his knife and began rubbing the edge on a flat stone, an action Duncan had seen Fitch perform a dozen times before. "Could be he thought the buildings were all going to burn."

"Killed by an Indian in a settlement after so many years fighting them in the wilderness," Duncan observed. "You said he was the best Indian fighter you had ever known."

"I thought you had seen his body." Something close to contempt had entered Woolford's voice.

"I did."

"Then you looked and didn't see."

As the ranger continued to whet his blade, Duncan reconstructed the scene in his mind. "His belt," Duncan said in a muted tone. "His knife and tomahawk were still in it. His attacker took him in the chest."

"It isn't the forest we should be watching."

"God's breath!" Duncan gasped. "It wasn't an Indian who killed him."

"It would be as likely for him to have been killed by the dowager Duchess of Kent as by one of those Iroquois. Measure the wound, McCallum. It's five inches at least. No tomahawk did that." A wave of emotion seemed to wrack the officer. "Fitch," he whispered with bowed head. "I ran ten thousand miles with the man, in every kind of storm man and nature could conjure. He spoke a dozen native tongues, was welcome at every hearth, Indian or white, south of the Saint Lawrence. What do I tell his family? That he died in a make-believe battle in Ramsey's pitiful, make-believe world?"

"I was there, in his last moments. He could not speak, but he made these motions," Duncan said, and repeated the hand gestures Fitch had struggled to make with his last ounce of strength.

Woolford grimaced and repeated the sign of the fingers falling from head to shoulder. "The tribes use hand signals sometimes to speak with one another when they do not share a language. This means woman." He stared with a puzzled expression as Duncan repeated the gesture of the fist with the moving fingers underneath, then sighed and looked away.

Duncan repeated the motion for himself. The fist. Something hard. A rock, a stone. The moving fingers underneath. A moving stone. A running rock. "Stony Run," he declared. "He was saying Sarah was being taken to Stony Run. How did he know?"

Woolford ignored the question, but it seemed to trigger something in his mind. He cast a worried glance toward the forest, toward the Edge of the Woods place. "Someone could not afford to have that message spread."

"Not want her rescued? Impossible. No one could . . . ." His voice faded, not certain how to complete the thought.

"We are in the land where all things are possible," Woolford replied in a bitter tone.

They watched in silence as the boy gathered more stones.

"It was like a military operation," Duncan said with grudging respect. "A precisely planned strike. The fire at the cabins was a diversion."

"What did they take from Ramsey's desk?"

"The most valuable thing in Edentown. The only thing that cannot be replaced." There had been many arguments in the law courts about the nature of such charters, Duncan knew. Judges had decreed that the charter itself constituted the right, that without the piece of paper there was no right. And more than once a king had changed his mind about such charters, but was powerless to change them unless they were returned. "They must have been looking for valuables and took it on a fancy. A pretty painted piece of paper signed by the king of England."

"The charter?" Woolford asked incredulously. "They left behind swords, hunting guns, mirrors, silver, glassware, blankets? Instead they forced his locked desk and took a hidden parchment? I was in the library, McCallum. Only the desk was touched."

"Who is the king to them?" Duncan asked after a long, perplexed moment.

The ranger leaned forward, his eyes lit with an intense curiosity as he contemplated Duncan's question. "A portrait at the governor's house," he replied. "A silhouette on peace medals and coins."

"To the Iroquois," Duncan said, "who is the giver of lands?"

"The Iroquois are perplexed about such things. Their old ways cannot account for men owning land."

"You said before, many of them feel the old gods are leaving them. If they were trying to adapt the old ways," Duncan pressed, "who would be the giver?"

Woolford swallowed hard. When he spoke his voice had gone hollow. "A god."

Each man in turn opened his jaw as if to speak, but no words came out. They watched, mute, as Jonathan brought back another handful of pebbles and returned to his foraging on the bank.

Duncan extracted the notched council stick and dangled it in front of the ranger. Woolford's eyes lit with sudden interest, but as he tried to grab the stick, Duncan closed his fingers around it. "Are the men who raided us from Tashgua?"

"Likely so," Woolford replied in a simmering voice. "I must see that stick."

"Are there Scots with Tashgua?"

"There were, months ago. The ones who survived are probably safe in Carolina by now." Cold anger was building in the ranger's eyes.

"Did you find my brother's body at Stony Run?"

"No." Woolford eyed Duncan's hand as if he were about to pounce on it.

"Was Tashgua at Ticonderoga?"

"I would not swear it," Woolford said in something like a hiss, "but I would guess it to be so, watching from the hillside."

"Where my brother disappeared." Duncan dropped the stick into the ranger's hand. "Where would the Onondaga hold a council?"

"Not all the Onondaga, but the prophet of the Onondaga, the great seer of the Iroquois people." Woolford bent over the little stick as he spoke, counting the notches. "And this," he said, lifting the stick in his open palm, "guarantees that every senior chief, every medicine man from every one of the tribes who believes that the old ways must be preserved will be there."

"Fitch had seen another message on a wampum belt," Duncan recalled, his breath catching. "It told where the council will be, didn't it?"

Woolford did not reply, only rose and trotted toward the barn, where he had left his pack and rifle. The message Fitch had seen hours before his murder. The council was being called at Stony Run, on the day the world was going to end.

After a moment, a shadow fell over Duncan. He turned and rose, facing Crispin. The big man, his face gaunt with melancholy, seemed to have shrunk. He said nothing, but gestured Duncan toward the barn.

"Lord Ramsey has a plan," Crispin announced in a worried voice as Duncan arrived at his side by the entrance. "He's called a meeting of all the town in an hour." The butler and a handful of Company men were staring at a row of smudges six feet from the loft ladder. They were the prints of hands covered with soot, rising straight up the wall, without accompanying footprints, spaced as if some great pawed spider had scaled the high wall. Duncan pushed though the men and climbed the ladder.

The hay had been pushed back from the center of the north wall of the massive loft, forming a ten-foot-wide semicircle of bare wood, above which a hideous red face hung from a beam, its crooked black mouth upturned at one end in a haunting smile, curled down at the other in a sinister frown. It was the mask from the island, the mask that had been on the prophet Evering, with the professor's black waistcoat suspended below it, but hung around its neck now were a dozen huge claws.

"It wasn't there yesterday," Crispin announced from behind him.

"But no one saw an Indian in the town during the raid. There were men watching everywhere, some with muskets."

"No one saw them in the house," Crispin reminded him in a bleak tone, "except the boy. Those who worship such a thing, they are creatures of the night."

"It's just a piece of wood, Crispin."

"They're bringing guns," Crispin said over his shoulder. "They're going to shoot it."

A new figure appeared, from a second ladder. Woolford stared in silence at the mask, then warily approached it, pacing in front of it, never taking his eyes from it. Then he paused, reached up, and ran his hand along its cheek, as if greeting an old acquaintance.

"Pull the damned thing down!" an angry voice boomed. Duncan turned to see Cameron, a sickle raised in his hand.

"You may pull it down if you wish, Mr. Cameron," the ranger calmly rejoined. "You can burn him. You can chop him. You can shatter him with bullets. But what happens when he reappears tomorrow morning? With another row of prints where he scaled the wall?" Woolford asked in a solemn tone. The men grew very still. "The Indians consider these masks alive, with a spirit inside. And this is a very powerful one. When it isn't in use, offerings of food need to be given it to keep it content."

The big keeper spat a curse but backed away to a rope at the far end of the loft, never taking his eyes from the demon. One of the Company men, watching in silence, reached into his pocket, hesitantly approached the wooden creature, and tossed a piece of sausage to the floor below it.

"Why here?" Crispin asked the ranger. "Why the barn?" Duncan recalled he had heard the same question twice before, when Sarah had chanted there and when Frasier had hidden a saw in the building.

Woolford's brow knitted, then he shook his head again. He had no answer. "Mr. Fitch always liked to camp near running water," the ranger said after a moment. "If you'd bury him near the river I'd be obliged."

Crispin nodded soberly.

"His Christian name was Ezekiel. He was born in 'oh-seven. In his pack you'll find a scrap of silk that belonged to his wife, who died of cholera years ago. Put it near his heart."

"Where are you going?" Duncan asked.

Woolford's gaze was filled with foreboding. "The crooked man comes from a crooked tree," he said, then turned and climbed down the ladder.

Ramsey was in no mood for one of his long speeches when the Company was finally assembled. His message was short, and the icy determination in his eyes seemed to unnerve many of those who watched. "I want six men, no more," he announced from his perch on a wooden crate in the barnyard. "It is an old game they play. For thousands of years, enemies have sought to steal princesses to use against a king. The way such villains are beaten is through wit and stealth." Cameron appeared at his side, bearing one of the big muskets.

"I am not empowered to change the duration of your servitude, for that is by order of the courts in England. But those who come back with my daughter," Ramsey continued, "and the parchment they stole from my office, shall have an extra hundred acres of bottomland at the end of their term."

Cameron pushed past Ramsey and stood in front of the crate. The assembly withdrew a step, eyeing the big keeper uneasily.

"As the first members of the Edentown militia, you will each be equipped with a musket, knife, and tomahawk," Ramsey added. "And all the ammunition and other supplies you can carry."

Two men pushed through the line, the red-bearded McGregor and another of the rough men who had accosted Duncan in the bilges of the *Anna Rose.*

"You will be led by my strong right hand, whom I have appointed major of our glorious new troop."

Duncan leaned forward, confused, and was shocked as Reverend Arnold emerged from behind Ramsey. Arnold was attired in the white shirt he usually wore, but over it he had donned a pocketed hunter's frock, opened to reveal one of the old metal breastplates Duncan had seen in the library. He carried Ramsey's engraved fowling piece. On his head he wore a new tricorn hat; on his feet, high-topped riding boots.

"We shall smite the heathen with the power of God in our hearts and in our weapons," Arnold declared in a loud but unsteady voice. He could not conceal the fear in his eyes. Had Ramsey forced the vicar to venture into the forest?

"It's work for soldiers!" a man called from the back of the crowd. "The captain's gone for help!"

"This is Company work!" Ramsey barked. "Every hour we wait, the greater the risk to our Sarah! Three more men is all I ask. With the prayers of Major Arnold and the strength of Mr. Cameron, you shall be invincible! Two hundred acres then!" Excitement rippled through the crowd. Within a minute, the ranks of the party were complete.

Duncan gave Ramsey ten minutes before following him inside the great house. Ramsey stood at his collection of arms, swinging a long saber through the air with grim determination.

"I am joining the search party," Duncan announced.

Ramsey returned the saber to its rack and raised another for testing. "Do you know much about Major Pike?" he asked in an absent tone.

"All I need to."

"He was stationed in Ireland once. A local conscript deserted and Pike went to his village, to his thatched farmhouse. Somehow a sister, a young maiden, died. Pike hid at the funeral and arrested him. The man was hanged and buried beside his sister before the sun set." Ramsey, sensing he had Duncan's attention, continued. "Pike only hated you before. I have made certain he knows you had a hand in the report to the governor. Take a step out of Edentown, and his agents will soon know it. There is probably nothing more he wants right now than to run a sword through your breast. He will then carefully spread word through the colony so your brother will know, before you are buried."

Despite what Crispin and Woolford had said about Jamie fleeing to Carolina, Ramsey and Pike seemed to think he was still in New York. "I know the Company sought me out because of my connection to my brother. I just can't understand why."

"Surely you can see we have more finesse, more humanity, than the army."

"Meaning that you won't kill me first?"

"You don't understand, McCallum. We are but advancing our plan. The party that leaves today is just to beat the brush, drive the game as it were, the vanguard of the Ramsey militia. You and I will march in two days with the remainder of the men to intercept the prey."

"The prey? Is that what Sarah is to you?"

"You are young and impatient. Let me teach you the ways of the world. I love my daughter, more than she knows. Having her in this house is like having my beloved wife back. But we act on the field of empire. She will soldier this out like the rest of us, and then we will see to her malady. She is not the one in imminent danger. And when we recover her, she shall have new physicians, the best in America."

"If you wish me to accompany you, then release Mr. Lister."

"You must read more Plato," Ramsey rejoined, lifting another sword before fixing Duncan with a cool gaze. "There are a handful who are destined to run society. All the others serve."

"Hawkins was seen arguing with Frasier, striking him, the evening before he was killed. He fled the next morning."

"Hawkins is not available for your purposes. His is the most important element in our strategy. His is the hand that will strike the final coup. And our victory will taste that much sweeter for having deprived General Calder of his glory. You and Hawkins will make it all possible."

Duncan turned to the window a moment, his heart in his throat. "You will use me to lure my brother, and Hawkins will kill him," he said in a hoarse voice. There was nothing mysterious about Ramsey after all. Everything he did was about his battle with General Calder for the governorship.

"Your brother's life is already forfeit."

Duncan fought to control his emotions. "But how does that return Sarah to us?"

Ramsey studied the ruin on Duncan's face and smiled. "A good tutor understands the basics of astronomy. There are days once every few years when all the planets are lined up."

Duncan collapsed into a chair and buried his head in his hands, images flashing through his mind. Lister rotting in his cell. Sarah weeping on his shoulder. Adam apologetically pressing the black bear stone into his hand. Jamie, always now at the edge of his consciousness, Jamie, whom Duncan had loved, cursed, and probably betrayed with his fiery letters, who probably didn't even know Duncan was in America but now was going to die because of it. He rose as if in a daze and found his way to the pantry closet by the dining room, selecting one of the fine linen tablecloths, warning away a protesting maid with a fiery glare. Edentown could afford the best of shrouds for its dead heroes.

As the vanguard of the Ramsey militia, led by Cameron and Arnold, slipped across the river an hour later, Crispin and Duncan explored the riverbank below the house, shovels on their shoulders.

"This will do," Duncan said after they had walked a quarter mile, and sank his shovel into the sandy soil at his feet. They were in a small clearing at the center of a grove of towering hemlocks, ringed with ferns. Small white flowers grew out of low, heart-shaped leaves. Water sang over the rocks of a small stream that entered the river a hundred feet away.

Crispin's only reply was a thrust of his shovel into the soft earth.

"This is the day," the house butler declared when they were nearly finished with the long, rectangular hole. "There is a good moon tonight. Slip into the woods along the fields while Ramsey takes tea. Stay in the shadows. Those who are watching keep their eyes on the river. Circle around to the road and walk all night. You can be twenty miles away by dawn."

"I could not. Not now."

"Now above all. You promised her." Crispin leaned on his shovel and wiped his brow. "The only thing I know for certain about those savages is that it is right for us to fear them. But I think she is in no physical danger. Why would they go to such trouble to steal her away if they meant her harm? To them she is just a runaway slave.

Slaves," Crispin said in a pained voice, "are property to be protected. There is only one thing you can do for her now. You promised her. I saw the relief in her eyes when you vowed it, an instant of contentment such as I haven't seen since she came back to us. She will be found, in a month, in a year. And a minute after I see her she will ask me about you. Do not force me to disappoint her. I would not have you betray her hope. Her hope is my hope. Do not betray *us*."

Duncan had no answer. He knew well about hope, and hope betrayed. He gazed across the river for perhaps the tenth time in as many minutes, then resumed his digging.

Only a dozen men gathered to lower the old soldier, wrapped in the Ramsey linen, into his grave. Crispin extended a Bible to Duncan, reminding him that Reverend Arnold was gone. Duncan recited a Psalm in a thin, tentative voice, then retreated to a rock, where he sat as the men closed the grave. He stared at the mound of earth, so lost in his thoughts he did not notice the men leave, rousing to his senses only in time to help Crispin finish laying small stones along the edge of the new-turned soil.

He stood, hesitated as Crispin headed back toward the town, then bent over the grave. With a stick he drew two waving lines on the grave, connected at the ends.

The Company crews were hard at work, cleaning the wreckage of the night before, as Duncan approached the rear of the charcoal crib, where Lister hummed one of his sea chanteys. When Duncan whispered his name, the old Scot crawled toward him.

"Did Mr. Fitch speak with you last night?" Duncan asked.

"An owl called, then another not far away. I saw Fitch run to the shed where the guns were stored, heard him curse when he found the door locked. Then the cabins caught fire. After that I saw him no more. He was a good man. May God have mercy on his thick-skinned soul. Pray for him in Carolina, Clan McCallum," Lister added.

"He's the last," Duncan vowed, an unexpected vehemence in his voice. "No more are going to die. Not by hammers, not by axes, not by nooses."

"We done fair by each other, you and me. Ye let me be me own man again, after pretending for too many years. No regrets." Lister shifted his chains and crawled to the far side of the crib. "Now I need ye to make that journey and start our cabin in Carolina. By the time the trial's done, I'll be fit to join ye. I've been thinkin' on it. I'll get a Percheron, a big gray plow horse like me father had. I'll buy one in Charleston and trot up to meet ye, grand as a prince."

"We'll need a cow," Duncan heard himself say in a dry, cracking voice.

"Aye, and some sheep. But ye'll be the one for the milking in the dawn."

Duncan jammed his hand through the slats, futilely trying to reach the old man. He had not felt the black thing that now grew inside him since the day of the storm when he had climbed the mast and decided to die. *We done fair by each other.* Since Lister had pledged himself to Duncan, the old man had been whipped, arrested, beaten, reviled, arrested again, and now, despite their banter, they both knew he was going to hang.

Lister began a sailor's song in a subdued, doleful voice. Duncan sat still, not sure he could summon the strength to move. "Good moon tonight," Lister observed when he finished his song.

"What do you mean?"

"Crispin and I spoke. When the great lord settles into his library for tea, Crispin will appear on the kitchen step and leave a broom leaning by the door."

"A broom?"

"My signal. Five minutes later I will start shouting that I see savages on the far bank. That's when ye break away. A few miles to the east and quick as Jack Puddin' y'er a free man. May God and Mary protect ye."

Duncan seemed to watch himself from a distance as he stepped to the schoolhouse, then rolled his papers into his spare shirt. Minutes later he was at the little cemetery, uncovering the pack and inserting the pipes. He had moved away ten paces when he paused and turned back to Sarah's gravestone. It took but a few moments to locate and clean the stone bear, which he pushed down beside his pipes. He slipped on the pack and made his way into the shadows. Ten minutes later he reached the Edge of the Woods place, where he sat staring grimly at the stone pedestal, as Woolford had done days earlier.

Images swirled in his mind again, the strange dreams that sometimes boiled out of despair. He would go to Carolina and send for Sarah. He saw her laughing and dancing with Crispin over the news that Duncan was in the southern mountains. Jamie and he were building a cabin as Lister plowed fields with a big grey mare. At a Highlands festival, Lister told old tales to freckled, kilted children. But then, like a frigid wave, reality broke over him and he found the words that had been squeezing against his heart. Sarah was a slave again, probably lying beaten and bloody that very moment in some squalid camp. He could only save her by breaking the solemn vow he had given her. And Lister could only be saved if Duncan preserved Hawkins, the man who was going to kill his brother.

He glanced at the map she had given him, and the name of the farmer who would act as go-between. William Wells. No one had told Sarah that the settler had been hacked to death the week before. The savages were close. The savages were everywhere. But slowly the realization had been building that there was another way to save Lister, as impossible as using Hawkins. There had been a witness to Frasier's murder, lingering in the shadows by the alder bushes, laying another message on the riverbank. Somewhere in the vast wilderness was a savage who had seen Frasier's killing.

When he finally rose, he lifted the stone cover of the lichen-covered cairn and draped the wampum belt over his forearm, the belt over which one could only speak the truth. He extracted his list of clan chiefs and held it before him, reciting the names without looking at the paper. He added a new name this time, in a firm, level voice aimed at the shadows before him. *Duncan McCallum.* Finished, he cupped in his hand the dried thistle he had carried since the day Lister had brought it to his cell and raised it toward the trees. He returned the belt, neatly folded, draped his list of clan chiefs around the thistle and set it on the belt before replacing the stone cover. As he did so men began shouting alarms from the town, and he saw figures running desperately toward the barn and great house. With a trembling hand he tore up the map to Carolina, then stepped toward the river and the black western forest. He wasn't going to throw his life away as Ramsey's puppet. But he was ready to die as the last chief of the McCallum clan.

Chapter Eleven

NEVER IN HIS LIFE HAD Duncan felt so alone, so helpless. He ran at a crouch as he climbed out of the river, ran until his lungs ached, until he stumbled on a root and fell, gasping for air. Without conscious thought he crawled into a gap between two boulders, leaning against one, his heart thundering.

Through the trees he glimpsed a low ridge, with a rock ledge jutting from its spine. Moments later he was in a small clearing at the highest point, surveying the top of the endless forest, where he laid out his few possessions on a flat rock. His pipes, his spare shirt, a blanket, a tomahawk, flints and a striker, the food left by Crispin. The papers he had grabbed from his schoolroom table. Finally, unexpectedly, a muslin pouch containing nearly a quarter pound of black pepper, a small treasure that must have been purloined by Crispin from Ramsey's kitchen, though Duncan could not fathom why.

A twig snapped nearby. Duncan recoiled in alarm, then he looked up into two moist black eyes. Twenty feet away a large stag stared at him. As he returned its gaze the majestic creature inched forward, tilting its head, and he realized he had seen its expression before, in the eyes of the Indians at the army headquarters, an intense, guileless curiosity, a countenance that seemed incapable of expressing fear. Duncan stayed motionless as the stag approached him, sniffing the articles he had strewn on the rock before him, cocking its head again as if expecting an explanation for Duncan's intrusion. He slowly uncurled his fingers, opening his palm for the animal to see what it held, the last object in his pack. The deer stared at the stone bear as if it recognized something in the stone, then stepped backward, pausing to investigate a blood-red mushroom before slipping back into the mottled shadows, following the rock ledge toward the north and west.

Duncan stared for a long time in the direction the stag had disappeared, then at the stone bear in his hand. Once, a lifetime ago, Adam Munroe had written that the bear would take Duncan where she needed to go. He gathered his meager belongings into his pack, took a step in the direction of the stag, and froze. There was a new sound in the distance, though approaching fast. The baying of large hounds. Against all odds, he had already been missed. The bear dogs were kept hungry, in case there was work to do.

He would never outrun them. With sudden realization he lowered the pack and retrieved the pepper. Crispin had foreseen the danger. He quickly spread some of the pepper on the rock, ran ten feet from the rock in three different directions, sprinkling more pepper behind him, then took off at a sprint down the bare rock of the ledge, leaving no prints and the barest of scents, which, Crispin had reckoned, would be of little interest to dogs whose senses were numbed by the pepper.

By the time he paused again, an hour later, the barking of the dogs had faded, then stopped, and he had begun to recognize the patterns of the forest. Though it held no roads, it had its own unique thoroughfares. Narrow trails of animals, some heavily worn, led to small watering holes along the streams, which themselves flowed down from the ridges to the northwest. Birds he could not recognize sang over his head, and he saw flashes of red and yellow and chestnut as they fluttered among the trees. Here and there golden leaves, harbingers of autumn, floated in the air. Squirrels and chipmunks stood on their haunches, some scolding him, others gazing at him before racing away as if to report his presence.

Suddenly in front of him was a small, ragged piece of green cloth, on the trail between two fallen trees. He halted, looking quickly about. The birds had stopped singing. The cloth was reminiscent of one of Sarah's green dresses. As he dropped to one knee to retrieve it, something slammed into the crown of his head. He collapsed, rolling, reaching for his hand ax, hearing a grunt of amusement, smelling an odor of rancid fat. As the ax cleared his belt, he lashed out at the quick, shadowy shapes that accosted him, landing a blow that caused a moan of pain, groping with his free hand to wipe the blood that was dripping into his eyes. A wrenching howl, like those he had heard in the Edentown raid, rent the air. As Duncan spun about to face its source, he saw only a blur of movement. Someone hit him in the back, slamming him to the ground; his tongue tasted the forest loam. He twisted futilely, saw the flash of a blade as someone straddled his back. Another man uttered a sound like a curse, and something hard hit him again. His last memory was the ring of a tiny bell.

Duncan floated in a terrible, dark place that echoed with the shouts of the Indians and remnants of Crispin's stories of Indian torture. Never before had he experienced such deep, piercing pain as that which now gripped his skull. As he gained consciousness, he stretched his hands to search the black night around him. Nothing but twigs and dried leaves. But he heard the music of morning birds, felt the soft, warm wind that came after dawn. A long, mournful groan escaped his throat. He was blind.

His heart rattling against his ribs, his breath coming hard and fast, he groped about and finally raised a trembling hand and discovered a cloth bandage tightly tied around his skull, covering his eyes.

"I'd rather we leave it for another hour," a deep, slow voice intoned from a few feet away. "Let the herbs draw out the filth. Those gentlemen seldom clean their blades."

Duncan lowered his hand and turned his head in the direction of the voice. He smelled smoke, sensed the dull heat of a fire.

"It took a stitch or two," the stranger observed. His voice was quiet and soothing, like that of the old priests Duncan had known as a boy. "The last of my good silk thread."

Duncan grew very still as the words sank in. "Are you saying they wanted to lift my hair?"

"I'm saying they did lift it. Or made genuine progress at it. I knew a man who survived the completed act," the stranger said in a whimsical tone. "Nothing but bone on top. He had seven wool caps of different colors, one for each day of the week."

There was movement, a hand reached around his neck, pulling him upward, and a hot tin mug was pressed to his lips. Its contents were bitter yet sweet. It smelled faintly of anise and roseberries. He sat up, fighting the stabs of pain in his skull, and eagerly drank.

"How did a gentleman such as yourself come to the deep forest?" Duncan asked when he had drained the mug, wondering who his savior could be, but quickly settled on an image of a well-schooled Englishman in a greatcoat, probably with an expensive fowling piece and a game bag. He remembered there were men of science who compiled descriptions of New World flora and fauna, who would know how to concoct a healing tea of local herbs. "Do you pursue natural philosophy then?"

He thought he heard a low sound that might have marked amusement, then sensed movement behind him. The man seemed to move without disturbing the debris on the forest floor. "Lean back," his companion advised. "I have made you a pillow of moss."

The tea, Duncan discovered, was quickly making him drowsy. "I have studied the sciences, too," he began, the awkward words blurring together as he eased back into the cool, soft cushion.

When he awoke, the pain in his head had subsided to a dull ache. The forest seemed alive with sounds he had never heard before. Where he had heard only a random whistling before, he now discerned half a dozen melodies from the trees, over the rustle of leaves and the chirping of squirrels. He slowly eased the bandage from his eyes for a glimpse of his benefactor.

It took a moment for his eyes to adjust to the late afternoon sun. Shielding his eyes with his open hand, he slowly focused on the back of a figure rummaging through a sack, a man attired in deerskin leggings and a ragged muslin shirt, his long black hair gathered together in the back with a strip of leather into which had been inserted a long mottled feather that hung downward.

With painful effort, Duncan seized a nearby limb from the forest floor and launched himself on the thief. "Murderer! What have you done to him?" he demanded as he slammed the limb into the heathen's spine, knocking him to the ground. The kind Englishman who had saved him had been killed by this Indian. All the anger and frustration of recent weeks erupted within him, filling him with a wild, dark energy. At last he had found an enemy he could deal with.

The savage groaned as Duncan hit him again and again, repeating his furious demand, then rolled away as Duncan faltered, swaying as his head began spinning. The Indian leaned against a moss-covered boulder, his eyes filled with pain, as Duncan dropped to his knees, a hand to his temple. The throbbing returned, now a low, steady roll of thunder in his head.

"If you insist on this frantic activity," the Indian declared, gasping, speaking in the deep voice Duncan had heard earlier, "I fear your wound will open again."

Duncan stared at the man, his jaw agape, looking about the small clearing, then into the forest and back to the stranger again. The man's face was as worn as a river stone, and his bright, intelligent eyes fixed Duncan with a steady, if sad, gaze. Around his neck hung a necklace of glass beads from which hung a small fur-bound amulet. At the end of a second necklace, a leather braid that had had been freed from inside his shirt during Duncan's attack, were two small silver cones that made a tinkling sound when he moved. Like tiny bells.

"I didn't ... I don't ...." Words failed Duncan. Still on his knees, propping himself with his makeshift weapon, he silently gawked at the man.

When the stranger lifted his hand, Duncan thought it was to make a gesture of warning. But instead he slowly extended one finger, first to his lips, then to a shrub at the edge of the clearing. Duncan followed the finger to a bird, with scarlet body and black wings, that burst into a light melody as it studied the two men. They listened without moving for over a minute, until the bird flitted away.

"In the tongue of my boyhood we called him Firecatcher. I have never heard an English name for it. You English have so few names for the important things."

Duncan looked back at the man with the same curious gaze the bird had used. "I am called Duncan McCallum. In the tongue of my boyhood I would be called ungrateful."

A small grin stirred on the man's face. "If you wish you may call me Conawago."

"Scottish. I am Scottish, not English." Duncan nervously surveyed the forest again.

Conawago offered a nod toward the base of a big tree near the circle of their camp. "They are gone." At the bottom of the tree were splinters of wood and three long barrels, the remains of three muskets. "Without their guns those kind are like frightened children."

"Who else?" Duncan asked, watching the forest again. "Are your companions nearby?"

"As I grow older, I find the company better when I travel alone." Conawago returned Duncan's stare with the same inquisitive, slightly amused gaze he had fixed on the scarlet bird, then with a wince of pain he rose and resumed loading his bag.

As he did so Duncan noticed streaks of red on the back of the man's shirt. "I injured you," he said, stricken with guilt. Conawago was probably three times Duncan's age. He had not only viciously attacked an old man, he had attacked the man who had saved his life.

"It is nothing," the Indian muttered without looking up.

"I studied to be a doctor. Let me help."

Conawago continued his packing. "I'd as soon turn myself over to one of the old witches in the Iroquois towns than to a European doctor. Bleed this, they always say, bleed that. Take some opium. Try some Peruvian bark. Swallow some cathartic. Treat a wound by making a bigger cut."

"I know enough to wash your wounds."

Conawago tightened the drawstring of his bag and straightened, ignoring Duncan, looking toward heaven and making an upward spiraling motion with his hand.

"I struck you. It was . . . ." Duncan searched for words. "I wronged you. Allow me to render a kindness. You saved my life."

Conawago's face betrayed no emotion. "It remains to be seen whether that should be considered a favor."

"Then you at least saved me from wearing a hat for the little time I have left to live."

A flicker of a grin crossed the old Indian's face. "There is a stream with a pool two miles north where I can clean my wounds. I was going there in any event. Farewell. If you truly know something of doctoring, you will know you will lose consciousness long before you could get there, so do not try to follow." He swung the bag onto his shoulder, lifted his staff, and began walking down the narrow trail that led toward the high ridges. For the first time Duncan noticed on his belt a long, curving club, its ball-shaped top carved like the head of a bird, whose bill was a lethal iron spike.

Duncan rose, staggered a few steps, and collapsed. By the time his head cleared, Conawago was out of sight. As he sat there, summoning his strength, he realized for the first time that his medallion, Adam's medallion, was gone.

He knelt, swaying on his knees, fighting not dizziness now but shooting pain from his head and ribs, and then forced himself to his feet. With his hand ax he cut a staff, then sliced a four-inch section from a small limb, inserted it between his teeth, and began walking. He stopped every two or three hundred paces, wiping away blood that dripped down his forehead and into his eyes, clutching his head, cutting a new plug of wood when he bit through the first. The trail branched with no sign of the old Indian's path, and he halted, trying to understand the signs he knew the people of the woods could instinctively read. There was a pool, Conawago had said. It would be the kind of place where animals would congregate. He chose the wider, more heavily used fork and kept walking.

When he finally reached the shaded, forty-foot-wide circle of water, Conawago was stripped to the waist, his back to Duncan, standing under a narrow flow of water that spilled into the pool from a ledge a few feet above his head. With a pang of shame Duncan saw the bruises and broken skin his attack had caused.

Conawago was muttering something unintelligible, catching the water that missed his head in a cupped hand and pouring it over his chest, looking up when he spoke, as if addressing the huge chestnut tree whose roots hung over the ledge above. Duncan collapsed at the bank, dropping his bag and lowering his head to the cool water, drinking it from his hand, then sluicing it over his own head.

"I have a spare shirt," Duncan said to the Indian's back. "I can make bandages."

Conawago's only response was to raise a palm toward him, to silence him. The old Indian continued speaking, sometimes to the water itself, but mostly facing upward, toward the ledge above. The old Indian had said he was coming to the pool in any event. He had come, Duncan realized, to pray to the massive tree.

He felt strangely embarrassed, wanted to turn away, but Duncan could not take his eyes from the old man. His grandfather had sometimes prayed like that, standing in an ebb tide under a full moon, refusing to come out when his mother had begged him to, laughing when their priest cursed him for a pagan.

After several minutes Conawago stopped speaking and backed a few inches away from the small waterfall. He caught more water in his hand and stared at the glistening drops. "I did not expect you," he said in a voice like that used in a church. "Now that you are here, there are words you, too, must say."

"I do not know your language," Duncan said awkwardly. "I cannot remember the words you said."

"I was apologizing for the spilled blood, and the foolishness of men. No good thing ever comes out of violence. You must always cleanse it away." He looked for the first time at Duncan, and stepped toward him, stopping eight feet away, knee deep in the water. "The words you must use are different. Say this," Conawago instructed, and began reciting words in the tongue Sarah had used.

Slowly, clumsily Duncan repeated the sounds.

Conawago nodded, then continued, speaking a few syllables at a time. Duncan echoed each phrase without comprehension, recognizing only one word of the many spoken. *Ohskenonton.* Deer.

"What does it mean?" Duncan asked when they finished.

"A prayer to the forest spirits. Difficult to translate. First, you asked for forgiveness for being so ignorant as to enter the forest without trying to know it, without respecting it. You said you knew you will die soon, but you just want another day or two to be able to show homage to the spirits, to try to find your true skin. You said you were no better than a pile of moldy deer droppings, but sometimes you will remember to put a hand on a tree and give thanks. It is a prayer taught to children in case they get lost in the forest." There was no amusement, no mocking on Conawago's face. "Now take something you need and give it to the forest."

A sharp retort leapt to Duncan's tongue, but he kept silent, breaking Conawago's harsh, penetrating stare to kneel and open his bag. He extracted the small, hard loaf Crispin had packed for him, then cast the bread toward the current that flowed along the far side of the pool and watched as it gradually floated down the stream, slowly sinking.

When he looked back, Conawago was holding a large river pebble under the waterfall, whispering to it. After a moment the old Indian turned, shouted out several words in his native tongue, and threw the stone high, so that it disappeared into the chestnut towering above.

Duncan bent to pick up his bag, realizing the sturdy old Indian truly did not need his help. "I thank you for your kindness, and I shall trouble you no—" The words fell away as Conawago turned to squarely face him, for the first time allowing Duncan a view of his naked chest. The bag slipped from his hands and Duncan found himself in the water, an arm's length from the Indian, staring at the intricate tattoo on Conawago's chest. "The wolf clan of the Mohawk," he declared in a cracking voice, then pointed to the pattern of rays that radiated from the Indian's left shoulder. "The sign of the dawn chasers."

Conawago's hand went to the club that still hung from his belt. "Where did you steal such secrets?" he demanded, his voice suddenly sharp.

"The last time I saw that wolf, it was on a man's chest. He wore his sign of the sun over his ear."

The Indian surveyed Duncan, head to foot, as if he had never seen him before. "You are a friend of Jacob the Fish?"

Duncan shook his head uneasily. "I helped to clean his body with some who were his friends."

Conawago leaned forward, intensely studying Duncan's face as if looking for the truth in his words, then he seemed to sag. The old Indian released the club, stepped to a flat boulder at the side of the pool, and collapsed onto it. "When the black snake wind blows, it must be obeyed," he said in a sorrowful tone.

"He was attacked near the Dutch inn after the Ramsey Company crossed the Hudson. They tried to scalp him."

"As it happened to you," Conawago said in a tight voice.

It was Duncan's turn to settle onto the bank. Conawago was right. What had happened to Jacob had also happened to him. A drop of blood fell from his bent head onto his hand. He stared at it for a moment, then began explaining what he knew about Jacob's death.

When he finished, the old Indian was silent a long time, withdrawn into himself.

"The wolf," Duncan ventured. "You were of the same clan?"

"Not exactly," Conawago said absently and looked up at Duncan. "He was Mahican. I am Nipmuc. He knew no one else left alive from his tribe. I know no one else of mine. But we always believed we would find them. He thought if he just stayed on his ancestral lands, someday they would come back. My tribe's land, in what you call Massachusetts, was taken so long ago, I look elsewhere. The last time I saw Jacob, he said he had had a dream in which we discovered that our peoples had been living together on an island in a lake that I had overlooked. He thought it was very funny. But," the old Indian sighed, "like all of his dreams, he thought there was truth in it. He made me promise to find the island, then come for him so we could go live there together."

Conawago fell silent again, looked at the old tree. "You should go back," he declared. "You, too, will die from your wounds if you push too hard."

Duncan looked over his shoulder toward the east. "There is no back for me. I am a fugitive, an escapee from the Ramsey prison company. I can only go forward. I am looking for a place called Stony Run, somewhere in the north."

Conawago winced, then tossed a pebble into the water and watched its ripples until they had disappeared. "If you knew what lay north, you would beg me to finish the job those fools started." The old Indian rose and put on his shirt. "You will not make it there. Return to the settlements. Stay here. Go north and die if that is your wish. You will snap like a twig in the hands of a Huron raider."

"You saved me. I thought Indians believed that when they saved someone they are responsible for them thereafter."

"I know not what you mean when you say Indians," Conawago replied in a weary tone as he lifted the shoulder strap of his pouch around his neck. "There are Lenni Lenape, Mohawk, Seneca, Susquehannocks, Nanticokes, Oneidas, Onandagos, Tuscaroras, Cayugas, Huron, Abenaki, a handful of Wappingers left, and fifty other tribes I have known personally, the nations living here before the Europeans. Just as across the ocean there are tribes called English, Scottish, Irish, French, Dutch, Hessian, Catalan, Danish, Welsh, Italian, and, if you credit the tales in taverns, Hungarian."

The old man glanced at Duncan and seemed to relent. "I was schooled by Jesuits at an early age," he declared with a shrug. "They cured me of many of my early notions."

"I don't recollect many Jesuits making offerings to streams."

"Jesuits," Conawago said with a sigh, "don't know everything."

Duncan gazed at the darkening forest. He could not recall ever feeling so weary, so lost. He needed Conawago, just for the night. "An innocent man is being held for murder at Edentown. I can find answers at Stony Run that will save him."

Conawago frowned again, then picked up another pebble, little more than a grain of sand, and tossed it into the pool. It barely made a ripple as it sank. "That is how much I care about the guilt or innocence of Europeans out in the broken land."

"Jacob the Fish was an innocent man."

"Lightning reaches down and takes you. If the spirits intend it, you will step around a tree into a swarm of hornets. It has nothing to do with innocence."

"Some of us fight the spirits when we have to. Jacob did. He didn't die because they wanted his scalp. He died because he had to deliver a message."

When Conawago reached for the paper Duncan extended, Jacob's blood-inked message, the old man's hand trembled. After a moment his eyes took on a distant expression as if looking through the paper at something far away. "I will light a fire and make tea for you," the old Indian said. "Then you will tell me everything."

Conawago spoke no more for nearly an hour, except to say they would need shelter from the storm, though Duncan saw not a cloud in the sky. Quickly, with an economy of motion that astounded Duncan, Conawago assembled a lean-to of limbs against a large, flat-faced boulder, covering it with pine boughs and a piece of tattered sailcloth from his bag. Then he tossed Duncan a flint and steel to begin a fire as he collected moss for a bed, laying Duncan's pack on it, and enough firewood to last for hours.

"I was in the Ramsey Company," Duncan began as the last rays of the sun hit them and the wood began to crackle in the flames.

"That is nothing, just what some other men did to you," Conawago said. "I am asking about you. Where was your mother on the day you were born, near water or mountain? What animals did you play with as a child? Were you scared of the ocean at first, or did your parents perhaps set you in it before you could walk?"

"How did you know I lived by the ocean?" Duncan asked.

"You can take no truth from a man without knowing the truth of his life," was Conawago's only reply. From the forest floor he picked up a flat stone, twice the size of his palm, set it at Duncan's side, then with two twigs lifted an ember from the fire and dropped it on the center of the stone. From his bag he produced a brown leaf and laid it on the ember. As the tobacco smoke rose in a small, slow spiral, he dispersed it with his hand around Duncan's head. He dug further into his bag and produced a folded piece of deerskin, which he reverently opened, exposing an inch-wide belt of white wampum. "Now the spirits are listening," the Indian declared somberly, as he laid the belt on Duncan's wrist, nodding, "now we shall see about you."

Thus began the most extraordinary conversation of Duncan's life. The old Indian would not have him speak of Jacob or Ramsey or any event of the past year, but spent an hour asking about the Highlands, asking the Gaelic words for rainbow and oak tree, trying to understand how Duncan had been raised. He became quite excited to hear that Highland cattle resembled bears and that they roamed freely around the hills like the guardians of the ancient clans.

"What do these creatures do at first snow?" Conawago inquired as he composed a soup of roots and leaf buds in a small copper pot. He seemed skeptical that such animals could truly be called cattle, and asked whether Duncan had ever caught any listening at doors and windows, as American bears were known to do.

"If as a boy you cupped a butterfly in your hand, did you notice the wind change direction? In living by the ocean, did you ever see giant fish circle about and make one of the great whirlpools that draw stars into the ocean?"

"I knew an old woman who said she had seen children change into seals," Duncan offered. The news brought an appreciative nod from his companion.

It seemed hours before Duncan reached the voyage of the *Anna Rose* and its prisoners, long after he had consumed Conawago's fragrant concoction and let the old man help settle him onto the moss bed against the face of the rock, which had absorbed the heat of their fire.

Did the great leviathans follow their ship, the Indian asked, and after a man had been lashed at sea did Duncan see the water around the ship glow the following night, as Conawago had himself witnessed? Thunder rose in the north, and lightning from over the horizon reflected on clouds above.

When Duncan came to the deaths on board, the questions came obliquely, about aspects he had not previously considered, as though Conawago's process of comprehending how men died was different than Duncan's. When they spoke of Evering, the Indian passed quickly by the circumstances of his murder and wanted to know if there were specks of color in the professor's dead eyes, whether he sang songs on his last day, and how he behaved at night on deck when the stars shined. He was intensely interested when Duncan related how Evering had predicted the coming of a comet.

"He died helping a woman named Sarah Ramsey," Duncan offered, having explained how the ship's most important passenger had attempted suicide, "and celebrating his love for his dead daughter." He could not understand why he felt so comfortable speaking of such things with a stranger.

"A fine way to die," Conawago affirmed with a slow nod.

Duncan paused, realizing he had never considered the point.

"And on that very day, this woman and you were summoned by the same spirits," Conawago summarized, as if Duncan had been called into the ocean to confer with some deity.

"I just jumped into the ocean to save her," Duncan countered.

The old Nipmuc gave a patient smile. "Do you remember anything at all about what happened in the water?"

"No," Duncan admitted

Conawago nodded, still smiling, as if Duncan had proven his point.

Duncan spoke on, of landing in New York, of the trip across the Hudson, of the duck Sarah had released, of the Stag's Head Inn and life in Edentown. He became aware of rain softly falling, though he could not say when it had started.

After one of the silences that punctuated their conversation, Conawago looked up, cocked his head, and spoke quite somberly. "Tell me, Duncan McCallum, how many are left of your tribe?"

It somehow seemed the wisest and most terrible question the Indian could ask, and it took a moment for Duncan to fight through the ache in his heart to answer. "My tribe, like yours, is almost gone. There is one other with my blood."

Conawago did not seem surprised, and he spoke on, softly, asking about the color of lightning in Scotland and the books in Lord Ramsey's library.

Finally words seemed to fail the old Indian, and he stared into the embers of the dying fire.

"Am I permitted some questions myself?" Duncan asked as he reverently lifted the wampum from his arm. Conawago looked up with wary eyes but did not object when Duncan laid the belt on his own arm. He lifted a stick in the dirt and traced the shape of a round creature with round, flat tail and wings. He had not forgotten the signs Adam had left on the mast.

Conawago stared at the drawing, then a slow, reverent sweep of his hand obliterated it. "We do not speak of sacred totems with human words. It is between a man and his totem, his protector spirit."

"Why would it have wings?"

"A greeting, from one who is about to become entirely a spirit being." Conawago dropped another leaf of tobacco on the embers and fanned the smoke toward Duncan, as if he needed particular attention from the deities.

"Do you know a man named Hawkins?" Duncan asked suddenly.

Conowago studied Duncan's wound again, cupping smoke over it, before he replied. "I know many like him in the forest north of here. I wouldn't necessarily call them men. More like wolves on two legs."

"*Okewa,*" Duncan tried. "What is the meaning of the word?"

The old Indian stared into the embers before answering. "A dance," he said in a voice suddenly gone hoarse. "A ritual. It starts at dusk and goes until morning. Women sing all night long."

"A ritual for what?"

"The dance of the dead, performed with the family a year after the death. It allows souls to make the final crossing to the other world." Conowago fixed Duncan with an inquiring glance. "Where did you hear this word?"

"It was written on a secret map in the home of Lord Ramsey."

Conowago's face went still as death. The old Indian stared into the fire again, added more tobacco to the flat rock. Duncan watched as his companion silently brewed one more cup of tea for him, then held his hand over Duncan's injured head and offered a whispered prayer. Duncan fell back, able to comprehend neither the reactions of the old Indian to much of what he had said, nor the unexpected calm that had settled over him when speaking with Conowago.

In the morning he awoke slowly, groggily, a strange dream about swimming with otters flickering at the edge of his consciousness. He tried to rub his eyes but could not feel his hands. He shook his head several times but still had difficulty understanding his surroundings. Conowago's last mug of medicine had done more than relax him.

He lay in the stream. His legs, nearly covered in water, were pinned by a heavy log that he could not budge no matter how hard he flexed and pushed his legs. His hands were behind him, arms straddling a tree, bound at the wrists behind the trunk. Their campsite, fifty feet away, was abandoned, with no sign of Conowago. Duncan's pack, neatly tied at the top, sat on a rock two feet away, a piece of white bark pinned to the side with a sliver of wood, bearing words inscribed in a neat, decorous hand.

The storm in the north last night means the stream will rise by noon and lift the log that imprisons you. When it does, push up against the tree. Your ax is embedded at the height of your waist and will cut the strap around your hands. Then run south and thank Ramsey for preserving your life by allowing you to be his servant. If you survive to wisdom, you will see there is no mystery about Jacob, Adam, or myself, only one simple truth. There is no better death, at any age, than standing up to an overwhelming enemy to defend the bones of your fathers and the refuge of your gods. There will be another Okewa, twelve months from now. Stay alive, and sing then for the red men and the plaid men.

Duncan stared at the note, reading it again and again, leaning back against the tree, listening to the forest, sensing the warm, subtle pulse from inside the tree, reading the note once more, trying to grasp the war within a war of which Conawago seemed to be speaking. His anger soon burned away, replaced by an unbidden ache in his heart and a question that tugged at the edge of his mind.

The final realization came slowly, only after countless readings, only after recalling everything that had happened between himself and the old Indian, every word they had spoken the night before. He might not have recognized him from Lister's description of a dark, educated gentleman who traveled with Sarah, or from the careful way the old man's questions had sidestepped Sarah. But the handwriting, the unique looping of the double *O*'s, left no doubt. Duncan had discovered Socrates Moon. He had found, and lost, the one man at the intersection of the mysterious paths of Sarah, Jacob, and Adam, and the only way to find him again was to reach Stony Run, where, Moon seemed to warn, everyone was going to die in seven days.

Chapter Twelve

KEWA. THE FULL SIGNIFICANCE OF the death rite did not dawn upon Duncan until the pool was an hour behind him. Conawago's instructions had proven perfect, and once the water had risen he had quickly freed himself, stuffed the Indian's note in his pack, and headed north. Now, as Duncan read the note again while he rested, he understood Conawago's alarm when he had heard that the word appeared on the map in Ramsey's safe room. Ramsey might not have known about the council of old chiefs called at Stony Run, but he had been advised, probably months earlier, that the Indians who had enslaved his daughter—and who controlled much of the land to the west—would all be back at Stony Run on the anniversary of the massacre.

With new determination he tightened the bandage over his head and rose from the log he sat on. He had taken two steps when his heart stopped beating.

The massive black creature that stared at him, though fifty yards away, looked as big as a horse. It was watching Duncan, its head cocked to one side. Duncan retreated a step. The bear took a step forward, approaching a fork in the trail. After a moment the beast turned its gaze toward the path that led to the north, Duncan's trail, then opened its huge mouth, revealing its long, treacherous teeth. The biggest of the beasts could pluck off your head like a ripe berry, men in the Company had told him. Duncan felt his knees weaken. The meager confidence he had been building since he left the pool evaporated with one glance at those fangs.

The sound that rose from the creature as it opened its mouth was not the ferocious roar he expected. It was more of a long, weary groan. But the animal continued to bare its teeth at Duncan after the sound died, in the manner of a patient predator, confident of its kill. It smelled the blood of his wound. It would never let him pass.

Duncan lost track of time as he stood motionless, replaying in his mind the past half mile of travel, considering and rejecting each tree, each outcropping as a possible refuge. Finally—had it been fifteen or fifty minutes?—he took a single step toward the trail by the bear, then another. The creature did not move, but did not take its eyes from Duncan. Duncan willed his hand toward the tomahawk on his belt only to find its fingers were full. They had already found, and clenched around, Adam's carved stone. For no reason he understood, he raised the stone, then, for good measure, shouted out the name of the McCallum chieftains. The bear cocked its massive head as he spoke.

With agonizingly slow progress, step and stop, step and stop, his knees shaking, he reached the fork and the well-worn northern trail, passing within twenty yards of the terrible creature, close enough to smell the wet musk of its fur. The bear followed him only with its eyes, which seemed to take on a chiding, impatient expression. Duncan backed down the first fifty paces of the trail before turning. When he paused and turned to look back after another fifty paces, the bear had not followed, but was still there, watching.

Hours later, aware of little but the throbbing in his head, he reached a river. He extracted Ramsey's map, realizing he had no way of determining if it was indeed the river shown on the map, the river that connected Edentown to Stony Run, but he had crossed no other in his journey, and he had no strength to push on. He found an overhanging ledge and covered himself with leaves. When he woke in the dawn, his head no longer spun, no longer roared out in pain at every movement. He washed himself, had a quick, cold meal, and began following the bank northward.

It was nearly midday when he glimpsed three towers of rock by a bend in the river. He found himself trotting, pulling Ramsey's map from his pocket, and relief surged through him as he searched for the cabin or farm, a resting place at last, he expected to find. He had, against impossible odds, navigated the wilderness alone, had found his way to the Chimney Rocks, the first landmark marked on the route to Stony Run. He slipped on a root and fell, then rose, his head now throbbing again, and hobbled past stands of small, dead saplings, his shoes crunching on dried sticks; then he was touching the vertical stones as if to confirm they were real, confirm he was not losing the thread of his sanity, that he actually had a chance of finding his way in the wilderness. Then he froze.

He was not in a grove of dead saplings. They were poles, arranged in groups of four, platforms of cut limbs at the top of each group. Objects were hanging from some of the poles, dangling from the platforms. Feathers. Strips of fur. Necklaces strung with clamshells and beads. Human legs and arms. He had not crushed dried sticks, but old bones. He was surrounded by pieces of the dead.

There were at least three dozen of the scaffolds, some so old as to have been overgrown with vines. Fitch's description of what he and Woolford had done with Old Jacob's body echoed in his mind. He pressed against one of the rock columns, the fear he had wrestled with now breaking free and overwhelming him. He slid down the rock, utterly sapped of strength, dropping to the moss below.

He had been gradually steeling himself against another encounter with the strange living natives of the forest, but dead Indians were far worse. He had entered a nightmare, for now he saw that the inhabitants of the platforms, who communicated with birds and visited from the world of the snakes, had been moving about the terrible field. Pieces of skeletons were scattered across the ground, as if the dead had simply collapsed at the end of the night. In a new paroxysm of fear he had a vision of himself, still trapped there hours after sunset, surrounded by sacks of skin and bone dancing in the moonlight, waving snakes in the air.

Then the sound of a solitary thrush cut through the miasma, and his senses revived. He remained very still, as he had seen Fitch and Woolford do, studying the scene with a new, calmer eye, examining the forest floor, the platforms, the stumps of poles that had been freshly hacked away. Nowhere did he see a complete skeleton. The dead had been disturbed, bones dragged from the burial platforms. A skull lay in pieces ten feet away, recently broken, stomped, he suspected, by a boot. The poles of many of the broken platforms had not rotted away but had been hacked with axes.

He discovered he had risen, had taken a step away from the chimney, toward a long, fresh rut in the moss-laden earth, along which lay remnants of several necklaces, old withered feathers, the carpals and tarsals of hands and feet. The track ended at the water's edge. The dead had been pulled from their platforms and thrown into the river. He took another step, numbed now with a new feeling, lifting a strand of intact beads from the bank, and found himself staring into the clear, fast-moving current. A piece of buckskin clothing clung to an overhanging branch fifty feet downstream. Much closer, several feet under water, a skull, some skin still attached, had been trapped by a submerged limb. It seemed to be looking up at him, asking why.

The thrush was joined by another sound, a low murmuring that he might have mistaken for the working of the wind were it not so constant. He pursued it slowly, consciously placing each foot so as to remain silent, to the far side of the second chimney, where on a wide, flat bank more platforms lay ravaged. Something frigid clutched his heart as he first thought he had discovered one of the sacks of bones, crusted with grime and blood, come to life.

Then with a stab of pain he recognized the gentle old man collapsed against the stone. Conawago had stripped to his loincloth, had covered all his skin except for his tattoos with dirt. He rocked back and forth, uttering low, prayerful sounds as with his knife he made a row of cuts on his arm. One leg was already oozing blood from two dozen parallel slash marks along his thigh. Tears rolled down his cheeks.

When Duncan reached out and pried the blade from his hand, the old Indian continued the cutting motion as if he still gripped the knife. Duncan closed his hand around the blood-soaked fingers. It took a long time for Conawago to become aware of him.

Finally the Indian scrubbed at his eyes with the back of his hand and looked up. "Who would do such a thing?" he asked forlornly. "Who would kill our dead again?"

It was nearly an hour before Duncan finished ministering to Conawago. The Indian moved like one of the decrepit aged when he rose, letting Duncan lead him toward the water, advancing in short, hobbling steps, pausing to silently lean on Duncan every few feet. He was as ruined as the cemetery.

Finally they sat on a rock ledge at the edge of the river, with Conawago's limbs washed but still oozing blood. He began speaking in his native tongue, not to Duncan, but toward the sky, then toward the water, in low, anguished tones. Eventually he fixed his gaze downward. Duncan looked away awkwardly then, as Conawago began what sounded like one side of a conversation. When he turned back toward his companion, another chill crept down his spine. The old Indian was speaking to the head under the water.

Duncan lowered his gaze and watched Conawago's blood drip from his fingertips into a still pool at the edge of the river.

"When I was young," he began when the Indian finally grew silent, "some English soldiers came up the coast seeking enemies of their king. My family sailed away to distant islands for a month. When we returned, we found that the English had slain all our livestock. My grandfather paid it no mind, said there were always calves and lambs in the mountains. But the next day I found him speechless, weeping on a rock by the sea. Our ancestral graveyard was in a small vale above our croft. The English had pulled up the grave markers and smashed them to pieces. They opened several graves.

The most recent was that of an uncle three months dead, whom they hung from a tree, with a note pinned to his chest saying he had been tried and found guilty of treason. Other bodies, mostly just bones, were scattered over the hillside."

Conawago said nothing. Now he, too, was watching his blood mix with the river water, desolation in his eyes.

"We reburied our uncle. My mother wanted to try to determine which pieces of which ancestors went into the other graves. My father said it didn't matter, so long as we showed proper respect. So we just put a few of the bones in each of the old graves and covered them up. We were almost done when my father looked past me and groaned. My mother had cut off her beautiful red hair, had shorn herself like a spring ewe, and was dropping a lock of her hair tied around a sprig of heather into each grave.

"My grandfather disappeared when the sun went down, and we found him playing *pibroch* in the graveyard, under the moon. Every night for a month he did that, and every night more of our people came to listen, until at the end of the month there was a great gathering and a bonfire with the clans swearing blood oaths to support each other. My grandfather declared it enough that the old ones in the graves were peaceful again."

Conawago, still staring at the blood as it slowly swirled downstream, gave no sign of hearing his words. Duncan fought an unexpected torrent of emotion as he relived the pain of that long-ago day when his family had found their own ancestors scattered across the slope.

"Pibroch?" the old Indian suddenly asked.

"It means the Great Music, the old music . . . ," Duncan began. "I don't know how . . . ." He stood, slowly surveyed the cemetery again, and stepped to his haversack. Conawago gave no notice as he extracted his precious pipes, inflated the bag, and began to play at the base of the tallest chimney. But as he played, his companion's head slowly rose, until he was solemnly staring into the sky.

Minutes later Conawago rose and slowly began collecting the remnants from the ground and arranging them on the surviving platforms. Duncan played for nearly an hour, then set down the pipes and helped Conawago. They worked until dusk, when at a distance from the cemetery Duncan made a small fire and a bed of moss for his companion.

"Hawkins," he said, breaking a long silence. "You asked who would do such a thing. It was Hawkins. He left Edentown last week with Ramsey men who were familiar with handling the dead."

"But why?"

Duncan had no answer.

"I had a dream last night," Conawago said after another silence. "I was at Stony Run. Men flew through the air like birds. As I was speaking with an old woman, rocks began pouring from the sky. There was great lamentation, though the *okewa* had not even begun."

"I, too, had a dream," Duncan rejoined, his heart racing now. "I was with Sarah Ramsey. She sat in the shadow of a great bear, and Hawkins was sneaking up on her with a knife between his teeth."

Conawago nodded slowly. "It is the way of things for her," he said in a weary voice. "She becomes only bone and starts over."

"I don't understand."

"She is dead again. The last time, I believe." Conawago gestured him around the outermost of the tall pillars, which towered over a bend in the river. A new scaffold had been raised, the only one left standing. On it lay a dead woman in a familiar green dress, with crows sitting at her head.

With a mournful sob Duncan leapt forward and in an instant was on the cross support of the scaffold, hoarsely yelling at the birds, with blind horror lashing out at them. Then he began to see the thing. It was Sarah's dress, he was certain, as was the small gold chain around the neck. But inside the dress were old bones, including a skull from which long hair still clung, with skeleton arms, even skeleton hands clasped together. He fell away, dropping from the scaffold, and gazed at the thing in horror. He wanted to weep.

After a long moment he steeled himself enough to examine the thing on the scaffold. Around the scaffold were the recent prints of moccasins, many overlain with boot marks. Indians had been there after the destruction of the burial ground and erected the scaffold. And the men who come after, probably Arnold and his party, had been too frightened to touch it.

A terrible despair tore at Duncan's heart. He gazed out onto the ruined dead. He felt so weak, he dared not ask the Indian to explain.

Conawago pulled him away, back toward the fire. "You still mean to go north?"

It took Duncan a long time to answer. "I have begun to understand the truth of dreams." he said. "An innocent man is going to hang. The truth of the murder he is charged with lies in the north. I know of no other way to go."

Conawago gestured to the broken bodies. "This is what Hawkins and the others will do to you," he said in a calm, matter-of-fact voice.

Duncan stared into the fire, fighting images of Sarah and Lister being chased by skeletons. He had also begun to grasp why Woolford had warned about speaking of dreams with the Indians. "I shall boil some tea," he declared at last.

"No tea," the Indian said in a dry, creaking voice. "The pipes. I never knew of these, but your grandfather understood. The dead can hear those pipes." He gestured out toward the desolation. "Call them home, like before."

Naked trees. "Look for naked trees," Conawago had said when Duncan had left him at dawn that morning. "Follow the naked trees to Bark Hollow by the mission at German Flats." After Duncan had spoken of his dream, the old Indian had spoken no more of Duncan fleeing south, but he had also denied any interest in traveling north himself now.

"Here is where I am needed," Conawago had said with a deathbed air. "I should go across, I should explain and apologize." He was, Duncan had realized with a chill, speaking of dying.

Duncan had felt as if he were bidding good-bye to another of his great-uncles, never to see him or his ways again. He had lit another small fire for Conawago and left him staring at the flames. "Mourning must be done," Duncan had said as he stood to leave, "but mourning is not standing up to the enemy."

Conawago had given no sign of hearing him.

Ten miles from the Chimney Rocks he reached the first of the naked trees, a huge hemlock, over five feet in breadth, stripped of its living bark for ten feet above the earth. Soon there were others, all oaks and hemlocks, all huge, all stripped to a uniform height. The swath became broader as he approached a rumbling sound that rose from behind a low ridge. He paused just before he reached the crest of the ridge, and looked back at the dozens of debarked trees he had passed. They were all going to die.

Bark Hollow had been aptly named by Conawago. Except for a small log house at the far end, the small valley was piled with bark. In the center, a heavy log had been mounted on a central hub fixed to a stump. Two-thirds of the way along the length of the log was fastened a huge roller stone, like a thick mill wheel with heavy striations along its rim. Harnessed to the end of the log was a great brindled ox, pulling the wheel along the circle, crushing the bark under the wheel. Leading the ox was a boy of perhaps twelve years. Duncan settled onto a rock and watched, his interest suddenly intense. Another riddle was answered. Evering had written that the third ghostwalker would be found at an ox wheel.

As Duncan took a step down the hill, still in the shadows of the trees, the boy's head snapped up, not at him, but at the forest, as if sensing something had changed. The ox slowed and bent its heavy head toward the cabin. Duncan paused, then squatted in the shadows, studying the cabin. It was a rough, squalid place. Two men lay stretched out on benches beside the cabin, jugs beside them. A thin horse tied to a tree gazed longingly at the stream that ran by the cabin. A small, fur-covered creature lay dead on a stump, a crow pecking at its head. Beyond the cabin stood a decrepit wagon at the end of a cleared track that wound behind the ridge. On it sat three bales of the crushed bark, bound for a tannery, where it would be steeped in water for its tannic acid.

Duncan's gaze drifted back to the boy, who was facing the ox, standing idly now, stroking its snout. Something was fastened to the boy's waist at the rear. A rope, he saw as the boy turned and began walking again. The ox was tied to the axle of the great wheel. And the boy was tied to the ox.

Duncan stepped back over the ridge, circled the valley, and walked up the track toward the cabin. The two men on the benches, reeking of rum, did not move as he untied the horse and led it to the stream, then knelt and washed the grime from his own face.

After a moment the hairs began rising on the back of his neck. He looked up to see a musket barrel extended from one of the windows, aimed directly at him.

"I only mean to water him," he explained in a loud voice.

"Git inside or git dead," came a high, nervous voice. "Put him back where he was." More gunbarrels had appeared, two others extending from rectangular holes recently chopped into the log wall.

Duncan rose slowly, tied the horse to a sapling, then moved toward the building, hands opened at his side.

"I tie him like that so when they come for him I have a clean shot," the gaunt man inside explained as soon as Duncan entered the musty cabin. There was an accent in the man's voice Duncan could not place.

"Wolves?" Duncan asked.

The man gestured toward Duncan's scalp. "Man with a wound like that shouldn't have to ask." Welsh. It was a Welsh accent.

"Indians want to steal your horse?"

"Steal everything but the air you breathe. 'Tis a raw, cruel season. Every farm for fifty miles along the river up in smoke."

As Duncan's eyes drifted around the dim chamber, he saw tools tossed in one corner, several clay jugs like those outside in another. One of the guns stuck into a loophole was heavily crusted with rust, its stock split. The weapon the man carried, though appearing too heavy for him, was of much sturdier quality. Burned into its stock was a familiar *R*.

"You have a Ramsey gun."

"Been through many hands, I daresay. The great laird won't complain if I kill a few red bucks with it."

"I came to speak with the boy," Duncan ventured.

The announcement seemed to disturb the Welshman. "I don't reckon so," he said, cradling the gun in his arm now, the barrel a short swing from Duncan's face, "since everyone knows he don't speak. Who the devil are you?"

"How is he named? Where does he sleep?"

"He sleeps with the ox, if that's what you mean. You be a Ramsey, too," the Welshman concluded, chagrin in his tone.

"He does not sleep here." The ox, Duncan knew, was the most valuable asset of the mill. At the end of the day it would not be left to shift for itself at the forest edge.

"Up at the Flats," the frightened man explained. "Come nightfall every sane Christian is at the Flats, with the mission folk. His name is Alex, just Alex. He was too young to have remembered his family name, or from where he was taken, though most likely his kin all died the day he was enslaved, those many years ago."

For a moment Duncan had a vision of savages closing in on them from every direction, and he had a compulsion to take up the old musket and join the man's worried vigil. The man's fear was contagious. "Who are those men outside?

"Hands from the farms. Came with two loads of bark last week, went back to find the families they worked for dead and scalped."

"Sarah Ramsey. Have you seen her?"

"'Course not. And the Reverend's party got a good head start if you be seeking the bounty on her."

"Reverend Arnold is at the mission?"

The hollow-faced man studied him with a sour expression. "Gone north. I told him he best be charging for burials, 'cause he'd be a rich man by winter. It's the way of Ramsey business. Where it goes you need lots of prayers and lots of rum," he said with a twisted grin. He inserted his gun back through the window and resumed his vigil.

Duncan paced along the dirt floor of the little cabin. A pile of molding pine needles in one corner might have been a pallet. An iron cooking kettle hanging on a peg looked like it had been used for years without a cleaning. A pile of squalid rags might have been spare clothes. He paused at the jugs, all but four of which were turned on their sides, empty. Behind the four was something hollow and shiny. He bent and pulled it into the light, its metal gleaming now. It was the ornate breastplate Arnold had worn into the woods. Except now it had two large bullet holes, dark stains along their jagged edges.

He carried the plate to the Welshman, who glanced at it and winced. "Like I said, got to keep your prayers up around those Ramsey captains."

Duncan considered the words. "You mean it wasn't Reverend Arnold wearing this."

"They spent a night with us, the Ramsey men. One of them was so scared he just sat in the corner of the stable shaking, clutching an iron nail in his hand. That Hawkins had come in with another group, telling what the Indians would do to any man who tried to flee when they moved north. That wretch kept shaking, wouldn't even join in Arnold's prayer service outside. He was useless. In the morning Arnold said he needed a man to deliver a message to Lord Ramsey. The poor lug would have none of it, then Arnold said he could wear the breast plate. He took the message, put on the plate, grabbed his gun and was gone. A few hours later those two outside come in carrying the plate and the gun, asking if they could trade for a jug. They found his body less than two miles from here. The fool didn't know the plate was made to stop arrows, not bullets." The Welshman tightened his grip on the gun.

"And the message?"

"That be the business of the Ramsey captains."

Duncan stepped outside, studying the little hollow, noticing for the first time a faint scent of smoke in the air, coming, judging from the wind, from over the next ridge. He stroked the horse's back, considering the scene, then approached the rumbling millstone.

He spoke greetings to the boy, offered to get him some water, even complimented the brindled ox. The boy did not acknowledge his presence. The ox stared at Duncan with its huge black eyes.

Duncan stepped directly in front of the mill axle. "Alex," he said, naming the boy for the first time. "I have been called a ghostwalker, too," he ventured. "I am a friend of Sarah Ramsey," he tried, still without result.

He paused frequently as he walked down the rough, rutted track that led out of the hollow, looking over his shoulder, unsettled by the Welshman's expectation of imminent attack, watching the northern horizon with deep foreboding. Suddenly he stumbled over a freshly plowed furrow. He was at the edge of a cleared field, with a team raising dust on the far side, dragging a stump.

A broad-shouldered man with long blond hair, not much older than Duncan, stood with his back to him, making a speech on a low rise a hundred feet away, his black britches unbuckled at the knees, a wide-brimmed black hat on the stump beside him. Duncan hurried forward, anxious to find someone in the man's audience to speak with, then halted as he reached the top of the little hill. There was no audience. The man was energetically addressing a field of stumps, in German. Duncan paused, not certain how to extract himself, then lowered his pack and settled onto the nearest stump as the stranger greeted him with a wave and kept speaking.

He listened awkwardly, casting about to confirm that he was the only human in the audience, then strained, able to make out a few German words. *God,* Duncan heard repeatedly, and *beggar,* and *bread.* As the dust began to clear, he saw a collection of buildings beyond the field. Beside a few struggling apple trees lay a pile of black material he took to be charcoal, beyond which was the roof of a building dug into the hillside with a tall stone chimney out of which a line of smoke curled. A girl in a black dress milked a cow. Children worked at a fence woven of twigs and branches that enclosed a vegetable garden. Dogs played along the bank of the meandering river.

Duncan found his hand absently rubbing his neck. If Reverend Arnold or Hawkins were at the mission, he could be in an iron collar by dusk. He became aware that someone was speaking to him. "Did you?" the stranger in the white shirt was asking, switching between German and English. "Did you think it too long?"

"I could find no fault with it," Duncan offered.

The German worked his tongue in his cheek as he weighed Duncan's words. "In a month I will depart for Saxony to recruit new settlers to join us. My father, the Reverend Zettlemeyer, says they will expect me to offer a sermon about faith in the New World. If we are to pay for their passage, then we must be certain they are committed to our missions."

"This is Reverend Zettlemeyer's mission? The Moravian mission?"

The German confirmed with a nod.

"I came about the boy."

"We have four boys."

"The boy with the ox."

"Ah. He's not a—" It almost seemed the German was going to say Alex was not a boy. He pushed the long blond hair from his brow and settled his hat on his head. "That one's not right in the brain. I am afraid that's all you *can* do, is see him."

"He lived with the Iroquois."

"And something of him died with them. His soul. My mother says an old Indian named Tashgua ate his soul."

"If I cannot speak with him, I will be satisfied to have him listen."

"We've tried things, for months we have tried things. There are secret ways, from the old country," the Moravian continued. "Last month my mother read the Book of Job to him, backwards," he added in a meaningful tone. The young Zettlemeyer surveyed his audience of stumps, offered them a mock bow, and gestured back toward the buildings. "My sisters bake bread today," he said, and then extended his hand. "I was christened Martin."

Duncan, shouldering his pack, reached out and took the hand that was offered, introducing himself by his Christian name only. He studied the little community as they walked toward it. "An impressive enterprise, for you to be able to pay for new settlers," he ventured. Moravians were known for their missionary zeal, not their wealth.

Martin laughed softly. "Never a profit from our hard-scratched fields, nor even the furnace. Father has arrangements," he said, then waved and called out to the milkmaid.

Ten minutes later Duncan sat in the shadow of the cowshed, drinking from a ladle of fresh milk as the freckled adolescent girl who had been tending the cow, one of Zettlemeyer's younger sisters, blushed at his side. The Moravian village, consisting of ten buildings other than the furnace, seemed a world away from the bark mill. All the inhabitants he encountered as he wandered along its paths—a soot-stained man on the bank above the furnace who fed charcoal down its chimney, two woman doing laundry in a wooden tub, the children in the garden—seemed peaceful, even contented. But the graveyard by the little chapel held over three dozen graves, a third of which appeared to have been dug in recent weeks.

He walked among the graves, most of which were marked with crosses of hewn wooden slabs, whitewashed and lettered in an ornate hand, many only in German. As he straightened a leaning cross, anchoring it with a stone, he saw half a dozen markers set apart from the others, not new but perhaps only months old. *Private Albert Simpson,* he read, then *Corporal Robert Griffin,* and *Ensign Bernard Atwood.* Soldiers. There were some old moccasins at the base of one of the six identical crosses, a faded green cap on another. Not exactly soldiers. He had found the rangers who had been murdered the year before. As he paced along the graves, he trod upon a long, unyielding object obscured by a clump of wildflowers. A narrow slab of precious iron. He paced the graves and found four more, all embedded in the ground. Someone, a

Highland Scot, had protected the graves with iron pigs, straight from the furnace.

He tidied the graves of Woolford's men, then sat in the shade of an old maple at the edge of the cow shed, watching the track from the bark mill for signs of the ox and his keeper.

"They have a wagon to fill by the morrow," a voice suddenly said, stirring him from a half sleep. "So they will work until the light fails. Come eat with us. You failed to mention you knew my father from Edentown." Martin Zettlemeyer helped him to his feet, and Duncan hesitantly followed him to dine at a table of planks set on barrels under a tall tulip poplar tree. He had deliberately not mentioned it, had hoped to avoid the elder missionary, the only person in the village who could put a full name to his face, who could name him as a fugitive.

The Moravians engaged in polite conversation at their hearty meal of sausage, boiled potatoes, maize pudding, and fresh bread, carefully avoiding personal questions. But clearly they had been informed about Duncan's intentions at the mission.

"He has lost all the talents of society, the young one," declared the solemn, gray-bearded senior Zettlemeyer. "He faithfully performs his duties and sits through all our worship services. That has to suffice, and perhaps that is the way it will always be. When Herr Weiser comes next month, we will send the boy back with him."

"Mr. Weiser?" Duncan asked.

"Conrad Weiser, of Berks County, in the Pennsylvania colony. He comes on errands for the government, to speak with the tribes. Conrad will know a farm safe from the war that needs an honest hand. The boy is no trouble."

"He is nothing but a beast of burden," Duncan said.

"In the eyes of the Almighty," Reverend Zettlemeyer opined, "we are all beasts of burden. If we can each find the particular burden we are destined to carry, then it is a blessing."

"Find our true skins you mean."

Duncan's words stopped all conversation at the table. Everyone looked toward the old reverend, who worked his tongue against his cheek, as Duncan had seen his son do. The Reverend cast an oddly pained glance at Duncan, then, too loudly, asked for the potatoes.

Duncan insisted on helping to clear the meal, carrying the empty dishes to one of the tubs where the Zettlemeyer daughters worked with scouring rushes and hot water, singing a spirited hymn in German. Still the ox stall was empty. As he carried his last load to the washtub, one of the women appeared with another bucket of hot water. But when he turned from his task, she was gone—and the bucket hadn't been emptied over the dishes. He found no sign of her as he circled behind the buildings, but discovered behind the woodshed a makeshift laundry line of white linen strips, pieces of old bedding torn into bandages.

From the shadows he studied the buildings with new interest, rubbing the head of one of the mission dogs that had followed him. The furnace and charcoal shed. The neat cabins that housed the inhabitants of the mission village. The cow shed, a wagon shed, the summer kitchen. A large springhouse with the door slightly ajar. Why would the woman take hot water into the building used for cold storage?

Duncan broke off a small piece of the sausage he had saved from dinner, wrapped in a leaf, coaxed the dog to follow him, and tossed the morsel into the open door. He slipped in behind the dog, hugging the inside wall. From behind a blanket hung on a rope at the rear, the woman gave a half-hearted reprimand to the dog, but did not rise from her work. As the dog nosed the blanket open, a sturdy hand reached out and patted its head. But the woman did not look away from her patient.

The man lying on the straw pallet was a few years older than Duncan, with long reddish hair clubbed at the rear. His face was puffy, his jaw clenched against pain as the woman lifted a poultice and began washing an ugly, oozing wound on his right calf. On the wall behind the man hung a black leather cartridge box, beside a knife sheathed in deerskin.

As the man flinched and twisted, Duncan saw the ugly color of the leg in the sunlight. Without conscious thought, he stepped forward around the edge of the blanket.

"Gangrene." The terrible word leapt out uncontrolled, as if he were suddenly in his Edinburgh classroom again. "It will be rotten soon."

The woman gasped. The man stretched for his knife but recoiled in agony, his only resistance a curse as Duncan knelt beside him to examine the wound, then sniff it. It was an old bullet wound, poorly healed over, which had broken open and festered. "How long ago were you shot?" He sniffed the poultice, then nodded with approval. Oatmeal and linseed.

"Nigh a year," the man grunted, clenching his jaw again in obvious pain. "It was wedged into the bone. It's been no problem until now."

"It has become dislodged and is moving about," Duncan declared, "mortifying the flesh. If we do not cut, the gangrene will take hold."

"Cut?" the woman asked in a stunned tone.

"I studied with surgeons. We need more water, scalding hot. Your best knife, freshened on a stone. Rum. Lots of rum. Have you knitting needles?"

The woman nervously nodded. "But my uncle allows no spirits here, none closer than the bark mill."

"Then he must be carried outside to the table, with men to hold him down and a strap in his mouth. And cover his eyes. He must not watch the blade."

The man's eyes had gone wild and round. "Like hell you'll cut me." His words were few but enough for Duncan to recognize the Scottish burr.

"Then you will die," Duncan declared, the firmness in his voice surprising even him. "As certain as daybreak you will die a terrible and slow death if we do not remove the offending metal and clean the wound inside. This time next week you'll be in the ground."

The words took all the fight out of the man on the pallet.

In a quarter hour all was ready, and in another quarter hour Duncan was done, sewing up his incision with the mission's finest thread. He looked up at last to find an audience of eight wary faces. "Now," he said, finding his confidence rapidly leaving him, "all we can do is pray."

"That," solemnly replied Martin Zettlemeyer, "is what we do best."

A great wave of fatigue surged through Duncan as he watched them carry the man back to the springhouse, then gazed at his hands, which had begun to tremble. It was the first time he had ever cut into a living human being.

As he lowered himself onto the bench by the table, the cowmaid appeared with a jug of cold milk, then with a nervous glance toward the house produced from her apron a piece of bread dipped in precious sugar. As he reached for it, the girl stopped his hand and wiped the blood from it before he ate.

"Do you speak English words?" he asked when he finished.

"Oh, yes. Papa says if his Indians can speak three or four tongues, then we can try two at least."

On the table Duncan absently rolled the round bullet he had excised in the surgery. "His Indians?"

"It's why we are here, to christen the Indians." She cast a worried glance at Duncan. "But you mustn't think we condone . . . ." Her mouth twisted in confusion. "You're a Ramsey," she added, as if it were the cause of her sudden discomfort.

"I have an Indian friend as well," Duncan assured her. Only after the declaration left his tongue did he realize how strange it sounded, though it was perhaps the hundredth time that day he had thought of Conawago, left with the dead at the Chimney Rocks, preparing himself to become one of them.

"I was wondering about the iron on the graves," Duncan said. "It reminds me of my old country. Is he the one who does it?" he asked, nodding toward the springhouse.

"Different ones come," the girl said, gazing now at the cemetery. "They usually appear at dawn, smoke a pipe or two with my father, and are gone."

They spoke of small things. Duncan pointed out a hawk soaring over the field. "Were you here last year when the ghostwalkers arrived?"

The girl shuddered, then silently nodded. "That was the second day, after all the killing. Brought in like captives, with the red-coated soldiers."

"Major Pike?"

"Oh, yes," the girl said dreamily. "On his fine white horse. He made sure Miss Ramsey got a bed, and a real dress. One of mine. I was happy to offer it."

"And Adam Munroe?"

The girl nodded again. "When he arrived he had his hair in braids and animals painted on his skin. I thought he was playacting, like my brothers and I do sometimes among the stumps. Some play the Indians, some play our fine brave soldiers in their red tapestry."

"Did you ever hear the boy speak?"

"Twice he spoke."

"Only two times?"

"I mean his tongue was open, then closed, then opened once more before it went numb forever. At first, when he arrived, he wanted to tell everyone about the tribes. Then Miss Ramsey spoke to him after they beat Mr. Munroe, and he was silent."

Duncan looked up in surprise.

"Poor Mr. Munroe, we pray for his soul. That first night Mr. Munroe and Alex escaped. But the pickets caught them because the boy fell and twisted his ankle. The soldiers dragged them both back and beat Mr. Munroe with sticks, cut off his braids, and scrubbed off his paint with rushes. Miss Ramsey, she spoke in the tribal tongue to the boy, like a mother chastising her son. But weeks later, when the great lord came, Alex talked a lot. They gave him sweets and paid my mother to make new clothes for him. He talked and talked as they made notes. Then one day while they were here, an old ranger came, asking about the men who had died, asking about the traders who come from the north, and Alex stopped again. His tongue has not worked since. My brother says when he gets older you'll be able to put a harness on him like another ox and he won't say a word, just mind the gees and haws."

"An old ranger named Fitch?"

The girl nodded and smiled. "A nice man. He carved a bird for me."

A figure emerged from the biggest cabin, Reverend Zettlemeyer, holding a Bible. As Duncan rose to follow him toward the spring-house, he pocketed the musket ball and turned back to the freckled girl. "When you playact among the stumps," he asked, "who wins?"

"Why, the soldiers, of course. Always the soldiers."

For the second time in a month, he entered a room filled with a woman's quiet German prayers. But this time the man on the pallet, though asleep, was still alive. He stepped past the Reverend's wife reading the heavy Bible, and noted for the first time a long bow with a quiver of feathered arrows beside it. He turned over the cartridge belt hanging on the peg above the pallet and froze. The knife was out of the sheaf, the cold blade expertly pressed against the artery of Duncan's thigh.

"I don't recollect offering to pay my butcher," came a dry, rough voice. The Scot was awake, and surprisingly nimble.

Duncan did not release the small leather box on the belt but slowly traced the two digits of its tarnished brass adornment. "The Forty-second saw rough service at Ticonderoga."

The man did not reply, but did not press the knife when Duncan shifted away, kneeling to inspect his sutures. "You must drink twice as much as usual. One part water, one part milk. Keep a poultice on the incision." He paused, glancing out the window for the milk-maid. There was another question he should have asked her. How could she know Adam Munroe was dead? He turned back to his patient. "Do not try to walk for a week; then use a crutch. If you open the wound, the flesh could mortify."

"Right," the man muttered. "Then ye'll be back and announce

it's time to saw it off anyway. I know doctors. I leave on the morrow, and I'll slice anyone who tries to stop me."

"Mrs. Zettlemeyer," Duncan turned to address the woman in a level voice. She looked up from her Bible. "When the skin turns yellow because he has walked on it too soon, then you must take him to the woodshed and have one of the boys chop the leg off." Duncan leaned over to the cool water in the stone trough at the head of the springhouse, moistened his fingers, and touched the moist earth. "Right here will do," he said, and with faint marks of mud drew a broken line on the man's skin above the knee.

His patient's face turned white as he tried to squirm backward, out of Duncan's reach. The woman's hand closed around his good leg and he moved no more. "If you think that was painful," Duncan said, "wait until the ax. By then you will scream in agony each time someone touches the skin of your leg. There will be unbearable pain for a couple hours, then you will likely die anyway." He turned to the sturdy German woman. "Dig his grave by those of his friends the rangers."

The Scot moved no more, just gazed abjectly at the line drawn on his skin.

"Were you at Ticonderoga?" Duncan asked.

The man accepted a drink of water from Mrs. Zettlemeyer. "All the regiment was at Ticonderoga," he replied sullenly. "I was a sergeant. It's sergeants who run the battle."

"Who was on the ridge above?"

"Onondagas. Then we saw the Hurons on the ledge above them, where they could destroy the old man and the other Iroquois with five minutes of musketry."

"Tashgua? Tashgua's band was there?"

The Scot nodded.

"You mean the Hurons were preparing to attack Tashgua's band?"

"That's what we thought, that's why we ran up there. But they weren't attacking, they were waiting."

"If Tashgua wasn't there to fight, why was he there?"

The Scot's thin mouth twisted. "You wouldn't understand. None of us really understood for months."

"Try me."

"Gods get new faces."

"Do not speak in riddles of such important things. I must know!"

It was Reverend Zettlemeyer who answered, from the shadows where he had hovered. "It is what old Tashgua does," he said in an already strained voice. "He stands between his people and their gods, to explain to his people the demands of their spirits. If he fails, the spirits will abandon them, and the people will die. But he knows that spirits can change, just as men can change."

Duncan searched their faces. "I still don't understand."

"Everyone says the French won that day," the deserter said in a bitter voice, "with nigh on two thousand British lying dead and wounded, and no more than one-tenth that on General Montcalm's side. But not to old Tashgua, not to all the Iroquois chiefs who came with him. To them, the British and French gods were battling it out on that field, and they had never seen anything like the British one. What else could explain thousands of men willingly throwing themselves to the cannons? He had never imagined such a powerful god. He was so shaken, his daughter had to lead him away."

"That's when he began doubting himself," Duncan said.

"That's when—Mother of Christ!" the man gasped, raising his knife again. "Look at you!"

Duncan stared in confusion. Nothing had changed about him, except he had stepped closer to the full sunlight cast by the chamber's small window. Outside, during the surgery, the man had been blindfolded. For the first time he was seeing Duncan's countenance in direct light.

"Step further into the light!" the man demanded. "Do it, or I swear I'll rip your stitches out of my leg."

Duncan took an uncertain step forward, into the pool of light.

"He said he had a brother," the Scot declared in a suddenly

wrathful voice, "an English doctor who sold out their clan, betrayed an old uncle to the gallows to please his lacy lairds."

Duncan's mouth went dry as tinder. "Where is he? Where is Jamie?"

The man seemed to have forgotten his pain. He studied Duncan with a cool, thin smile. "Many a night I've sat and listened to him recount the ways all traitors must be dealt with. Last time he said his brother the doctor would have a medical kit with cutting tools. He vowed to use each one on you before you breathed your last."

Duncan felt the cold scalpel in his heart already. "It isn't like that. They traced my uncle to me. I never—"

The man lurched upright and launched a hand at Duncan, hitting his chest before collapsing in pain.

Through his own agony, Duncan saw the man had ripped the tartan sash from inside his shirt.

"You'll not use this for your lying and cheating of true Scots."

"I am the eldest of the Highland McCallums, I—"

"There be no English boots to lick here. Save your song for when you're tied to the post. He's learnt a thing or two from the tribes, about making men sing." The deserter stuffed the plaid inside his own shirt, then seemed to brighten. "My nurse this afternoon told me ye be a Ramsey slave. The river's up, high enough for Ramsey canoes to journey here in a day or two, with Major Pike not far behind. Ye got nowhere to run but into the arms of y'er heathen brother." Despite the obvious pain it caused him, the man burst into a harsh, wheezing laughter.

A hand was suddenly on Duncan's shoulder. Reverend Zettle-meyer was at his side. Duncan let himself be led out of the springhouse like one of the living dead.

Chapter Thirteen

A GOAT TIED TO A TREE. Woolford's words from the night on the Hudson echoed in Duncan's mind as he sat on the bench where Zettlemeyer had led him. He had thought he could escape that fate, even save Lister and Sarah in doing so. But now his brother wouldn't come for him because the army dangled Duncan like bait; he would come because he hated Duncan as much as Duncan hated the English aristocrats. Either way his brother would die; either way Duncan would be powerless to save his friends. The deserter in the springhouse was right. He didn't deserve the piece of tartan. He was an arrogant fool to even playact as a clan chief. The Ramseys and Pikes of the world were destined to win, would always win. He would wear an iron collar around his neck for years, and every time he touched it he would think of Lister and his brother rotting in their graves, because of him.

A low, throaty rumble disturbed the still evening air. The sound of an angry ox. Duncan was on his feet before he heard the second sound, the hissing rhythm of a switch being jerked through the air. He did not pause as he reached the shed, did not hesitate as he launched himself at the Welshman, seizing his uplifted arm as it was about to slam the stick onto the boy's back again. He thrust his foot against the man's knee, spinning him violently backward against a post.

Quickly turning to examine Alex's injuries, he lifted the boy's torn shirt and froze. The ox's tether was stretched tight, its nostrils were flared, its eyes bulging. With another ounce of effort the massive creature could snap the line and, in its current temper, could destroy anything in its path.

But Alex, without even a glance at Duncan, darted to the ox and began stroking its neck. Instantly the tether went slack and the animal's angry breathing quieted, replaced by the gasping of the Welshman, whose breath had been knocked out of him.

Duncan ventured a step closer. The boy spread his arms and the ox buried its mighty head in them. As Duncan paused, unwilling to disturb the embrace, a slab of firewood struck a painful, glancing blow on his shoulder. A second blow knocked Duncan to the ground, and the Welshman charged forward, switch in hand. He landed another two strikes on the boy's back before the ox hurled him aside with a thrust of its horn, then Duncan reached him, seizing his free arm, pulling it behind him, bending it until the man cried out in pain. Learning the treatment of injuries at the pugilist matches in Yorkshire also meant he had learned their causes.

"Do you feel that?" Duncan asked in a simmering voice, twisting the man's arm. "The way the pain rises as I turn it? A little more—" the man gasped as Duncan turned it again, "—and you won't use it for a day."

"He gave the brute double rations," the Welshman groaned. "He has no right."

"Working until dusk, that is double duty," Duncan suggested.

"You be the one! The McCallum fugitive that has the great lord so furious! Fifty pounds on your head!"

Duncan increased the pressure on the man's arm. "If I twist some more you won't use it for a week. And then how will you raise that musket when the savages come for you?"

"I can fix things for ye," the Welshman groaned. "I'll give ye to Ramsey when he comes. Then I'll split the bounty with ye and let ye go. We can be rich!"

Duncan pressed harder, and the Welshman let Duncan pull the

switch from his hand. Duncan released his hold and broke the switch on his knee. As he turned to toss the pieces into the darkness, he saw a bearded head watching from the shadows. Reverend Zettlemeyer, his body all but obscured by his black clothes, wore a sober, almost melancholy expression but offered not a word. As the Welshman followed Duncan's gaze toward the missionary, he gave a defeated sigh. But he turned with a vindictive gleam before slipping away into the night.

"Ain't just Ramsey who wants ye, boy. There's a price on y'er hair. Ye be worth more to the Huron dead and scalped than presented intact to the great lord. In a few days ye'll be begging to be turned over to Ramsey."

Duncan stared into the darkness after the man, his heart racing. Ramsey and the French savages were competing for his head. It was impossible. Why would the French want him dead?

Duncan turned to the boy, who had taken the Welshman's final blows like an old sailor, without breaking his embrace of the brindled beast. He lifted the boy's tattered shirt only a few inches before Alex jerked it out of his grasp and slipped to the other side of the ox. But it was enough for Duncan to see the marks left by many such beatings in the past.

The boy's eyes went wild as those of the ox as Duncan tried to approach him again. Duncan retreated, began stroking the opposite flank of the ox, rubbing him down with a rag that hung on a nearby peg. After a few strokes the boy pulled the rag from his hand and began using it himself.

Duncan offered greetings, offered apologies, offered to find Alex some extra food for himself, but nothing prompted so much as a glance from the former slave to the Indians. What had Reverend Zettlemeyer said? The boy had lost all the talents of society.

When Duncan finally abandoned his effort and stepped out of the shed, Reverend Zettlemeyer was still standing there, watching with the same melancholy expression.

"If this is what Moravians do for orphans," Duncan spat, "then the New World can do without your settlers."

Zettlemeyer seemed to accept the words like a well-deserved blow. "I wake in the middle of the night thinking of Alex," he said. "I find myself stopping amidst prayer thinking of the boy, and the Ramsey girl. I know not how to reach them."

Duncan's head snapped up. "Sarah? You've seen her?"

"Ten days ago. But ever since she first visited last year, she is in my thoughts, sometimes my nightmares."

Duncan stepped closer to the missionary. "Sarah was here ten days ago?"

"Just for a night. She rode away at dawn, in the direction of Edentown, right toward the raiding parties. She has powerful angels over her, that one."

"She saw Alex?"

Zettlemeyer nodded. "It was like she needed to be certain he was still alive."

Duncan turned, looking up to the night sky, his mind racing, and stepped toward the open fields.

The German kept speaking to his back. "My wife says you saved the life of our guest in the springhouse." Duncan kept walking. "Just a word, McCallum."

Duncan did not respond.

"Sarah Ramsey didn't just speak to Alex, McCallum. She spoke to me about a dead man named Evering."

Duncan halted, slowly turned. The old Moravian gestured him toward the moonlit field above the village and began walking. He had settled onto one of the stumps near the top when Duncan reached him. When he spoke again, he had none of the confidence of a man accustomed to the pulpit.

"She told me to protect the boy, to keep him safe, away from any visitors. But the boy will have none of it. I brought him into the house to sleep the night after she left, and he climbed out the window."

"But what of Evering?" Duncan asked.

"She said a man named Evering had been given a vital message from Adam Munroe, who had known he was going to die. Evering was to have warned me, she said."

"Warn you about what?"

"That was the source of her greatest agony. Adam Munroe had decided she could not know, that it was to be the job of the Ramsey tutor to carry the warning. She sat up here with me and wept as she watched Alex settling into the stable. She asked me strange things. She asked if I had ever met the English king. I would have thought it a jest but for her solemn expression. She asked me if I had had dreams since the massacre last year. She gave me something in a leather pouch I was to pass on as a message."

"To whom?"

"She made me pledge not to reveal that."

"Then what was the message?"

"I don't know what it meant. There were no words, no writing." Zettlemeyer sank his head into his hands a moment. "A pouch. Inside were a claw, a bear claw with little red feathers tied around it. At the bottom were a dozen purple beads." He looked up, searched Duncan's face. "You are the Ramsey tutor. Explain the catastrophe that comes."

"Huron raiders. Lord Ramsey. Major Pike," Duncan said. "We are rich in catastrophes about to break upon us." He felt the Moravian's gaze again. "I don't know. Evering was murdered before he could speak with me."

They sat in the cool stillness, gazing at the stars.

"My son leaves soon to bring back more settlers," Zettlemeyer said at last. "He has a grand speech about property and land ownership. I told him I cannot go because of my health, but the truth is I cannot go because I don't know what to tell them about this place, about how a good Christian goes about taming the wilderness."

"Do you fear the wilderness?"

"We'd be fools not to. Most nights one of the children wakes up screaming from nightmares about Indian attacks. But that's only a part of it." The missionary went silent again. "You think you bring your old identity with you when you come as a settler," he began at last, "your culture, your values, your knowledge of what it means to be human. But when you settle onto the new land, you soon learn that all that is gone. You are naked. You have nothing of the Old World to rely on. There is only what is in here—" Zettlemeyer tapped his chest, "and what is out there." He gestured toward the forest. "When I first came, I met an old Indian named Conawago. I said, 'this is Eden.' In reply he said, 'Yes, except it is the eighteenth century.'" The German fell silent again.

"This is God's great experiment on earth," he continued. "Here He reduces everyone to a common denominator, to see how they start over. And there are others who have pursued a spiritual life in the forest far longer than we have." He ended with an unexpected motion, two fingers extended, spiraling upward. Duncan had seen it before.

"Is it something about the heavens, Reverend, that sign?"

"They use many names. The Great Spirit. The Guardian of the Forest. Most of the old ones just call it the Great Mystery."

Duncan considered the Moravian's words as they gazed at the stars. "Are you saying, Reverend, you have lost your appetite for converting the Indians?"

Zettlemeyer seemed to struggle to get his response out. "I am only asking the question. What if our spirits are blinded by what we bring from across the ocean?"

A shiver ran down Duncan's spine. "Why do you say these things to me?" Something small in the forest began screeching in terror, its cries gradually subsiding as it died.

"Because I am the one who betrayed the ghostwalkers," Zettlemeyer blurted out in an anguished tone. "The price for doing so has been far heavier than I expected."

"But they were captured by soldiers."

"The three asked me to release them. I refused, for the good of their souls. I kept Sarah Ramsey locked in a room until she could be safely conveyed to New York."

There was more, Duncan sensed. The missionary still was not

telling him what weighed most heavy on his heart. "You visited Edentown last week," he ventured.

Zettlemeyer sighed heavily. "We had nothing, hardly enough to feed ourselves, no hope of anything so costly as an iron furnace."

Gradually Duncan fit the pieces together. "There was a reward paid by Lord Ramsey," he concluded.

The Moravian's head moved up and down in the moonlight. "A wagonload of food at the start of the winter. It was a great blessing. We gave thanks to Ramsey in our prayers. But I did not understand something about Ramsey."

"A man like Ramsey," Duncan suggested, "doesn't pay rewards. He pays retainers."

"Crates of Bibles. The equipment to build the furnace. More cases of Bibles, even copies of the Greek philosophers."

"Money for transport of new settlers," Duncan said.

"Even our bishop prays for Ramsey now. And I get letters from Edentown asking about things."

"Things?"

"How many Indians have we baptized. How many Indian children in our school. Send the last known location of the shaman Tashgua. Make two maps of the location of all the settlers' farms we know of. It doesn't seem like much, does it? Ramsey sent me a passage from the Old Testament about how true believers must destroy the temples of the idolators. When he was here two days ago, Reverend Arnold announced that the hand of God soon will make a fist."

The words left a smell in the air, like the smell after a lightning strike.

"Once every few days I see a huge bear at the edge of the fields, by the northern trail," Zettlemeyer said in a thin, weary voice. "Sometimes it brings the body of something to eat there. It eats, then it sits and watches us. I couldn't bear to tell Sarah about my dreams when she asked. I often wake in cold sweats, my heart pounding from a dream in which I find the bear sitting at our hearth in a chair, reading our Bible."

Duncan did not respond, in that moment did not believe himself capable of responding. The old Moravian began whispering a prayer, in German. Duncan studied the thousand stars overhead. When he looked back down, Zettlemeyer was gone.

He retrieved his pack from the shadows by the furnace and found his way to the cow shed, then located the small, slender form lying against the slumbering ox and settled onto the straw-covered earth beside the boy, pulling straw over them both. He listened for a long time to the strangely harmonized breathing of the two creatures.

"Alex," he whispered at last, "I know not how to reach you when you are awake. But my grandfather taught me there are parts of us that listen while we sleep." The breathing of the ox seemed to grow in volume, the great hairy back heaving up and down.

"My name is Duncan McCallum," he began. "And I live between worlds, as you do." After these first difficult words, the others came out with surprising ease. He explained how he had been arrested and transported, how he had met Adam Munroe, how Adam had died, then spoke of Reverend Arnold and Ramsey and Pike and Woolford. In a lower voice he spoke of Sarah's kidnapping, and of Conawago and the ruined Indian graveyard where he had left him. "There are questions left by the dead, Alex, which will never be answered unless you and I help."

When he finally fell silent, the ox turned its great head toward him, as if it had been listening and knew that Duncan had left something out. After a moment he whispered his final, brittle confession. "I built a dream around finding my brother, and all the while he has wanted me dead." When he settled back onto the straw, he realized his hand had closed around the stone bear, his fingers rubbing the head. So often it had done so in the past weeks, it had become something of a reflex.

He rose before dawn, when he could still fix the North Star, and quietly slipped out of the shed, after piling added straw over the sleeping boy, pausing to touch the crown of the ox, who watched him intently, and pausing again with a grateful grin when he found a pouch of food lying on top of his pack. Five minutes later, on the far side of the fields, he halted. Someone had lit a small fire at the head of the trail to the north. Looking about for a sign of the Moravians, he warily advanced and was almost upon the fire when he glanced down and froze. It was a small mound of tobacco leaves, carefully laid over burning coals. He gasped in alarm as a hand closed around his shoulder from the back. His assailant did not speak, and was already returning his war club to his belt as Duncan turned to face him.

"Conawago!" Duncan exclaimed.

The old Indian acknowledged him with a slight nod, then solemnly pointed to the trail and began a slow trot toward the north. Duncan squatted by the fire a moment before following, cupping the smoke in his hand as he knew Conawago must have done, washing it over his face.

The old Indian did not speak the few times they paused to rest, but somehow Duncan did not expect him to. He was in mourning still, for the dead who had been killed again by the Ramsey men. He had made no more lacerations on his limbs, and, to Duncan's relief, those he had made were healing well, though they gave the old man a fierce aspect, the look of an ancient and awful warrior.

As they sat on a high, stony ridge, silently sharing a piece of bread from the mission, Duncan began to notice the wariness in Conawago's eyes. Pushing ever northward, he watched uncomfortably as the old Indian knelt several times to study the trail, sometimes pressing his ear to the ground. Suddenly he gestured Duncan off the well-used path, leading him at a run to a smaller parallel game trail on the ridge above, then pausing at a stout oak to gaze back, his hand on his club.

The explanation came half an hour later, as they moved along a series of high outcroppings. They had slowed to a walk, Duncan in front, and he had cleared the end of a long pile of huge boulders when he spotted a solitary figure moving at a steady lope nearly a hundred yards away on the main trail. It was an Indian, adorned not unlike those he had seen at the army headquarters, a musket strapped upside down on his back. When he turned to point the man out to Conawago, his friend was nowhere to be seen.

"There is—" he began, then a figure materialized in the air, leaping onto Duncan, knocking him to the ground, clamping a small hand over his mouth. Duncan frantically tried to free himself, then realized his assailant was not trying to hurt him, but was using his free hand to cover them both with dried leaves. A small face appeared near his own, aimed not at Duncan but at the trail below. It was Alex.

A moment later more figures appeared. Alex tensed, seemed to stop breathing. Twenty-four, Duncan counted, all appearing much the same as the first, except for two men in the center who wore white fringed tunics with green wool caps and green leggings. They all trotted at a uniform pace, fleet and silent as deer.

For five minutes after the party had passed, the only part of Alex that moved was his eyes. His hand stayed clamped on Duncan's mouth. He made no effort to shift the debris from their prostrate bodies.

Finally came a low, warbling whistle behind them, and the boy was up, brushing off his clothes.

"They won't hurt you, Alex," Duncan said to the boy. "I know they must terrify you after all they—"

The boy ignored Duncan, stepped eagerly to Conawago's side. They clamped their forearms together, their hands gripping near the elbow in a silent, emotional greeting. There was a new aspect to the boy, a feral quality that had been absent at the mission. He had unthreaded the sleeves of his shirt and removed them, leaving his arms bare. A length of rope hung around his waist, from which hung a small pouch. Around his neck was a necklace woven of familiar tawny hair. Alex had braided it from the hair of his ox.

"I thought you had grown more particular about your scalp," Conawago chastised Duncan.

"But they were like—" Duncan suddenly felt weak. He lowered

himself onto a rock. Despite his first impression, obviously they had not been like Conawago, not like the army Indians.

"Hurons. And a few Abenaki, if I'm not mistaken. Two French soldiers, at least one an officer. If they'd seen us, we wouldn't have lasted five minutes. They are not inclined to be merciful, or to take prisoners, this deep in enemy territory."

Duncan fought a shudder. "A raiding party? Why here? The farms are along the river."

"Raids on farms are usually by just a handful of Hurons," Conawago replied. "Which means the better question is why a party so large should be here at all. A party that size acts as skirmishers between units of the main armies. But the armies are far north of here, where General Wolfe is moving on Quebec. They shouldn't be here."

They shouldn't be here, Duncan repeated to himself, just as they shouldn't even know who Duncan was. But they were here, and the French were paying the Hurons to kill him.

Five hours later Duncan was about to drop from exhaustion when Conawago abruptly halted his relentless pace, dropping to a knee beside a fallen tree. Again Duncan knew the old Indian had seen, or sensed, something invisible to him. It was evening. They had been climbing a series of ledges that rose stairlike up a steep ridge, eating dried meat on the run. In the still air came the call of a bird, a low, two-tone whistle, which caused Alex's head to snap up with a broad grin. Conawago answered the call, and a figure in green emerged from behind a rock a hundred feet ahead.

Captain Woolford looked worn out. The left side of his face bore a long bruise; one hand was wrapped in a bloodstained rag. He offered a weary nod, then led them to a campsite nestled among rock outcroppings beside a fast-moving spring. It was a base camp of some kind, Duncan realized, for inside the shadows of an overhanging ledge he spied several leather pouches, a kettle, and half a dozen rolled blankets.

After greeting the boy with a long, silent embrace and conferring in low, hurried tones with Conawago, the ranger confronted Duncan.

"Do you have any idea what Ramsey will do to you when he catches up?" Woolford snapped. "You're going to wish you had chosen to stay on the ship and face Jamaica. With fifty pounds on your head, you'll probably be better off if it *is* Ramsey who takes you. He is paying for you alive, but barely alive will be good enough for him."

"I must start traveling with a clerk," Duncan replied, his voice heavy with fatigue, "to keep tally of all those who wish me harm." He decided to tell the ranger about the French bounty on him, leaving the officer gazing in confusion at him. "Now let me see that hand," Duncan said in conclusion.

The ranger did not object as Duncan unwrapped the makeshift bandage. It had been an ugly gash across the back of the hand, but was healing well. Duncan did some quick calculation. "This was done not long after you left Edentown."

Woolford gestured to Duncan's own wound along his temple. "It could have been the same knife that did that. They jumped me at a stream. They had more blades, I had faster legs. And they knew nothing of reloading on the fly." He sensed the question in Duncan's eye. "Rangers are trained to load while running, at least one shot a minute, including time to twist about and aim." His gaze settled on Alex, who was helping Conawago light a fire. "How does he fare?"

"I left him at the mission this morning, thinking he was lost to the world of men. Three hours later he just appeared from thin air. Saved my life. Or more accurately, kept my foolishness from killing us all."

"The Hurons aren't supposed to be here. Headquarters tells me all the French Indians have been called back north, to harass Wolfe's army marching on Quebec. When I sent an urgent message reporting they were wrong, that every farm from Edentown to German Flats has been raided, all I got back were orders to move north myself." Woolford explained that he had already dispatched most of his men north, then studied the forest with a worried expression. "One of my men had been tracking this party. They were headed north and changed course three days ago, turned back for here."

"Why?"

Woolford shook his head in frustration. "It's like a war within a war."

"We must be close to Stony Run," Duncan declared.

"No more than ten miles now."

They fell silent again. "If he had lived, Adam would have found a way to be there now, because of his wife," Duncan said with a tone of query.

"Because of his wife," Woolford agreed. "If things had been different."

It had been one of the many layers of mystery surrounding Adam Munroe. But Duncan had finally realized that he had kept his wife a secret because she was part of the secret of his Indian captivity, because he had married while with the Indians. "Will she be there?" Duncan asked.

A low sigh escaped Conawago's lips.

"Butterflies," a small, tentative voice said. "There is a valley full of butterflies where she lives now." Alex had found his tongue. "She used to visit it often, would tell me about it." He spoke very slowly, seeming to struggle for each word. "She makes meal with a magic pestle, never having to add more maize. And there are . . . ." His lips twisted in frustration and he made a sign of something large and round with his arms, then turned and spoke in a tribal tongue to Conawago.

"And pumpkins," Conawago translated, "fields full of pumpkins."

"Pumpkins," Alex nodded. "She likes pumpkins."

Duncan dared not speak for fear of spooking the boy. In the spreading darkness only his gaunt face was visible, lit by glowing embers.

"When we arrived at the German mission, Adam said we weren't prisoners," Alex continued, "but they all treated us as if we were."

"When she came to visit him, he sent her away," added a new voice, low and strained. Woolford, turning halfway so he could still watch the night.

"Not right away," Alex explained. "They spoke first, Adam and Sarah and she. They didn't know I was watching. Adam gave her something, told her she had to flee to the farthest of the Indian towns. I don't think they even saw when I followed her, hanging out the Reverend's cabin window. I thought no one else saw. I caught up with her behind the furnace. We slipped into the forest past the charcoal piles and ran. One of the Germans knew the trails, though, and led the soldiers onto the path that goes over the ridge, while I took her around it, because of my twisted ankle and because she was with child, four or five months with child.

"Suddenly they were there, leaping down the hill, calling out. She was terrified, pushed me ahead, clutching the sacred thing in both hands, the thing that Adam had saved from an old chief at the massacre, the thing he ran down the waterfall with and had given her for safe-keeping. I didn't understand the ways of those men in red. I was in front of her when she fell on her knees, and I turned to see the thing that grew out of her breast. She stared at it, touching it with one hand, not under-standing. She even tried to get up, but that metal had taken all her strength. Not a night passes when I don't see her like that, her hand on the metal growing out of her, covered with her own blood. I was as con-fused as she was. I, too, had never seen one of those things before."

"What things?" Duncan asked, his throat tightening.

"A musket sword."

Woolford spoke again, in a desolate whisper. "Bayonet. A bay-onet in her back."

The tale opened a frigid chamber inside Duncan's mind. He was back in Flanders, learning for the first time what the English soldiers had done to his family.

"Sometimes I find a snake in the forest and ask to visit her," Alex said. "They live in the valley of the butterflies, just like Adam prom-ised they would. By a river, because of Adam."

"They?" Duncan asked. "Who else is there with her?"

"Adam. He just came a few weeks ago."

A new chill crept down Duncan's spine as he exchanged a haunted glance with Woolford.

"What do you mean beside the river, because of Adam?"

Alex looked up uncertainly, then gazed into the embers. "A spirit totem is his secret, not for words of men."

But Duncan did not need to be told. The beaver. The beaver had been Adam's sacred sign, the beaver who had been carved on the mast when Adam died, the beaver who swam deep.

"She didn't want to leave him at the mission that day. Adam said she had to save the ancient thing, or the soldiers would find a way to use it against her people. He promised she would be safe, that there was nothing to worry about, that he knew she would never let go of it, never let it fall into enemy hands, that it would protect her, that if anything happened to her he would know. He vowed on the spirit of their child that if she went to her sacred land before him, he would know and he would join her." Alex poked at the embers. "Sometimes when I see them, there is a small shape in the shadows behind them. It's him, I think. Their son."

There was no sound for a long time, none except the distant lonely call of an owl.

"I killed them," Alex said in a tiny voice, filled with pain.

"Impossible," Duncan said.

"I didn't understand until later, when I heard those soldiers complaining. They had been told there would be a large reward paid for Sarah. They thought I would have family who would pay as well. It's why they followed, because of me. What they took from her only paid for a few mugs of rum."

When Duncan finally stirred, Alex was asleep, his head on Conawago's leg. He rose and stepped across the fire. "You knew about the thing she was protecting, the ancient thing," he said to Woolford's back. "You recovered it."

"Like the boy said, it took awhile to understand. When I did, I rescued it from those who stole it. But Adam decided to flee that very night, as far from the army as he could go."

"But why didn't he run back into the woods?" Duncan asked.

"Because he knew there were men who would use him against the Indians. Because he heard that Major Pike was coming the next day to interrogate him, and if he went among the Iroquois, Pike had ways to find him."

"You recovered the ancient thing and then it was stolen from you on the ship." The bear, Duncan knew now, had been in the blood-stained doeskin pouch passed around the prisoner's hold. He glanced at his pack, where the bear lay snug against his pipes.

"I was trying to keep it safe. I never expected Adam to take it with him. He must have decided it was the only way for it not to be used against his wife's people."

"Or he could not abide that it was in your possession. You belonged to the ones who killed her."

Duncan regretted the words instantly. For a moment the sturdy ranger looked as if he might weep. "It was a mistake, McCallum. Those soldiers didn't understand. Some may have wanted a bounty. But all of them assumed she was stealing Alex back into slavery."

Duncan settled onto the ground by the fire. It was a long time before he slept. When he awoke two hours before dawn, he saw that Conawago had replaced Woolford as the sentry. He rose and gestured the old Indian back to the sleeping forms by the fire, to take his turn on watch.

Crickets chirped along the spring. An owl called in the distance. Duncan lay back on a rock and stared up at the stars.

It wasn't the sunlight that woke him, nor the morning calls of the birds. It was the cold steel of an army sword pressed against his jugular.

"Breathe wrong and you're a dead man, McCallum."

Duncan resisted only for a moment. The instant he twisted his neck he felt his skin begin to break, sensed something warm oozing down his neck. He froze and looked up into the cool gray eyes he had first seen at the army headquarters in New York. Major Pike had abandoned his wig, but had added a pistol and a silver-hilted dagger to his belt.

"Careless of you to venture forth without your patrons," the officer hissed. "No royal cousin to interfere. No soft-hearted general."

Someone at the edge of his vision lowered a pack and extracted something, clinking of metal. A red-coated soldier stepped beside Pike carrying a set of manacles. As Pike looked up, Duncan twisted slightly, trying to see the rest of the camp. It was empty. What had Pike done to his companions? He had failed them, had fallen asleep while on watch. Duncan's hand reached for his belt. His tomahawk and knife were gone.

"Where is he?" Pike demanded. He placed a foot on Duncan's belly, jammed the sword's point against Duncan's heart. It was the action of a hunter about to dispatch his wounded prey. The soldier, a brawny man with a face like a hatchet, bent over Duncan and fastened the manacles around his ankles.

"Lord Ramsey?" Duncan said, struggling to keep his voice level. "Much closer than you think."

A cool satisfaction entered Pike's eyes. "My Indian fighters report a charming habit among the heathen," the officer declared. "Making necklaces of their enemy's body parts." He extracted his dagger and handed it to the soldier with the manacles. "A man with medical training might regret the loss of some fingers. Sergeant, the right hand first." The sergeant offered a cool smile as he bent over Duncan again, so close Duncan could smell the tobacco on his breath, so close he could see the pockmarks on his cheek, oddly set in two pairs, four inches apart.

"Maiming a member of His Majesty's rangers," a cool voice interjected, "could raise regrettable questions when General Calder hears of it." Pike's sword relaxed enough for Duncan to twist and see Woolford, squatting at the fire, calmly rebuilding it.

"This is not your concern, Captain," Pike growled. "Do not dare to meddle in affairs of my office."

"Above all it is my concern. This man is a member of my company."

"Ridiculous."

"His left waistcoat pocket."

Pike angrily gestured to the sergeant, who probed Duncan's left pocket, offered a low curse, and rose with a large round medallion, one of the rangers' identification badges. It had not, Duncan was certain, been there the night before.

Woolford produced a small, dog-eared, leather-bound book from his own pocket and waved it toward Pike. "Duncan McCallum was entered on my rolls yesterday."

Pike's face went crimson. "You have no authority."

"A combat officer in a combat zone has worlds of authority," Woolford countered in a casual tone, then shrugged. "You could challenge it, Major. But you would have to do so in Albany or New York town."

"Bold words for one officer alone in the wilds."

Woolford fixed Pike with an unblinking stare. "Many have made the mistake of underestimating the strength of a ranger in the field."

"And many have made the mistake of thinking they can mock me," Pike snarled.

Woolford stood, suddenly quite sober. "If you are looking for satisfaction, Pike, I am your man."

"Easy words when you know the king's officers are forbidden to duel." A different kind of hunger seemed to build on Pike's face. "The ranger company was ordered toward Canada, Captain. You are in violation of your orders."

"Hurons are here in strength, Major. My skirmishers have engaged them several times. A party of that size could pose a threat to the supply trains behind the lines. The general will not second-guess my decision to keep a few men behind while we gauge their intentions."

"You are mistaken, sir. Leave this forest. Not being in the west is a dereliction of duty. The general waits my assessment of the situation here. I shall report that your failure to follow his orders destabilizes our efforts."

"The integrity of a report is but as good as the integrity of the officer who pens it."

Pike's eyes flared again. He took a step toward the ranger, sword extended low at his side. Strangely, he did not look at Woolford, but at the half-dozen soldiers of his own party, as if silently assessing them. Duncan slowly sat up and pushed himself against a rock. Pike's burly sergeant placed a boot on Duncan's leg.

The whistle of the thrush came so perfectly pitched, so clear, that only when it was repeated did Duncan realize it came from Woolford. A moment later it was echoed from somewhere else among the rock ledges. Instantly Pike's men raised their weapons, some taking cover behind rocks. Woolford whistled again and the reply quickly came, though this time fifty feet from where the first had come, then another, from the rocks above them.

The sneer on Pike's face disappeared.

Duncan pulled his leg free of the sergeant, who gazed with a worried expression into the forest. He rose and hurried to the other side of the fire, looking for a rock, a stick, anything he might use as a weapon. Another thrush sounded, behind them now. He spotted his knife and tomahawk, near the sergeant's feet, and calculated whether he could reach them before the sergeant shook off his distraction.

"We are all good soldiers of the king," Pike ventured. "Call them out. We shall make breakfast."

"No. Rangers eat cold breakfast, at dawn, or not at all. And you smell too much. Toilet water, soap, brandy, talcum, boot polish. My men spend weeks taking on the scents of the forest. Your stench could endanger their lives."

"You address a superior officer, Woolford." The cold fury had returned to Pike's voice.

"Your stink is unbearable, *sir.*"

For a moment Pike seemed about to explode. Then he studied the surrounding ledges with a worried eye, muttered quick orders to his men. In less than a minute they had shouldered their packs and were gone.

Duncan watched in confusion as Woolford squatted at the fire, stirring the coals, then rose to pack his few belongings for travel. Five minutes later Conawago and Alex materialized beside the nearest outcropping, the old Indian signaling to Woolford with a thrust of his hand toward the northwest as the ranger warily watched the forest in the direction of the redcoats.

As Woolford gestured for Duncan to pack his own bag, the truth began to dawn on him. "There was no one else," Duncan concluded. He recalled the location of the bird signals. The Indian and the boy, as fleet and silent as they were, could possibly have shifted to most of the locations, though he never would have expected it from one of Conawago's years. He pointed to the high rock opposite them, the source of the last whistle. "But you couldn't have climbed that," he said to the old Indian.

"The creatures of the forest choose their sides, too," Conawago explained.

A slight grin grew on Duncan's face, answered by one on the Indian's countenance. It had been an actual thrush, joining the skirmish. A low sound of amusement rose from Woolford, breaking the brittle air of the camp. For the first time since Duncan had known him, Conawago laughed.

Their lightheartedness quickly faded as they moved northward. Woolford insisted on scouting ahead, always running, waiting every quarter hour until they caught up with him, conferring with Conawago before setting off again. It was midmorning when they abruptly changed course.

Duncan was about to ask for an explanation when he began to detect the scent of burning wheat.

They reached the source of the smoke half an hour later, pausing at the edge of a wide clearing along the river. The overgrown field of ripened grain, the garden of insect-pocked vegetables, the half-burned stumps, the scrawny cow, indicated the little farm by the river had been struggling. But now its struggle was at an end. The small cabin was in ruin, collapsed into embers. The field was smoldering. The cow was dead. Woolford took a step forward and froze. A moccasined foot extended from a tree in front of him. The ranger bent, raising his rifle, then as quickly relaxed as he advanced another step.

It was a man with long, ragged hair, clad in buckskin, slumped against the tree, his eyes opened forlornly toward the farm. But he could not see. An arrow had pierced his breast, leaving a long streak of blood down his leather tunic. A gourd canteen was upended at his side. He had taken time to die.

Woolford made a hand signal to Conawago and they separated, circling around the ruined building. Duncan saw the empty way Alex gazed at the dead man and pulled him away.

They found Conawago bent over a soot-stained woman who sat on the ground, cradling the head of a man on her lap, stroking his face. Tears streamed down her cheek. Her calico dress was torn and stained, her hands bloody.

Duncan dropped his pack and urgently leaned over the man, looking for injuries, then froze and backed away. The man was beyond his help. Blood had congealed on half a dozen wounds in his belly and chest. A four-inch strip of hair at his crown had been sliced away.

Alex appeared, carrying water in a charred wooden bowl draped with a rag. Conawago knelt, pulling down the lids of the man's unseeing eyes as he murmured strange words to the woman, who still not did not respond.

Ramsey's painting. The image recoiled in Duncan's mind as vividly as the hour he had seen it in the aristocrat's library. The woman at the cabin at the edge of the woods, cradling a man's head. Except this woman and this man were Indian.

"Moravians," Woolford explained when Duncan stepped to his side. "Part of Reverend Zettlemeyer's flock."

"But the cabin. The field. The cow. . . ."

"Go to any large Iroquois town and you'll see acres of maize and pumpkins. They understand farming. This is the way of the peaceable kingdom, the Moravians tell them. These two would often travel to the mission on Saturday to be there for the Sabbath." Woolford began lifting pieces of debris, bending over a footprint here, the mark of a heel there, studying the landscape as if to reconstruct the attack.

Duncan, too, surveyed the rolling field, the stream, the blue mountains in the distance. It was the kind of place where, in his own dreams, he might have started a farm for his clan. But in the world in which he was living, every dream ended in something smoldering and bloody. He gazed in confusion back toward the trees where the man in buckskins had died.

"It was quick, hot work here," Woolford said, as if to answer the question in Duncan's eyes. "They didn't linger, didn't even finish everything. Like they were in a rush to be elsewhere." He knelt, studying the dark, moist earth, then the ranger rose and circuited the house, examining footprints and breaks in the plant stems that had been trampled by the raiders. Finally he motioned for Duncan to help lift a half-burnt roof beam that had fallen into the cabin ruins. He raised a charred blanket from the remains of a bed and stepped back to the woman, who had refused to leave her dead husband. Conawago gently coaxed the woman to her feet, then led her to a bench at the side of the cabin that had escaped the fire. As she walked, Duncan noticed the slight, low roundness that said she was with child.

Woolford laid the blanket beside the dead man and motioned Duncan to his side. They silently laid the body on the blanket and carried him to the stream. When they had finished washing the body, Duncan extracted the ranger badge from his pocket and handed it to Woolford. "You probably saved my life with this."

"There are accounts to balance." The ranger made no effort to accept the badge.

"Accounts?"

"You buried Fitch."

"As any good Christian would have." He searched Woolford's face, which had gone cloudy. "Say what you mean, Captain. You are thinking of Adam and his wife."

Woolford looked away. "I knew her. A lot like Sarah, only happy. Always a song in her eyes, yet wise about many things."

"I saw her run with Alex that day at the mission, but I made the mistake of following them on the same trail. The infantrymen crossed the ridge and got there first. I arrived but a minute too late. They had already . . . . I stood over her body and ordered them away."

Woolford washed the dead man's arm for the third time.

"Already what?"

"Like Alex said. They had business."

Duncan closed his eyes a moment as he finally understood. "They scalped her," he whispered after a moment. "But the army is prohibited."

"We're a long way from headquarters. There's always someone with money for scalps. Trappers move between here and Canada. I caught one last year with twenty-five scalps hidden between his beaver skins. More of it goes on than ever before. Fitch and I swore if we ever found the one who opened those purse strings, we'd fill his throat with coins until he could breathe no more. It was what Fitch had been doing while I was gone to Europe, trying to track those who paid for hair, back along the trails to Canada." Woolford looked down at Duncan's hand, which still clasped the badge. "Keep it."

"I will not serve the king," Duncan insisted.

"The ocean is wide, the king is far away."

"The king is as close as Lord Ramsey."

Woolford winced, then stared into the face of the dead man, as if consulting him. He glanced back at the cabin, reached to his belt, and produced his knife, extending it to Duncan hilt first. "Like you announced once, you are a wondrous doctor to the dead," the ranger said as he lifted one side of the blanket, obscuring the view from the direction of Conawago and the woman.

"I don't follow."

"The wounds. I want to know what caused them. Do it," he insisted as he saw the hesitation in Duncan's eyes. "Then we'll wrap him tight in the blanket and dig a hole. He would have wanted a Christian burial. We'll have to make a marker."

Duncan slowly closed his fingers around the hilt, then knelt at the stream, slapping the cool water over his face before beginning the grisly work. In ten minutes' time he had produced two round musket balls. The other wounds had been stabs from short blades. Duncan washed the bullets off and handed them to Woolford, who gazed at them grimly before stashing them in his pocket.

They buried the man on a knoll under a tall sycamore. Duncan had begun a second grave when Woolford stopped him with a hand on his arm, gesturing toward the tree where the man with the arrow had died. The body was gone.

Duncan trotted to the tree in alarm. He could understand enough of the signs on the ground to see that the body had been dragged to the river by someone in moccasins coming from the homestead. Conawago. Conawago had dumped the body in the river while Duncan and Woolford had been digging the grave.

He asked no questions when they gathered at the grave. When no one offered words, Conawago spoke, first in a native tongue that Woolford did not seem to understand, then switching to English, solemnly reciting a Psalm. Duncan gazed at him in surprise, then remembered that the old Indian had long ago been educated by Jesuits. Alex stood beside the grief-stricken woman, holding her hand, showing no emotion as Duncan and Woolford began closing the grave, standing there with the Indian woman until they had finished. When she finally turned from the grave, she walked deliberately toward the ruined cabin. They followed and helped her pry up a charred floorboard, from under which she retrieved a long object wrapped in leather. She unrolled the wrapping to reveal a well-used hunting rifle, with a powder horn carved with deer. She spoke to Conawago, who shook his head, then she pressed, her insistent tone unmistakable, though Duncan knew not the words that were spoken.

When Conawago at last accepted the rifle, Woolford turned to Duncan. "She says the world is upside down. She says she could not bear for Conawago to be buried this season as well."

Alex helped the woman gather her few surviving possessions into a blanket, which he slung onto his shoulder, and then the two began walking across the field. When Duncan grabbed his own pack, Conawago put a restraining hand on his arm.

"They have a different path to take," he said.

Duncan looked in confusion from the old Indian to the boy. "But Alex . . . all those years a prisoner. Surely we can't just let him think he's a slave again. We must . . . ."

"God's breath!" Woolford snapped. "After all this, you cannot see? His nightmares aren't caused by all those years with the Indians. To his mind, he only became a prisoner when he was taken by Europeans."

Duncan looked from the ranger to Conawago, both of whom gazed at him; perplexed, he looked down at the earth, at his feet, with unexpected shame. He was a fool to think he was progressing toward the truth. All he ever found was more confusion.

"Do you think he suffers from anything you and I do not?" Woolford asked in a forgiving tone.

"What are you saying?"

"His days spent with Arnold and Ramsey at the mission. You asked once when the Company was started. That's when."

"At the mission? But that was where Alex explained the Iroquois to them, tried to explain their trade routes, their concept of religion, how the shamans were the lifeblood of their people, how . . . ."

"Exactly," Woolford interrupted, as if Duncan need say no more. The ranger turned, retrieved his pack and rifle, and began jogging back up the trail.

They moved in silence, Duncan's companions so wary now that he retrieved a heavy piece of wood from the forest floor to defend himself. As they climbed the final mountain before their destination, Conawago and Woolford stopped running. They acted as though they were stalking game now, crouching, moving in perfect silence, keeping Duncan between them. Once, in the distance, there was a cracking sound. It could have been a tree snapping in a gust. It could have been a rifle shot.

Woolford signaled for a halt and sat on a rock under a hemlock, as if waiting. Conawago, seeming to sense something as well, crouched beside a boulder twenty feet away. After several minutes, a man in a fringed linen hunter's frock and green leggings material- ized from behind a tree a hundred feet away, running toward the north until Woolford gave a soft warbling whistle.

The leathery-faced man offered a broad smile to Conawago, eyed Duncan suspiciously, then hastily reported to his captain. Wool- ford's face tightened as he read a slip of paper handed him by the ranger. He handed it to Duncan. "Never have I met a man who made friends so quickly," he said.

The note was in French. It offered a princely sum for the scalp of Duncan McCallum.

"The corporal says some of the Ramseys mixed it up with that party of Hurons," Woolford reported after a moment. "He came across two of them running through the woods, the Hurons tracking them, not far behind. One with a beard that's red and gray, with another half his age." He turned to Duncan with question in his eyes. The ranger was asking if the men were worth saving.

"The old one's named McGregor. They're all just trying to work off their indentures."

"Working off indentures at Chimney Rock?" Woolford rejoined with a bitter frown, then turned and conferred with the corporal again. The soldier nodded several times, drank from a small wooden canteen that hung from his shoulder, then dashed away in the direc- tion of the camp they had left that morning.

Five minutes later, as they climbed a steep ridge, another cracking sound echoed through the forest, this one unmistakably a gunshot, and much closer than the first. Woolford pointed to the top of the ridge and ran. The ranger led them into a formation of rocks that was like a small fortress, squared at the top but with natural open- ings like the crenulations of a castle wall, a flat-topped tower of rock above the wall. As Duncan collapsed behind the rocks, Wool- ford and Conawago took up positions, guns at the ready. Moments later Woolford raised his rifle and fired. There was a muffled cry of surprise, then a flurry of footsteps. As Duncan ventured a look down the ridge, McGregor burst into view, stumbling, running, pausing to offer a call of encouragement to a companion in the shadows behind—a call that ended in an abject cry as the second man fell and was instantly covered by an Indian kneeling on his back. McGregor paused only a moment, for another Huron appeared from behind a tree thirty feet away, a tomahawk raised in one hand, a rifle balanced in the other, quickly closing on the old Scot.

Woolford, having quickly reloaded, leapt past Duncan down the slope several feet, dropped to a knee, and fired. The Indian staggered backward, slumped onto his knees, and fell face-first onto the ground. McGregor summoned a final burst of energy, reaching Woolford, who grabbed his arm and shoved him toward Duncan.

"McCallum! Never thought I'd find . . . ," the old Scot panted. "God's life!" he groaned, stricken with fear again as Conawago leapt toward them, battle ax raised for throwing. "Another!" McGregor bent, grabbing a rock as if to defend himself. But the ax, tumbling end over end, landed in the upper arm of an Indian aiming a bow at McGregor only twenty feet away. The arrow discharged as he spun about, the bow knocked from his grasp. With one fleet glance, the Indian took in Conawago and Woolford, then vaulted over the rocks down the slope, the war ax dropping from his broken arm, dripping with blood.

McGregor straightened, looking first in confusion at Conawago, then at Duncan with an air of guilt. "Arnold said Ramsey was to be given the paper, down the river, said to watch for you, for the bounty," the old Scot said, apology in his tone. "But we wanted no more of it, McCallum. We thought if we could get back to that mission, we could go take that road east and . . . ." With a hiss of air, McGregor's words choked away. It wasn't pain on his face when he looked down, but surprise. Three feathered shafts had materialized in his chest. By the time the Scot turned his numbed gaze to Duncan, blood was oozing from the side of his mouth. With a trembling finger, McGregor touched the pocket of his tattered waistcoat. *"Redeat,"* he said in a rattling voice, then dropped to his knees. As he collapsed onto the ground, Woolford fired shots, then Conawago. Whistles and animal calls rose in the forest, sounds Duncan had not heard before.

"Retreating," Woolford declared, then leapt over the rocks toward the Indian who had died when charging at McGregor. Duncan bent to the old Scot, clasping his wrist, touching his neck, calling his name.

"He is dead, Duncan," Conawago said over his shoulder. As Duncan kept futilely searching for a pulse, the Indian extracted the arrows, working the heads back and forth, seeming to take great care not to damage them.

Duncan stroked the old man's hair, emotion welling within. He felt as though he had somehow failed the old man. He straightened McGregor's long, graying hair, began brushing the soil from his clothes.

"No time for niceties, McCallum," Woolford interjected. As Duncan looked up, the ranger leaned a long rifle on a rock beside him, dropped a leather cartridge bag and powder horn beside it. "This is yours. Do you know which end to aim?"

Duncan touched the gun, then withdrew his hand.

"Take it or die," Woolford said in a matter-of-fact tone. "Without a decent weapon, you haven't a prayer of reaching what you seek." The ranger lifted the gun, gauging its balance, gazing approvingly at the finely worked walnut stock. "A good piece, near as good as my own. A Pennsylvania gun, likely taken in the raids in the Wyoming Valley south of here."

Duncan gazed with revulsion at the weapon. "You mean the man who owned this was killed by that Indian lying out there?"

"Most likely." Woolford stepped away, conferring with Conawago.

Duncan could not bring himself to touch the gun. To do so not only seemed to show contempt for its dead owner, but more, it seemed to mean he was joining the ranks of the king he hated so much. He left the gun where it lay as Woolford and Conawago began moving their belongings to the top level of the rock formation, a flat ledge enclosed by more rock formations.

"Leave him," Woolford said as he saw the way Duncan looked at McGregor's corpse. "He'll do us no good up there."

But Duncan somehow could not leave the old Scot. He heaved McGregor's body over his shoulder before climbing to the little protected table of land. They looked down steep rocky slopes on three sides. The fourth was a cliff that dropped away to a fast-flowing river fifty feet below.

As his companions watched the forest below, Duncan laid the body flat on the rock ledge, cleaned McGregor as best he could, then reached into the pocket the old man had touched, extracting a piece of paper. Arnold had said Ramsey had to have it. It took him a moment to understand, then he stared at it numbly. On one side was a plan for constructing a gallows, complete with detailed measurements, on the other an outline for conduct of Lister's murder trial.

"There's a grave to be dug," Duncan said.

"Not on this rock," Woolford rejoined without taking his gaze from the forest.

"Below then, where he died."

"No."

"We can't just—"

"Go down there with McGregor and there will be two sets of bones for the wolves to pick tonight."

For the first time Duncan saw real worry on the ranger's face.

"Usually they would move on," Conawago explained, "especially with a ranger sharpshooter against them. But they caught the scent of a real treasure now. And they know there's three of us, with perhaps twenty of them left." The Indian lifted his gun, watching a shadowy patch of forest.

"Treasure?" Duncan asked.

"You heard the old Scot. He called out to you by name. Your scalp is worth more than any of them would earn in an entire trapping season. And the hair of a ranger officer always carries a premium."

"Woolford!" Duncan exclaimed. He suddenly realized the ranger had slipped below them and was working feverishly along the base of their little fortress, gathering dried brush and tree limbs into piles spaced twenty feet apart, prying up a large boulder that could be used for cover and letting it roll into the forest.

With a single fluid motion, Conawago raised his rifle to his cheek and pulled the trigger. The top of a rotting log two hundred feet away burst into fragments. Woolford kept at his task without a pause.

Five minutes later, as Woolford dove over their covering rocks, the Huron rushed them again. Duncan loaded rifles for the ranger as he kept up a hellish fire, alternating between his own gun and the salvaged Pennsylvania rifle. The Huron reached within a hundred feet before withdrawing under the answering fire, carrying three of their companions with them.

Woolford and Conawago exchanged a troubled glance. "Your ax," the ranger said, and tossed Duncan a sharpening stone from his pack. "Make it ready for work." He rummaged deeper into his pack and produced a knife, much bigger than the one Duncan had been given at Edentown. "This was Fitch's. Use it half as well as he did and you might live."

"But your rifles—"

"There's powder enough but only ten balls. The work will be hot, and close, by dawn."

Duncan clamped his jaw tight, fighting a new surge of fear, and began whetting the stone on his new blade. Conawago followed suit with his knife. They worked with silent, grim determination as the sun set. Duncan suddenly stopped to reach into his pocket and tossed Woolford the bullet he had extracted from the Scot at the mission. "Thirteen balls. This and the two from the farm."

Woolford silently lifted his rifle and placed the ball on the end of the barrel. "These three are all the same size, all seventy-five caliber, made for the Brown Bess standard of the army. Rangers and Indians use long rifles, with smaller balls, fifty caliber and less. Even the

French soldiers use a smaller caliber. If I had a mold, I could melt these down, but I left it at the base camp."

Duncan looked out into the darkening forest a moment. "I cut it out of a deserter from the Forty-second," he explained as he tried to reason out the puzzle. "He took it in his leg a year ago. He was a survivor of Stony Run."

Woolford leaned forward, his eyes flashing with excitement as he hefted the three balls in his palm. "You're wrong. There were no survivors, only Adam."

"There were other Indian prisoners who survived."

"Sarah and Alex weren't there. Tashgua had sent the council to Stony Run. He was performing a rite nearby. When they came back the carnage was done."

"You don't know for certain, Captain. A deserter would never speak with you."

"No," Woolford admitted after a moment. "He wouldn't."

Duncan bent over his pack and pulled out the high-domed hat he had secreted there, wrapped in a scrap of muslin. He tossed it to Woolford. "Why would Ramsey have this, hidden like a great treasure?"

"Grenadier," Woolford said as he turned the cap over and over in his hand. "The Forty-ninth. You lied about finding that match case?"

"I found it, but with this hat in the Ramsey cellar. Where were the Forty-ninth Grenadiers last year?"

"In the north. Lake George. Lake Champlain." Woolford's face darkened as he threw the cap back to Duncan, and he turned back toward the forest. "They'll try before the moon gets higher, to use the dark," he predicted.

"We can jump in the river," Duncan said, "swim away in the dark."

"They will have thought of that and will be watching. Right now they don't know we are short of rounds. Drop in the water, and they will know for certain we could not shoot, even if we kept the rifles, for our powder will be wet. They have enough men to straddle the river and spear us like fish."

Duncan watched as Conawago lit a small fire then began tying dried grass around the ends of the arrows he had extracted from McGregor.

"The brush at the bottom," Duncan concluded. "You're going to light fires. But there's a gap."

"Exactly," Woolford said in a flinty voice and lifted his rifle. "That's where we greet them."

It happened exactly as the ranger planned. As Duncan watched in surprise, Conawago produced a long string, which he inserted into notches at the end of his staff, converting it into a bow. The old Indian waited until there was movement at the base, then lit the brush below with carefully aimed shots. With a thundering heart, Duncan watched their attackers move into the darkened gap and climb halfway up the slope before his companions opened fire. He reloaded with shaking hands, spilling precious powder, his gaze shifting often to the sharpened tomahawk lying on the rock beside him. Then there was silence. Below them someone moaned; the fires crackled and subsided. There were bullets left for only two more shots.

Woolford and Conawago arranged their blades in front of them.

"If you keep holding that ax so tightly," the ranger warned Duncan, "your fingers won't respond when it comes time to use them."

Duncan forced himself to set the weapon down and wiped the sweat from his palms. He gazed up at the moon, which had risen high enough to cast a silver glow over the hill. He had a strange sudden desire to be near the ocean. The McCallum clan chiefs almost always died on or near saltwater.

By the end of the first hour, the waiting became unbearable. Duncan found himself shifting positions like a nervous child, then began to notice how differently his companions waited for the final onslaught. Woolford, ever the soldier, watched the shadows with a cool, treacherous anticipation. But Conawago had stopped watching the woods. He had found a small white flower growing out of a crack in the stone, glowing in a small patch of moonlight, and was studying it with a serene expression.

As he watched the old Indian, Duncan found himself growing

calmer, inching closer, watching the flower himself, watching the stars reflected in a small pool of rainwater on the ledge by the flower.

"It thrives only in rocks and other harsh places," Conawago said of the flower as Duncan reached his side. "I found one like this when I was very young, and asked my mother why it would bloom in the night. She said that was a secret between it and the moon, from a time before man."

Duncan looked away for a moment as he realized he had also been studying the Indian's face the same way Conawago had looked at the little silver pool. "I'm sorry," he said clumsily. "It's just that here we are, with two bullets left and. . . ."

"Here we are," Conawago repeated when Duncan could not finish the sentence.

"I don't even know who you are."

"Men can only know one another by their actions."

"I don't know who your people are."

The old Indian offered a sad smile and looked up at the stars. "It's just another story of old clans fading away."

"You said they were called the Nipmucs, from Massachusetts."

"A very old and peaceful tribe," Conawago said after a moment. "Our troubles began with the Dutch, who enticed us closer to the Hudson for trade, then gradually wore us down. There were wars, small wars that few took notice of. My people were finished by the time I was born, nothing but small family groups left to wander along the river, under the protection of the Mohawks and the Mahicans who were left. When I asked about our tribe, my mother said one day we would all be together again, that for now our family was our tribe. Then some Jesuits came and offered me a new life. They were kind men. They showed my mother the magic of written words, told her that if I could learn the European ways, I could protect what was left of our people. My mother said go with them for five years, that she and the family would not leave, they would be there at their camp by the river waiting when I returned." Conawago looked at the flower in silence before continuing.

"But the Jesuits kept me for seven years, took me to Europe. I came back with gifts, with books, with new European clothes, with great plans for building a new village for my people. But they were gone. There was a new trading post there, new farms. I could barely recognize the land. There was only one of my family left, an old uncle who had become a drunk. He laughed when I said who I was, said I was dead. I discovered that my mother had refused to leave the land, saying she was waiting for me, until the trader there convinced her I was dead, made up a letter saying so and read it to her. She believed written words were magic, that they could never lie.

"For years I tried to find them, following the trail of every camp of Indians forced to move by the settlements. Some old Lenni Lenape said I should go to the Ohio for them. In the Ohio country they said maybe I should look along the Niagara. There they said to try the Kentucky lands. Eventually I went back to the Mohawks, lived with Hendrick, sometimes Tashgua."

"In New York harbor," Duncan ventured, "there was a man with a staff walking away after the attack. It was you who shot those arrows, and the staff was your bow."

"It was a signal Adam had arranged, to let the Ramsey tutor know I was there. We were supposed to meet at a tavern the next day. I waited two days, but you never came."

"The first arrow wasn't a signal."

"I had seen how the captain mistreated the old one, kicked him even when they were dragging him to the wagon. I feared he was about to do the same to you."

"If it weren't for that arrow," Duncan offered, "I would be on the way to Jamaica."

"You gave up all that sunshine for this," Conawago said.

They exchanged small, melancholy grins.

Their silence was broken by the loud crack of Woolford's rifle. An arrow whirled overhead, then another. Two rifles answered the ranger's shot. Conawago leapt to Woolford's side, his ax in his hand. The Huron war cries seemed to come from every direction. Duncan grabbed his tomahawk. Then, as suddenly as it started, it ended. His companions settled back as Woolford loaded the last round in his rifle. The forest went deathly quiet.

"I want to attend to McGregor," Duncan announced after another long silence.

"Attend?" Woolford asked.

"A funeral of some kind. A farewell for an old Scot forced from his Highland home."

He felt Woolford's withering gaze through the darkness. He expected a rebuke, a curse, even a bitter laugh. "What would you say to a burial at sea?" the ranger asked instead.

Woolford joined in preparing the body as Conawago watched the moonlit forest. With small vines they tied his feet together, then bound his arms across his chest after setting several flat rocks inside his shirt. Duncan retrieved his pipes from his pack as Woolford dragged the body to the edge of the cliff, then began a slow, sad tune. When he finished, they flanked the body.

"He died on his feet, in battle," Duncan offered.

"'He who dies pays all debts,'" Woolford added, ever ready with Shakespeare. Then they tipped the body over the edge. Duncan lingered, gazing into the silvery water, then lifted his pipes again.

"Enough," the ranger said. "It just makes you a better target."

Duncan ignored the warning. He played another lament, and another, not aware of when Woolford returned to Conawago's side. An icy hand gripped his heart as he realized it was for his own funeral, too. By dawn he would be scattered in pieces among the rocks, his scalp hanging from some Huron's belt.

The thought caused him to falter, to break the rhythm of his song. But then he smelled fresh heather and the scent of wool long steeped in the smoke of peat. He dared not turn for fear of ending the spell, but he knew his grandfather was lingering close by. He remembered that in the old Highland regiments there were those who did not fight but only played the pipes throughout the heat of battle. They were always conspicuous targets, but they never stopped playing. If a piper received a mortal wound, he would be braced against a tree and keep piping, his last breath on earth exhaling through the reeds.

He played as he had never played before, drawing the notes out, pausing only to slip the tomahawk and knife into his belt, at the ready. After several minutes he leapt atop a tall, flat column, silhouetted against the moonlit sky. He would make it a Highland death after all, with a blade in one hand, pipes in the other, and his grandfather at his side.

Chapter Fourteen

THE FIRST RAYS OF THE SUN woke him where he had leaned against a rock an hour before dawn. He leapt up with a groan, tomahawk in hand, shamed at not having maintained the vigil.

Conawago and Woolford were watching the forest intently, chewing on strips of dried venison from Conawago's bag. Woolford's weary countenance remained fixed on the shadows below as Conawago nodded to Duncan and offered him a piece of the meat.

"They never came," Duncan said in a confused tone.

"In the forest," the old Indian said, "there's always a bigger predator to steal your kill."

Duncan looked down the slope in alarm. The three bodies that had been visible were gone. The forest was silent. No birds greeted the dawn, no small animals scurried among the trees. He shuddered to think of what possibly could have frightened the fierce Huron warriors.

Duncan bent to stow his pipes in his bag, wondering whether he should ballast it and throw it over the cliff to rest with old McGregor instead of allowing the pipes to be destroyed in the final attack. He chewed the venison, gazing for a moment at the pool below, where the old Scot lay, then took a step toward Woolford and abruptly flung himself against a rock. A warrior stood at the bottom of the hill.

Duncan grabbed the third rifle, aimed, and was about to pull the trigger when Woolford pushed the barrel down. "Aiming a gun, even an empty one, is not what you want to be doing to this gentleman," the ranger said in a strained voice.

"Haudenosaunee," Conawago whispered. "An Onondaga," he added, though there was no relief in his voice.

Duncan would never have guessed the man was an ally. He was dressed in a breechcloth and leggings, his body adorned with red and black paint in a speckled pattern, a war ax in one hand. In his other hand the warrior held a painted stick on which was impaled a small creature, clad in white fur. He searched his memory for what he had learned of the Iroquois tribes. The Onondaga were the center nation, the keeper of the council fires for all the tribes.

Woolford warily stepped away from his cover, his palms open and empty at his side, then uttered a syllable of greeting.

The warrior did not reply.

Conawago stood, also without his weapons, and motioned Duncan to do likewise. Duncan did not miss the hesitation in the stranger's eyes as he saw Conawago, the brief look of human chagrin before the predator's face returned.

As the stranger took several steps forward, Conawago called out, speaking quietly in the Iroquois tongue, asking questions. The warrior softened slightly but did not reply except to ask his own question, pointing at Duncan.

Conawago spoke again, gesturing to Woolford and himself. The Iroquois' face darkened and he turned toward Woolford. He seemed to know Conawago and did not wish to speak with him. There was no need to translate the anger in his voice when he replied.

Conawago sighed and turned to Duncan as the Iroquois stepped to within thirty feet of them. "He wants you to go with him."

Duncan studied his companions, not comprehending the worry on their faces. "Who is he?"

"From the ones all in the Six Nations fear. The protectors of the sacred one. The singers of death. From the bear spirit himself."

"Tashgua." The name escaped Duncan's lips like a moan. "Why me?"

"Because," Conawago said in a hesitant tone, "he says you were the one who spoke with the gods last night. His name is Ravencatcher."

"You know him?"

"He is the son of Tashgua. When he was young, I spent several seasons in his camp. Since last year, he no longer trusts Europeans or those who have lived with them."

"The dead thing on the stick," Duncan said. "What does it mean?"

Woolford spoke this time, gesturing to the stick in the Iroquois's hand.

The response came in a low, impatient voice.

"He says he did not come to weave words in empty air," Woolford explained. "He wants to know if you are coming or not."

"If I say no, are they going to attack us? If I say yes, are they going to attack you?"

"I don't know," Woolford admitted. "They're angry as hell. It's a killing season like no other."

Duncan searched Conawago's face. The old Indian shrugged. "The tracks before us are like none I have seen before."

If he left his friends alone, Duncan realized, they still could face the Hurons, with one bullet left. Before he could reply, the Onondaga took another few steps forward and lifted the dead thing in his hand. Something in Duncan wanted to laugh, something else wanted to cringe. It was a wig, one of Ramsey's short powdered wigs. Exposed underneath it, at the end of the stick, was the skull of a young bear. "Tell him the three of us go or none of us go."

Woolford studied Duncan a moment, betraying no emotion, then translated.

The Iroquois spat an unhappy syllable, spun about, and without another word stepped back down the hill.

"He reluctantly accepts your terms," Woolford explained, hastily gathering his equipment. "But he's waiting for no one."

Moments later they were leaving the rocks, Woolford in the lead. Duncan followed for several paces, then paused. The Pennsylvania long rifle was still leaning against a boulder. He hesitated a moment, scrambled back to retrieve the gun and its powder horn, then ran to join his friends.

The uneasy procession increased in number as they reached the adjoining ridge, with warriors materializing from behind trees and boulders, some even rising from shallow hollows in the forest floor, until they were a dozen in total, moving silently along the well-used trail at the gait of the forest runner. The scalp lock of one of the men in front of Duncan showed russet hairs. Another man, the only one with long locks, wore them plaited and pinned at the rear in the style of a sailor. His hair was the color of ripe barley.

As they paused at a spring to drink, Duncan approached the man with the plaited hair, who dressed with the breechcloth and leggings of the other Iroquois. To his arrow quiver was tied a small swatch of black-and-green tartan. Duncan asked him in Gaelic if he were a *Gaidheal*, a Highlander. The man's reply was in the Indian tongue, spat over his shoulder as he rose and resumed the trail. Duncan recognized only one word. *Haudenosaunee*. When he looked to Woolford for an explanation, he saw the ranger on his belly, drinking from the stream. A passing Indian paused long enough to kick him in the ribs.

They were nearly inside the village before Duncan noticed the bark-covered longhouses in the shadows along the bottom of a low, steep ridge. At first the camp seemed abandoned. There were no dogs, no children, no crops, no sign of any activity. Four of the five habitations were in the shadow of large trees, beyond which lay a long, sandy groin at the edge of a river. In the distance was the low rumble of a waterfall. The fifth house was set apart from the others, beside two tall outcroppings like pillars, which flanked a well-worn trail up the ridge. The entry to the thirty-foot-long lodge was hung with animal skulls of all sizes and shapes. Over the door was one so huge it seemed impossible that it could ever have belonged to a flesh-and-blood creature. Its massive teeth seemed ready to close over anyone who dared trespass inside. A long string of massive bear claws hung down one side of the entry. Duncan found himself clutching the stone bear in his pocket as the Indians gathered up the rifles he and his friends carried, and he fought the temptation to offer it up and flee.

He was led to the far side of the clearing, a hundred feet from the solitary lodge, where a heavy log, stripped of bark, had been sunk in the ground. It was covered with painted images of animals and men. At its base, the bare earth was covered with ominous stains. With a start he saw that Woolford and Conawago were being led into the shadows by the other longhouses. As three somber warriors moved toward him, Duncan retreated, until suddenly he found himself backed against the painted post. His hands were seized from behind, and before he could resist, they were bound behind the post. Three more Indians appeared. Not Indians, he saw. Though their hair was darkened with grease, all of their locks were fair.

"My name is Duncan McCallum," he declared in a taut voice. "From the Highlands nigh Lochlash." He saw that each of them held stout lengths of wood only an instant before the nearest one hit him.

The blow to his abdomen doubled him over. "I am called Duncan, of Clan McCallum," he gasped in Gaelic as he straightened. "From the—" The next blow took him on the shoulders, slamming his head against the post.

"From the English sewers where spies and other rodents are bred," spat a lean, muscular man with the left half of his face painted black. The blows came quicker now, on his legs, on his ribs.

"The Pied Piper for all the redcoats," one of the Scottish warriors snarled.

"The king's lapdog," muttered another as he landed a club on Duncan's thigh.

But then he forgot the blows, let them fall as they would as he stared into the blue eyes of the black-painted man who seemed to be the leader of the Scottish warriors. His blond hair was shaved deep along the temples, but the remainder was plaited down his neck. There was hate in his eyes as he returned Duncan's stare, but there was also something familiar.

"Jamie!" Duncan gasped. "Don't let it be like this!"

His brother muttered something in the Iroquois tongue. A man produced a switch and slapped Duncan's shoulder, raising a sting like a cat o'nine tails.

Words rose behind Jamie, Iroquois words in a low, forceful voice. Two of the Scots instantly backed away. The words grew sharper. Jamie launched the club from his hand into the air so that it tumbled end over end above them. As everyone else, even Duncan, watched it, Jamie seized the club in the hand of the nearest man and pummeled Duncan again, with a quick, vicious rhythm. "Don't ever use the name of my clan again," he warned in a scalding whisper. "You forfeited the right long ago."

"Cut me loose and I'll teach you not to speak to the eldest of your clan so," Duncan shot back, in the Highland tongue.

Jamie's club, aimed now for Duncan's head, slowed, then twisted downward. Someone was pulling the end. He resisted with a violent shove, knocking the interloper to the ground, raising the club again only to have it seized in mid-swing.

Everyone seemed to freeze for a moment. As Jamie spun about in anger, all the other Scots stared uneasily toward his feet. Duncan's mind, clouded by pain, saw only a pile of feathers at first, then as the onlookers gasped and rushed toward the feathers, they took on a feminine shape. It was a cloak of feathers, Duncan saw, and inside it was a woman with russet braids.

"Sarah!" he cried, twisting in his bindings, struggling now to be free, to help her.

But she needed no help. As Jamie looked down, he seemed to shrink. He released his grip on the club and silently watched as half a dozen hands reached down to help Sarah to her feet.

"What have you done?" she asked in an injured tone. It took a moment before Duncan realized she was addressing him, not his brother. "You made a promise."

Before Duncan could reply, more Iroquois appeared, pulling Sarah away as he stared after her. She was alive. She had changed.

She was no longer pale, no longer fearful. The Indians who escorted her did not have scorn in their eyes, but worry.

In a moment no one was left but his brother. Jamie's eyes flared as a blade appeared in his hand. For a moment his brother hesitated, as if deciding where to sink it, then it flew downward to cut his bindings, and Jamie slipped away as a new figure materialized in front of the post, glaring at Duncan.

It was the Indian who had brought him from the ridge that morning. His paint had been wiped away, so that for the first time Duncan saw his face clearly.

"A crow," Duncan heard himself say as he saw the tattoo above the Indian's jaw. "You have a crow on your cheek."

"A raven," the Indian replied in a calm voice, the first time Duncan had heard him speak any English. "When I was young, my father found me in a nest of ravens on a cliff, playing with the birds. When I became of age, I was given the name Ravencatcher, though I always thought it was the ravens who had caught me," he added. Then, to his utter surprise, Duncan saw a small, quick grin.

"This morning at the ridge you didn't—" Duncan began, then started over. "You speak English well."

"I had a good teacher when I was a boy," his voice seeming to wander for a moment. "An old Nipmuc."

"I am called Duncan."

The Iroquois replied with a sober nod, then turned, gesturing him to follow. As Duncan followed him, an adolescent girl in a deerskin dress darted out of the bone lodge. With a shy smile she handed Duncan a turtle shell filled with water, motioning for him to drink. He drained the shell, then she handed him a small, round, yellow loaf, no bigger than his palm. He brushed off the soot from its edges and bit into it. It was of cornmeal, and to his long-deprived palate it tasted like the finest of cakes. She smiled again as he quickly devoured the bread, then darted back into the bone-covered entrance. Inside, Sarah lingered, shrouded in shadow, gazing at him. He moved toward her, returning her stare, question in his eyes. She had not been mistreated. She was no slave. But he could not decipher her strange behavior. What did the feather cloak signify? He had heard of cultures where captives were feted until they were offered in human sacrifice.

Duncan had already taken a step toward her when Ravencatcher touched his elbow and gestured him toward the other lodges. Woolford and Conawago were there, stripped to the waist, washing from woodcarved basins, scraping their skin with narrow slabs of fragrant cedar. A boy was helping them, dumping fresh water into another basin. It was Alex, still wearing his shirt without sleeves, looking more at ease than Duncan had yet seen him. As Duncan stepped toward his friends, Ravencatcher held up a restraining hand and gestured at his belt, then at a log at the side of the nearest lodge. Their rifles lay against it, as did his companions' other weapons and carrying packs. Duncan quickly laid down his tomahawk and knife, then stripped off his shirt.

As they finished cleansing themselves, Ravencatcher stirred the embers of the fire, placed several coals on a flat stone, and dropped tobacco leaves over them. He stepped to each man with the stone in his hands. Duncan followed the actions of Conawago, cupping the smoke in his hand, washing it over his face, rubbing it over his skin before putting his shirt on again.

When they finished, no word was offered, no gesture made. Ravencatcher simply set the flat rock on a log, turned, and walked away, up the steep trail. It was a very old path, rutted from decades, perhaps centuries, of use. As they climbed, painted images appeared on the rock walls at its sides, of varying complexity and design, of varying age, though all were of forest animals. On the downward side, all the paintings were of snakes.

As they descended through the maze of rocks, Conawago began a low, whispered prayer. Woolford kept glancing back uneasily at Duncan. Suddenly they rounded a huge boulder and emerged into a half-mile-wide bowl through which a boulder-strewn stream flowed. The valley was almost perfectly symmetrical, with steep rocky walls rising up on either side and dense groves of white birch trees at either end. In the center was the most remarkable living thing Duncan had ever seen.

It was a tree, though to call the massive oak before them a tree was to call the mighty Atlantic a lake. It was as tall as the grandest cathedral he had ever seen, its canopy as broad as any village square, its huge lower limbs spreading out like the beams of a castle hall. Its vast trunk, easily a dozen feet in diameter, was split by a jagged, three-foot-wide hole, as high as a man, that seemed like the entrance to a deep cave.

Conawago noticed the awed look on Duncan's face and waited as he slowly advanced. "Stony Run is just the name of the stream that feeds into the river over the waterfall," the old Indian said. "It is the name Europeans use for the place because no one of the tribes will utter the name of the sacred tree itself."

"It must be ancient." Duncan was whispering.

"Once I met a natural philosopher in Philadelphia who insisted you could age a tree by the number of rings in its cross-section. When limbs blow off in a storm, there is a ceremony for burning them. Years ago I was here when it happened. I counted two hundred rings in the limb alone.

"The shamans of the Iroquois have been coming here since before memory," Conawago continued as they walked toward the tree, "since before the Iroquois were even a nation. It is the most pure place on earth, Tashgua says. Wampum beads are not needed here."

Duncan weighed his words as he studied the small group of men sitting at the base of the tree. "You mean the tree makes people speak the truth."

"When I was young and came here the first time with my mother, there was a woman of over a hundred winters who lived in the bone lodge. She said if a human were to be deceitful here, the limbs would reach down and tear him to pieces."

The Iroquois who sat against the far side of the oak seemed to have grown out of the tree itself. He sat between two massive, gnarled, lichen-covered roots that disappeared into the ground at his feet. The lines on his worn face seemed to match the grooves in the surface of the tree. The gray strands in his hair made it blend with the bark. He had a profound stillness about him, like the power of the sea in repose. Nothing moved but his eyes, brilliant as obsidian. Duncan did not need to ask. He had found Tashgua.

Before the shaman were a dozen men. Ravencatcher and another of their band sat to his left and right, facing eight other Iroquois, older men, though clearly not so ancient as the man who sat against the tree. Together they encircled two men from Edentown. Reverend Arnold was patiently speaking, seemed to be giving a sermon, as Cameron warily watched the Indians. Arrayed on a hewn log before Arnold were printed pages—more of the pages, Duncan saw, that had been ripped out of Evering's Bible. Beside the pages was the brass cross that had been stolen from Edentown. Every few moments Arnold paused as one of the Indians, a sinewy man wearing the skin of a fox over his crown, translated for the others. They were, Duncan realized, testing the words of the Bible.

As they spoke, Ravencatcher's hands began to work at what looked like a linear drum, a hollowed log, perhaps six inches wide and four feet long, carved with images of forest animals. The sound Tashgua's son drew from it was soft and undulating, like a distant moan of wind on a winter night.

"Tashgua and the tree are listening," Conawago whispered, and dropped to the ground, folding his legs beneath him. Woolford, then Duncan, silently followed his example. Though the old sachem gave no acknowledgment of their presence, Arnold stopped his discourse in midsentence, his cheeks filling with color as he jabbed a bony finger toward Duncan.

"This man is a lawbreaker," he declared loudly, all patience gone from his voice, "cast out from our God! He must be removed! My man will take him away."

Tashgua leaned forward, squinting. A smile lit his leathery countenance as he recognized Conawago; then he studied Duncan, cocking his head, his eyes growing round as if he were surprised at something he read in Duncan's face. The shaman turned back to Arnold and shrugged. When he spoke, his voice was like leaves rustling in a breeze. "The reason we are here, Major," he said in slow, imperfect English, "is because it not be for mere men to say who is cast out from the gods."

"He has broken his word!" Arnold protested. "Broken his bond! Broken our law!"

Suddenly Tashgua was standing in front of them, though Duncan had not seen him rise. He examined Duncan again with a gaze that seemed to be aimed at something under his skin. "He has been summoned here, this one, summoned to be dealt with," the shaman declared to Arnold. The words raised a shiver down Duncan's spine.

But Arnold seemed unable to contain his fury. He rose, pulling Cameron up, shoving him toward Duncan. Suddenly a long object appeared in Tashgua's hand. At first Duncan thought it was a club. Two feet long, ending with a carved head of a raven, the top third consisted of a flattish, ridged turtle shell, the handle below it carved with snakes. As he shook it over Arnold's head, it rattled with the sound of many small objects inside. Cameron froze, then slowly lowered himself to the ground. Arnold's eyes flared, but he seemed able to endure Tashgua's stare for only a moment before relenting and sitting again. The shaman circled the two men, solemnly shaking the rattle, his eyes somehow wild and serene at the same time.

"Inside," Conawaga whispered without looking away from Tashgua, "are bones. It is very old, handed down from the first of the holy ones who sat at these roots. They say it has bones of the most powerful shamans from every generation since. Some say it is the most powerful object in all the Six Nations. Like the Jesuits," he added.

Duncan could not curb his question. "The Jesuits?"

"They also carry about old bones of their saints, and ascribe great power to them."

As Tashgua returned to his seat, the strange ritual continued, Arnold pointedly not looking at Duncan as he resumed speaking, though Cameron continued to cast resentful stares. Duncan struggled to understand why Arnold would tolerate the demands of the shaman he hated so, but soon forgot about this and drifted into a dreamlike state, somehow mesmerized by the voices and the slow, sibilant sound of the drum. Arnold's words, about an all-powerful and wrathful god, seemed but a backdrop against something vitally more important, something very old, something that seemed to bridge the spirits of men and the forces of the forest. The fact that Duncan could not name it, could not put it into words but could only feel it, seemed only to make it more vital. What was it Fitch had said to him, a thousand years ago? *The most important things can never be put into words.*

Arnold, finding his pulpit voice, finished with a flourish, with words about Christian soldiers and judgment day. He seemed about to rise when the old chief in the fox skin stood and entered the center of the circle, where he bent over the Bible pages.

"Seneca," Conawago whispered, "an old friend of King Hendrick." The chief spoke in the tongue of the tribes, the ears of the fox head bobbing up and down as he nodded toward Arnold and Cameron.

"A great man was at your side when you journeyed across the salt-waters," Ravencatcher translated. The Seneca chief reached inside his shirt and produced a folded piece of paper.

"The Ramsey Company does great work," Arnold rejoined.

The Seneca unfolded the paper and stretched it on the flat rock, over the printed Bible pages. "But your god is wrathful, your god is jealous. He could not abide the starspeaker who was coming among us."

Arnold's patience seemed to be coming to an end. He glanced warily at Cameron and sighed. "Starspeaker?"

The fox dipped and rose as the Seneca lifted the paper for Arnold to better see. It held a maze of lines, words, circles, and arrows. Arnold's jaw dropped. Duncan stared at the paper in disbelief. It was the missing chart from Evering's cabin. Cameron's head jerked up, and he seemed about to rise until he noticed that one of Tashgua's warriors had materialized behind him.

The fox-draped chief spoke again. "Why would the god you

describe take such a powerful shaman from his people? Can you speak to the stars? Can you persuade them to tell us where they will be at the rise of the next full moon?"

"Evering," Arnold sputtered. "Evering was no shaman. He was a . . ." His voice trailed off and he cast an accusing glance toward Duncan. "You could not have known this man. We cannot know what these scratches on this paper are."

"But we do," the Seneca said, and turned Evering's chart over. "There is a prophesy of miracles this year. A water miracle, an earth miracle, a sky miracle that will confirm our gods are still with us." Cameron moved again, as if to snatch the chart away, then froze as the hand of the warrior behind him settled on his shoulder. Arnold's face swirled with emotion as he gazed at the reverse of the paper.

The back of the chart offered a chaos of words, drawings, and Iroquois symbols. An image of a feather, not just any feather, but the vermilion-marked feather that had been left at the bloody compass. Iroquois words, sounded out in English. Crude images of men and animals like those Duncan had seen on the wampum belt at Edentown, but also images of snakes and longhouses and birds. Some had been drawn by Evering, but some, Duncan realized, had been drawn by Sarah Ramsey.

The Seneca chief turned the chart over, back to the sky map, and stared gravely at Arnold. Tashgua's eyes, fixed on the paper, had a strange longing in them.

"Your god is wrathful," the Seneca said. "He could not bear to have such a prophet on the earth."

Duncan watched as Arnold's eyes flared with emotion. Then the vicar seemed to collect himself. "You and I," he said to the chieftain in a strained voice, "have our own appointed turn to leave this world, and it is useless to resist it. Even a prophet has such an hour."

A single syllable from Tashgua broke the silence that followed. The Indians began to rise.

"We have received our benediction," Conawago announced, and rose, offering Duncan a hand.

But Duncan, as if under a spell, did not rise, only stared at Evering's chart. He extended a finger, touched the whitened edge of the chart, then brought his finger to his tongue. For one raised in a seaborne clan there could be no mistake. The paper had been soaked in the ocean. He suddenly realized the others were gone, all but one. He was alone with Tashgua, and the tree. The shaman fixed him with a calm, weary gaze. For a moment Duncan considered bowing his head to the ground. But then the shaman lifted his hand, closed it into a fist, tapped it against his chest, then raised the hand, extending two fingers as he lifted them in a spiraling motion toward the sky. Duncan, without thinking, repeated the motion. The wrinkles on the shaman's face rearranged themselves, and Duncan realized he had smiled. The shaman motioned Duncan toward him, and he advanced and lowered himself onto the ground between the outstretched roots. With a chill he watched Tashgua's rattle rise, and fought an impulse to flee as the rattle shook at one side of his head, then the other.

The shaman smiled again, capturing Duncan with his eyes. Suddenly Duncan was aware of Tashgua's hand on his, guiding it over the hollow log, letting his fingers touch the carved bears, then showing him how to make the subtle rubbing, tapping motion that produced the undulating, otherworldly moan of the log. Once, twice, three times Duncan opened his lips to confess he was carrying the sacred stone bear, but each time something held his tongue until finally he knew words were unnecessary. Tashgua's tired, wise eyes watched him with an odd contentment, and Duncan realized the shaman's hands were clasping the roots again and Duncan alone was making the quiet throbbing sound, like the heartbeat of the ancient tree.

He slowly pushed back the chaos of his thoughts, letting the murmur of the log take over his mind and body. When he finally rose, Tashgua's eyes were closed. He studied Evering's chart one more time then stepped backward for several feet before turning toward the trail. He understood little of what the shaman had done that day, but somehow at the tree he had finally seen the truth of what had happened on board the ship. At the trailhead, he paused for another look. From the distance Tashgua looked like part of the tree.

As Duncan climbed back over the ridge, a dozen men in ill-fitting red coats, some stinking of tar, were being herded into the camp from the river by a mixed group of Scots and Iroquois, under Jamie's command. Lord Ramsey had deployed the rest of his militia. He hesitated, fighting an impulse to flee, then saw Sarah.

The Company men, disarmed and terrified, seemed to sink into a paralyzing confusion when their captors began throwing Gaelic taunts at them.

"In the king's name!" came an angry voice behind the Company soldiers. Red-coated men were shoved aside as a furious Lord Ramsey appeared.

"How dare you treat us like this! Are we at war with the Iroquois?" Ramsey demanded. "Is not our beloved King George a constant friend of the Six Nations?"

Jamie, at the edge of the clearing, called out in the Iroquois tongue, presumably translating for the Indians who had no English. Iroquois and Scottish warriors reacted alike, with quick whispered mutterings and bitter frowns.

"You will return our weapons!"

"This is a sanctuary," Jamie declared to Ramsey. "For as long as memory serves, no weapons but those of the guardians, no act of war has been allowed here."

Ramsey glared at Jamie. "I come as colonel of the Edentown militia to treat with our Iroquois friends," the patron replied. "Not with Scottish brigands." Arnold, who had worked his way through the assembly, leaned into Ramsey's ear. "And certainly not," Ramsey added with a victorious gleam, "with a traitor to the king. You, sir, will consider yourself under arrest." His furious gaze rested on Duncan for a moment. "Along with your contemptible brother," he added. "The army knows how to deal with traitors. But an escaped bond slave will know Ramsey justice," he hissed at Duncan.

Amusement flashed across Jamie's face. "You should take to the stage. The public ever thrills at those who playact as soldiers." His smile disappeared. "The great shaman desires dialogue with you, so you are guests in this camp. Otherwise we would have stopped you and your toy soldiers ten miles downstream. I am here to assure that you abide by the rules of the sacred place."

Ramsey surveyed the camp. "Do not mock me," he snarled. "There is but mud and bones and forest debris here."

"This is but the antechamber. Over the ridge lies the cathedral, as Reverend Arnold will surely attest. There is a cleansing ceremony for any wishing to go beyond."

"I cannot proceed until what was stolen from me is returned," Ramsey barked, his hand on his pistol. "I will not endure your ceremony until the thieves clean their own hands. You have a Ramsey paper. You have a Ramsey heir."

A tall figure stepped in front of Jamie. Ravencatcher did not speak but motioned Ramsey toward the bone-fronted lodge. The patron seemed about to erupt again, then gestured Arnold to his side and followed the tall Iroquois, with Duncan, Woolford, and Conawago a few steps behind.

It was dark inside, the air tinged with fragrant smoke. At the far end, under one of several holes in the ceiling, the chief in the fox skin sat at a small fire, beside a sturdy Iroquois woman in a doeskin dress adorned with dyed quills. The woman extended graceful hands to push the smoke toward the visitors as they sat. From the shadows, Ravencatcher produced a long cylinder of birch bark sewn with leather strips and extracted a large rolled parchment.

Ramsey seemed about to launch himself toward the charter. "It is mine! Return it this instant!"

The Onondaga ignored the patron. "Its words shall be spoken tomorrow at the tree, and we will see. Your man of god has read his Bible. You will read this paper."

"You, sir, will not dictate to me!"

Ravencatcher leaned toward Duncan and Woolford. "Our people are disturbed. They wonder whether the old spirits hear them anymore. They rightfully puzzle over this new one with the power to give the owning of land." He turned to Ramsey. "You will go to the tree and speak the charter, to test its truth."

Ramsey's face flushed with color. "Truth? These are the words of the king!"

"For as long as trees have grown and waters have flowed, no one of our people has ever taken land for his or her own. We borrow land from the gods, a maize field here, a pumpkin field there, a town of houses sometimes. We give it back when we are finished. Now a new spirit arrives and pushes men to change all that, so that some men must have land and others must not.

"We do not doubt you have a strong spirit behind you. We try now to understand if the old spirits who have ruled this land since its creation now wish for your spirit to also become the god of the Haudenosaunee. Then we will finally know about your war."

"*Our* war!" Ramsey simmered. "Now you mock the king! Treaties have been signed in Albany. Pledges have been made."

"For those who have to fight and bleed," came a quiet voice, "war is a very personal thing." Conawago spoke toward the fire. "It is easy to speak of distant kings and distant battles. It becomes very different when it is the blood of your own sons and daughters being spilled."

"There shall come a reckoning for what you have done with my own daughter," Ramsey spat. "You shall see—" His threat died as his gaze froze on a figure framed by the opening of the lodge. Sarah, in an elegant quill-worked dress, was in the clearing outside, moving with Alex and an older Iroquois woman among the Company men, offering ladles of water and cornmeal loaves. Ramsey leapt to his feet, rushing out, but halted after a few steps, as if uncertain of what he was seeing. The Company men who saw him awkwardly looked away, though Sarah took no notice. She was acting like the matron of the village, the hostess receiving guests. And the look Ramsey gave her was that which Duncan had seen on those who called Sarah a witch.

"Your daughter is no prisoner," Woolford said to Ramsey's back.

"Then she fled to follow those she saw stealing my charter,"

Ramsey said after a moment. "It is the Ramsey blood in her. They acknowledge her due rank."

"She is not part of your campaign, sir," Duncan interjected.

Ramsey's face filled with color again as he turned to face him. "Were it not for this—this sanctuary, I would have you hanging by your arms from a tree to begin your punishment. When we are ready, McCallum, we will drag you home in chains." The patron watched his daughter again. "Reverend Arnold and I have decided what must be done with her. There is a surgeon in Philadelphia who treats brain disorders. He has agreed to a trepanning."

"You would open her brain?" Duncan gasped.

"Drill into it. An accustomed procedure. Based on her behavior, he says there must be a mortifying growth that needs to be excised."

"I have heard of soldiers who have had the surgery," Woolford said in a haunted voice. "Afterwards they stare without seeing, have to be led from place to place. It's like they are empty inside."

"The doctor in Philadelphia has had great success," Ramsey shot back, then fell silent as his daughter approached. She spoke to him as she had the other men, offering a greeting in the Iroquois tongue, pushing a small loaf into his hand. For a moment father and daughter stared at each other, then Ramsey let the loaf drop to the ground. Sarah seemed about to speak again when suddenly a man in one of the militia uniforms burst out of the woods, gasping for breath, blood streaming down the side of his face.

"The Hurons!" he cried. "The Hurons approach!"

Jamie surveyed the confused assembly of men then began barking out orders.

They made a slow procession over the low, steep ridge after dawn the next morning, Tashgua and the Iroquois first, then Ramsey, Arnold, and Conawago. Woolford and Duncan, in the rear, kept pausing to look back. They had spent much of the night in the forest with several of the Company men, searching for the Huron to no avail. At the crest of the ridge, Tashgua called an unexpected stop, sending Ravencatcher down the trail with all the Iroquois warriors, then waited until his son appeared on one of the rocks below and whistled. The reason for the delay became obvious as soon as they reached the opening into the little valley. Other visitors had appeared on the sacred ground. Cameron sat guarded by the Iroquois, in front of seven scarlet-coated figures. Pike and his squad glared angrily at their guards, who had made a pile of their weapons at the edge of the stream.

Duncan and Woolford exchanged an alarmed glance. There was not supposed to be another access to the little valley.

Ramsey, however, seemed not at all surprised by the new arrivals. He simply greeted them with a nod, then pointed to a figure emerging from the trail behind them. It was Jamie, wearing a small fur cap and wolf pelt on his shoulders against the chill. Pike rose and also pointed at Jamie, as if he needed to be sure his soldiers understood that the traitor they had so long sought was at last before them. Jamie glared at Pike then quietly ordered his men to carry away the soldiers' weapons. He stepped to a thin old chief who stood with his arms clasped together, clearly suffering from the cold dawn air, and good-naturedly set the cap and pelt on the chief, then with a worried expression began to walk downstream. The waterfall. Alex had mentioned that Adam had fled down a trail along the waterfall.

More Indians started arriving from the camp. The *okewa*, the death anniversary ceremony, was due to begin later that day. Tashgua's work with Ramsey, Conawago had warned, was likely to take all morning. There were prayers to offer, tobacco to be burned, pipes to be lit and shared, and Tashgua would not want Ramsey to recite the charter until his full council was present.

As the new arrivals spoke with the other Iroquois, Duncan and Woolford slipped away, walking along the high walls, looking for anything Pike might have brought with him—a secret weapon cache, evidence of a trap—and, finding nothing, their anxiety mounted.

"You're nigh to offending our host," came a voice from the rocks as they approached the waterfall. Jamie stepped in front of them, blocking their path.

"You're the guardian of this place," Woolford said in an accusing tone. "How did they get through?"

"There are too few of us," Jamie said. "Some had to watch Ramsey and his men in camp. Some had to watch for Hurons in the forest."

"A distraction. The warning was a distraction. What did Pike and his men do here?" Duncan asked his brother.

Jamie pointed at Woolford. "Here's one. Ask him."

"You know that is not true," Woolford snapped.

"Is not your paymaster the same as Pike's?" Jamie demanded with a chill tone. "You all look after your own. Back home in your New York mansion houses, you can't wait to pour the brandy and boast of all the heathens you killed."

"A damned lie and you know it!" Woolford spat. He seemed about to launch himself at Jamie.

"If I am not mistaken," Duncan said to his brother, "their paymaster was also yours for a few years." He looked over Jamie's shoulder. "Did they come up the waterfall?"

"Aye. We usually keep a sentry on the path to the tree. Tashgua said it was no longer necessary. He has no fear. He is incapable of fear. The spirits have already decided what is to happen—this is what he said when I tried to argue."

"It's not spirits I am worried about," Duncan pressed. "It's Pike and Ramsey. They hate each other, but suddenly they seem friends. Did you follow the trail they took up here?"

"There were marks of three canoes on the bank."

"Canoes?" Woolford asked. "Pike had no canoes."

"Ramsey," Jamie said. "The Ramsey militia had canoes. There were two covered with canvas, big cargo canoes with kegs of rum and flour."

"Then someone must find them," Duncan urged, "see what was taken."

"And walk into another trap? Not my men."

"The trap," Duncan shot back, "is already laid."

"Pike's men have no weapons," his brother said. "We took the flints from their guns, hid their blades."

Duncan surveyed the valley, tasting fear now. "You must run, Jamie. Pike wants your blood more than anything in the world. He would not give up his weapons with you so near, not unless he had another plan."

Jamie gazed down the valley, at the tree where the old sachem sat. "I'll not leave Tashgua. He kept us alive after Ticonderoga, shielded us when the other Iroquois said we should be surrendered to Albany. When most of his men died last year, those who were left of us vowed to protect him."

Woolford took a step forward, toward the waterfall. "I'm going down there, to read the trails."

Jamie raised the war club in his hand.

"Woolford had men who died last year, too," Duncan reminded his brother.

"Aye. And the army blames us for that as well."

"Perhaps they have reason to blame you," Woolford observed in a brittle tone.

"To hell with you, Englishman. You are not interested in the truth."

"He crossed the Atlantic to find Adam, just to hear the truth," Duncan said.

"Then why ask me?"

"Because Adam died," Woolford shot back. "Because he refused to speak with a king's officer."

"You did a lot of traveling for no good reason. To Scotland. To here. All in search of Scots who will not speak with you."

Woolford looked away, the pain in his eyes obvious. "We once ran in the woods together, Jamie," the ranger said after a moment.

"That was a different life."

"Rangers and your men, they have much in common," Duncan ventured.

"Don't presume to speak of my men," Jamie snapped. He raised the deadly spike of his war club toward Woolford's head as the ranger inched closer.

"They were together a year ago," Duncan said, "trying to track the killers from Stony Run."

"You don't know that."

"Odd, that you and your men would hate the rangers so yet tend their graves at the mission. I saw him at the mission, Jamie, the sergeant who was shot when he was with the rangers last year, the only one to escape."

Jamie said nothing. Duncan pulled the musket ball from his pocket and tossed it to him. "I took this out of his leg, where he had carried it for the past twelve months."

Jamie's face darkened as he rolled the ball between his fingers.

"Ramsey hates the army," Duncan continued. "Why is he so friendly with Pike?"

"You're a Ramsey man, you tell me."

Duncan pulled the grenadier hat from inside his belt, holding it in front of his chest. "This I took from a safe room of Ramsey's, hidden as if it were his greatest treasure."

Jamie's eyes stayed on the cap as he spoke. "The Forty-ninth has been deployed in the north. Nowhere near here."

"It doesn't necessarily mean the Forty-ninth was here," Woolford said. "Just someone with access to central stores, where uniforms are shipped out. Like someone on the staff of a general who works in secret."

"What if the killers last year didn't come to kill the Iroquois?" Duncan ventured. "What if they came to kill the Black Watch deserters and the Iroquois just happened to get in the way, happened to be witnesses to something that could never be spoken of?"

Jamie grew very still. "They wouldn't know. What happens here is secret, even to many of the Iroquois. Outsiders don't even know where this place is."

Woolford made a small choking sound. The color drained from his face. "Last year Pike asked for the ranger companies to report where the Iroquois sacred sites were so he could assure troop movements would avoid them."

"The bastard doesn't care what—" Jamie began, then his voice trailed away as realization struck.

"What happened on that hill above Ticonderoga?" Duncan asked.

"Someone was there, in an unmarked English coat, speaking to Hurons and a man in a white hunter's frock."

"A traitor!" Woolford spat.

"We never saw his face. He sent the Hurons after us, cut us off from the battlefield. They would have cut down Tashgua if we hadn't stayed with him."

"Pike," Woolford said in a whisper, "has always lost heavily at the gaming table. His debt was huge. But last year he started wearing lace and gold rings."

All three gazed down the valley in stunned silence.

"It shouldn't be difficult," Duncan said, "to find out how soon afterwards his debts were retired."

"There was one mistake after another made the day of the battle," Woolford said in a taut voice. "Mortar barges directed into the wrong channel so that they came under French cannons. Units sent to attack abandoned positions."

The painful silence returned. Jamie braced himself against a boulder, as if he had difficulty remaining on his feet. After a moment Woolford pushed past him and disappeared in the direction of the waterfall.

"It isn't about Pike today," Duncan said to his brother.

"He still wants me dead."

"And me half a minute later, if he had his way. And if not Pike, then Ramsey."

"I do not fear a lout like Ramsey," Jamie said, though worry had entered his voice.

"If it was Pike with the Huron last year at Ticonderoga, then surely they must work together. The warning yesterday, it was Huron meant to draw your men away. Half the Ramsey Company, and Hawkins, are still missing." Duncan turned to face the assembly at the great tree. "Ramsey can't abide a victory by Pike. He wants you dead, Jamie. Hawkins is his weapon. For God's sake, take your men and leave." But when Duncan turned back, his brother was gone.

Tashgua had been recounting the spiritual history of his people and was inviting Ramsey to speak when Duncan reached the tree. The patron seemed to have trouble controlling his emotions, and raw hatred burned in his eyes as the sachem lifted the charter from its bark tube. For a moment it seemed Ramsey was about to berate the old Indian again. But a slender figure dressed in white doeskin appeared between them. Sarah accepted the parchment from Tashgua, then unrolled it and held it in front of her father. Ramsey glanced uneasily at his daughter, cleared his throat, and began reciting the king's words. At the end of each phrase, Sarah lowered the parchment and translated for the assembled Iroquois, now numbering over thirty. The chieftains listened solemnly, some studying the tree as they did so.

When Ramsey finished, he looked up expectantly, only to find Ravencatcher standing with one of his dress wigs extended on his bear skull stick. "Now become this one, and read it again."

"Nonsense," Ramsey said, in the tone he used for addressing servants.

Ravencatcher turned and indicated more wigs lined up on a log. "You will speak it as each of the people you claim to be."

Ramsey clenched his jaw, glanced at Arnold, and accepted the wig.

It was the chief with the fox skin who stood and addressed Ramsey when he was done. "What is it you will do with the land if your lord presents it to you?" he asked in a contemplative tone.

"I will make it yield to men," Ramsey replied. "I will build great towns. I will turn rocks into a gun, a tree into a house, a stream into a mill that feeds five hundred. What have you done with the land?" he asked, gesturing toward the wooded ridges. "It is but a wasteland in your hands. Have you improved it in all these centuries?"

Ravencatcher translated, then walked around Sarah and Ramsey as his father watched with an expression of deep curiosity. "What you say is that your way requires you to make things from the land." Tashgua's son was speaking for himself now. "Is that the source of your magic?"

For a moment Ramsey seemed intrigued. "Yes. It is the destiny of men to use the tools they have been given."

"And when all the land is gone there will be only things in your world. Will those things have life?"

"No. They will allow for more people, for stronger people."

"So you treat the land as a dead thing. You will take the strength out of it. But without the land, without the bear, without the otter, the owl, the deer, what spirits will live in the people? Those spirits will never be stronger than they are today."

Duncan inched away. Woolford had reappeared among the rocks.

"Ramsey's two cargo canoes are empty," the ranger reported when Duncan reached him. "Pike's men carried the contents up here. I'll search the far side," Woolford added, and sprinted away.

Duncan moved obliquely, as inconspicuously as possible, toward the back of the oak. Boot marks, many of them, in the moist soil at the base, showed repeated back-and-forth movements. A shadow flashed over his shoulder. Pike's ox-like sergeant, the man who days earlier had towered over Duncan with manacles, stared at him with a hungry glint, his fists opening and shutting as if preparing for action. Duncan shifted one way, then another, darting around the man's side to appear in the open beside the seated Iroquois.

Arnold was speaking, the rolled charter in his hand now, his words like some rehearsed homily. As he finished, he stuffed the charter into the sleeve of his coat, draped it over the log he had been sitting on, then stepped toward the soldiers who, as if on cue, rose from the log some of them sat on and parted, pulling away the blanket that had covered the log to reveal two wooden kegs. The sergeant appeared by the kegs, lifting one onto a rock, and with a flat stone pried up the sealed ring of willow that had secured the cap. Arnold began lifting objects out, unwrapping the leather scraps that covered many of them, passing them out among the Indians. Combs. Flint strikers. Horn cups. Pewter spoons.

A murmur of excitement moved through the Iroquois. Raven-catcher watched with chagrin. Tashgua remained expressionless. The sergeant lifted the second keg, settled it onto two logs, and pulled out the bung at the bottom. A thick yellow substance oozed out. Honey.

Arnold gestured the Indians forward, led them back to the tree and into its dark hollow. Duncan, every instinct screaming alarm, followed. The soldiers had turned the hollow into a warehouse. Kegs were stacked five high, thirty kegs, perhaps forty, all stamped with the Ramsey *R*—the very kegs he had seen in the Ramsey cellar. As Arnold began speaking about how the gifts would be distributed among all the tribes, Duncan watched soldiers tending a new fire two hundred feet away, holding up tin mugs for the Iroquois.

Duncan lingered as the chieftains filed out for the hot tea being offered by the soldiers. In the light that filtered through the holes and slits along the base of the tree, he quickly searched for hidden weapons. There were none, only the stacks of kegs packed with bribes for the Iroquois, proof of the power of Ramsey's protecting spirit. He exited the dark chamber and circuited the massive trunk again, to no avail. On the log in front of him were Arnold's coat and hat. Lying nearby was the carved drum log Tashgua and his son had used the day before. Arnold was at the fire, beside Ramsey, serving out tea from a tall kettle. Tashgua was ten feet away, his eyes closed now as he chanted in a whisper. With one swift motion, Duncan pulled the charter from Arnold's sleeve and slipped it into the log drum. He lifted the log, a hand at both ends, and ceremoniously carried it into the tree chamber, kneeling to set it in the center of the pool of light cast through the entry. He glanced up to see Arnold watching him now. He offered the vicar a nod, then solemnly ran his hand along the log drum. Arnold shot him a peeved glance, took a step toward Duncan, then was interrupted by Sarah's outstretched hand. She looped her arm through Arnold's, then led him in the opposite direction, back toward the fire.

Suddenly Duncan spotted Woolford splashing across the stream, sprinting at a desperate pace up the trail to the camp. With terrible foreboding Duncan watched him disappear behind the outcroppings. He dared not follow, dared not leave Ramsey with the Indians.

The Iroquois were admiring the gifts from the keg, hefting some of the powder horns the sergeant had produced, responding when another of Pike's soldiers set the keg of honey on a root at the foot of the tree and gestured for them to come and sweeten their cups.

"Your heart," said a quiet voice at Duncan's side. "She has your heart in her dreams."

Duncan turned to see Tashgua, sitting in his chair of roots. The old Indian's wrinkled face seemed beyond age, so ancient, so full of secrets from other centuries, other worlds. Duncan longed to sit with him for hours, for days, to learn something of life in the forest before the Europeans came, to absorb some of the things that could not be spoken. Then he realized that in the middle of the long-awaited ceremony, the old shaman wanted to speak of Sarah.

"There was a terrible storm at sea," Duncan said. He had never felt more humbled, more insignificant, before another person.

"A mother storm," Tashgua declared, as if he had been there.

"I was going to die. Then she was going to die. Then the storm swallowed us and spat us back out."

"We know," the shaman murmured. "It was the first miracle. The water miracle."

Duncan's breath caught in his throat. The Iroquois had decided that his saving Sarah had been one of their prophesied miracles.

"Part of both of you died in that storm," Tashgua said before Duncan could respond.

Duncan swallowed hard. He looked up at the massive tree and with a strange sense of release knew it to be true. Since the hour he had saved Sarah there were parts of his life that were indeed dead, never to go back to, just as new parts had been created. "I am not strong enough to be in Sarah's dreams." The words came out unbidden, and Duncan looked up with an expression of surprise.

Tashgua, strangely, smiled. "Her dreams are for all of us. We do not control them. She does not need our strength. She needs our understanding. It is not an easy thing to live in this world and another at the same time."

Duncan realized he did not know for certain which worlds Tashgua spoke of. But then he gazed out among the Iroquois and knew they would have to speak of it another time. "You must tell them to leave," he pleaded.

Tashgua offered another small, serene grin. "We will all be the same, you know, all of us linked forever by this day."

"The soldiers and Lord Ramsey, they . . . ." His voice trembled as he felt the quiet power of the man beside him. "Please," he added in a whisper, beginning to lift the stone bear from his pocket.

Tashgua, seeming to anticipate his intention, raised a hand to stop him. "We came so the spirits could speak to us. Nothing else matters," Tashgua said, then lifted his hand and gently placed his palm on Duncan's heart. "Do I have your blessing?" the shaman abruptly asked him.

Duncan stared in disbelief as the stiff old hand reached down and clasped Duncan's. He returned the grip, squeezing tightly, then the aged prophet rose and stepped inside the tree. Tashgua gazed at the log drum in the pool of light in wonder, as if it had magically transported itself into the center of the tree cave, then sat beside it, his fingers running along its ranks of carved animals, the motion slowly converting to the quiet, steady heartbeat sound.

The final realization came in pieces as Duncan walked out among the Iroquois gathering before the tree, some taking honey, some settling onto the ground as Tashgua's drumming grew louder, amplified by the hollow chamber of the tree. For the first time, he noticed a grenadier's match case on the chest belt of one of the soldiers. He saw the soldiers all moving, though not in the same direction. One, with a long horn from the keg of gifts, stepped into the shadows at the side of the tree. There was a faint scent of sulphur in the air. Pike stood with Ramsey by the fire, far from the tree. The images came faster. Something red flashing on the rocky cliff above them. The soldier with the match case moving toward the tree. Arnold retrieving his coat from the log by the tree. Conawago, searching among the rocks by the stream, waving something at Duncan. A tool, a large hand auger. As the soldier disappeared around the tree, Duncan saw that the match case was off his belt, in his hand now.

His feet reacted faster than his mind, propelling him toward the shadows as a long, anguished moan escaped his lips. He tackled the soldier from the back, knocking the man to the ground, but as he fell, the soldier adeptly tossed the piece of smoldering match cord to the burly man, Pike's sergeant, who was emptying the contents of the horn into a hole drilled into the tree wall.

Duncan struggled to his feet and launched himself at the sergeant, who spun about and kicked him as the slow match did its job, lighting the line of black powder now leading into the oak. As the soldiers sprinted away, Duncan staggered to the front of the tree. Arnold shouted at him, holding up his coat, his hand in the empty sleeve, his face draining of color as he understood what Duncan had done. The vicar dropped the coat and flung himself toward the drum in the tree chamber.

Duncan cried out for the Indians to flee. Most of them stared at him uncertainly, then looked back toward Tashgua. Pike snapped furious orders and two soldiers charged at Duncan. There was a sharp crack from the hillside, and the old chief wearing Jamie's wolf pelt stumbled forward, caught by his companions. Some of the Indians began to move as Conawago took up the warning, then another figure dashed through them, calling frantically in their own tongue. Duncan spun about as Sarah paused in her sprint to push some of the chieftains away, then launched herself toward the opening through which Arnold had disappeared.

Duncan leaned forward as he reached her, his shoulder to her belly, scooping her off her feet, maintaining his frantic pace as she pounded his back, screaming out the same Iroquois word, over and over. He threw her behind a boulder, covering her with his body as with a massive roar the world came to an end.

Chapter Fifteen

UNCAN WAS THE FIRST TO rise in the awful stillness. The scene was like a battlefield. One of the two soldiers who had tried to stop Duncan sat on the ground, blood gushing down his chest, staring numbly at him, holding the end of a thick splinter of wood that had pierced his neck and emerged from the opposite side. The second soldier lay lifeless on the ground, his body perforated with at least a dozen wooden shards, some curved, from the kegs that had held the gunpowder.

Most of the Iroquois lay on the earth, many dead or dying. Duncan slowly pushed himself up, saw that Sarah was numbed but unharmed, then ran to the Iroquois, stopping at the chief who had worn Jamie's cap and blanket. The back of the man's head was shattered. He had not been killed by the explosion.

"He flew through the air," a desolate voice said from behind him, as Duncan bent to the old Seneca with the fox headdress. Conawago was looking at another figure, lying on the ground a hundred feet away. "I saw his face. There was no fear. There was no surprise." The chief at his feet was dead. Duncan straightened, looking past Conawago, then ran to the inert form as several of the surviving Iroquois began a terrible lamentation, accompanied by loud words from the cooking fire. Ramsey was shouting at Pike, pointing to the ridge above.

Tashgua's body, incredibly, was intact. He had been at the entry, had ridden the force of the explosion outward. The bones of his back were crushed, his skull indented where it had slammed against a rock. As Sarah rose with an anguished cry, Duncan's hand shot into his pocket, then pushed under the dead shaman. He stood as she reached him, tears flooding her cheeks, then stepped aside as she collapsed onto the body. As he turned back to the other Iroquois, patches of color appeared on the path from the camp. A line of forlorn men in ill-fitting red coats emerged. Ramsey's harangue of Pike choked away as the patron recognized the figures on the trail. It was the remainder of his militia, along with Hawkins and his trappers, each man bound by rope to the next. They were being escorted down the ridge by Jamie's men and half a dozen others wearing the colors of Woolford's rangers.

An agonized moan brought Duncan back to the carnage behind him. The wounded Iroquois were not reacting to their own pain, Duncan saw, but to the fate of the sacred tree. They all gazed in the same direction, at the massive burning stump before them. Most of the tree lay in huge, smoldering pieces, some blown far from the stump. The remainder, a thirty-foot-tall section at the rear, was moving, swaying, groaning. The long, wrenching screech as it separated from the base was the most terrible sound Duncan had ever heard, the dying sound of the centuries-old creature. They watched in stunned silence as it toppled, shaking the earth so violently that rocks on the ridges above were loosened and rolled down the cliffs. Ramsey had brought the wonder of his science to the Haudenosaunee.

As he recovered his senses, Duncan moved more quickly from one Indian to the next, clenching his jaw against the gore. The torso of one of the old Iroquois had been nearly severed in half by a slab of wood the size of a plowshare. Every one of the Indians who had been directly in front of the chamber was dead, including the old woman, the smiling matriarch who had helped Sarah in the village. Several of them had no evidence of injuries, except the blood seeping out of their ears and noses. He watched, his heart in his throat, as Conawago moved among them, closing their eyes, lifting dead hands and folding fingers around the leather totem pouch each wore around his or her neck. Duncan steadied himself, lifted the tail of his shirt, and began ripping bandages. There was work to do among those who still lived. He labored without break for an hour, staunching wounds with moss brought by Conawago, removing long, bladelike splinters from legs and arms, vaguely aware of Jamie's men ordering Pike's surviving soldiers to remove their shirts for more bandages. As he finished with each of the wounded, they struggled to their feet, refusing assistance, insisting on limping to the dead shaman.

"Twenty-two dead," Woolford announced in a grim tone. "Including the two who were inside the tree."

Arnold. Duncan paused in his work, looking about for signs of the vicar.

"We found Arnold's hand, with his vicar's ring, blown halfway across the valley. The rest is mostly ash, inside the stump."

"You reached the militia."

"With only moments to spare. They had orders to open fire on the surviving Indians and deserters."

The tone shifted among the survivors. Something like joy entered the voices of several nearest the shaman's body. The oldest of the surviving chieftains had his hand in the air, lifting a black object to cries of awe.

Conawago cocked his head in confusion for a moment. "It's a miracle," he said, gazing pointedly at Duncan. "They seemed to have discovered their ancient bear, missing since the massacre last year. They say the blood of Tashgua has drawn the sacred bear out of the earth. They say this is the true word of the tree, the last word, the reason Tashgua brought them together. It is the earth miracle they awaited."

"But it can't be . . ." Woolford said with a muddled expression. "Munroe took it into the . . . ." The ranger slowly turned toward Duncan, realization lighting his eyes. He lowered himself onto a rock, a strange mix of guilt and gratitude on his face.

"What was it she spoke?" Duncan asked after a moment. "The word Sarah kept repeating when she realized what was happening."

Conawago whispered the answer. "Father. It means father."

They burned the red coats of Ramsey's militia in the embers of the sacred tree, then returned to camp and released all but ten of the Company men at the canoes, ordering the confused, subdued men to Edentown without Ramsey or the head keeper. Cameron spoke quietly to Ramsey, who despite his victory seemed confounded, looking about, calling for Arnold. When the patron offered no protest, made not even a demand that the remaining men tied in the shadows be released, Cameron began directing the loading of the canoes. When the keeper complained the men had no weapons against the Huron, Woolford ordered four of Pike's privates and one of his own rangers to join the party.

"My men only take orders from the major and me," Pike's sergeant groused. Pike, who had not left Ramsey's side since the explosion, watched his men readying their packs, then inched toward his own.

"Major Pike," Woolford declared in a loud voice as two of his rangers appeared at his side, brandishing manacles pulled from Pike's equipment, "is under arrest."

Ramsey's head snapped up. "By you?" he snapped. Woolford's defiance had broken the patron's spell. "Ridiculous. He is under my protection."

The deserters of the Forty-second seemed to have developed a new respect for Woolford. The ranger officer made a quick, impatient gesture toward Pike, and in an instant the manacles were on his wrists. Two of the Scottish warriors dragged him, shrilly protesting, sputtering curses, to the post at the entrance to the camp, where they began to tie him. Ramsey uttered a weak protest, then turned to Sarah, his countenance sagging as he saw the dark emotion in her eyes. When she had called to her father that afternoon before the explosion, it had been toward the shaman. Tashgua had raised her from a child. Duncan recalled how she always referred to the patron as Lord Ramsey. He had misunderstood her fearful prediction at Edentown. *They want my father dead,* she had declared, *they want to spread the pieces of his body over the forest.* She had not meant Ramsey.

She had one true father, the man who had first brought knowledge into her heart, and Ramsey had killed him that day.

"Deserters! Traitors!"

Duncan spun about to see a tangle of arms and legs on the ground near the post. "Leave him, God rot ye!" Pike's burly Irish sergeant had charged into the Scots tying Pike and was lashing out with fist and foot at the former soldiers, who responded with equal vehemence. One of the Scots fell to the ground, doubled up in pain. The sergeant was repulsed with a blow of a club to his back, which sent him sprawling onto a pile of knapsacks belonging to the half-dozen rangers who had arrived in time to help confront the militia. He threw one of the packs at his opponents, strewing the contents over the ground. As he did so, four of the Scots warriors fell on him, dragging him backward, pinning the sergeant against a rock, tying first his hands, then his feet, then connecting the two bindings with a short length of rope so he could not straighten.

"Major Pike," Woolford declared in a dark voice, "is under arrest for treason. Perhaps, Sergeant, you need to join him at the post."

"A pox on ye!" the Irishman snapped. "We know the traitors in this camp! We sent a runner back. The army knows where to find ye! Ye'll all swing from trees before the winter, ye damned whores of the heathen!"

Duncan had never seen the ranger move so fast. In an instant Woolford was before the man, the back of his open hand pounding his jaw. "Major Pike is under arrest for treason," he repeated as the sergeant reeled backward. "And for the murder of six of my rangers. There may well be room for you on that particular gallows, Sergeant."

The man spat in the dirt at Woolford's feet. "Treason, my arse! We'll see about charges! Aiding the McCallum deserters, that be worse than murder in some esteemed ranks."

As the two men glared at each other, Duncan began helping the young ranger who was retrieving the articles that had tumbled out of the knapsack. A flint striker, a bullet mold, a wool cap. He paused as he lifted an unfamiliar object. It was a flat piece of iron, four inches long, with short legs at each corner ending in sharp points, two small loops at each end on the side opposite the legs. He gazed at it, not understanding what about it was gnawing at his awareness.

"We never know how long we'll be out," the young ranger explained as he reached for the piece of iron, "don't know if we'll get back to a quartermaster before winter." He saw the confusion in Duncan's eyes. "An ice creeper. You strap it to the bottom of your boots."

Duncan quickly pulled out the grenadier's cap from Ramsey's cellar. The four pointed legs matched the four small holes perfectly. "Who is issued these?" he urgently asked the soldier.

"Rangers. The other troops stay in winter quarters."

The curses of the Irishman died away as Duncan approached Woolford, extending the creeper, silently demonstrating how the legs matched the holes in the cap.

"Meaning what?" Woolford still hovered over the sergeant as if about to pounce again at any moment.

Duncan replied by holding the cap and the creeper in front of the sergeant.

"A pox on y'er mother!" the sergeant spat.

"His left cheek," Duncan said. When the sergeant resisted, turning the cheek against the rock, two of the Iroquois Scots held the man, forcing his head around. "It's hard to see for the grime," Duncan said, and before he could continue, Woolford had grabbed a kettle sitting by the cold firepit and tossed its contents onto the man's face. The scars were there, as Duncan had seen at the ranger camp—two pairs of small circles spaced four inches apart. He held the creeper to the man's cheek. On the skin, as with the hat, the marks were perfectly aligned to the ice spikes.

"A ranger did this to you," Duncan stated. "A ranger stripped of his weapons, fighting with the only thing he could find."

The sergeant glared at Duncan, then shot an uncertain glance at Woolford. "Not rangers. French. Spies. Infiltrators in army clothes. The major gets information about such."

"Where are the others who were with you that day?" Duncan demanded. "In the boats to Edentown?"

"Not them. The others be gone. Assigned to new posts, every last one. India . . . some to Jamaica."

"How convenient."

"Damned your eyes! They were French we killed by the tree that day. Scouting targets for the Huron raiding parties. The major warned us that they sometimes used ranger uniforms, for deception."

"You did not think it strange that Pike had you change your own uniforms to those of the Forty-ninth?"

"Confuse the enemy about troop placements, that's why. That's part of what his office does. They were French, I tell you!"

"Sergeant!" Pike shouted. "I command you to hold your damned tongue! Do not be beguiled by these outlaws!"

One of Jamie's men pounded a slab of firewood against his temple. Pike slumped, slid down the post to the ground.

"Not French," came a ragged, angry voice from the shadows. Two new rangers had appeared, carrying between them in a litter the blond Scot Duncan had left at the mission. "You murdered them in cold blood." One of the rangers carried a crutch, hung with a shoulder strap along his rifle. He removed the crutch and extended it to the wounded Scot. The man refused help as he struggled to his feet.

"Ten of you bastards," he hissed, "six of them, all but one asleep. I was helping them after the massacre at the tree, following the tracks of those who had done it, was running back in the dawn to tell them I found a fresh camp not far away. A camp for ten men, abandoned before dawn. I ran back with the news but stopped when I got near, because I didn't understand what I was seeing. A grenadier walks up to the ranger lighting the morning fire, talking all friendly-like, then quick as lightning he has a dagger to the ranger's throat, warning against any sound. I thought it was me they wanted, for desertion, so I hid. I didn't really understand until it was over. It took less than a minute. A volley of muskets, then they finished those still living with bayonets. Only one lived long enough to fight you, you bastard, and that only with his ice creeper, because you took all their weapons. Then his skull was crushed from behind with the butt of a Brown Bess."

Duncan angrily threw the grenadier's cap at the sergeant's head. "A blow with the ice creeper to your cheek. Another blow to your crown into your borrowed cap, with enough force to knock the cap off. You didn't bother to pick it up."

"Because by then he was running after me," the wounded Scot explained.

"But someone else picked it up later." Duncan glanced toward the shadows where the bound Ramsey men sat watching, all except Hawkins, who leaned against a tree, sleeping. "Probably Hawkins. He found it and gave it to Arnold. Hawkins and Arnold eventually understood the significance." Duncan looked up to Woolford, whose face was dark with anger. "It was how they got Pike to help them this time. Pike showed them how it was done, finding easy unarmed targets at the sacred tree. And once they understood about the death ritual, Ramsey knew it could repeat it a year later to destroy the remaining old chiefs." Duncan leaned over the sergeant. "Just hide on the ridge and fire down on them when they were lined up by the sacred tree. Is that how you did it last year?"

The sergeant cast a baleful glance at the Scots. "Those deserters last year were going to die no matter what. No one said anything about the others there being Iroquois. If Indians were with the traitors, they had to be Huron, the major said. They were just Indians," he added, his voice gone hollow.

"Tell me, Sergeant," Duncan asked, "did someone try to transfer you, too?"

The burly man seemed to be shrinking before their eyes. He nodded slowly. "The major gave me papers for the East Indies. But I took sick with the flux the day before sailing. When I was finally fit for duty, they needed every able-bodied man, so transfers were cancelled." His face, turned to the ground, had become gaunt. "God's breath!" he groaned. "I never . . . I wouldn't have . . . our own rangers," he said in a desolate whisper, and kept repeating the words. "Our own rangers . . ."

• • •

"Nothing is settled," Woolford said as they sat in front of one of the back lodges an hour later, giving voice to the new foreboding that had been growing in Duncan's own heart since returning to the village. Duncan poked with a wooden spoon at the corn mush they were eating for supper, nodding his agreement. A gallows was still being built in Edentown. Those of Tashgua's band who survived could no longer stay in the village, for the army knew where they were now. Duncan's heart still wrenched every time he thought of Sarah, who was to be taken back to have her brain opened. And Woolford, Duncan knew, was beginning to understand what for him may be the harshest reality of all. They had no assurance that once back in their world either Ramsey or Pike would pay for what they had done.

"But the tribes," Duncan ventured. "The tribes know what Ramsey did."

"And they will do what?" Woolford interjected in a bitter tone. "Bring a suit of law against Ramsey?"

"The war. Official action will have to be taken, to protect the alliance."

"No," the ranger sighed. "The ones killed were the ones who wanted the Iroquois to end the alliance, to stop taking sides in the affairs of Europeans. This just makes it easier for the tribes to keep sending warriors to Albany. For the old ones, what will be remembered is that the sacred bear is revived, a sign that the old ways are not totally dead. For the young ones, what will be remembered is that the sacred tree is gone, that it destroyed itself and Tashgua with it. At many of their council fires, there will no longer be voices speaking up for the old ways."

"There are other trees," came a quiet, sad voice. Conawago leaned and stirred the embers of the fire before them. "When your lodge is burnt, you find another." For a moment Duncan remembered how Conawago had sometimes paused when they traveled together to seek out sacred places, some of them rock formations, some of them old trees. "There are ceremonies, to introduce spirits to new homes."

"And of those who know such things, old friend," Woolford asked, "how many of you are left?"

Conawago gazed into the flames. "Every time the wind takes a leaf from a tree, the world is forever changed."

They were silent a long time. When he spoke again there was a hard edge in Conawago's voice. "You don't know Ravencatcher. He will not let Ramsey forget his visit to his father's temple."

Woolford and Duncan exchanged an uneasy glance as Conawago stepped toward the path to the far side, where the Indians, with Sarah, still prepared their dead.

"Ramsey will not forget," Woolford said. "He lost his vicar."

"No," Duncan said, "what he will remember is that he lost his ten thousand square miles, lost his private kingdom." The patron, like everyone else, had been numbed by emotion after the explosion, though in his case the true remorse had not struck until he had found Arnold's coat sleeve empty.

"I know what you did with the charter, McCallum," Woolford announced. "I consider it—" as the ranger searched for words, several phrases ran through Duncan's mind. An act of treason. A blasphemy against the king. A theft of vast dimensions. "I consider it to rank with your other miracles, McCallum." The ranger offered his hand. After a moment Duncan took it, and the two men solemnly shook.

"There will still be a trial in Edentown," Duncan pointed out.

"I am overdue at Quebec. And you are on my register of rangers. Come with me. I can protect you, give you a different name on the payrolls."

"I will not abandon Mr. Lister."

"They will take you back in chains."

"Which is why I need help. Someone who can watch out for Sarah, at least until she is with Crispin. Someone to take a message to the mission. Someone with soldiers who can be trusted. And you must not interfere with what Ramsey is going to do to me. Let him work his fury on me." Woolford gazed into the fire, then looked up with a conspiratorial gleam as Duncan began to explain what he needed.

• • •

At dusk the remainder of Tashgua's warriors filed down from the ridge. They did not pause to eat or drink, but immediately surrounded Lord Ramsey, who sat alone at one of the cooking fires as Cameron and the remaining Company men readied the canoes at the river landing under the watchful eyes of several rangers. The warriors were freshly painted, as if for war. The patron was so alarmed, he was not able to find his tongue as the Iroquois led him away, did not protest until, his face turning chalk white, they began tying him to the post.

"Woolford!" The call came out as an anguished groan. Ramsey called again and again, the words coming out as a scream, fading to a moan as he saw the ranger at the side of the camp. Woolford, having settled onto a log, extracted his pipe and was lighting his tobacco as he calmly watched the Iroquois. Ramsey's gaze fell upon Hawkins, awake at last, still bound, watching with amusement in his hollow eyes. In the last light of dusk, more of the Iroquois emerged from the shaman's lodge. As they arranged bundles of dry grass in a ring around the pole, a figure in a white doeskin dress appeared in the doorway of bones.

"Sarah! God on earth, daughter!" The cries were frantic now. "Stop them, dear Sarah! You must stop—" The words choked in the patron's throat as his eyes met those of his daughter, who now approached at a slow, ceremonial pace. Sarah Ramsey returned his terrified gaze with a look of cool pity.

Ramsey fell back against the post as if struck, making small whimpering sounds as Sarah helped the Iroquois arrange the tinder.

"Not this way!" Duncan cried. His hand went to his tomahawk. As he took a step forward, the shaft of a war ax pressed against his belly. He looked up. Conawago did not speak, only soberly shook his head from side to side.

The Indians, now including most of their adopted Highlanders, began moving in slow rotation around the post, beginning a low, steady chant. Torches appeared, stuck in the ground outside the circle of warriors. Ramsey started shouting in a trembling voice, something about money, something about the King of England, but his words were drowned out by the chant, now louder and louder. Suddenly the voices reached a crescendo and abruptly halted. Duncan stopped breathing for a moment. A spirit had materialized inside the circle.

The spirit's crimson face was wrinkled, and its white eyes, round and hollow. Its mouth was strangely puckered. On either side of the wooden mask hung what appeared to be lengths of horsehair. The spirit's arms and legs, though human, were painted white. In one hand it held the bone rattle of Tashgua.

The spirit dancer shook the rattle at Ramsey as the circle began to move again, with a new, more animated chant. The masked dancer circuited the post as well, with gruesome, writhing motions. Each time he completed a circuit, he shook the rattle at either side of Ramsey's head.

Duncan glanced at his rifle. Conawago, who never seemed to miss a motion, touched him with the shaft of his club again, gesturing for him to sit beside Woolford, who, puffing his pipe, watched in fascination.

From the shadows beside Duncan, the Indians and Scots who had been watching suddenly burst into activity. Cameron and his Company men had emerged from the river trail and were trying to reach the English lord. There was a brief flurry of silent motion, and when it settled, all the men except Cameron were pinned against trees, some with blades pressed against their throats to prevent further movement.

The circle was moving faster now. A spark of defiance kindled within Ramsey, and he began berating the men as vulgar savages, swine of the forest, reminding them that he shared blood with the king. But the spark quickly died as one of the warriors, who had sliced open his own palm, passed his hand over Ramsey's head, leaving blood dripping down the Englishman's cheek. The patron's eyes were frozen in terror. Ramsey's jaw opened and shut without making sound. As snakeskins were draped over his shoulders, his bladder emptied.

The chant of the shaman warriors grew almost unbearably loud. A torch appeared in the hand of the spirit dancer, and Ramsey found enough voice to scream as the masked man lit the grass.

Only Duncan and Ramsey reacted to the fire, Ramsey screaming louder, Duncan leaping to his feet. A calm, expectant glance from Sarah stopped him. Then he saw the tobacco leaves being laid on the fire by the dancers. The ring of burning grass, already ebbing, was no closer than two feet from Ramsey. It was a purification fire, a fire to cleanse the man at the post. The Indians knew they could not exercise their full fury on an English lord. But they were not going to leave the source of their misery untouched.

The chant renewed itself as the tobacco fumes spiraled upward, the masked dancer again using the bone rattle, the circle moving faster. Duncan, mesmerized by the chants, the smoke, the rhythmic music, lost track of time. Suddenly he was aware that the masked dancer was gone.

The other dancers gradually widened their circle, until they eventually disappeared into the shadows. To Duncan's surprise, it was Conawago who cut the patron's bonds. The old Nipmuc was speaking in a low voice to the stunned Englishman, with words that were strangely familiar. Conawago, he realized after a moment, was giving Ramsey the prayer he had once taught Duncan, the prayer used by children lost in the forest. Suddenly another figure was there, pushing Conawago aside. Cameron wrapped a blanket around Ramsey's trembling shoulders and led him toward the lodge where the Ramsey prisoners were being taken for the night.

As Duncan watched Ramsey disappear into the shadows, something landed at his feet. His haversack.

"Go now," Sarah urged. She had already packed and tied his sack.

"There's an old Scot in a prison cell," he reminded her.

"They may well kill you tonight, Duncan." There was a new strength in Sarah's voice, along with her foreboding. "One of the soldiers saw what you did with the king's paper. He told Cameron."

The camp settled quickly for the night, with the Ramsey men tied to the posts of one of the lodges. Duncan waited for nearly two hours, then rose from his blanket and stepped into the shadows, carrying his loaded rifle. He walked the length of the trail to the canoe landing at the river and back, studying each bend and curve, each pool of moonlight, trying to mimic the soundless way the Indians and rangers moved through the forest. Upon his return, he watched the slumbering camp for several minutes, confirmed that the Iroquois were all still on the far side of the ridge, preparing the dead by torchlight, and then retreated to the back of the lodge where the prisoners had been taken. The lodge was old and in disrepair. He had made a point of being there as the men were being tied, joining Alex as the boy offered a gourd dipper of water to each prisoner, noting the position of the men and the lodge poles they were bound to. He had marked one of the posts on the outside of the lodge with a white stone, and now, glancing one more time to confirm no one watched, he drew his knife and quickly sliced through the leather strap around the post. Then he rose and slipped back down the river trail.

He had waited only ten minutes behind a boulder where the trail opened onto the river flats before he made out the sound of running feet. His timing was not perfect as he sprang in front of the man, but it was good enough for him to land a glancing blow to the man's temple that knocked him to the ground.

Hawkins had begun to squirm away when he saw the rifle leveled at his chest.

"You murdered an old Iroquois today," Duncan growled. "A bullet in the back of his head."

"And here I thought no one appreciated my work," Hawkins sneered. The trapper glanced left and right. As his hand inched toward a stone, Duncan kicked it away. "He would have been dead a moment later anyways."

"But then you would have lost the bounty," Duncan continued in an icy tone. "If Jamie had died in the blast, you would have had no claim to the money. Except you shot the wrong man."

"An honest mistake," Hawkins spat. "Who would have thought he would give his coat to some old buck?"

Duncan pulled back the hammer on the rifle. "Leave Jamie be, Hawkins."

The oily trapper studied Duncan's moonlit face. "Y'er the one who set me free? That be y'er bargain, boy? My freedom for y'er brother's life? I don't deal with slaves. And Ramsey would have me free on the morrow anyways."

"Then why do you run, Hawkins? Because you fear I get close to a truth you can't have others know? Like how Frasier died? That's the price. Take a bullet now or tell me what happened at dawn that day."

It was the lowest of pugilist tricks that undid Duncan, a quick hook of a foot around his calf that caused him to totter long enough for Hawkins to grab the barrel of the rifle. The trapper sprang up like a cat, wrenching the rifle away, clubbing Duncan with it. Suddenly Duncan was on the ground, the end of the rifle pressed against his neck as Hawkins probed his belt, lifting away Duncan's ranger knife. Pressing the blade against Duncan's throat, tucking the gun under an arm, the trapper deftly opened the frizzen pan and blew away the priming, rendering the gun useless.

"Ye've only a wee bit of a killer in ye, boy," the trapper said, amusement in his tone as he tossed the gun aside. "Not near enough to survive in these parts."

Duncan made a slight movement of resistance, twisting his spine, and the blade flashed downward, slicing into his arm before returning to his throat.

"I need money, boy."

"I haven't any."

Hawkins sighed, raised the knife again, slower this time, toying with Duncan, bringing it down to slice the other arm. But suddenly it was frozen, immovable against the head of a war ax whose iron spike suddenly protruded through the flesh of Hawkins's forearm. He uttered a long groan before grabbing the knife with his other hand, poised to throw it at the old Indian who held the ax. Then he froze once more, his entire body solid, as if it had gone numb. The knife slowly came down.

With a quick, crablike motion Duncan moved out of reach, then followed the trapper's gaze. Hawkins looked not toward Conawago, who still held the ax that had impaled his arm, but toward a round, shimmering thing that floated in the moonlight.

It was an image of a raven, black against yellow. It was Adam Munroe's medallion, stolen by Duncan's attackers the day he had left Edentown.

"Drop the blade," Conawago said in a cool, fierce voice. "McCallum wants an answer about a murder."

The knife did drop, but Hawkins did not speak. For a moment he had the look of one of the doomed animals that thrashed in his traps. Then his hollow, cold-blooded gaze returned. With impossible coolness, he pulled his arm free of the ax spike. His muscles coiled. He seemed about to leap at the shadowy figure with the medallion. But when he launched himself, it was backward, out onto the flats.

Duncan grabbed his knife and raced toward the canoes, a step in front of Conawago, thinking Hawkins was intent on stealing one. But when they reached the vessels, none were missing, and they could see a dark figure raising silver water as he hurried across the waist-deep river.

When they returned to the trail, the one who had been holding the medallion was sitting on a moonlit boulder, staring forlornly at the black bird in his hand.

"Sarah said you knew my brother," Ravencatcher said to Duncan.

"Adam Munroe was your brother?"

"The husband of my sister is my brother," Tashgua's son explained. He cradled the medallion in his fingers. "You were there, when he died?"

"He died strong. He died for your sister."

"I gave this to him, on the day they became husband and wife."

"I lost it, the day I left Edentown."

"And I found it," explained Conawago, "on the dead man lying against the tree at the cabin."

Duncan stared in the direction Hawkins had fled, then slowly tuned back toward Ravencatcher. "You should keep it," he said.

"No. It is right that you have it, McCallum," said the Iroquois.

"Adam would wish it so. My second sister would wish it so," Raven-catcher added, then thrust the quillwork medallion into Duncan's hand and slipped away into the shadows. His second sister. He meant Sarah.

"Don't go back to the camp," Conawago warned. "Tashgua's men are all at the embers of the old tree, with his body, which is where Ravencatcher and I go now. Ramsey woke to find Woolford gone, and untied his men."

But Duncan knew the only way he could return to Edentown was in Ramsey's chains.

A bright fire was burning as he entered the camp, with Ramsey and his head keeper standing beside it. A new fury had risen on Ramsey's face. He had revived, and had spoken with Cameron.

The patron stepped toward Duncan as soon as he saw him. Something wild and hot had grown in Ramsey's eyes. With surprising speed he lifted an arm and slapped Duncan, hard.

"Sedition!" Ramsey hissed. "I curse the day the good reverend laid eyes on you!" He turned to Cameron, standing in front of the remaining Company men. "Seize him!"

Cameron glanced toward the ridge path, then leapt forward. He held Duncan at both sides as Ramsey slapped him again, and again. "You were the one who encouraged her. You were the one with the impudence to defy me, to steal my trust. You were the one who destroyed my charter!"

Duncan's head swam, his vision blurred. The Company men swarmed around him. He was vaguely aware of movement at his back, of something cold on his shoulder. By the time he understood and tried to resist, it was too late. One of the hinged iron collars was on his neck, with a small, bent hook fastened in the holes at the rear.

"Your hot Scottish blood blinds you to the simplest of facts," Ramsey hissed. "The Ramsey Company requested your transportation to America. The Ramsey Company can rescind its request. You, sir, will be shipped back to England in irons with a long list of new crimes, signed by myself as magistrate. I vow to you, McCallum, you will rot away the rest of your miserable life in a moldy English cell."

A figure appeared beside Ramsey, and a hand seized the patron's arm as it rose to slap Duncan again. Woolford was instantly surrounded by Cameron's men.

"And you, Captain Woolford, will be mucking barracks stables in India by the time I finish with you."

Woolford surveyed the hungry faces of the men around him. The ranger had only a handful of his own men to back him up, and once they were out of the wilderness, the world belonged to Ramsey. As Duncan watched, Woolford cast a glance toward the path to the sacred valley. They both knew it would take little encouragement for some of the Scots there to deal permanently with Ramsey. But if they let him be killed, none of them—neither Duncan, nor Woolford, nor Jamie—could ever face Sarah again. The ranger dropped his hand and retreated, pulling Sarah with him.

Ramsey watched as the ranger faded into the shadows, then turned toward the post and spat a quick command. Duncan saw the motion of a thick piece of firewood being swung through the air. It knocked him to his knees. As he fought for his breath, a second blow connected with his skull and flattened him against the ground.

When he regained consciousness, Duncan had been untied from the post and a rope had been fastened to the collar. He watched as if from a distance as Cameron strung the rope over a limb and heaved, tightening it so that Duncan had to stand on the balls of his feet. They left him there in the chill autumn air and returned to their blankets. By the time someone loosened the knot, in the small hours of the night, he was so wracked with pain, he could only collapse onto the ground.

At dawn he was awakened with cold water on his face as the Company men made ready for travel. Cameron pulled Duncan to his feet in time to see Ramsey throw his pack into the underbrush, then the keeper led him down the trail to the river like a leashed dog, out of the now-abandoned Iroquois village.

Duncan stared at the earth as he walked, reliving a memory of his long-ago day on the mast. A black wave was speeding toward him again. Ramsey was pushing him into it, and afterward he would have no life.

Suddenly Cameron spat a warning and lifted the club in his hand, then relaxed as Woolford stepped onto the trail, followed by Sarah, in a green dress, her hair neatly combed, her face scrubbed. "The rangers are taking Major Pike downriver," she announced in a flat voice. "We have readied more canoes. If we leave now, with so many men to help with the portages, we can be at Edentown tomorrow afternoon."

"This escapee," Ramsey said, with a gesture toward Duncan, "receives a hundred lashes when we reach Edentown. And I have decided that two days after we return, the old man hangs."

"You cannot!" Duncan's protest came out so loud every man turned toward him. "The governor must approve first."

"I have decided to ask his forgiveness," Ramsey explained in an imperious tone, "rather than his permission. I will explain the crisis of law and order that we face and the need for a speedy resolution. He will understand when I explain that our town is populated with Scottish convicts. But before we hang him, McCallum, we will bind him to the scaffold and make him watch as we flay the skin from your back."

Sarah and Woolford turned down the trail without reply. On one of Woolford's shoulders hung Duncan's haversack; on the other, an extra rifle. Duncan's rifle.

Three strangers waited at the first of the ranger's canoes, all wearing Highland bonnets and dark plaid kilts, their top half naked save for sleeveless waistcoats and chest straps. Not strangers, Duncan realized with a start. Jamie and two of his men, having scrubbed off their paint and shifted to a semblance of European dress, were traveling with them. His brother offered no acknowledgment as Duncan caught his eye before being dragged toward a canoe, did not seem to notice as Cameron shoved him downward to soak his clothes, assuring he would shiver in the cool air.

The river was faster than Duncan could have imagined. The canoes shot downstream until sunset, then the party stopped to camp on an island, where two fires were lit—one for the Ramsey men, the second for Woolford and the others. Duncan, tethered to a tree, was given a strip of dried meat to chew and otherwise ignored as his captors covered themselves for sleep. Then a shadow appeared at his side. Sarah arranged a blanket over his legs, then rolled herself in another blanket, to sleep beside him, though they did not sleep at first, only leaned against the tree, her head nestled in his shoulder. There were no words between them, not simply because the others might hear, but because he knew it was the not the way of Sarah or the Iroquois who had raised her to give words to what rose in their hearts, only to show it. And in these moments he felt their roles reversed, as if he were the wild deer about to bolt.

He only spoke when the moon was high, when he was certain the Company men all slept. "They were going to use you as bait to attract Tashgua," he said. "You realized it, and with Adam and Evering gone, you did not know how to stop it. It's why you made the ritual at the compass, then went out on that mast in the storm."

He could feel her nod against his shoulder. "Adam was arranging for Evering to help me escape," Sarah whispered. "Evering would meet Conawago in New York town, and Conawago would take me away."

"But Adam and Evering died," Duncan said, weighing her words. "You ran away from the inn to the mission. You could have gone into the forest. Why did you go to Edentown?"

"Because of you, Duncan, and what happened to Mr. Lister. When I heard about that, at the inn, I knew Lord Ramsey would destroy you both."

"Why the barn, Sarah?" he asked after weighing the puzzles of the past ten days.

Her reply, slow in coming, sent a shudder down his back. "Because Lord Ramsey and Hawkins share the same skin," she said in a cracked voice.

He touched her cheek. It was soaked with tears.

Duncan gazed at the moon a long time, mentally reciting the list of the McCallum clan chiefs, then asked her to find Woolford. She returned with the ranger and a god. The Indian wearing the spirit mask gazed at him with hollow eyes as Duncan explained the battle to come.

Chapter Sixteen

*T*HE GALLOWS WAS NEARLY COMPLETE when they arrived at Edentown, a whipping post with an iron ring already sunk into the ground beside it. The men of the Company would not look Duncan in the eye as he stumbled along the main street, pulled on his leash by Cameron. He resisted as he passed the smithy, and though the jerk of the rope nearly knocked him off his feet, he paused long enough to make out the silent shadowy form in the charcoal crib, and to see the bony fingers that gripped the slats. Lister, looking like a ghost, was watching the finishing touches on his gibbet.

Ramsey's spirits had risen steadily as they approached the town, and by the time he climbed onto the bank near his massive barn, he was snapping orders, calling for men to clear the desks from the schoolhouse, to line the classroom with benches, to straighten a fence rail here, clean a harness there. He completed his promenade when he reached Duncan, now tied to the hitching post at the schoolhouse steps.

"I shall bathe and take a large meal," he announced airily as Crispin arrived with a cup of tea, "then we shall have our justice. Mr. Lister will be tried for murder, and you, McCallum, shall be tried for theft. We shall—" Ramsey paused, looking at a group of strangers huddled at the cooper's shed—a dozen men, women, and children, their clothing torn and soiled. "Who are these trespassers?" he demanded.

"More settlers, sir," Crispin explained. "Burned out of their cabins. Some escaped the Huron, fled as soon as they heard the cries in the night."

Ramsey surveyed the ragged group with a frown, then his gaze was captured by movement on the riverbank. Sarah had arrived, and was being helped ashore by Conawago. Ramsey silently pointed her toward the great house and waited to enter until she had disappeared inside. Moments later Crispin returned to the schoolhouse with food, drink, and a basin to wash Duncan's wounds.

By the time the patron emerged more than an hour later, bewigged and dressed as if for church, Jamie and his two men were moving among the Company workers, several of whom uttered small sounds of joy at the sight of their kilts. Wherever they touched the ranks, the men dispersed, fading away behind the barn. Ramsey, busy positioning and repositioning his freshly powdered wig, noticed their actions only as he climbed the schoolhouse steps.

"Fools!" he snapped at the keepers, who now held Lister, so weak he had to be supported, at both shoulders. "Summon the men back! The trial commences!"

But the keepers did not move. Their eyes, wide and worried, were focused on the new rank of strangers who, as if by magic, had appeared along the riverbank.

They were larger than life, huge bronzed men—some adorned only with paint, leggings, and loincloths, some in britches and boots wearing remnants of uniform tunics. Three wore kilts; two, incongruously, wore swords. All were armed, with rifle, war ax, or bow. Their faces were solemn, their spines rigid and straight. The remainder of Tashgua's band had arrived, and stood as if ready for battle.

At the center, beside Tashgua's son, was Woolford, freshly shaven and in a spotless uniform, wearing, for the first time since Duncan had known him, the brass gorget of rank at his neck. The ranger stepped forward. "The trial commences," he repeated in a loud voice.

"Do not mock me, Woolford," Ramsey growled.

"Do not mock the king," Woolford shot back as he approached. He paused at the water trough, filled a ladle, and handed it to Lister, who ravenously gulped it, then marched to the foot of the steps. "This is a theater of war. I am a captain in His Majesty's army. I have records showing that one of your defendants is enrolled as a ranger in my own company. There is the murder of my sergeant to resolve. There is evidence of a crime committed by a king's officer."

Ramsey had the look of a hungry predator whose fresh meat was being threatened. "You cannot have McCallum."

"You mistake me, sir. A court-martial is required, but I respect your desire for efficiency in the administration of justice. So we shall proceed with two judges."

Ramsey glared at the ranger. "I am aware of military procedure, Captain. You have no authority."

"In the wilderness," Woolford said in a treacherous tone, "in the midst of war, we are all used to asking forgiveness rather than permission. Major Pike has been relieved of command. Until countermanded by a more senior officer in the regular army," he said, "I speak for the military."

"I am colonel of the Edentown militia. If you wish to exercise authority, then you may clamp James McCallum in chains, Captain."

"A regular army officer is not beholden to the militia," Woolford declared in an even tone. "And we shall try one McCallum at a time."

Ramsey paused and glanced at Duncan. The patron's temper seemed about to erupt anew when he saw five figures emerge from the house. Sarah was attired in a dark blue dress trimmed in lace, one Duncan had not seen before, with her hair pinned back, giving her the look of a woman several years older. Flanking her were Crispin and Conawago, each holding the hand of one of the younger Ramsey children. Sarah stepped forward and curtseyed to the patron. But for the leather pouch that hung beside the gold chain on her bodice, she would have been a match for any young woman of elegant breeding on any promenade in London. The dress had a French flair to it. It was, Duncan realized, most likely borrowed from her mother's closet. Her appearance struck Ramsey dumb.

"We shall convene in the barn," Woolford announced, and he turned without waiting for a reply.

Sarah, Crispin, and Conawago followed the ranger into the huge structure that dominated the town—Ramsey's precious Palace of Husbandry. The patron watched in confusion for a moment, then darted inside the school, returning with an ornate gavel and his copy of Plato, and followed, gesturing for the keepers to bring their prisoners. Duncan took a step toward Lister, who, leaning on a makeshift crutch to relieve his broken ankle, seemed about to topple at any moment. But with a satisfied grunt, Cameron pulled back on Duncan's collar, then shoved him toward the barn.

Two wide planks had been placed on trestles, nearly spanning the center aisle. Two stools were placed behind this improvised bench for the judges, and a third at the end of the table, for witnesses. Ramsey, scowling, was about to sit when he froze and pointed above their heads. "Remove that monstrous thing!"

Old Crooked Face had been shifted within the loft, so that the Iroquois spirit mask hung on a barn post directly above the judges' bench, as portraits of the king hung in English courtrooms.

When Cameron stepped to the ladder, Jamie was there first, blocking his way. "There was a great debate, Your Highness," Jamie said to Ramsey in an exaggerated Scottish burr, "about whether an Iroquois should sit as judge, given the crimes committed against them. It would be one of the older women most likely, since they are often deemed the wisest among the tribes."

"The king's justice," Ramsey replied in a chill tone, "will never bend so far."

"But my aboriginal friends agreed," Jamie continued, "that we need not have a third justice beside you, so long as there is one listening overhead. Perhaps we might borrow a wig for him?" Two of his band appeared overhead, in the loft, flanking the mask as if to guard it. "He is a grand god, you know. Old Crooked Face. He was working in the skies, helping create the world, when he began frolicking with the other deities—racing, as it were—and got a wee bit carried away. In his excitement, he fell against a mountain and smashed his face. The Iroquois love him. I think it is for his honesty. He still goes out in the world and admits his ugliness. He lets the world know that sometimes the almighty can go too far."

Ramsey's eyes flared again. "I want him—I want that thing in the smithy furnace," Ramsey demanded, turning to Crispin. Duncan glanced at the forge. The furnace had been lit. When the trial was over, the smith would drive a hot bolt into Duncan's iron collar and crimp it permanently down, sealing his fate.

As Crispin took an uneasy step forward, Ramsey gazed anxiously at the assembly of Company men, Indians, and Scottish deserters, then sighed and raised a restraining hand. He rose, lifted his stool, and placed it on the opposite side of Woolford. The mask was no longer in his field of vision. With a stroke of his gavel, Ramsey commenced the proceeding.

The trial, he had once proclaimed, would be a grand ritual, an instruction in biblical commandments and Plato's logic. Now he extracted a sheet of paper folded within the volume of Plato. From his seat five feet away, Duncan had no trouble recognizing Arnold's handwriting, and realized the vicar would have had time to rewrite the notes he had sent with McGregor, and lost. Ramsey stated the murder charges against Lister and the charges of theft and breach of indenture against Duncan, then straightened the paper on the plank in front of him and read the first name on Arnold's list. He worked the witnesses in quick succession, taking testimony on the deaths of Evering and Frasier, following the advice of Arnold from beyond the grave.

"We have no end of comments about circumstances," Woolford interjected after the fifth witness, "but not a word on the criminal acts of the accused."

"Mr. Lister was found bending over poor Frasier's body, the boy's blood on his hands," Ramsey snapped. "The night Evering died, everyone was accounted for except Lister. He killed Evering because of his hatred for everything English, more particularly because Evering had doubtlessly discovered his lie. He killed Frasier because Frasier had discovered evidence of the first crime."

"There are other circumstances to be considered," Woolford declared. "I call on Mr. Lister's advocate to explain," He pointed to Duncan, in the front row.

"McCallum?" Ramsey gasped. "Impossible! You cannot ask a prisoner to—"

Woolford ignored Ramsey, motioned Duncan to rise. "There are other motives to consider," the ranger said, "and other men who were unaccounted for the nights Evering and Frasier were murdered. And there is the science of their deaths. Science does not lie." He addressed Ramsey now. "Science, like justice, instructs the truth."

Ramsey's anger seemed to subside. Here, at least, was the kind of talk Plato would have preferred at a trial.

Duncan quickly led them through the scientific evidence, explaining how it proved Evering had been killed in his cabin with two blows from a hammer, how Frasier had also died of a hammer blow, a single blow to the head. Before being killed, Evering had smashed one of Sarah's dosing vials of laudanum, had, as Sarah could confirm, been allowing her to awaken, had been speaking with her of her plight and of the Ramsey Company. Jacob—another friend of Sarah, Duncan added— had died when his path had crossed that of the Company.

"The ferryman? He was a heathen," Ramsey scoffed, his patience paper-thin now. "Two killings will be sufficient to stretch this man's neck."

"There were four murders, counting Sergeant Fitch," Duncan rejoined, speaking to the assembly in front of him. "All arising out of Ramsey Company affairs."

"Do not presume," Ramsey simmered, "that by digressing you will save a minute of this killer's life."

"I call my first witness," Duncan said in reply.

Ramsey pounded his gavel angrily. "You will not mock this tribunal, sir. You have no authority!"

"I call my first witness," interrupted Woolford in a loud voice. The officer gave Duncan an inquisitive nod.

"Reverend Zettlemeyer of the German Flats mission," Duncan announced. Woolford repeated the name.

The Moravian, dressed for the pulpit, emerged from the back of the assembly. Duncan lost no time in asking him about the settlers in the lands between Edentown and the mission. Of his own accord, Zettlemeyer produced a piece of paper—a map. When Ramsey objected, Woolford ordered Duncan to proceed. Pike, sitting between two soldiers on a front bench, rose as if to leave; his sergeant, the Irishman, blocked his path. The major hissed an order. The sergeant pointed him back to the bench. Duncan held the Moravian's map for all to see, pointing first to two crosses marking German Flats in the north and Edentown in the south.

"What are the little squares?" he asked the missionary. There were over two dozen squares scattered around the map.

"Each is a homestead, a farm," the German replied, "all those within forty miles of the mission."

"Who has such a map?"

"I made this copy from two identical ones I sent to Reverend Arnold four months ago."

"We must know all our neighbors," Ramsey said, as if in protest. "The Reverend had to know all the sheep of his flock."

"Are some of that flock present?" Duncan asked the missionary.

Zettlemeyer nodded and motioned a man and a woman forward, introducing them as the survivors of two different homesteads. Duncan asked them to mark their farms on the map, then all the others that had been attacked by Indians. He soon displayed the map to the assembly, now showing many *X*s, all along the river.

When Duncan called the next witness, Pike growled out a futile protest. All the way to the stool, Pike's sergeant looked at his feet. The big Irishman quickly confirmed that Major Pike often consulted a map kept in the leather cartridge case on his belt. Pike made a quick sideways motion as if to slide off his bench, then felt the chill stare of his sergeant and moved no more. He said nothing as a ranger approached and pulled the leather cartridge box from his belt. Duncan accepted the case, opened it, and pulled out another map. He held it up beside Zettlemeyer's map.

Duncan showed how the map had been folded, addressed on the reverse, and marked for postage. "Why, Major Pike," he asked, pointing to the addressee's name, "would Reverend Arnold send you one of his maps?" When Pike did not reply, Duncan paced along the front of the assembly. "And why would it be precisely the same map, with the same marks as those we've made today by the homesteads that were destroyed?"

A confused murmur swept through the crowd.

Pike make another effort to slip away, and was stopped by one of the rangers.

"The map sent by Arnold," Duncan declared, "wasn't an intelligence report. It was a plan." He held the map back up for the assembly to see. "Arnold and Pike knew where all the raided homesteads were, three months before the raids."

The stunned crowd was silent as Duncan placed the maps in front of Ramsey on the table. The patron seemed confused, and then worry creased his brow as he noticed Pike's stricken expression. Ramsey had begun to grasp that it was not Lister who was on trial now. He stared so intensely at the maps that he took no notice of Duncan's next witness, until Jonathan replied to Duncan's question about the time spent by the Ramsey children with Reverend Arnold.

"An hour each day, sir," Jonathan said in an eager tone. "Father said we must have religious instruction at least an hour each day."

"And did not the vicar offer lessons drawn from life here in Edentown?"

"Oh, yes, sir, we—"

"How dare you!" Ramsey shot up from his chair, color filling his face now. "Crispin! Remove the children this instant!"

Crispin's response came without hesitation. "I may have the

power to remove the Ramsey children, sir, but I have no power to remove a witness."

"I believe you were describing how the vicar escorted you around the works of the town," Duncan continued.

Jonathan's gaze now rested on his older sister, standing at the wall, her hands on the shoulders of young Virginia. "Yes, sir. The smith, the carpenter, the butcher, the cooper."

"The butcher?"

"Oh, yes, sir. Every day the butcher. Reverend Arnold helped arrange the meals, said there were great lessons to be had in a butcher shop. He spent time in his own cousin's butcher shop as a boy, and told us that each creature on earth had a destiny in life and death. He said those years had shown him how every human endeavor could be anchored in the teachings of the Bible, how his cousin operated a most Christian meat shop."

"What would a young assistant do in a Christian butcher shop?"

"Sweeping clean. Killing the animals."

"And how does a good Christian butcher dispatch those creatures meant by God to serve him in their death, Jonathan?"

Looks of confusion passed through the assembly. Ramsey looked up from his paper.

A small hand shot up from one of the rear benches. "I know, Mr. McCallum! I know!" Virginia Ramsey did not want her brother to have all the attention. The girl jumped up, blurting out her answer without waiting for her schoolmaster's bidding. "If you please, sir, if God wishes to use our hand when he requires another creature to be dispatched to heaven, we must seek to avoid their suffering. First you say the words 'God wills it so'."

"Virginia!" Ramsey said, rising from his stool. "This is no place—Crispin! At least take—" The big butler began moving through the crowd.

But Ramsey's youngest daughter made sure her answer was complete before Crispin reached her. "Then a quick hammer to the skull—that does the trick," she blurted out.

The words stopped Crispin, and everyone else present. Virginia, pleased with her correct reply, grinned up at the mask of Old Crooked Face.

Ramsey was the first to break the stunned silence. "It means nothing," he said in a tight voice. "You mean to obscure the truth. You build no logic in your case, only distractions."

"It means everything," Duncan countered, and called his next witness.

Cameron settled onto the stool by the judge's table with a peeved expression.

"Reverend Arnold was a busy man, was he not, Mr. Cameron, being the Ramsey business agent as well as the vicar?"

Cameron only frowned.

"At least he had your valuable help. As a former merchant, you no doubt had a hand in the bookkeeping." Sarah Ramsey stepped forward, extending to Duncan an object covered with a flour sack. Cameron watched her retreat with resentment in his eyes. When he turned back, Duncan had extracted the account book and opened it in front of the keeper. "Your writing, is it not, for these recent weeks?"

"Aye."

"About stores. I see familiar entries in the first part. Flour. Bacon. Spices. Wheat. Linens." Duncan raised the pages for all to see. "I don't understand the second part, the one at the back," he said, opening now to the pages he had first read in the cellar safe room. "Names from outside the Company. Numbers. Payments. Dates. For what, Mr. Cameron?"

"That's the vicar's writing. Ask him."

"A lot of trouble, keeping such accounts locked in the safe room."

Cameron glared at him.

"The Company's first day ashore," Duncan said abruptly, "did you kill a bear cub?"

"That was Hawkins."

"Why do you suppose Mr. Hawkins has fled?"

"He is a trapper. Trapping season is starting."

"A pity." Duncan put a finger on the first line in the secret accounts. "Mr. Hawkins is the first entry, with over a dozen marks. Was he getting paid for bear cubs, Mr. Cameron?"

When the keeper didn't reply, Duncan set the ledger in front of Ramsey and turned back to the witness stool. "What did *you* kill that first day, Mr. Cameron?"

The keeper's eyes flared. "When vermin step in your path, you don't preserve them to plague you another day."

Duncan returned his icy stare. "You lost your family in an Indian raid, in Pennsylvania. Did you explain that to Reverend Arnold when he recruited you?"

A thin, cool smile formed on Cameron's lips. "He said the Company needed leaders who would not shy away from the duties of avenging angels. Sure, I killed that old Indian, as good as done, judging from the blood he lost. And ye'll not find a judge in America who would condemn me for it."

Duncan stepped closer, spoke quickly as Cameron kept his gaze on Ramsey. "Exactly how many Indians have you killed, Mr. Cameron?"

"An even dozen so far. Four for each of mine they—" Cameron's tongue stopped working. He slowly turned to face the assembly, from which at least a dozen Iroquois stared at him.

"An odd thing, that Arnold had to keep the work of his avenging angels so secret." Duncan gestured toward the ledger. "This list has your name at the bottom, the most recent entry. The first date by your name was the day Sergeant Fitch was killed. Was he your price of admission to these ranks? Were you paid for Fitch as well as for Indians?"

"There is no charge against me!" Cameron spat. "Fitch died of a tomahawk to the chest. An Indian weapon."

"No," Duncan countered. "I measured the wound when I cleaned his body. Not a tomahawk. The blade was much wider. It was a hewing ax, the kind kept in the barn by the sharpening wheel. Passed out among the Company the night of the raid."

"Fitch had found that damned Welshman at the bark mill," Cameron muttered, "asked him a lot of questions about what

Hawkins's men spoke of when they drank. When his captain wasn't here on his return, Fitch came to me about whether to tell the Reverend of what he had learned."

"What did he learn?"

Cameron offered a cold smile. "Nothing much. Just that when they got drunk, they were always practicing their Indian war cries."

"Is that an admission, Mr. Cameron?"

"I admit to nothing. Like Woolford said, the killing of a soldier be a military matter. Not a damned thing you can do it about, McCallum. This trial is about Frasier and Evering. You can't—" His words choked away again as movement above caught his eye. The assembly followed his gaze upward. A tall, stately figure stood beside the mask, staring intensely at Cameron.

"You may remain there, Mr. Cameron, as my next witness speaks," Duncan announced. "His name is Ravencatcher, of the Onondaga tribe."

The gavel began pounding on the table; Ramsey worked it so feverishly, his wig came ajar. "This circus stops now, McCallum!" Ramsey shouted, turning for a moment to Cameron. "The chains! I want him in chains again! You'll feel the lash this very—"

Ramsey's arm was stopped in midair as Woolford gripped his wrist. When the patron tried to shift the gavel to his free hand, another strong arm blocked him. Pike's sergeant loomed over him and silently pried the gavel from his hand. "Sergeant," Woolford acknowledged with a grateful nod, and then he turned to Duncan. "Please continue."

Another figure appeared by Ravencatcher. Conawago draped a wampum belt over the Onondaga's raised arm. Tashgua's son stepped into a pool of light cast through the hayloft door. Not a man below spoke.

"You were near here, in the forest, for several days before you came for Sarah in the night," Duncan began.

"It is true," came the reply from above.

"You and Sarah exchanged messages, using signs on the riverbank."

"She would put signs out at dusk. I would come at dawn to reply."

"But young Frasier saw them and tried to destroy them."

"I did not know his name," explained the Onondaga. "A young one with red hair. He had much fear. The day before Sarah came away with me, I saw him, by the barn in the early light. I thought to wait for him, to explain I meant him no harm, to ask that he stop destroying our sacred signs. I crouched by the alder, wrapped in the ground mist."

"But he didn't make it to the bank."

"Another man came, carrying something on his shoulder. The one you call Frasier spoke in a low voice."

"Did you see the other's face?"

"No. He was in shadows all the time. There was only the beginning of light. It was over quickly. Four words, then a swing of that thing on the second man's shoulder and the sound of bone cracking."

"What did you do?"

"I stepped back across the river. It was town trouble, not for me."

"And the four words. Did you hear them?"

Ravencatcher nodded solemnly. "'God wills it so,' the man said—only those words. Then the young one fell."

Duncan turned to the judges. "There was no Scottish murderer on the ship," he declared. "The same one who killed Frasier killed Evering—also with a hammer." It had taken his time with Tashgua for Duncan to understand. Only one person could have taken the chart, which had been crusted with sea salt, from Evering's cabin. Sarah never would have done so, never would have taken it into the ocean with her—unless she had known Evering was dead already. That certain knowledge had caused her to lash out at the Company with the ritual at the compass, and then to mount the spar for her suicide. Only Arnold had something to lose by Sarah's awakening. Perhaps Evering's life would have been spared if Arnold had only found him with the dosing vial he was to have given to Sarah, but he had seen Evering's notes, too, which he burned in the chamber pot after killing him. Only Arnold would have understood their significance, would have known that Evering had become the junction, the ally, of the only two people who could do his plans harm.

Ramsey's head sank into his hands. Ravencatcher and Conawago disappeared from sight. Duncan nodded to Woolford, who rose and quietly spoke to Pike's sergeant. Duncan found himself gazing at Sarah, who stared at the floor, a single tear on her cheek. Duncan became aware of movement around him, of a growl of protest abruptly cut off. When he turned back to the table, Ramsey was finally raising his head. Pike was standing to one side, a ranger holding each of his arms, a gag in his mouth. Conawago stood beside Duncan. Lister was standing, leaning on his crutch, rubbing his wrists where the manacles had been.

Duncan motioned to Woolford, and the ranger pushed Pike's leather belt box in front of Ramsey. "Open it," Duncan instructed, "there was more than a map in the case." Ramsey glared at him, then lifted a small, cloth-wrapped object from the box and, with an impatient sigh, flung the cloth open.

As the glittering object inside was revealed, all color left the patron's face. A choking moan escaped his throat. "Impossible!"

It was a small, elegant cross, worked in gold and rubies. Duncan had seen it once before, in the portrait of Lady Ramsey.

Ramsey looked as if he had seen the ghost of his wife. "She took it with her," he declared in a hoarse whisper. "It went down with her."

"No," Duncan corrected. "Arnold stole it when she left, knowing you would think Lady Ramsey had taken it on her travels, then gave it to Pike to seal their bargain."

"Bargain?"

Duncan nodded to the sergeant, who pried off Pike's gag for a moment. "How many acres of land, Major? How many did Arnold pledge to you?"

Pike looked up defiantly. "Five thousand. And you haven't authority to lift a finger against me, McCallum. You will pay, you all will pay," he said, with a malevolent glance at Woolford.

"Five out of how many promised to Arnold, Lord Ramsey?" Duncan asked.

"Fifty," Ramsey whispered, his gaze still locked on the cross. "Fifty thousand."

"You and Arnold used the grenadier cap against Major Pike," Duncan said to Ramsey. "You kept it because it could implicate him in the massacre. But you also needed a way to clear out the settlers from your new land. The homesteads were too haphazard, too random, to suit your plans, and most of all, they weren't yours. All the clouds on your title had to be removed. This was Arnold's one chance at greatness, a chance to own his own estate. Everything depended on meeting the terms of your bargain with the king. You had to clear the land of the Iroquois, and you would destroy them by destroying their chiefs. But Arnold knew you would need the settlers cleared, too."

"It was where he had chosen his acreage, the tract between here and the mission along the river," Ramsey said, still in a whisper.

"Once Arnold realized why Pike had massacred everyone at Stony Run, it would not be difficult for him to connect Pike to the French. A bargain between Arnold and Pike was the obvious next step. Pike worked for the French for money, for Arnold for land. They would help each other accomplish their goals. Pike would use the Hurons to finish the work he started last year at Stony Run, and to help you exact vengeance on Tashgua for taking your daughter, to help the Ramseys take the land offered by the king. But Pike needed some security. So Arnold gave him the cross."

Duncan lifted the map taken from Pike and turned to the major. "Arnold needed help clearing out the homesteads. You had Hurons at your beck and call. Arnold had men in the south, you had the Hurons in the north." The phantom raiders under Hawkins had attacked Duncan, he knew now, which was why Conawago had found his medallion on a dead raider at the burnt cabin, and why Hawkins had been so frightened by its sudden appearance in Raven-catcher's hand.

No one spoke. The assembly in the barn was like a tinderbox. And the fire in the eyes of the Iroquois and the settlers was enough to ignite it.

Ramsey seemed to slowly sense the baleful stares directed at him. "I didn't . . . . You have no proof that I . . . . How could I have known?" he sputtered. "Arnold was responsible for details. He just had to get the land ready, that was all."

Duncan lifted the ledger book and turned to the back pages. "But the entries in the ledger, before Cameron and Arnold arrived. They are all in your hand."

Ramsey had no reply. He shifted in his seat, seeming to grow smaller, then stared at the cross again.

Duncan moved to the place where Sarah had sat and chanted the month before, facing the storeroom. He opened the storeroom door as the spectators shifted to watch him. "Codes and secrets, bounties and bribes. The lifeblood of the Ramsey Company."

"Let us move to the schoolhouse," Ramsey suddenly blurted out, standing, gesturing toward the great house. "Refreshments. We should have refreshments in the garden before we continue. Rum. Rum for everyone!"

"What would your wife think, Ramsey," Woolford asked, "if she knew how many deaths were built upon her cross?"

The words seemed to stab Ramsey. He sagged, dropping back onto the stool, gazing once more at the cross in his hand.

As Duncan began pulling away the barrels that lined the back wall of the room, he recalled another day, on the ship, removing barrels to find Evering's body trailing in the sea. He felt a strange closeness to the gentle professor, as if now he were taking Evering home.

More men, Iroquois, Company men, and rangers alike, joined the effort. When the wall was cleared, Duncan called for lanterns and began to examine it, began to study each joint, each plank and peg. After a long moment, he surveyed the objects in the room, settling on an open barrel in which spare shovel and ax handles had been stored. He explored the contents of the barrel and then the shadow behind the barrel, pulling out a short pole, beveled at one end like a three-foot-long wooden chisel. It took only a few moments to find the board on the wall it fit under, at a narrow gap by the floor that could easily have escaped notice. He pried the pole under it, levered it upward, and a three-foot section of the wall swung out on hidden hinges.

A rank, fetid odor wafted out of the sealed room. On a small table by the door sat several writing leads, a candle in an iron holder, and a candle box. Duncan slid back the lid of a small candle box. Inside were several more pieces of jewelry. Brooches and necklaces, most of gold, some with Dutch-worked diamonds.

"The treasure room!" someone in the rear called out as Duncan lifted a necklace into the light. "Bring out the rest of the treasure!"

Duncan stepped into the darkened doorway. "This is what Arnold stole. There is no more treasure," he said, a new sort of fear tightening his throat, "only the seeds of the Ramsey empire."

But the men, having seen the gold and jewels, would not be stopped. Duncan found he had no strength to resist as they pushed forward, grabbing the lanterns. The tide pushed him toward Sarah, who leaned against a barrel, her head down, one hand wrapped around the leather pouch at her neck. All color had left her face. He gently pulled her head against his shoulder.

Within seconds the men were fleeing, pale as ghosts, two of them emptying their stomachs on the barn floor. Woolford and Jamie soon stood alone in the doorway, their faces as old and gray as stone.

Here was the essence of the Ramsey Company, here was the warehouse of Ramsey's and Arnold's ambitions. They hung from slats like drying tobacco, row after row of patches of skin and long black hair.

"Over a hundred at least," Woolford announced. "They weren't particular. Young and old. Men and women." Some of the braids still held small feathers; some had beads and ribbons woven into them. Along the wall were other trophies—elaborately carved drums and war axes, and Indian clothing, enough to meet the needs of any troupe seeking to masquerade as Hurons.

"What do we do?" Crispin asked in a derelict voice.

Duncan gestured to Sarah, who, of Ramsey flesh and Iroquois heart, seemed inconsolable. "It's not up to us."

They waited until finally Sarah had no more tears. She stood, straightened her dress, and began speaking in low tones, to Crispin, to Jamie, and to the Iroquois. They burst into activity. Men began leading livestock out of the stalls, rolling out barrels of stores, carrying away tools. Many of the Company men returned, listened to Jamie's warriors, and started helping. No one complained, no one questioned Sarah's instructions.

Ramsey took a long time to notice the hurried effort but still did not speak until Sarah helped him to his feet. Men began collecting water buckets.

"Not my barn, daughter," he said in a tiny voice, "not my beautiful barn." But he made no other complaint as she helped him hobble outside, as if he were an aged cripple.

Only the Iroquois carried the torches, touching them to hay and wood chips, then throwing them into the loft. In five minutes flames were leaping up the posts of Ramsey's palace. In ten, the roar of the fire had pushed the livestock to the far side of the pasture. In fifteen, the crews that had been throwing buckets of water on the adjoining structures had to retreat from the heat.

As the last vestiges of the day disappeared behind the western forest, the shingle roof caught. Night had settled over the compound by the time the posts gave way and the building started to collapse. Not long after—whether by design or accident, Duncan never knew—Lister's gallows began to burn.

Chapter Seventeen

*T*HE CONFLAGRATION ILLUMINATED THE FACES of its inhabitants like actors on a well-lit stage. Ramsey sat on the great house steps, his face empty as he watched the destruction, the house staff too frightened to go near him.

The men of the Company returned to dowsing the adjoining buildings, often pausing to gaze at the crackling fire. They cut a wide swath around the solitary figure who stood staring at it from the riverbank, wrapped in a blanket brought by Crispin. Sarah's face was flooded with emotion. Duncan saw hate, fear, guilt, melancholy on her features, but also a different kind of fire, a fierce yet somehow inquisitive determination that Duncan had seen in the eyes of her Indian father. Her lips were moving, he saw. She was reciting her Haudenosaunee prayers.

"Brace y'erself," a gruff voice said behind him.

Duncan turned to see Lister and two Company men, one bearing tongs from the forge. Before he understood what they were about, the two men had grabbed both sides of the collar, and Lister, balancing on his crutch, took the tongs and began unbending the hook that fastened it at the rear. The old Scot held the collar in his hand a moment, held it up for all those nearby to see, then flung it, whirling like a top, into the fire. As it disappeared into the red-hot embers, some cheered. Some pounded Duncan on the back, some shook his hand, then hurried on as they followed his gaze toward Sarah. She still scared them.

Duncan ached for a way to help her but knew that, like the barn, her fire would have to burn out on its own. He turned back to the men with the buckets and worked with them far into the night, dousing the wall of the cooper's shed when it burst into flame but preserving all the other buildings, with only few charred timbers.

It was long after midnight before it seemed safe to rest, and many of the men sat in the river to wash the soot away, staring at the long, wide pile of glowing embers and low flame, staring at Sarah, who had risen and was leading Crispin toward the door of the kitchen. The fear had burned out of the men, replaced by something Duncan could not at first name. There was a new, solemn strength about them, as if they understood something important had happened that night, something that changed Edentown forever, something that made them closer to whole men again. The burning of Ramsey's English barn had released something inside the prisoners. It wasn't a barn that burned so much as the bridge to Ramsey's world.

As Duncan walked around the huge bed of coals, he found Lister gazing outward, toward the starlit pasture. A knot of men were in the center of the cleared land. He could not make out the words they spoke, but their tone of excitement was unmistakable.

"'Tis those savages," Lister said in a worried voice. "They took that mask out there."

Duncan took several steps into the pasture, then turned and gestured for Lister to join him. The Iroquois were there, with several of Jamie's men, gathered around Ravencatcher, who wore the mask, facing upward, arms extended toward the sky.

None of the Indians seemed to notice them as they walked around the circle. They were all watching Old Crooked Face as he studied the eastern sky. Duncan followed the gaze of the mask, not understanding. Then he saw it—a long, glowing slash in the sky. A small gasp of joy escaped his lips. "What day is it, Mr. Lister?"

"Wouldn't know, sir. Late September, nigh October."

The Iroquois had found Mr. Evering's comet. And from their excited tones, he knew they had decided it was the third miracle, the miracle of the sky that proved the old spirits had not abandoned them.

Ramsey still sat on the steps of the great house in the morning, gray and empty, another cinder left by the night. In all the long hours of darkness it appeared no one had gone near him, no one had dared to offer help. Duncan, having collapsed onto a bench in the carpenter's shop three hours before dawn, rubbed the sleep from his eyes as he approached the patron. He ventured a quiet greeting. When Ramsey did not reply, did not even seem to see him, Duncan pulled him to his feet and led him, hand on his elbow, into the house.

Inside, the second floor bustled with activity. Duncan led Ramsey into the quieter sitting room of the first floor. Like a man robbed of his senses, the lord let Duncan lay him down on the day bed and cover him with a blanket. In seconds, he was asleep.

Outside, Iroquois, Company men, and rangers worked alongside one another, clearing away the debris of the barn, stacking its salvageable building stones as they cooled, raking embers into piles, gleaning pieces of hinges and pintels, some gnarled by the heat, for reuse by the smith. Duncan found a shovel and joined the effort. The sun was nearly overhead when they finished, and Duncan was washing himself at one of the water troughs when he heard an alien, unexpected sound. A child's laughter. He looked up and stared in wonder. Jonathan and Virginia were ankle deep in the water, with poles and line, being taught to fish by Lister, who sat on the bank, crutch at his side. Virginia squealed with delight as a long, bronzed arm appeared around an alder bush, holding a huge, flopping trout.

"Come see, Clan McCallum, 'tis Mr. Moon!" Lister exclaimed to Duncan as the old Indian appeared around the bush. "The very one I sailed with!" Duncan smiled and nodded. Conawago had put on his European clothes, though a feather dangled in his braided hair and his legs were bare below his britches. Conawago showed the fish to the children and let Virginia stroke its rainbowed side before setting it back into the stream.

Duncan lay back on the bank, luxuriating in the sun, watching with an unexpected contentment until he saw Jonathan staring uncertainly across the river. People were quietly moving in the shadows, pushing canoes in the water. Tashgua's band was preparing to travel.

"To the west," Conawago said as he settled beside Duncan.

"I didn't think you would leave so soon."

"Not me, not with them. Our ways will no doubt cross again, but we are not on the same path. They promised to keep an eye out for my people."

"They would be welcome here, to rest for a few more days." Incredibly, he told himself, it was true. As they had worked side by side the night before, the inferno seemed to have welded something between the Company men and the Iroquois.

"Soldiers will be coming," Conawago reminded him.

Duncan found himself on his feet. Canoes were already shoving off, heading downstream, some paddled by the warrior Scots. He quickly waded through the thigh-deep water to the far bank, shaking a hand here, offering a word of encouragement there, accepting from one of the Iroquois warriors a bundle of feathers wrapped with a strip of fur. Tashgua's son was there, arranging large leather pouches that Duncan suspected held the ceremonial masks. Ravencatcher soberly lifted a leather necklace from his neck and placed it around Duncan's neck. A claw of a bear hung from it. "In all your life," the Indian said, "you will never need to fear a bear again." He turned and stepped into a canoe.

Suddenly a small, round face was in front of him.

"You can stay here, Alex," Duncan said. "Study in the schoolhouse."

Alex seemed to have lost years from his once weary countenance. He was no longer a ghostwalker. He was a boy. He nodded. "She made me promise to come back in a year. Sarah says that I must learn the drawing of words, that I must become a bridge between peoples."

"And with oxen perhaps," Duncan said with a grin.

Sadness crossed the boy's face for a moment. "Before I left the mission, I cut all his bindings. I told him a strange Scottish man had come to save us. I asked him to come with me. He followed me for a few steps and stopped and gazed at me with those huge eyes of his. Then he turned and walked down the road to the bark mill."

They stood in silence, struggling for words. Adam Munroe was there, beside them, between them.

Someone called out the boy's name. Alex's new mother was gesturing him toward a canoe.

Duncan suddenly searched his pockets for something, for anything. He loosened his belt and slid off the sheath with the ranger knife, pushing it into the boy's hand. Alex solemnly accepted the gift, then backed away several steps, his eyes locked on Duncan's, before turning and darting to the canoe.

Conawago waited for him on the other side. They watched in silence as the last canoe disappeared down the river, an emptiness building inside.

"He would not go like that," the old Indian said after a long moment.

Duncan had met many men in America who could expertly decipher the signs of the forest, but only one who could always read the tracks of his heart.

"He waits."

"Where?"

"There is a place where people from different worlds go to find words for each other."

He ran. With no thought except that he would be too late, he ran.

But Jamie was there, sitting on a log, staring at the lichen-covered cairn, his gun and pack beside him. He did not turn when Duncan stopped at his back.

"There was an old pantry in the rooms I let in Edinburgh," Duncan said after a long moment. "He stayed in there with a cabinet pushed across the entry to hide it. At night we spoke about the old times. I was trying to find a ship for him to Holland. I was going to buy him passage and give him what little money I had. But one morning he said it was his birthing day, and he wanted a jar of whiskey. I never knew what exactly happened when he was alone that day. There was a pounding on the door after I returned. The magistrate's men knocked me down with their staffs, began beating me. I woke up in a cell. At the trial my neighbors testified they heard Highland singing from my rooms. He got drunk and sang. He survived all those battles, all those storms, and in the end it was the old songs that killed him.

"They took me in chains to the hanging. He spat in the eye of his hangman. The hangman was so mad, he broke his arm. He shouted out the name of our clan. They broke his other arm. He sang one of his songs until he had no breath left." Duncan's heart felt like a vise was closing around it. "I was a coward. I should have sung with him."

"They would have broken your arms, too," Jamie said, still facing the cairn of the old tribes.

"I should have sung with him," Duncan repeated. After a moment he sat on the log beside his brother. "You're going west. You mean to go to the Iroquois towns."

"No. Tashgua understood before he died. The old ones there understood."

"Understood what?"

"Do you know how many settlers there are in the English colonies?"

"A hundred thousand, perhaps two."

"Hundreds of thousands, nigh a million, and increasing every day. There's maybe thirty thousand Iroquois, far fewer of the Lenni Lenape and other tribes. Every year another twenty or thirty miles of forest is taken. Tashgua understood it. Conawago understands it. Woolford understands it."

"What exactly?"

"About the future. The tribes all look to the future as a time when white men and red men live beside one another. But the white men, they assume that in the future there will be no more Indians."

The words raised an unexpected pain. Duncan buried his head in his hands a moment. "The army, Jamie. We can explain things. You have a future—"

Jamie reached into his pocket and pulled out a well-worn letter. "Woolford found this on Pike. It cautions me about trusting the king and the king's army. It reminds me of what the army did in the Highlands, and to the Highland way of life. The one who wrote it suggests that naught but disaster comes when men without conscience take on the mantle of command."

Duncan stared at the ground. It had taken many weeks, and it had gone through many unintended hands, but the letter Duncan had written the night before Evering's death had finally reached his brother. "You mean to go far," he said at last. He was having trouble making his tongue work. He had waited years to speak like this, brother to brother, and now Jamie was leaving.

"There are places beyond the Ohio that will see no settlers for two or three more generations at least. If there had been such lands back home, we would have done the right thing long ago."

"So you'll do it now for a few Scots and some of the Iroquois."

"We'll do it for all Scots, and all Iroquois." Jamie stood and, as Duncan watched, opened his pack, pulling out an inch-wide strip of wampum. He placed it over his wrist and finally looked into his brother's face. "We wish you to come with us. There is a place for the McCallum clan out there, away from the world." He bent and pulled something from behind the cairn. It was Duncan's own pack.

It was Duncan who broke his brother's earnest gaze, looking out into the dark forest as he struggled for words. "You forget who I am. A transported convict with a warrant to send me back to prison."

"Run. You would not be the only wanted man among us. The wilderness is wide. The king is far away."

"The war will be over in a year or two. The army will turn toward Europe and Asia and the Caribbean. They will forget you. But Ramsey will never forget me. He would hire more men like Hawkins to find me. And once they did, your secret would be lost."

Jamie silently paced around the old cairn, his hand on the top stone, then reached into his pack and extracted a tattered piece of wool. "I took leave once from the barracks in Chester, told them I was going to Glasgow. But instead I went back to the old house. It was all in ruins, with gorse and heather growing out of the crumbled walls. But I found this under the remnants of a smashed chest." He unfolded a piece of tartan, a foot wide and two feet long. It was the brown-and-green plaid favored by the McCallum clan. He handed it to Duncan. "The chief of my clan should have this."

Duncan's hand trembled as he reached for the wool. He had never expected to see the plaid again.

"In the shards of the chest were small stockings and britches," Jamie added in a brittle whisper. "Mother was saving it for him, for when he grew older."

"Angus," Duncan whispered back, a new pain rising in his heart. Angus, their younger brother, who had not survived the bloodbath after Culloden.

It was a long time before either spoke. They barely moved, Jamie standing with the truth-speaking wampum on his hand, Duncan with the tartan on his. Finally Duncan stretched the cloth in front of him. "I remember the looms," he said, an unexpected calm entering his voice. "Out in the islands. The women washed the wool by the sea."

"Sometimes grandfather piped as they worked. And you and I romped among the seals. He watched us close, because sometimes the seals would take children away for their own."

With one firm stroke, Duncan tore the cloth in half. Jamie's momentary chagrin turned to solemn acceptance as Duncan handed him his half. As Duncan set his piece in his pack, he paused, looked at his brother, and pulled out the pipes.

He played tunes from their youth, bringing faraway smiles to their faces, before switching to one used by their clan in battle, facing Edentown as he played. When he finished and turned back to the log, Jamie and his pack were gone.

When he finally emerged from the forest, the coach that had

brought the Ramsey children was at the front of the house, its team hitched, baggage being loaded onto it. Duncan hurried to the house, reminding himself that he had not seen Sarah all day, remembering with a shudder Ramsey's vow to dispatch her to the trepanning surgeon in Philadelphia.

His throat tightened as Sarah emerged from the house with a load of baggage. But she wore no travel clothes, and instead of returning into the house she began speaking with the bearded driver, who was nodding repeatedly, nervously, as if receiving directions from a new employer.

Duncan left his pack on the schoolhouse steps and eased himself onto the end of the porch of the great house, staying in the shadows, then settled into the one of the chairs near the door. He had no reason to believe she had noticed him until after she had retreated inside.

"Please fetch Mr. McCallum a mug of cold milk," he heard her call through the open door as she hurried upstairs.

Duncan drained the milk when it was brought, then slipped inside, aware that Ramsey could explode out of his library at any moment. But then his eye caught movements in the sitting room, where still the curtains were drawn. Crispin was there, looking as frightened as Duncan had ever seen him. Ramsey was sitting on the day bed where Duncan had left him, mindlessly letting Crispin lift his limbs as the houseman dressed him.

Crispin's fear spread to Duncan. He backed out onto the porch, but as he turned, he found himself face-to-face with Sarah. She offered a shy smile and seemed about to speak when her gaze abruptly shifted over his shoulder.

"There are blankets and pillows in the coach," she announced in a flat voice.

"Are you traveling, daughter?" came a thin, unsteady voice from behind Duncan. Crispin had led Ramsey outside.

"When our business is complete, you are traveling, sir," Sarah explained in a new, resolute tone, then pointed to a small table that had been placed on the porch beyond the door, with an inkpot, a quill, and several documents secured under a candlestick holder. She was wearing her mother's ruby cross.

Duncan edged away, was about to step off the porch when Sarah touched his sleeve and pointed him to one of the chairs by the table.

"I don't understand." Though Ramsey had slept for hours, he seemed as weak as when Duncan had led him inside at dawn. Crispin appeared, carrying a cup of tea, which he set on the little table. The tea seemed to persuade Ramsey to sit. He lifted the porcelain cup, holding it in midair. He seemed to see something in his daughter he had not noticed before.

"You are leaving Edentown," Sarah announced. "Go to New York town. Go back to England. Go to your southern plantations. Anywhere but here. I am staying here, with Jonathan and Virginia."

Ramsey slowly lowered the cup. A spark flickered in his dull eyes. "You cannot just—"

"I have not finished." Sarah seemed to have lost interest in his words. "Crispin stays with us." It was indeed a new Sarah, wrought from the fire of the night before. "And you will sign these papers. The first withdraws your request for Mr. McCallum to be sent back to prison in Scotland. The second sets forth your finding as magistrate that Mr. Lister is innocent of all charges related to the murders. The third certifies over your name as magistrate that the deserter Captain James McCallum and his men are all dead, killed by Hurons. The fourth grants a power to me for the conduct of all affairs related to the Ramsey property at Edentown. The next states your decision to convert the Ramsey Company to a true commercial enterprise. One half will go to me, for the betterment of this settlement. One half will be shared among all the men of the Company, the proceeds to be held until the end of their indentures."

Duncan tried in vain to read the papers from where he sat, but he could see that two different hands were used in their drafting. Crispin's and Conawago's.

"You go too far." Ramsey's voice was still weak, but now not entirely without venom. "I will not tolerate—"

"Mr. McCallum, would you please summarize the new report you and Captain Woolford will prepare for us to dispatch to the governor if Lord Ramsey does not comply?" Sarah did not look at Duncan as she spoke. He saw now that she was struggling to keep control. Crispin stepped closer, to her side. Another figure had appeared by the steps. Woolford was wearing his dress uniform again.

Duncan glanced at Ramsey, then chose to speak to the stack of papers. "There would be many pages dedicated to review of the evidence. But the conclusion will be straightforward. Agents in the employ of Lord Ramsey were the murderers of four men."

"You're nothing, McCallum!" Ramsey spat. "A convict, a damned Highland mongrel!"

"Lord Ramsey," Duncan continued, "persuaded the royal court to create the Ramsey Company under false pretenses."

"You wouldn't dare!" Ramsey snarled.

"Then Lord Ramsey further obtained a land charter from the king under false pretenses, knowing he could never meet his promise to the king without committing crimes against homesteaders and our Iroquois allies. In time of war, Lord Ramsey violated the governor's orders against the taking of scalps. He joined with a traitor in the ranks of His Majesty's army who had conspired with the French at Ticonderoga, who had murdered the king's own rangers to hide the evidence of his treachery."

"I never knew about Pike and the French!" Ramsey protested.

"It would not take a stretch of a barrister's tongue to suggest that Lord Ramsey conspired against the king himself," Duncan continued. He looked out over the town, his gaze sweeping across the bitter homesteaders and the former members of Ramsey's militia. "We could obtain fifty, nay a hundred, signatures to vouchsafe every word."

Ramsey threw his tea into Duncan's face. As Duncan calmly wiped it off, the patron began signing the documents.

When he finished, Ramsey fixed Duncan with a poisonous glare. "You're still a Ramsey slave for seven years," he spat. "By order of an English judge. There is naught anyone here can do to change that."

Without another word, with no effort to bid good-bye to Jonathan and Virginia, who watched from the doorway, Ramsey mounted the coach and snapped orders to the driver.

"But Pike," Duncan said to Woolford. "He and Cameron—"

"Four of Tashgua's warriors left in two canoes before dawn," Woolford said in a solemn voice. "With Pike and Cameron both trussed and gagged. His sergeant and I will report they both disappeared in an engagement with the Huron. They will be taken far west and sold as slaves to some unknown tribe."

Duncan shuddered. It was, he had to admit, perfect justice for such men, and they could never be trusted to an official court without betraying secrets best left unspoken.

"Hawkins?" Duncan asked.

"Not a sign. There's not a man, Indian or European, he will be safe with, not for hundreds of miles. Five of the surviving settlers have already left to track him, and they *will* find him, in some camp in some forest when he least expects it. They will know how to deal with him." The ranger lifted his hand. "I'm leaving as well." Duncan saw a cluster of men waiting at the forest's edge—Woolford's remaining rangers.

"You're one of us, Duncan. You'd be welcome running at my side."

Duncan took his hand and the men exchanged a long, sober stare. "You do me honor, Captain, and those are words I never expected to say to a British soldier."

"American," Woolford said, as if correcting him. "And not a soldier—a ranger."

"No Shakespeare for our parting?"

Woolford grinned, and glanced at Crispin. "'We few,'" he said, "'we happy few, we band of brothers.'" He unhooked the shiny gorget from his neck, stuffed it into a pocket, and stepped away to his men.

The dust from the coach had barely settled when Sarah summoned the keepers and told them to begin dismantling the palisade, and to use the wood for new cow sheds. She declared that a large meal would be served at the end of the day, under the trees by the house. Duncan joined Conawago and Lister as they worked at the palisade, prying out logs, chiseling new joints so the beams could be reassembled into long lean-tos.

When the men were washed and the meal finally served out in steaming bowls and chargers, the members of the Company hung back, staring at the U-shaped table arranged by Sarah by the garden. They had never eaten with the Ramsey family, knew better than to expect to sit at the same table. But Sarah bent to her brother and sister, then the three of them stepped into the throng, pulling hands, directing men to the benches. When Sarah finally sat, Jonathan pulled Duncan forward and put him beside him his older sister.

The men listened at the end of the meal as Sarah explained the changes in the Company. There would be no more keepers, only foremen, the chief of which would be Mr. Lister, henceforth to be known as Mr. McAllister, who would sleep in one of the rooms in the great house. There would be a new barn, but first the settlers' cabins would be rebuilt, then some new cabins at Edentown, for Sarah was sending to Philadelphia for a score of women who wanted honest jobs as cooks, laundresses, and weavers. When she described the final change, the sharing out of the Company, few seemed to understand. Then the men who had served on whaling ships described how the proceeds of the work on board were shared out to every member of the crew. Jaws dropped, eyes went round.

"I thought they would rejoice in the news," Sarah said as they cleared away the table. Most of the men had left with sober, contemplative expressions.

"Their eyes. Did you not see their eyes?" Duncan asked. "They were different men when they left, chewing on something they had not tasted for a long time. You have given them hope." And he had learned well enough that here, in this strange new land, hope need not be the poison it had been on board their prison ship.

The rejoicing came soon enough. Men began trickling back to the now lantern-lit table, some with musical instruments. There was singing and dancing and, for the first time at Edentown, the sound of grown men laughing.

Sarah brought out a blanket and she sat under one of the trees with Duncan, studying Professor Evering's comet. Eventually Crispin and the young ones went inside, and as the men wandered back to their barracks, Sarah rolled the blanket over their legs and she put her head on Duncan's shoulder.

He woke alone in the morning, the blanket empty beside him. Sarah was sitting on the kitchen steps, holding a slip of paper. "He's gone," Sarah said with a tone of surprise. "He left a note."

Spirits do not die, Conawago had written, *they just take on new shapes.* Duncan turned it over. There was nothing else.

"He was on the porch at dawn and asked if there was a scrap of paper that might be found," Sarah explained. "I showed him an empty ledger in the library. He spent an hour in there, at the desk, then appeared with his pack and bow. Later, when I checked, he had taken only a page, from the back of the book."

Duncan found the journal still on the desk, ran his finger along the edge where the page had been cut out. He held the book on edge at the window, seeing the faint indentations on the page underneath. Moments later he was rubbing a quill along the fresh soot in the fireplace. Soon the indentations took shape as he lightly ran the edge of the feather over the page. It was another map, showing rivers and ranges to the north and west. He studied it with an odd longing, trying to make sense of the dozen small circles Conawago had carefully drawn on the map, trying to reconcile them with his strange parting words. Then a glimmer of recognition rose as he examined the lowest circle, the nearest one, and its position between river and range.

Sarah was still on the steps when he returned. "I told him yesterday I had a room for him in the house, that he had a family at last." Her voice had a strange quiver in it. "I hope you will take it now, Duncan."

He looked at her without replying, then gazed out into the forest. They sat in silence for several minutes, then she rose and faced him, staring into his eyes. She offered another of her small, knowing smiles and stepped back into the kitchen.

Sarah returned ten minutes later, carrying his pack and rifle. "It seems I am always packing for you, Duncan McCallum," she said, trying to push strength, even whimsy, into her voice. She tied a small pouch of food to the top of the pack. "You need to be with your brother, and who am I stop you?"

He looked in confusion from the pack to Sarah. "You know I am bound. Still a prisoner in the eyes of the law."

"I cannot change what the law has decreed," Sarah admitted. "But you are not an escaped prisoner unless you are reported as such. And the only one who can legally complain of your absence now is myself," she explained, catching him again with her deep green eyes. She flushed and looked down. "My heart will complain," she whispered toward her feet. "But that is a crime I choose not to share with the government."

"They're inside," she said after a moment, and stepped toward the riverbank.

He needed but a stride into the kitchen to find all those he sought. Crispin, Lister, and the children sat at the kitchen table, eating bacon and bread. Lister gestured Duncan to sit beside him, then seemed to sense that something had changed. The old Scot glanced outside, saw the pack and rifle past the open door.

"Ah," he sighed, and his face tightened for a moment, then he rose with a forced smile. "A clan chief has business in many parts."

Duncan took his hand with a great knot in his throat, unable to speak for a moment.

"I owe you everything, Clan McCallum," Lister said.

"Not so. It is I who owe you everything."

"We still have a clan to build."

"We still have a clan to build," Duncan confirmed with a smile.

"I didn't think this would come so soon," Crispin said when Duncan turned to him.

"You know you'll see me again," Duncan promised, extending his hand. "It's the way of particular friends."

"I know." There seemed to be no other words they could speak. The former slave covered Duncan's hand with both his own, clasping it in silence for a long moment.

Duncan embraced each of the children. "You have a new teacher now, much wiser than me," he told them. "His name is Crispin."

Outside on the riverbank, he embraced Sarah tightly, for a long time. As he kissed the top of her head and they stepped apart, she entwined her fingers in his for a moment, as they had on the ship. His shoulder was still wet with her tears when he stepped out of the river, into the forest. He had traveled for several minutes downstream, in the direction Jamie had gone, before he halted, looking at a small flower growing out of a rock in a pool of dappled sunlight, finding himself on his knees as he gazed at it.

At the steady gait of a forest runner, it took him less than two hours to reach the broad chestnut above the pool he had visited after he had fled Edentown—the only mark he had recognized on the map made in the library that morning. The old Indian was praying beside the huge tree, his hand on a root, but surprise froze his tongue a moment as Duncan silently knelt beside him. A wise and kind grin rose on his wrinkled face. As Conawago resumed his prayer, Duncan produced several leaves of tobacco and began gathering wood for a fire, watching the sky as he worked, wondering how long it would be to first snow. It would take them at least a month if they were to visit all of the ancient trees Conawago had marked on his map.

Author's Note

During the late 1750s a peculiar complaint began arising from officers in the British forts north of Albany in the New York colony. They questioned the practice of allowing Iroquois allies to bivouac near their combat garrisons due to the unruly behavior that resulted when the Indians mingled with the Highland Scot troops—who seemed, by British army standards, little more than heathens themselves. The bonds between Scots and Iroquois that anchor the plot of this novel are indeed not a novelist's fancy but rooted in historic fact: for a few years in the mid-eighteenth century these two extraordinary cultures briefly and sporadically overlapped. In retrospect the connection should come as no surprise to anyone who has studied the two peoples. The Highlanders and Iroquois were both steeped in warrior traditions, shared a rich heritage of storytelling, chafed against authority, and were each in their own way deeply spiritual. A particular headache for British officers—and a particular delight for those of us with Scottish blood who gaze back into history—was the tendency of certain Highlanders and Iroquois to perform war dances together before engagements.

Where such bonds formed between Scots and Iroquois, they may well have been nurtured by a mutual recognition that both their cultures were under siege by the same forces. They were living in turbulent times, years of unprecedented change that were altering their ways of life, and those of many others, forever. The period in which this book is set marked in a very real sense the beginning of the modern era. Science and literature were blossoming. The proliferation of printing presses had begun to connect and empower people, politically and culturally, in ways never before known. The common man had begun to discover his own identity, with profound implications for society. The first conflict that can truly be called a world war had begun, ignited in the forests of Pennsylvania by a young officer who was later to play the leading role in the American Revolution. These years became the pintle upon which many events of the following centuries swung.

Yet the history of this period, like too many others, has been taught to us in flat, sterile terms. We learn it through maps, charts, and trend lines, almost never through the eyes of actual human participants, and as a result most of us have lost our connection with the remarkable people of this remarkable time. It is largely a forgotten period, eclipsed by the more dramatic upheaval that began in 1775, but for me it has always held great fascination. Pick up a text and you might read of the dilution of monarchy and religion that occurred during these years, but those were only the symptoms of much more important transformations under way in the hearts and minds of the immigrants—mostly Scots, German, Irish, and English—who set out across the Atlantic and entered the endless forest. Traveling to the American wilderness was like traveling to another planet. Nothing in their experience could prepare those immigrants for what they encountered, just as nothing could prepare the natives of the woodlands for the Europeans who began appearing on their trails.

The mysteries on these pages are not far removed from the broader mysteries that transformed these people. How did the Highland soldier feel when he charged into battle for the very king who had destroyed his way of life? What words hung in the air at deep forest campfires when Scots and Iroquois spoke in the night? What was at work in the heart of the Indian who stood at the edge of the forest and watched the plows that were burying his traditions? It wasn't just the bloodthirsty fury reflected in Hollywood images of such natives, for these were intelligent, curious, and spiritual people.

The woodland tribes had a rich, vital culture with much to teach us—most of us are oblivious to the reasons our Founding Fathers incorporated aspects of the Iroquois confederation into our government. How is it that in these violent times the Moravians—well-educated Germans with a zeal for God and exploration—went among the tribes even in the midst of war, yet not one was ever killed? What irresistible force drove those families who, with full knowledge of the dangers, packed up their belongings and headed into the wilderness? What was the explanation given by the many European settlers captured by the woodland Indians who, when later given their freedom, chose to stay with the tribes?

These are the riddles that keep this period alive for me, and given the scarcity of direct answers in our chronicles, this may be a case where fiction can strike closer to the truth than history texts. Historians, after all, are handicapped by the fact that they can only celebrate the explorers who went into the wilderness and came back to speak of it. I, for one, have always been more interested in those explorers who went into the wilderness and decided not to return.

—Eliot Pattison

$\mathcal{T}ime\ \mathcal{L}ine$

1746   APRIL   At Culloden Moor, near Inverness, the Scottish Jacobite rebels, including many Highland clans, were defeated by British forces, breaking the rebel army and forcing the Jacobite leader, Bonnie Prince Charlie, to flee into exile. In the aftermath of Culloden, the British send punitive expeditions into the Highlands, wreaking havoc in many traditional Highland clan communities. These campaigns, and the concurrent Act of Proscription that outlawed the bearing of arms and even the wearing of Highland kilts, effectively ended the traditional Highland life for many clans.

1754   MAY   Great Meadows. As British settlers moved into the Ohio River valley during the 1750s, the French deployed troops to protect what they considered their domain. The Virginia governor sought to defend that colony's western land claims by sending a small militia force into the region led by twenty-three-year old George Washington. In May 1754 Washington raided a French camp at Great Meadows in what is now western Pennsylvania. The action marked the opening of armed hostilities between France (and its allies Austria and Russia) and Great Britain (and its ally Prussia), which spread to the Caribbean, Asia, and the African coast, in what became known as the Seven Years' War in Europe and the French and Indian War in North America.

    JULY   At Fort Necessity, erected by Washington near Great Meadows, an overwhelming force of French soldiers and Indian allies attacked the Virginia troops. Washington was forced to surrender the fort and leave the Ohio country. The defeat galvanized the

British government, which began deploying regular army troops along the western frontier.

1755	JUNE	A small British force captured Fort Beausejour (a French fort in western Nova Scotia), an action that resulted in the expulsion of the local Acadian population to the British colonies.
	JULY	A British army under General Edward Braddock was defeated at the Monongahela River by combined French and Indian forces. This defeat, in which Braddock was killed, painfully demonstrated that rigid European military tactics would not succeed against the wilderness style of combat, resulting in a new emphasis on irregular ranger forces and light infantry. The French and British began cementing relations with Indian allies—the French with the Huron, Ottawa, and Abenaki and the British with the six nations of the Iroquois (Seneca, Tuscarora, Cayuga, Mohawk, Oneida, and Onandaga).
	SEPTEMBER	William Johnson, who had forged close ties with the Iroquois, led a mixed force of colonial soldiers and Mohawks in defeating French forces at the southern end of Lake George. Iroquois chief King Hendrick (Teyonhehkwen), who was part Mohawk and part Mahican, died at the age of eighty while leading a Mohawk attack against the French.
1756	MAY	England and France formally declare war after two years of hostilities.
	AUGUST	French forces under General Louis-Joseph Montcalm attack and seize the British force at Fort Oswego, on Lake Ontario.
1757		August General Montcalm attacks and captures Fort William Henry at the southern end of Lake George. After the surrender of British forces, French Indians, ignoring Montcalm's orders, massacre the retreating British troops. This battle and the ensuing massacre were immortalized in James Fenimore Cooper's *The Last of the Mohicans.*

1758	JULY	A vastly superior British force under General James Abercromby attacks the French under Montcalm at Fort Ticonderoga. After a series of costly mistakes, including ordering Black Watch Highland troops to charge heavily manned entrenchments without artillery support, Abercromby withdraws with heavy British losses.
	AUGUST	After a month-long siege, British forces capture the French port of Louisbourg on Cape Breton island, the strongest fortress in North America. In retaliation for the massacre at Fort William Henry, the British expel eight thousand colonists from Cape Breton.
	SEPTEMBER	At a battle outside Fort Duquesne (present-day Pittsburgh), British forces under Major James Grant, acting on faulty intelligence about the strength of the garrison, are defeated by enemy forces consisting primarily of Indians.
	OCTOBER	At Fort Ligonier in Pennsylvania, the British repel a French attack. British troops advance again on Fort Duquesne.
	NOVEMBER	The outnumbered French retreat from Fort Duquesne, burning it as they leave. The British rebuild the fort, renaming it Fort Pitt.
		During 1758 the British embark on negotiations to win over woodland Indians who had been supporting the French, particularly the Lenni Lenape (Delaware).
1759	JULY	British forces attack the French at Fort Niagara, seizing the fort and moving on to occupy Forts Venango and Presque Isle, eliminating the last French operating bases in the western theater. The French blow up Fort Ticonderoga and withdraw as General Jeffrey Amherst advances with a large British force. Amherst dispatches Rogers' Rangers on a long-distance raid to destroy the Abenaki operating base at St. Francis.
	SEPTEMBER	After a bloody three-month campaign, British forces capture Quebec. In the final battle on the Plains of

Abraham, both the French and British commanding generals, Montcalm and James Wolfe, are killed.

1760   APRIL   After enduring a winter-long siege in Quebec, British forces are attacked by the French and win a second battle on the Plains of Abraham.

             SEPTEMBER   Montreal is captured by British forces, the last significant engagement of the French and Indian War in North America.

1761–1762   Fighting between the French and British continues in India, the Caribbean, and Europe and on the coast of Africa.

1763   FEBRUARY   The Treaty of Paris formally ends the Seven Years' War / French and Indian War.

A note on American Rangers: The irregular rangers fighting for the British during the French and Indian War were one of the most remarkable military units in American history. After Braddock's devastating defeat in 1755, the British military responded by forming such units in all theaters of the war. They were largely home-grown colonials who quickly proved they could rival the woodland tribes for stealth and endurance. Their discipline was lax by military standards, an aspect readily overlooked by senior commanders after the rangers delivered remarkable victories in lightning raids on enemy encampments and forts. The diversity of their ranks was not matched until modern times—included in ranger units were freed slaves, affluent landowners, impoverished farmers, and many men of mixed Indian and European blood. In 1759 three ranger companies at Lake George consisted entirely of Indians. Rangers were routinely assigned tasks that would have been virtually impossible for traditional units and, unlike other troops, were kept in the field during all seasons of the year. In July 1756, when asked to harass the French on Lake Champlain, Rogers' Rangers promptly cleared a road through miles of mountainous terrain and hauled whaleboats to the lake. Their sudden appearance far behind enemy lines to raid the Abenaki base at St. Francis was a feat of superhuman endurance. One of the most remarkable operations in American military history was the rangers' four-month mission to Detroit and back in 1760. Several ranger officers went on to become generals or colonels in the American army during the revolution. The "rules for ranging" taught by the most preeminent of the rangers, Robert Rogers, are still taught to U.S. special forces troops and are posted at U.S. Ranger headquarters in Fort Benning, Georgia.